AND SO IT BEGINS . . .

Ally felt her consciousness start to wobble. She reached out and seized the edge of the bed for support.

"Kristen, talk to me."

Her eyes went blank again, and Ally could just barely make out what she mumbled next. In fact, all she could catch were random words, words that only drifted through her consciousness and failed to stick or make any sense. It was as though Kristen were in a séance and sleepwalking among the words of some alien language.

"Young," Kristen seemed to say. "You want to be . . . to stay. Old is so horrible. Time. You're young and then suddenly you're old and it turns out you can't . . ."

Ally heard the words, but they didn't make any sense.

"I'm sorry, Kristen. I'm feeling a little dizzy."

"It's started," she said, abruptly coherent again and focusing in on Ally. "That's how it began with me. At first they said everything was okay and then it wasn't."

"What are you talking about?"

"It's happening throughout my body." She sobbed. "Everything is . . . changing."

The words drifted through space, and Ally felt like she was hallucinating, in a place where time was sliding sideways. The images were all retro, things from her past that floated through her vision in reverse chronological order.

That was it. In her mind, time was going backwards. But was it just . . . ? She looked again at Kristen and gasped. Finally, *finally* she understood the horror of what was really happening. . . .

Oh my God.

BOOKS BY THOMAS HOOVER

Nonfiction

Zen Culture

The Zen Experience

Fiction

The Moghul

Caribbee

The Samurai Strategy

Project Daedalus

Project Cyclops

Life Blood

Syndrome

SYNDROME

THOMAS HOOVER

PINNACLE BOOKS
Kensington Publishing Corp.
http://www.kensingtonbooks.com

"The potential [of stem cells] for saving lives . . . may be unlimited. Given the proper signal or environment, stem cells, transplanted into human tissue, can be induced to develop into brain, heart, skin, bone marrow cells—indeed any specialized cells. The scientific research community believes that the transplanted stem cells may be able to regenerate dead or dying human tissue, reversing the progress of disease."

Michael J. Fox
The New York Times (Op-Ed), November 1, 2000

Chapter 1

Sunday, April 5
6:49 A.M.

Alexa Hampton was awakened by a sensation in her chest. The alarm wasn't set to go off for another eleven minutes, but she knew her sleep was finished.

Not again! She rolled over and slapped the blue pillowcase.

That little sound from her heart and the twinges of *angina*, that catchall for heart discomfort, was happening more and more now, just as Dr. Ekelman had warned her. But she wasn't going to let it stop her from living her life to the fullest as long as she could, and right now that meant having her morning run.

She curled her legs around, onto the floor, reached for a nitroglycerin tab, and slipped it under her tongue. Known as a vasodilator, the nitro lowered the workload on her heart by expanding her veins. It should get her through the workout. . . .

That was when she felt a warm presence rub against her leg.

"Hi, baby." Still sucking on the tab, she reached over and tousled Knickers's gray-and-white hair, then pushed it back from her dog's eyes. Her Old English sheepdog, a huge hirsute off-road vehicle, turned and licked her hand. Knickers was ready to hit the trail.

She'd been dreaming of Steve when the chest tightness came, and maybe the emotion that stirred up had caused the angina. She still dreamed of him often, and it was always someplace where they had been together and loved, and they were ever on the brink of some disaster. That frequently caused her heart to race, waking her.

This time it was the vacation they took six years ago, in the spring. They were sailing off Norman's Cay in the Bahamas. She was raising the jib, the salt spray in her hair, but then she looked up and realized they were about to ram a reef.

She felt the dreams were her unconscious telling her to beware her current precarious condition. If, as is said, at the moment of your passing, your entire life flashes before your eyes, then the dreams were like that, only in slow motion. It was as though she were being prepared for something. The dreams were a premonition. She had a pretty good idea of what.

Ally had had rheumatic fever when she was five, which went undetected long enough to scar a valve in her heart. The formal name was rheumatoid aortic stenosis, a rare, almost freakish condition that had shaped her entire life. The pediatrician at Mount Sinai had told her parents they should think twice about allowing her to engage in any vigorous activity. Her heart's function could be deceptively normal during childhood, but when she got older . . . Well, why stress that organ now and hasten the inevitable day when it could no longer keep up with the rest of her body?

She had refused to listen. She'd played volleyball in grade school, basketball in high school, and she became a disciplined runner when she went to Columbia to study architecture. She wanted to prove that you could make your heart stronger if you believed hard enough and wanted to live hard enough.

Now, though, it was all catching up. She'd had a complete checkup two weeks ago Thursday, including a stress test and

Doppler echocardiogram, and Dr. Ekelman had laid out the situation, gazing over her half-lens glasses and pulling at her chin. The normal twinkle in her eyes was entirely absent.

"Alexa, your condition has begun worsening. There's a clear aortic murmur now when your pulse goes up. How long can you go on living in denial? You really can't keep on stressing your heart the way you have been. You can have a normal life, but it's got to be low-key. Don't push your luck."

"Living half a life is so depressing," she'd declared, not entirely sure she meant it. "It's almost worse than none at all."

"Ally, I'm warning you. If you start having chest sensations that don't respond to nitro, call me immediately. I mean that. There's a new drug, Ranolazine, that temporarily shifts your heart over to using glucose as a fuel instead of fatty acids and provides more energy for a given amount of oxygen. It will make the pain back off, but I only want to start you on that as a last resort. That's the final stop before open-heart surgery and a prosthetic aortic valve."

Day by day, the illusion of normality was getting harder and harder to maintain. She had been playing second violin in an amateur string quartet called the West Village Oldies, but a month ago she'd had to drop out. She didn't have the endurance to practice enough to keep up with the others. Blast. It was having to give up things you love that really hurt.

Still, she was determined to keep a positive attitude. There was your heart, and then there was *heart*. You had to understand the difference.

She lay back to wait for the alarm and try to compose her mind. This Sunday morning was actually the one day of the year she most dreaded. *The anniversary.*

It had been back when Steve was still alive. They were living in the Chelsea neighborhood of New York, in a brownstone town house they were renting. The rent was high, but they were doing all right. Steve was a political consultant, who had helped some fledgling candidates overcome the odds and win important elections. In between campaigns here, he also got work in the nominal democracies in Latin America.

She was a partner in a small firm of architects who had all been at Columbia together and decided to team up after graduation and start a business. There were four of them— she was the only woman—and it was a struggle at the beginning. For the first three years they had to live off crumbs tossed their way by the big boys, subcontracts from Skidmore and other giants. They felt like they were a high-paid version of Manpower, Inc., doing grunt work, designing the interiors of shopping malls in the Midwest and banks in Saudi Arabia, while their prime contractors got to keep all the sexy, big-budget jobs that called for creativity, like a glass-and-steel office tower in L.A.

But then interesting work finally started to trickle in, including a plum job to convert a massive parking garage in Greenwich Village into a luxury condominium. Through a wild coincidence (or luck) she had personally designed the apartment she later ended up buying for herself.

Just when everything seemed to be turning around and going her way, an event happened that stopped her in her tracks. Five years ago on this very day, April 5, her mother, Nina, phoned her at six-thirty in the morning and, in a trembling voice that still haunted, announced that her father was dead.

Arthur Wade Hampton was fifty-nine and he'd been cleaning his Browning shotgun for an early-morning hunting trip to Long Island—so he'd claimed the night before— and . . . she was awakened by the explosion of a discharge. A horrible accident in the kitchen of their co-op in the West Village.

Like Hemingway. Thinking back, they both realized it was the wrong time of year to hunt *anything*—but they both also knew he wanted the world to think that. Moreover, it was precisely the kind of vital lie they'd need to get through the pointed questions and skeptical looks that lay ahead. It was a knowledge all the more palpable for being unspoken. There's no time like those first moments after a tragedy to create a special reality for yourself.

It was only in the aftermath that she managed to unravel the reason. He owned and operated an interior-design firm in SoHo called CitiSpace, and he had mortgaged it to the hilt. He was on the verge of bankruptcy. (That was why Ally had not spoken to her younger brother, Grant, in the last 4 1/2 years.)

She felt she had no choice but to try to salvage what was left of the business and her father's reputation. She left the architectural firm and took over CitiSpace. It turned out she was easily as good an interior designer as she had been an architect, and before long she had a backlog of work and was adding staff. She restructured and, eventually paid off the firm's debt; it was now on a sound financial footing.

These days CitiSpace specialized in architectural rehabs in the Greenwich Village area, with as many SoHo and TriBeCa lofts as came her way. The work was mostly residential, but lately some lucrative commercial office jobs were beginning to walk through the door. Anything dependent on luxury real estate can be vulnerable in dicey times, but she'd been able to give everybody a holiday bonus for the past couple of years. She'd even given herself one this year, in the form of this new condo apartment, which she loved.

Another major reason she'd taken over CitiSpace was to try to provide her mother some peace and dignity in her twilight years. But then, irony of ironies, Nina, who was a very lively sixty-six, was diagnosed eighteen months ago with early-onset Alzheimer's. Now her consciousness was rapidly slipping away.

All the things that had happened over the last few years had called for a special kind of heart. She had known Steve Jensen, a freelance political consultant, for eight years, and they'd lived together for three of those, before they got married. He was warm and tender and sexy, and she'd envisioned them in rocking chairs forty years down the road. They'd been married for only six months when he got a job to help reelect the president of Belize. At first he was reluctant, concerned about human rights issues, but then he decided the other candidate, the alternative, was even worse. So he went.

How many things can be destined to go wrong in your life? Exactly seven months after her dad died, she received a phone call from the American Embassy in Belmopan, Belize. Steve had been flying with the presidential candidate over a stretch of southern rain forest in a single-engine Cessna when a sudden thunderstorm came out of the Caribbean and the plane lost radio contact. That was the last, etc.

She rushed there, but after two weeks the "rescue" officially became a "recovery" mission. Except there was never any recovery. After two months she flew back alone, the loneliest plane ride of her life.

She still had his clothes in her closet, as though to keep hope alive. When you love someone so much you think you could never live without them—and then one day you're forced to—it resets your thinking. Her dad's death and then Steve's . . .

She wanted to love life, but life sometimes felt like it was asking more than she should have to give. She currently had no one special to spend her weekends with, but she hadn't given up, nor was she pushing it. All things in time, except time could be running out. . . .

Brrrring went the alarm and Knickers responded with a lively "Woof!" She was anxious to get going.

"Come on, baby," Ally said. "Time for a treat."

She struggled up and made her way into the kitchen and got down a box of small rawhide chews. It would give Knickers something to occupy her mind for the few minutes it took to get ready.

Since she lived at the west end of Barrow Street, right across the highway from the new Hudson River Park esplanade that defined that mighty river's New York bank, she had a perfect course for her morning runs. She usually liked to run down to the park at the rejuvenated Battery Park City and then back. She didn't know what the distance was exactly, maybe three-quarters of a mile each way, maybe slightly more, but it fit her endurance nicely. The weather was still cool enough in the mornings that Knickers could accompany her at full trot. In the heat of summer, however, they both had to cut back.

She'd put on blue sweats, got her Walkman prepped with a Beethoven quintet, and was just finishing cinching her running shoes when the phone jangled.

Sunday, April 5
7:18 A.M.

Grant Hampton listened to the ringing and felt the sweat on his palms. For a normal person, this would be an insane time to call, but knowing his nutbag sister, she was probably already up and about to go out for her daily run. And this on a Sunday morning, for chrissake, when rational people were drinking coffee or having sex or doing something sensible like retrieving the *Times* from the hallway and reading the columns in the Business section. He had left Tanya, his runway model live-in, to get her beauty sleep and had driven downtown at this unthinkable hour on a mission. He was chief financial officer of Bartlett Medical Devices, Inc., which was in imminent danger of going under and taking him with it.

Come on, Ally. Pick up the frigging phone.

He gazed out the windshield of his blue Porsche, now parked directly across the street from Alexa's lobby, and tried to calm his pulse. He hadn't entirely worked out the pitch, but that was okay because he wanted to sound spontaneous. Who was it who said, "Sincerity, if you can just fake *that,* you've got it made?" That was what—

"Hello."

Thank God she's picked up.

"Hi, sis, remember the sound of my voice? Long time, right?" *Come on,* he thought, *give me an opening here.*

There was a pause that Grant Hampton thought lasted an eternity.

"You picked a funny time to call."

Is that all she has to say? Four and a half frigging years she shuts me out of her life, blaming me, and then . . .

"Well, Ally, I figured there's gotta be a statute of limitations on being accused of something I didn't do. So I decided to take a flier that maybe four years and change was in the ballpark."

"Grant, do you know what time it is? This is Sunday and—"

"Hey, this is the hour you do your Sunday run, right? If memory serves. So I thought I might drive down and keep you company."

He didn't want to let her know that he was already there. That would seem presumptuous and probably tick her off even more. But by God he *had* to get to her.

Again there was a long pause. Like she was trying to collect and marshal her anger.

"You want to come to *see* me? *Now?* That's a heck of a—"

"Look, there's something really important I need to talk to you about. It's actually a big favor for you, sis. You've surely heard of Winston Bartlett?"

"I've also heard of Donald Trump. So?"

"Well, he's got a clinic out in New Jersey that—"

"Grant, I know you're a big shot in his medical conglomerate or whatever it is, but I'm not interested in whatever you're peddling. I'm going out to run now."

He heard the sound of the phone clicking off, without so much as a good-bye.

Jesus, he thought, *she really* is *ticked. This is going to be harder than I thought.*

Okay, here goes Plan B.

He started the Porsche and slowly backed to the corner of Washington Street, where he parked again and then hunkered down, loving the smell of the new leather seat. Ally was going to come charging out of the front door in about two minutes, with that damned sheepdog that Steve gave her, assuming it was still around.

Grant Hampton was three years younger than Alexa and he lived in a different world. Whereas she'd never wanted to be anything but an architect, he had aimed directly for NYU School of Business. After that, he had gone to Wall Street and gotten a broker's license and begun an extremely lucrative career as a bond trader for Goldman Sachs. He discovered he had the nerves, as well as a gift for handling big numbers in his head. Soon he had a duplex co-op on the twenty-sixth floor of a new building on Third Avenue in the East Sixties. He loved the money and the pad. He also liked how easy it was to pick up models at downtown clubs if you had your own co-op, a Porsche, and were six feet tall with a designer wardrobe.

That was where he met Tanya, also six feet tall, a striking (natural) redhead who did a lot of runway work for Chloé.

He thought he was making a lot of money, but Tanya, who could order a two-hundred-dollar bottle of Dom Pérignon to have something to pass the time while the hors d'oeuvres were being whipped up at Nobu, taught him he was just barely getting by. She was accustomed to screwing men who had some depth to their money.

But when he tried a financial endeavor on the side, it turned into a disaster. Time to move on. He sent around his résumé and managed to get an interview with BMD, which was looking for someone to help them hedge their exposure in foreign currencies. The next thing he knew, he was trading bonds for Winston Bartlett's personal account.

When Bartlett's CFO died of a heart attack at age forty-nine (while undergoing oral sex in the backseat of a chauffeured Lincoln Town Car), Grant Hampton got temporarily drafted to take over his responsibilities. That was two years ago. He was aggressive enough that there was never a search for a replacement. He had made the big time, and he had done it before he was thirty-five.

But now it all hung in the balance. If this didn't work out, he could end up cold-calling widows out of Dun & Bradstreet, hawking third-rate IPOs. Tanya would be gone in a heart-beat.

Ally, work with me for chrissake.

Sunday, April 5
7:57 A.M.

As Alexa stepped out of the lobby, the morning was glo-rious and clear. Spring had arrived in a burst of pear and cherry blossoms in the garden of St. Luke's Church, up the street, but here by the river the morning air was still brisk enough to make her skin tingle. The sun was lightening the east, setting a golden halo above the skyscrapers of mid-town. Here, with the wind tasting lightly of salt, the road-ways were Sunday-morning silent and it was a magic time that always made her feel the world was young and perfect and she was capable of anything.

This was her private thinking time—even dreaming time—and she shared it only with Knickers, who was trotting along beside her now, full of enthusiasm. Ally suspected that her sheepdog enjoyed their morning runs along the river even more than she did.

As she headed south, toward Battery Park City, she pon-dered the weird phone call she'd just gotten from Grant Seth Hampton. That was his full name. She called him Grant, but her mother, Nina, always called him Seth. Unfortunately, by whatever name, Grant Seth Hampton, an unremitting hustler, was still her brother. She wished it were not so, but some things couldn't be changed.

In truth, she actually thought Grant had exhibited a kind of sequential personality over his life. When they were kids, he'd seemed rakish but also decent. At the time, of course, she was impulsive and rebellious herself, admiring of his spunk. Now she viewed that as his Early Personality.

Later, when he was pushing thirty and the Wall Street pressure and the coke moved in, he evolved into Personality

Number Two. He lost touch with reality and in the process he also lost his inner moral compass. His character bent and then broke under the stress, proving, she now supposed, that he was actually a weak reed after all. Now she didn't know *what* his personality was.

Grant, Grant, she often lamented, *how did everything manage to turn out so bad with you?*

He'd been a bond trader for Goldman, and at family gatherings he'd brag about making three hundred thou a year. But he had a high-maintenance lifestyle involving downtown models he was constantly trying to impress with jewelry and expensive vacations, so that wasn't enough. He decided to freelance on the side. He set up a Web site and, with his broker's license, opened a retail business trading naked futures contracts on Treasuries. He managed to get some naive clients and for a while made a profit for them. But then the market turned against him, or maybe he lost his rabbit's foot, and he began losing a lot of other people's money.

A couple of his clients with heavy losses felt that he'd misrepresented the risk, and they were getting ready to sue. They also were threatening to file a complaint with the SEC. There was a real possibility he could be barred from the financial industry for life.

The only thing that would put the matter to rest was if he made good some of their losses. But Grant, who lived hand to mouth no matter what his income, didn't have any liquidity. *A reserve? That's for guys who don't have any balls.*

She pieced this story together after the fact. Somehow he'd gotten to their father, who bailed him out mainly to save the family from disgrace. In doing so, he had mortgaged CitiSpace right up to the breaking point.

When she finally unraveled this poignant tale, she realized her father believed he was going to have to declare bankruptcy and close the firm, laying everybody off and leaving Nina a pauper. He thought the only way to save the family from ruin was to collect on his life insurance. Unfortunately, however, he botched the plan. Nobody believed his death was accidental and suicide voided the 3-million-dollar policy. . . .

Grant had always inhabited another planet from her dad, but surely these days he was able to support any lifestyle he chose. For the last two years he'd been some kind of hotshot financial manager for the high-stakes conglomerate owned by Winston Bartlett, or so Nina said. He should be making big bucks. Had he managed to screw that up somehow? Anytime he came crawling back to the family for anything, it was because he was in some kind of trouble.

She hadn't seen him in so long she wondered if she'd even recognize him—not that she had any plans to see him.

But what could Grant possibly want from her now? Also, why would he pick this morning, this anniversary morning, to reappear? Didn't he know what day this was? Or maybe he didn't actually care.

He'd been living on the East Side that fateful morning of their dad's death, in a doorman co-op he surely couldn't afford, and she'd taken a cab there to tell him in person rather than do it over the phone. When she did, her voice breaking, she could see his eyes already filtering out any part of it that touched him. By today he'd probably purged it out of his memory entirely. . . .

She had reached the vast lawn that had been built on the landfill behind Stuyvesant High, the Hudson River on one side and the huge expanse of green on the other. It was manicured and verdant, a *La Grande Jatte* expanse of grass where you could see visions of wicker picnic baskets and bottles of Beaujolais. The space was deserted now and smelled of new grass. Knickers had gotten ten paces ahead of her, as though impatient that Alexa was slowing her down, but then she paused in midstride to sniff at a bagel somebody had tossed.

"Come on, honey." Ally caught up with her, wheezing. "Time to backtrack. My chest is getting tight again. Goodies at home."

Knickers glared at her dolefully for a moment, not buying the argument.

"Let's go." She resumed her stride back north, knowing— well, hoping—Knickers would follow. "Home."

Her senses must have been slowing down too, because she honestly didn't hear him when he came up behind her three minutes later. . . .

Sunday, April 5
8:29 A.M.

"Didn't think I could keep up, did you?" Grant Hampton quipped from ten paces back. "Guess you didn't know I've started playing handball every other morning. Half an hour, with the Man. Great for the stamina. Not to mention brown-nosing the boss, since naturally I let him win."

She doesn't look half bad, he thought. *Maybe she's getting out ahead of that heart problem. Maybe she's actually okay and I'm screwed.*

Fuck.

But why is she still so fried at me? Sure, I had a little trouble, but everybody has ups and downs. Nina, that hardhearted bitch, wants to blame me for Arthur's death, when it was nobody's fault but his own that the old fart pulled the plug. Hell, I was going to pay back the money. He just didn't believe in me. He never did.

"What are you doing here, Grant?" When she turned to look back at him, she realized she wasn't prepared for this moment at all, but here he was, complete with a trendy CK running outfit.

She'd only seen him a couple of times after the funeral, and he looked like life was treating him well. The perfect tan, the lush sandy hair with an expensive cut that covered the top of his ears like a precise little helmet. He was a touch over six feet, with athletic shoulders, a trim figure, and a graceful fluidity to his stride. *No wonder he scores with models. Damn. How could such a creep look that great?*

"I told you, I'm trying to do you a favor." He momentarily pulled ahead, as though to head her off, then looked back and grinned. She thought she detected a vaguely demented quality in his gray eyes. "Hey, I've turned my life around, Ally. Lots of good karma. I'm CFO for BMD, and W.B. lets me handle a lot of his personal investing too."

She put on a burst of energy, trying unsuccessfully to get out ahead of him. Even though she'd rehearsed this inevitable moment over and over in her mind, she hadn't realized that seeing him again would be this upsetting.

Why was he here? But now that he was, maybe she ought to momentarily let go of the anger long enough to find out what he wanted. Fortunately, they were almost back to Barrow Street. So this was going to be quick; no way was she going to ask him up.

"Look," Grant declared over his shoulder, "I think it's high time to admit I've been a shit. To you and to a lot of people." Now he slowed enough that she pulled alongside. "For a long time there, back when I worked for Goldman, I was an immature asshole. But at least I'm mature enough now to admit it."

"I think the window for owning up is past." She didn't need his belated mea culpa. Nothing was going to bring their father back, and having a scene on this anniversary day would only demean his memory. "Sometimes it's better just to let things rest."

"No, that's wrong, Ally, and I want to try and start making amends. For all the money Dad helped me out with. I want to do a kindness for you, to repay you and Mom as best I can." Now he was jogging along beside her as smooth as a stroll, barely breathing. It was adding to her humiliation.

"Grant, it's a little fucking late for that. Dad's gone. Money's not going to bring him back. And I'm okay, Mom's okay—at least for money." *Well,* she thought, *that's true for now, but who knows what lies ahead?* "So what's a couple of million or so between siblings, anyway? Right? It's the price of finding out who everybody is."

Just now, she told herself, *the biggest "kindness" he could do would be to disappear. Forever.* She'd thought she was over the bulk of the pain and the feelings of humiliation, but seeing him again, hearing his voice, and looking at his eyes was bringing all of it back. She realized she was never going to be over it.

"Ally, go ahead and say whatever you need to . . . Look, I can't really do anything about the money, at least not right this minute—though I've got a big ship on the horizon, assuming a deal I'm working on comes through. But right now I'm about to try to do you a favor."

"I think I can muddle through without any of your 'favors,' Grant. And I really don't appreciate your showing up out of the blue like this, bullying your way back into my life."

She glanced over and saw his gray eyes were hangdog. It was the soulful look he used to melt her resolve. But not this time. She was yelling at herself inside *not* to give an inch. If she let him anywhere close to her life again, she was sure she'd only regret it.

"Well, like it or not, I am here at the moment," he said, once more jogging a pace ahead, then twisting his head back. They were at the crossing and he could see her building from where they were. He had to get a hook into her before she disappeared into that damned lobby. Time for the bait. "By the way, Ally, how's your ticker doing these days? You still have to watch out for . . . that heart thing?"

"Look, Grant, I've got a busy morning. I'm going up to see Mom, not that you'd give a damn. So thank you for inquiring about my health, but frankly what do you care?" She paused. "Tell you what. If your 'favor' is so wonderful, I'll give you one phone call. Tonight, at home." She had Knickers's leash on a short hold and was waiting for the light to change. "But I've got to go now."

Shit, he thought, *the hook didn't catch.* "Can't be on the phone, I'm telling you. I needed to *see* you. Why the hell do you think I took the trouble to catch you before your day got started? You know I hate getting up this early." He stepped onto the curb and stopped. "Ally, please listen. This is something I can *do* for you. I won't insult you by saying it's for old times' sake, but in a way it is. I got you a shot at a big job. Bartlett wants to redo the ground floor of his place on Gramercy Park. I told him about CitiSpace, and he sounded interested and said he'd like for you to come by and meet him and help him kick around some ideas."

She looked at him, not believing a word.

"You hacked into my life at seven o'clock Sunday morning for *that*. You had to *see* me? Give me a break. What do you really want? And this better be good."

Okay, he thought. *Cut to the chase.*

"You're correct. It's about your heart."

"What about it?"

Make it real, he told himself. *This could be your only shot.*

"All right, here's the unvarnished deal. What I really did for you. About five years ago, Bartlett bankrolled a start-up bio-med firm called the Gerex Corporation. It was the brainchild of a Dutch doctor whose research project had just been sawed off at the knees by Stanford University. Then Bartlett moved the entire operation to a clinic at the BMD campus out in New Jersey called the Dorian Institute. It's all very hush-hush, but I can tell you Gerex has a new procedure in clinical trials that can literally work miracles. The head researcher, this Dutch doctor, has pioneered a new treatment using a stem cell procedure to trick an organ into regenerating itself, even a heart. It's like you grow your own transplant."

Now she was finally listening.

"I was talking to the Dutch guy late last week," he went on, picking up a faint positive vibe and hoping desperately he could build on it, "and he said he's looking for someone in their thirties with a rheumatic-heart thing—I think it's like what you have—to be part of this big clinical trial they're wrapping up. But they have to do it immediately, so they can put the data in their final report to the National Institutes of Health."

"And you thought about me? That's very touching, Grant. Your idea of doing me a favor is to let some Dutch quack experiment on me?"

"Hey, don't be so fast to turn up your nose at this." *Shit,* he thought, how *am I going to make any headway?* "His procedure operates at the cell level. The way they say it works is he takes cells from your bone marrow or blood or . . . whatever and makes them 'immortal' with this special enzyme and then injects them into organ tissue. It causes that organ to start regenerating itself."

"That sounds completely like science fiction. Besides, I'm not—"

"Well, he's doing it. Trust me. But there're only a couple of weeks left in the clinical trials, so everything's on a fast track now. If you're the least bit interested, you've got to call him tomorrow. If you don't, I'm sure he'll find somebody else by the middle of the week."

He reached down and tried to give Knickers a pat, but she drew away. *Good for her,* Ally thought. Then he looked up and his voice grew animated. "Ally, the Dutch doctor—his name is Van de Vliet, by the way—is the smartest man I've ever met. I'd say he's a good bet for the Nobel Prize in Medicine this time next year. I'd put my last dime on it. What he's doing is so incredible I shouldn't even be talking about it. At least not till the clinical trials are finished. But I wanted to do you this favor."

Uh-huh, she thought. What it amounted to was, he was coming to her with another one of his hustles. Probably they needed somebody to round out their clinical trials and she was conveniently handy. "You know, Grant, maybe I'll just pass. I already have a cardiologist."

She found herself wondering what Dr. Ekelman would say to this radical new treatment.

"All right, Ally, do you want to make me beg? I *need* you

to do this. When I described you to Dr. Van de Vliet, I could tell he was very excited. This could change everything for you." He paused, perhaps becoming aware of the pleading tone in his voice. "For chrissake, give me a break. Is there someplace we can have coffee? I'm not asking to come upstairs or anything. I just want to see if we can be on speaking terms long enough to help each other out."

In a way she was relieved, though she was secretly hurt all over again too. He wasn't crawling back to her to beg forgiveness for destroying lives. No, he was back and groveling because he thought she could help him butter up his boss. How could she not feel used?

God, that was so like him. At that moment she *knew* there was never any chance he'd change.

"Come on," he said again. "A lousy cup of coffee. There's that little French bistro on Hudson Street." He tried a grin. "Hey, I'll even buy."

For a moment she thought she felt her resolve slipping. It's funny, but after you break up a family, no matter how dysfunctional, you start repressing the bad memories. But then something comes along to remind you all over again.

"Grant, are you hearing yourself?" She stared at him. "You sound like you're selling snake oil."

"Why was I afraid you'd back off? You're really doing it because you're pissed. Okay, you've got a right. But I've brought you something I think you ought to at least look at." He was unzipping his fanny pack and taking out a Gerex Corporation envelope, folded in half.

Christ, he thought miserably, *why is she doing this to me? I've got to keep the door open.*

"Read this and then give me a call tonight, like you promised. It'll tell you more about him."

She hesitated before taking it. It was thick with papers and she was planning to spend the day visiting Nina. "I think I've heard enough already."

"Just look at his CV. Van de Vliet's. He's done a lot of

things. You've got to take him seriously." He urged it into her hand. "Look at it and call me. Please."

She took it, and then she reached down and patted Knickers. "Come on, baby. Let's go up."

He watched her disappear into the lobby and start shooting the breeze with the doorman, some red-haired jerk with a ponytail who'd just come on duty.

Damn. Maybe the best thing would be just to chloroform her and let her wake up in the lab. W.B. needs her.

Chapter 2

"Okay, you'd better take it from here," Winston Bartlett declared to Kenji Noda over the roar of the engine. He had lifted his feet off the pedals and was unbuckling the cockpit seat belt. He liked having a turn piloting his McDonnell Douglas 520N helicopter on the commutes between his corporate headquarters in Lower Manhattan and his medical research park in northern New Jersey, but prudence dictated a more experienced hand on the collective during descent and landing. For that he had Noda, formerly of the Japanese Defense Forces. A tall, wiry man of few words, Noda was also his bodyguard, chauffeur, and curator of his museum-quality katana sword collection.

With the sharp, delicious aroma of the pine forest below wafting through the cabin, Noda quickly put aside the origami he'd been folding, to center his mind, and slid around a special opening in the bulkhead. He strapped himself into the seat, then took the radio headphones. The sky was the purest blue, with not another craft in the visual perimeter. They were, after all, over a forest.

As Bartlett settled himself in the passenger compartment, he thought about where matters stood. There was the very real prospect he had rolled the dice one time too many. The daily blood tests at his clinic in New Jersey were showing he was disturbingly close to using up his nine lives.

To look at him, though, you'd never suspect. At sixty-seven he was still trim and athletic, confident even cocky, with a full head of steel dark hair and probing eyes that instantly appraised whatever they caught in their gaze. He played handball at a private health club near his Gramercy Park mansion for an hour every other morning and he routinely defeated men half his age, including Grant Hampton. Remaining a player in every sense of the term was the main reason he enjoyed flying his M-D chopper, even though his license had been lapsed for eight years. It was the perfect embodiment of his lust for life. As he never failed to point out, his lifelong business success wasn't bad for a City College grad with a bachelor's degree in Oriental art history. He had gotten this far because he *wanted* success enough to make it happen.

He'd started out in New York real estate, but for the last twenty years he had concentrated on buying up small, underpriced medical-device manufacturers with valuable patents and weak bottom lines. He dismantled some of the companies and sold off the pieces, always for more than he'd paid for the whole. Others he restructured with new management, and when a profitable turnaround was in sight, he took them public or sold them to a major player like Johnson & Johnson. The potential winners, though, the ones with promising pipelines of medical devices or drugs whose FDA approval was imminent, he relocated here at the BMD campus in northern New Jersey.

But competition was fierce, and the bigger players like Merck and J&J had limitless research capital. They could write off dead ends a lot easier. Thus it was that five years ago, when his pipeline was drying up, Winston Bartlett took the biggest gamble of his life. He acquired a cash-strapped new start-up called the Gerex Corporation, whose head scientist was at the cutting edge of stem cell research. Karl Van de Vliet, M.D., Ph.D., had just had his funding terminated and his laboratory at Stanford University closed after a political flap by right-wingers.

Bartlett had moved Van de Vliet here to New Jersey and poured millions into his stem cell efforts, bleeding BMD's working capital white and racking up 85 million in short-term debt just to keep the rest of the company afloat. Now, though, the gamble was paying off. This month Gerex was winding up stage-three clinical trials for the National Institutes of Health. These trials validated a revolutionary procedure that changed the rules of everything known about healing the human body. Already his CFO, Grant Hampton, was heading a negotiating team hammering out a deal with the British biotech conglomerate Cambridge Pharmaceuticals to sell them a 49 percent stake in Gerex. Over 650 million in cash and stock were on the table, and there were escalators, depending on the results of the trials now under way.

The problem was, Cambridge had only seen the financials and summaries of data from Gerex's *successful* clinical trials. They knew nothing about the fiasco of the Beta procedure.

"Karl called just before we left and said she's worse this morning," Bartlett remarked to Noda. He was removing his aviator shades and there was deep frustration in his eyes. "God, I feel so damned responsible. She was—"

"Having the Beta was Kristen's idea," Noda reminded him. "She *wanted* to do it."

What he didn't say was on both their minds: what about Bartlett himself? After Kristen Starr had had the Beta, and it had seemed successful, Bartlett decided to have it too. Now his daily blood tests here at the institute were showing that the telomerase enzyme was starting to metastasize and replicate in his bloodstream, just as it had in hers.

"Well," Bartlett went on, "Karl thinks he's got a new idea that might save us. Hampton is supposed to be on the case this very morning." He stared out the chopper's window, down at the rooftops of his empire. At the north end of the industrial park was the main laboratory, where stents and titanium joint replacements were tested on animals—mostly sterile pigs, though some primate testing also was under way. The central area had two large manufacturing facilities where the more complex devices were made.

The buildings were all white cinder block, except for the one they were hovering above now. It was at the far south end, a massive three-story mansion nestled among ancient pines and reached by a long cobblestone driveway. Though it was actually the oldest building of the group by a hundred years, it was the latest acquisition for the complex. It fronted a beautiful ten-acre lake, and had been a summer *palacio* of a nineteenth-century railroad baron. Around midcentury it was turned into a luxury retirement home, complete with nursing services. Its ornate appointments reminded patients of the Frick Gallery, if one could imagine those marble halls teeming with wheelchairs and nurses.

Bartlett had bought the defunct manufacturing complex next to it eighteen years earlier for the BMD industrial park, but it was only six years ago that the owners of the mansion, a group of squabbling heirs, finally relented and agreed to part with the property. It was now a flagship holding of BMD.

He had an eye for design and he had loved remodeling the old mansion and making it into a modern clinic and research facility. He had renamed it the Dorian Institute and moved in Karl Van de Vliet and the research staff of the Gerex Corporation. He also had put a landing pad on the expansive roof, along with a stair leading down to an elevator that could take him directly to the laboratory in the basement.

Kenji Noda settled the McDonnell Douglas onto the pad and cut the engines. Bartlett never let himself worry about the noise. The patients in the clinical trials were here at no charge, so they really couldn't complain, particularly since they were now part of what was possibly turning out to be the greatest advance in the history of medicine. If your Alzheimer's had just been reversed at no charge, you weren't going to complain about a little hubbub on the roof.

"I'll wait here," Noda said, opening the side door. His bald pate, reminiscent of an eighteenth-century samurai, glistened in the early spring sun.

Bartlett nodded, knowing that his pilot did not trust physicians and hospitals. Taking care of your body was *your* responsibility, Kenji Noda frequently declared, and he trained his own daily. He ate no meat and drank gallons of green tea. When he practiced kendo swordplay, he had the reflexes of a man half his age. He never discussed why he had left Japan, but Bartlett assumed it was for reasons best left in the dark.

Bartlett headed down the metal stairs leading to the self-service elevator. This daily ordeal of flying out to give a blood sample and to see Kristen was increasingly unsettling. As he inserted his magnetic card into the elevator security box, he felt his hand shaking slightly.

So close to the eternal dream of humankind. So close. How was it going to end?

Sunday, April 5
8:38 A.M.

"Dr. Vee, I'm feeling so much better, I can't tell you." Emma Rosen reached out and caught her physician by the collar of his lab coat, pulling him down and brazenly bussing his cheek. She'd been longing to do this for three weeks but hadn't mustered the nerve until now. "This morning I climbed the stairs to the third floor, twice, up and back without any chest pain. Oy, can you believe? It's a miracle."

Karl Van de Vliet was a couple of inches over six feet, with a trim face and sandy hair that some older patients judged too long for a physician. His English normally was perfect, though sometimes he made a mistake when trying to sound too colloquial. But everyone, young and old, adored his retiring Dutch manner and those deep blue eyes that carried some monumental sadness from the past. They also were sure he would soon be recognized worldwide as the miracle worker he was. The prospect of a Nobel didn't actually seem that far-fetched.

"Emma, please, I begged you to rest." He sighed and checked the dancing electronic pens of her EKG. They were in the basement of the Dorian Institute. Upstairs, the "suites"— nobody called them rooms—were intended to invoke a spa more than a clinic, so most of the heavy-duty diagnostic equipment was kept in a row of examining rooms down near the subterranean lab. "For another week at least. Why won't you listen? You've been a very naughty girl. I may have to tell your daughter."

He glanced at the seventy-three-year-old woman's readout one last time, made a quick note on his handheld computer, and then laid a thin hand across her brow for a fleeting, subjective temperature check.

She's all but fully recovered, he told himself. *It's truly astonishing.*

Five weeks earlier, she had come through the front door of the Dorian Institute in a wheelchair pushed by her youngest, a bottle blonde named Shelly. He took one look and scuttled the normal security precautions, the frisk for cameras and recording devices. Emma's low cardiac output had deteriorated to the point that her left leg below the knee was swollen to almost twice its normal size, owing to renal retention of fluid, and she was so short of breath she required oxygen. He hadn't wanted to complicate the clinical trials by taking on another patient at that late date, but she had been referred by a physician friend in the city, begging. How could he turn her away?

He had removed a microscopic amount of bone marrow from her right ankle, extracted the stem cells, applied the hormonal signal that told them to develop into heart muscle, and then injected a thriving cell factory into her heart. Since stem cells could be made to ignore the body's rules to stop replicating after a certain number, they were able to reproduce forever, constantly renewing themselves. The only other cells with that immortal characteristic were cancer cells. In fact, it was as though he had given Emma a new kind of cancer—one that produced cells as healthy as those in a newborn. Today she probably could have *run* up those stairs.

Although his stem cell technology was going to create a new era in regenerative medicine, he had experienced his share of bumps in the road. Five years earlier, Stanford University had canceled his research project there since the work he had been doing involved the special stem cells in unused fertility-clinic embryos. The university claimed there had been death threats to its president. The Board of Regents had finally decided, with a sham show of remorse, to revoke his funding. They called him in one sunny afternoon in May and pulled the plug. He thanked them and tore up his contract. By that time he had already demonstrated that, using the right chemical signals, stem cells could be coaxed into becoming almost any organ. Inserted into the heart, they became new heart muscle, replacing scars; inserted into the brain, they became neural tissue. No way was he going to be stopped now. They didn't know what they were losing.

What he needed was a "white knight." He did some poking around and came up with Winston Bartlett, then floated feelers to Bartlett's people. What if, he proposed, Bartlett acquired the Gerex Corporation for BMD and made it a for-profit business? No more public funding (and maddening administrative meddling). The research already completed was so close to a payoff, after years and years of grinding lab work and thousands of white mice, that the deal could be considered an investment where 95 percent of the seed money had already been supplied by taxpayers.

Winston Bartlett had liked the sound of that, and Karl Van de Vliet had his white knight.

Once his financing was secure, he decided to begin by solving the problem that had dogged him at Stanford. Since there would always be a distracting public-relations problem hounding any researcher in the United States who made use of aborted embryos, even if it was to save lives, he was determined to find a less controversial way to trick Mother Nature and garner "pluripotent" stem cells, the name given those that could give rise to virtually any tissue type.

He had. After he moved his research team into the Dorian Institute just over 4½ years ago, he had perfected a way to use a human protein, an enzyme called telomerase, to make adult stem cells do most of the miracles once only thought possible with embryonic cells.

The phase-three clinical trials over the past seven months had proved conclusively that the technique worked. Adult stem cells, when treated with the telomerase enzyme to arrest the process of cell senescence, could indeed regenerate everything from the human brain to the human heart, from Parkinson's to acute myocardial infarction.

Twenty-three days from now, when the phase-three clinical trials were formally scheduled to be completed, Karl Van de Vliet would have enough data for the National Institutes of Health to confirm one of the most important breakthroughs in the history of medicine.

Unfortunately, however, there was that other bit of data that he would *not* be sharing with the NIH. The Beta.

Thinking about that, his heart heavy, he turned back to the situation at hand.

"Emma, you're making wonderful progress," he continued on with the banter, "but don't push yourself too hard just yet."

She laughed, sending lines across her forehead. Her voice was deep and rich, sultry in its own way. "When you get as old as I am, honey, you do anything you can get away with. What am I saving it for? I just might go to Atlantic City next week and pick up a sailor."

"Well, then, I may have to have Shelly go along and keep an eye on you," he said with one last programmed smile. Then he checked his watch. Bartlett should be arriving any minute now. Time to get Emma Rosen the hell out of here and back upstairs.

He turned and signaled for Ellen O'Hara, the head nurse, to start removing the suction-cup electrodes that had been stuck on Emma for her EKG. Ellen had been with him when he was at Stanford and her loyalty was unquestioned. She had made sure that the Beta disaster with Kristen hadn't become the gossip of the institute. Still, how much longer could it be kept quiet?

Then Sandra Hanes, the lively, dark-haired woman in charge of the second floor for this shift, walked into the examination room. She knew nothing about Kristen.

"Perfect timing," he said. Then he drew her aside. "Keep an eye on Emma, will you? Try and keep her in her room and quiet as much as you can. The last blood work showed her white-cell count over twelve K/CMM. It could mean there's some minimal rejection rearing its head. Probably nothing to worry about, but can you just keep her away from the stairs for godsake? I don't want her tiring herself out."

"I'll tie her to the bed if I have to," Sandra answered. The clinical trials had required a mountain of paperwork, and her face was strained from working long shifts, including a lot of weekends, like this one. But he suspected she actually appreciated the overtime. She was forty-five, divorced, and putting a straight-A daughter through Rutgers.

She also was a first-rate nurse, like all the others at the institute, and her loyalty couldn't be more secure. Still, he knew that she and all the other staffers were bursting to tell the world about the miracles they'd witnessed. That was why Bartlett had insisted on an ironclad nondisclosure agreement in the contract of every employee to be strictly enforced. (And to put teeth into the security, all employees were body-searched for documents or cameras or tapes on the way in and out.) To violate it would be to open yourself to a life-altering lawsuit. During World War II the claim had been that "loose lips sink ships." Here they would render you a pauper for life. Nobody dared even whisper about the spectacular success of the clinical trials.

As the examining room emptied out, he checked his

watch one more time. Winston Bartlett was due any minute now and he had nothing but bad news for the man.

Trying to control his distress, he walked to the end of the hallway and prepared to enter the lab. Whereas the ground floor and the two above were for reception, common dining, and individual rooms, the basement contained the laboratory, his private office, the examination rooms, and an OR (never yet used, thankfully). There also was a subbasement, accessible only through an elevator in the lab or an alarmed set of fire stairs. It was an intensive-care area, and it was where Kristen, the Beta casualty, was being kept.

He zipped a magnetic card through the reader on the door and entered the air lock. The lab was maintained under positive pressure to keep out the slightest hint of any kind of contaminant. It was as sterile as a silicon chip factory.

The room was dominated by a string of black slate workbenches, then rows and rows of metal shelves with tissue-containing vials of a highly volatile solvent cocktail he had engineered especially for this project, along with a computer network and a huge autoclave and several electron microscopes.

He walked in and greeted his research team. He'd managed to keep the core group that had been closest to him at Stanford, four people who, he believed, were among the finest medical minds in the country. They were the renowned molecular biologist David Hopkins, Ph.D., the strikingly beautiful and widely published endocrinologist Debra Connolly, M.D., and two younger staffers, a couple who'd met and married at his Stanford lab, Ed and Beth Sparks, both Ph.D.'s who'd done their postdoc under him. They all were here now in the wilds of northern New Jersey because they knew they were making medical history.

David was waiting, his long shaggy forelock down over his brow as always. But his eyes told it all.

"Karl, Bartlett's blood work from yesterday just got faxed up from the lab at Princeton. His enzyme level has increased another three point seven percent."

"Damn." It was happening for sure. "Did you run—"

"The computer simulation? A one-standard-deviation estimate is that he's going to go critical sometime between seventeen and nineteen days."

"The Syndrome." Van de Vliet sighed.

"Just like Kristen."

"She faked us out. There were no side effects for weeks." Van de Vliet shook his head sadly as he set his handheld Palm computer onto a side table. Later he would transfer all the day's patient data into the laboratory's server, the Hewlett-Packard they all affectionately called the Mothership. Then he began taking off his white coat.

"Bartlett looks to be inevitable now." David exhaled in impotent despair. The frustration and the tension were getting to everybody. They all knew what was at stake. "It's in two and a half weeks, give or take."

What had supposedly been a cosmetic procedure had gone horribly awry. Van de Vliet wondered if it wasn't the ultimate vengeance of the quest for something you shouldn't have.

"His AB blood type is so rare. If we'd just kept a sample before the procedure, we'd have something to work with now," Van de Vliet said sadly. "We still might be able to culture some antibodies."

He hadn't told his research team yet about the other possible option—using somebody else as an AB blood–type incubator.

His last-ditch idea was to find a patient with a blood type of AB positive and introduce a small quantity of the special Beta telomerase enzyme into them. The theory was that this might induce their body to produce compatible antibodies, which could then be extracted and cultured in the laboratory. If a sufficient quantity could be produced, they could be injected into Bartlett and hopefully arrest the enzyme's pattern of entering the host's bloodstream and metastasizing into the more complex form that brought on the Syndrome. And if it did work, then there might even be some way to adapt the procedure to Kristen.

"Karl, if Cambridge Pharmaceuticals finds out about the Beta fiasco, how's it going to affect—"

"How do you *think* it's going to affect the sale? If this gets out, there'll be no sale. To anybody. Bartlett will be ruined, and Gerex along with him. That's everybody here, in case you're counting." He turned and exited the lab, pushing pensively through the air lock, and then he walked slowly toward his office, collecting his thoughts. He was just passing the elevator when it opened.

Sunday, April 5
8:47 A.M.

Winston Bartlett looked up to see Van de Vliet as he stepped off the elevator, and the sight heartened him as always. The Dutchman was a genius. If anyone could solve this damned mess, surely he was the one.

"First thing, Karl, how is she now?"

"I think you'd better go down and see for yourself," Van de Vliet said slowly. "As I told you on the phone, she still comes and goes. I think it's getting worse."

Bartlett felt a chill run through him. He had once cared for this woman as much as he was capable of caring for anybody, and what had happened was a damned shame. All he had intended was to give her something special, something no man had ever given a woman before.

"Will she know who I am? She still did yesterday."

"It depends," Van de Vliet replied. "Yesterday afternoon she was fully lucid, but then earlier this morning I got the impression she thinks she's in a different place and time. If I had to guess, I'd say she's regressing chronologically. I suppose that's logical, though nothing about this makes any sense."

Bartlett was following him back through the air lock and

into the laboratory. The intensive-care area below was reachable only by a special elevator at the rear of the lab.

All these once-cocky people, Bartlett thought, were now scared to death. Van de Vliet and his research team might actually be criminally liable if the right prosecutor got hold of the case. At the very least they'd be facing an ethics fiasco.

But I'm the one who's about to be destroyed. In every sense.

It had all started when Karl Van de Vliet confided in him that there was an adjunct procedure arising out of stem cell research that might, *might,* offer the possibility of a radical new cosmetic breakthrough. Just a possibility. He called it the Beta, since it was highly experimental. He also wasn't sure it was reproducible. But he had inadvertently discovered it while testing the telomerase enzyme on his own skin over a decade ago.

At the time he was experimenting with topical treatments for pigment abnormalities, but the particular telomerase enzyme he was working with had had the unexpected effect of changing the texture of his skin, softening it and removing wrinkles, a change that subsequently seemed permanent.

The idea had lain dormant while they were preparing for the clinical trials. But then Bartlett's *petite amie,* the cable-TV personality Kristen Starr, had had a career crisis that she blamed on aging, and he came up with the idea of having her undergo the skin procedure.

In a mistake with unforeseen ramifications, she had then been made an official part of the NIH clinical trials. After she had gone for over a month without any side effects, Bartlett had elected to undergo the procedure himself.

Then it began in Kristen—what David had solemnly named the Syndrome. Van de Vliet had immediately (and illegally) terminated her from the clinical trials, removing her from the NIH database. She was now being kept on the floor below, in the subbasement intensive-care area.

As they stepped onto the elevator to go down, Bartlett found himself wondering how many of the staff here were aware of the real extent of the crisis. Van de Vliet had said that only three of the nurses knew about Kristen and the Syndrome. Fortunately, they all were trustworthy. Two had even been with him back at Stanford. They would never talk.

But what about the rest? They'd all fawned over Kristen, starstruck by her celebrity, and they'd spill the beans in a heartbeat if any of them found out. The story would be everywhere from *Variety* to the "Page Six" gossip column. It would certainly mean the financial ruin of Bartlett Medical Devices. If Gerex went under, everything else went with it.

On the other hand, he thought ruefully, *what does it matter? If I end up like her, I won't even know it happened.*

"W.B., the telomerase enzyme is completely out of control in her now," Van de Vliet continued. "First it metastasized through her skin and into her blood. Then it began directing its own synthesis. I've tried everything I know to arrest it, but nothing has worked. I still have a faint hope, though. If we can make some headway on your own situation . . ." He paused and his voice trailed off. "In the meantime, though, I think it would definitely be wise to move her to another location. There are too many people here. The risk is enormous. Word is bound to get out sooner or later. You must have someplace . . ."

"Of course." Bartlett nodded. "I'd rather have her in the city and closer to me anyway. But let me see if I can talk to her first. I need to try to make her understand."

Though it's probably too late for that, he told himself.

They stepped off the elevator and entered a high-security area, a long hallway illuminated only with fluorescent bulbs. Using a magnetic card as a key, Bartlett opened the first door they came to. As always, he was dismayed by the sight.

For a moment he just stood looking at the thirty-two-year-old woman sitting up in a hospital bed, mutely watching a flickering TV screen showing the Cartoon Network. He had truly cared for her, perhaps even loved her for a time.

Then he walked over. "Kristy, honey, how're you feeling?"

She stared at him blankly. Kristen had been a vivacious blue-eyed blonde who'd had her own showbiz gossip show on the E! channel till it was canceled during a scheduling shake-up six months earlier. She had a nervous breakdown, declaring to Bartlett that her show had been canceled because she looked like a crone.

He'd told her it wasn't true, but if she was so distraught about her appearance, then maybe there *was* something he could do for her. Van de Vliet had once mentioned an experimental skin procedure. . . .

Bartlett turned back to Van de Vliet, feeling the horror sinking in.

"Karl, goddamit, we've got to reverse this."

"Let's talk outside," Van de Vliet said.

Bartlett kissed Kristen's forehead in preparation for leaving. Her lifeless blue eyes flickered something. He thought it was a flash of some old anger.

Who could blame her? he told himself. But back then, who knew?

He'd wanted to give her a gift like none other. Not quite the Fountain of Youth, but maybe a cosmetic version. Her skin would begin to constantly renew itself.

And he'd been right. The promise of having her skin rejuvenated was just what she'd needed to get her self-confidence back.

For more than a month the miracle seemed to be working, and there were no side effects. Her skin was becoming noticeably softer and more supple. She was elated.

Screw NIH trials and the FDA, he then decided. It was working for Kristen. By God, he would try it himself. He wasn't getting any younger.

But no sooner had he had the procedure too than Kristen started evidencing side effects. First it was little things, like lapses in short-term memory. Next, as it got progressively worse, she could no longer remember why she was at the institute. Then she couldn't recall her name, where she lived. And now . . .

Could it be that God can't be cheated? And when it's tried, God brings down a terrible vengeance.

When they were outside in the hallway, he said, "I have a place on Park Avenue that's empty. At the moment. We used to spend weekends there and I can arrange for a full-time nursing staff, all of it." He paused. "Has anybody called here about her lately?"

"Just her mother, Katherine, who's getting pretty frantic."

"The woman is unbalanced. Certifiable. God help us if—"

"I told her to see what she could find out from Kristen's publicist."

"Good." Bartlett had told Kristen's midtown publicity agent, the nosy Arlene of Guys and Dolls, Inc., that Kristen had gone to a private spa in New Mexico to rethink her career and didn't want to be disturbed. She desired complete solitude. Any communication with her would have to be handled through *his* office.

He looked at Van de Vliet. "Karl, tell me how bad it is for *me* now."

"For you?" He hesitated. This was the question he'd been dreading. "The telomerase numbers from yesterday's blood sample are not encouraging. As I told you, your topical enzyme application has metastasized into your bloodstream and started to replicate, just like it did in Kristen. We're seeing a process known as 'engraftment.' These special cells have learned to mimic any cell they come near. They become the tissue that those cells comprise and begin replacing the healthy tissue with new. In Kristen's case, we think it's now entered her brain and it seems to be supplanting her memory tissue with blanks. The same side effect could eventually evolve in you."

That doesn't begin to describe the real horror, Bartlett thought. *It's too impossible to imagine.*

"The only thing left is to find some way to cause your body to reject the enzyme," Van de Vliet said. "I'm optimistic that we might be able to grow some telomerase antibodies in another patient with your blood type, then culture enough of them to stop the Syndrome in its tracks. It's worth a try. Frankly, I can't think of anything else. But your blood type is AB, which is extremely rare. Also, the problem is that we'd possibly be putting that other person at severe risk too."

"Let's go back up to the lab," Bartlett said. "That idea of yours—Hampton thinks he's got somebody. A woman, her late thirties." He put his hand on Van de Vliet's shoulder. "We're going to get her on board, however we have to."

Chapter 3

Stone Aimes was staring at the e-mail on the screen of his Compaq Armada and feeling an intense urge to put his fist through its twisted spiral crystals. What do you do when you've come up with an idea that could possibly save thousands of lives using simple Web-based technology and then the piece gets spiked by your newspaper's owners at the very last minute because it exposes some important New York hospitals to unpleasant (but constructive) scrutiny?

What it makes you *want* to do is tell everybody down on the third floor to stuff it and walk out and finish your book—undistracted by corporate ass-covering BS . . . or, unfortunately, by a paycheck.

Around him the newsroom of the *New York Sentinel,* a weekly newspaper positioned editorially somewhere between the *New York Observer* and the *Village Voice,* was in final Sunday countdown, with the Monday edition about to be put to bed. The technology was state of the art, and the room flickered with computer screens, blue pages that gave the tan walls an eerie cast. Composition, spell-checking, everything, was done by thinking machines, and the reporters, thirteen on this floor, were mostly in their late twenties and early thirties and universally underpaid.

The early morning room was bustling, though it felt to Stone like the end of time. Nobody was paying any attention to him but that was normal: everybody was doing their own thing. Besides, nobody else realized he'd just had a major piece killed at the last minute. Now he felt as though he were frozen in place: in this room, in this job, in this life.

The book he had almost finished was going to change a lot of things. It would be the first major explication of stem cell technology for general readers. Stem cells were going to revolutionize everything we knew about medicine and the research was going further than anyone could have dreamed. The possibility of reversing organ degeneration, even extending life, was hovering right out there, just at humankind's fingertips. It cried out for a major book.

He had read everything that had made its way into the medical journals, but the study that was furthest along was privately funded and now cloaked in secrecy. It was at the Gerex Corporation, whose head researcher was a Dutch genius named Karl Van de Vliet. The company had been bankrolled by the medical mogul Winston Bartlett after Van de Vliet lost his funding at Stanford.

Winston Bartlett, of all people . . . but that was another story.

Thirteen months earlier, the Gerex Corporation had trolled for volunteers on the National Institutes of Health Web site, referring to a pending "special study." The notice suggested the study might be using stem cell technology in some fashion. If that study was what Stone Aimes thought it was, it would be the first to use stem cells in stage-three clinical trials. Nobody else was even close.

Karl Van de Vliet was the ball game. Unfortunately, however, his study was being held in an atmosphere of military-like secrecy. Why? Even the identities of the participants in the trials were like a state secret. Since Winston Bartlett owned Gerex, it surely had been ordered by *him*. You had to wonder what that was all about. . . .

Whatever the reason, Stone Aimes knew that in order to finish his book with the latest information he *had* to get to Van de Vliet. But Bartlett had forbidden any interviews, and Gerex's clinic, called the Dorian Institute, was off-limits to the public and reportedly guarded with serious security.

But, he thought, perhaps he had just come up with an idea of how to get around that. . . .

He stared a moment longer at the dim reflection coming back at him from the antiglare screen, which now informed him that his cover feature had been chopped. Truthfully, it was happening more and more; this was the third time in eight months that a major muckraking piece had been axed. Also, as he stared at it, the reflection told him he wasn't getting any younger. The hairline was no longer where it had been in his college photos—it was up about half an inch— and the blue eyes were sadder, the lines under them deeper.

Still, the tousled brown hair was thick enough, the brow mostly wrinkle-free, and he still had hope. He wasn't exactly young anymore, but neither was he "getting on." The "Willy Loman" years remained safely at bay. He was thirty-nine and divorced, with an ex-wife, Joyce, who had departed to be a garden designer in northern California, taking with her their daughter, Amy, on whom he doted. He had a one-bedroom, rent-controlled apartment in the East Nineties, on the top floor of a fashionable brownstone. He was socially unattached, as the expression goes, but he was so compulsive about finishing the book that he spent weekends hunched over his IBM Aptiva, nursing a six-pack of Brooklyn Lager and writing deathless prose. The truth was he was lonely, but he didn't allow himself to think about it.

He'd always vowed he'd amount to something by forty. And now it was as much for Amy as for himself. She lived with his ex-wife near El Cerrito, California, and she meant the world to him. The mortifying part was, he was a week behind with this month's support check. And he knew Joyce needed the money. It made him feel like a callous deadbeat dad, when the real culprit was an unlucky confluence of inescapable bills. He'd make it up next week, but he'd sworn he would never let this happen.

That was why he had a larger game plan. Get out of this frigging day job and *finish the book*. The time for that plan to kick in was approaching at warp speed. This last insult was surely God's not-so-subtle way of informing him that his future was in the freelance world. Every day out there would be a gamble, but he could write anything he damn well pleased.

There was a parable set down by the ancient Taoist philosopher Lao Tzu that Stone Aimes reflected on more and more these days. It was the story of two oxen: One was a ceremonial sacrificial ox who, for the year before he meets the ax, was feted with garlands of lotus flowers and plied with ox goodies. The other was a wild ox who had to scrounge in the forest for every scrap. But, the story went, on the day the ax was to drop, what wouldn't that ceremonial ox give to change places with that haggard, struggling, underfed wild ox?

That's the one he empathized with. The one who was out there, half starved but *free*.

The *Sentinel* was an iron rice bowl that normally never let anybody go except for grossest incompetence or flagrant alcoholism. On the other hand, getting ahead was all about office politics, kissing the managing editor's hindquarters, and copying him on every memo to anybody to make sure nobody else took credit for something *you* thought of.

On the plus side, he knew he was a hell of a medical journalist. There was such a gap between medical research and what most people knew, the field cried out for a Stephen Hawking of health, a medical Carl Sagan. The way he saw it, there was room at the top and he was ready for a major career breakthrough. He had done premed at Columbia before switching to journalism, and these days he read the *Journal of the American Medical Association* from cover to cover, every issue, along with skimming the many other journals now on the web.

The piece that just got cut was intended to show the world that investigative journalism was alive and well and trying to make a difference. He'd documented that hospital mistakes were actually the eighth leading cause of death in the United States. The Institute of Medicine estimated that medical errors caused between fifty and a hundred thousand deaths a year—rivaling the number from auto accidents or AIDS. (He'd gotten enough data to be able to quantify how many of those deaths were in leading New York hospitals.) Yet there was no federal law requiring hospitals to report mistakes that caused serious injury or death to patients.

The reason seemed to be that the medical lobby—he'd named names—had successfully turned back all attempts by Congress to pass such a law, even though it was a formal recommendation by the Institute of Medicine. The problem was, once you admitted you screwed up, you could get sued.

So there was no formal accountability.

But (and here was the constructive part) if patients' medical records were put on the Web—everything, even their medications—it could make a big dent in the all-too-frequent hospital medication foul-ups. That alone could cut accidental hospital deaths in half.

He'd pitched Jay Grimes, the managing editor, to let him do a five-thousand-word piece for the *Sentinel*. Jay had agreed and even promised him the front page. Jay liked him, but since all the real decisions were made by the owners, not-so-affectionately known as the Family, there wasn't much Jay could do to protect his people. Stone now realized that more than ever.

The e-mail on his Compaq's screen was from Jane Tully, who handled legal affairs for the paper. Apparently, Jay didn't have the balls to be the hatchet man, so he'd given the job to Jane, who could throw in a little legal mumbo jumbo for good measure. And she hadn't even had the courtesy to pick up the phone to do the deed. Instead, she'd sent a frigging e-mail: *See attached. Corporate says legal implications convey unacceptable risk. Consider an op-ed piece. That way the liability will be all yours. Love and kisses.*

And of course, by "Corporate," she meant the Family (or, more likely, their running-dog attorneys down on Nassau Street).

It was really too bad about Jane. She was a young-looking thirty-six and had her own legal practice with a large law firm in midtown, but she always dropped by before her Sunday brunch to answer any legal questions that might be pending before the *Sentinel* was put to bed. Stone knew pretty well how her mind worked. He should. Jane Tully was his former, *very* former, significant other.

They'd lived together for a year and a half on First Avenue in the East Sixties. But she was type A (tailored Armani suits and always on time) and he was a type B (elbow patches and home-cooked pasta). The denouement had been seismic and full of acrimony and accusations.

So was she killing this major piece out of spite? he wondered. Just to prove one last time who really had the *cojones?*

Actually, it would have been nice to think so. That would put a human face on this gutless travesty. But the attached memo had enough legal jargon that another reason was immediately suggesting itself. The owners of the paper, the Family, the fucked-up twins Harry and Bosco and their mother, Adeline, the heirs of Edward Jordan, actually *were* afraid of a lawsuit. The attachment had the fingerprints of the Family's attorneys all over it. Jane was just carrying out marching orders.

And sure enough, there at the bottom was a second message, unsigned and not part of the original memo. She had written clearly *ITMB.*

That was their old code for "I tried my best."

Well, Jane baby, who the hell knows. Maybe you did. Damn, it wasn't supposed to be like this. He wasn't trying to be a Carl Bernstein, for chrissake. For once, all he wanted was to report a story exactly the way it was, and then try to help. He ultimately wanted to fix, not fault.

He hit a button and printed out a copy of everything, then minimized the screen, grabbed his jacket, and walked down the hall. Was this the moment to quit? It was, except he couldn't afford to. He'd never managed to put enough aside to take off a year and live on air and write and still get that fifteen-hundred-dollar check out to Joyce and Amy every first of the month.

He got to the bank of elevators and pushed the button for the third floor and stepped on. The inspection sticker framed just above the controls actually told the whole saga of why his cover story about sloppy procedures in New York and national hospitals had been killed. The building was owned by Bartlett Enterprises, the real estate holding company of Winston Bartlett.

The *Sentinel* held a very favorable lease, renewable for another ten years at only a 5 percent increase when it rolled over in seven months. The Jordan family had gotten it in the early 1990s, when New York real estate was still in the toilet from the stock market crash of '87, and for once Winston Bartlett really screwed up. Now it was about a fifth of the going price per square foot.

So naturally he was about to do everything he could to break the lease. He was that kind of guy. The Jordan family, owners of the *Sentinel,* probably figured that a big lawsuit by the AMA or somebody would overtax their legal budget and give Bartlett a shot at their soft underbelly. Thus no boats were to be rocked.

The elevator chimed and he stepped off on three. This floor had subdued lighting and understated birch paneling, pale white, in the reception area. It was as though power didn't need to trumpet itself. Everybody knew who had it.

He waved at Rhonda, the receptionist, and strode past. She glanced up, then said, "Does she know you're coming?"

She knew full well he was headed down to see Jane. Unlike most organizations, which take Sunday off, this was always a big day for the *Sentinel,* with all hands on deck.

"Thought I'd give her a little surprise."

"No kidding." She was reaching for the phone. "I think maybe I should—"

"Not necessary." He was charging down the hall, feeling knee-deep in the thick beige carpet. "I've got a feeling she's expecting me."

Jane's door was open and she was on the phone. But when she saw him, she said something abruptly and hung up. He strode through the door, then slammed it. The decor was bold primary colors, like her take on life. Explicit.

"Okay," he demanded, "what the hell's going on? How about the *real* story?"

"Love, you know you can't hang the Family out with that kind of liability," she declared, then got up and came around her desk and cracked open the door half a foot. "And you're the one person here I can't have a closed-door meeting with. It'll just get people talking again."

"Good. Let the world hear. It's time everybody on this floor learned what a bunch of gutless owners we have." He watched the crisp way she moved, picture-perfect inside her deep blue business suit, complete with a white blouse and a man's red tie. Seeing her here, hair clipped short, glasses, in an office brimming with power, you'd never guess she liked nothing better than to be handcuffed during sex.

"Stone, have you ever considered growing up?" She settled back into her chair. The desk was bare except for her notebook computer, an expensive IBM ThinkPad T25. Power all the way. "The Family's attorneys are just trying to keep us from getting dragged into court. At least until we can get the paper's lease on this building renewed. We're going to need to focus on that negotiation, not be distracted by some massive libel suit brought on by an irresponsible, mudslinging piece. You practically accused the AMA of bribery, and you named three senators. One from New Jersey, for chrissake. Stone, there might be a time for that, but this is *not* it."

This was exactly the reason he'd expected. What it really meant was, the Family was scared stiff of Winston Bartlett. They figured he was going to go to court to try to break the *Sentinel*'s lease.

"Let me ask *you* a question. Whatever happened to journalistic ethics around here? Remember that Statement of Purpose they have everybody sign before they could be hired. 'All the news, without regard' . . . you know. We were both so damned proud to be a part of that. Now you're helping them kill anything that's the slightest bit controversial. Is that what we've come to?"

"Stone, what the *New York Sentinel* has come to is to try and stay out of legal shit till their lease is renewed." She brushed an imaginary lock of hair from her face, a residual gesture she once used to stall for time when she actually did have long hair. "Just let it go, won't you? To get the signed and notarized documentation we'd need to run that piece—assuming we even could—would cost a fortune in time and resources."

Well, he told himself, there was possibly something to that, from a legal standpoint. But this was not the moment to let sweet reason run riot.

"Okay, look, if you or the Family, or whoever the hell, believe I'm going to go quietly, you'd better get ready for some revisionist thinking. If this piece gets spiked, after all the work I put into it—and dammit, Jane, you know I can document everything I write; that's the way I work—then I bloody well want something back from this gutless rag. Actually, it's something I want from *you*."

"You're not really in a position to—"

"Hey, don't try to ream me twice in the same morning." He walked around her desk and gazed down at the street. The Sunday-morning traffic was light. He also noticed that there was a public phone on the corner. Good, he'd be using

it in about eight minutes. Then he took a moment to reflect
on how nice it was to actually have a window. Of any kind.
"You know the saying, the pen is mightier than the sword.
I'm about to prove that once and for all, but there's something I need. I need a half hour's face time with one of Bartlett's
employees. A certain Dr. Karl Van de Vliet. He runs a company that Bartlett bought out, called the Gerex Corporation.
Strictly for fact-checking. They've got some important clinical trials going on at a clinic in New Jersey that I need to
hear about."

She looked at him in sincere disbelief.

"Stone, how on *earth* am I supposed to—"

"You talk to the Family's lawyers. They've gotta be talking to Bartlett's attorneys by now. *Make* it happen."

"And why exactly—"

"Because I have a book contract, Jane. And in the process
I need to find out everything there is to know about Winston
Bartlett's biggest undertaking ever. He has bankrolled some-
thing that could change the face of medicine."

"You're doing a *book* about Bartlett?" Her astonishment
continued growing and appeared to be genuine. "Jesus, you
didn't tell—"

"Hello. That's because who or what I write about on my
own dime is nobody's effing business around here."

Now he was thinking about Winston Bartlett and wondering why he'd never told her the most important piece of information in his life. It was how he was connected to the
man. He often wondered if maybe that was why he was
doing this book on stem cells, knowing that half of it would
end up being about Bartlett's self-serving, take-no-prisoners
business career. His infinite cruelty. Was the book actually
revenge?

"You know you'll have to get permission to reprint anything you've published in the *Sentinel.* The paper owns the
rights to—"

"Didn't you hear me?" He smiled. "It's a book. *My* book.
There's no editorial overlap."

"Who's the publisher?"

"They exist, trust me."

His small publisher wasn't exactly Random House, but they were letting him do whatever he wanted.

"It didn't start out being a book about Bartlett, per se," he went on, "but now he's becoming a central figure, because of what's going on—or possibly not going on—at Gerex."

She was losing her famous poise.

"What . . . *what* are you writing?"

"The end of time. The beginning of time. I don't know which it is. You see, the Gerex clinic in northern New Jersey has clinical trials under way on some new medical procedure involving stem cells. At least that's what I think. They've clamped down on the information, but I believe Van de Vliet, who's the head researcher there, is perilously close to one of the most important breakthroughs in medical history. I just need to get all this confirmed from the horse's mouth."

"Is that what you want to interview him about?"

"He was available for interviews until about four months ago. I actually had one scheduled, but it abruptly got canceled. Bang, suddenly there's a total blackout on the project. They just shut down their press office completely. When I call, I get transferred to his CFO, some young prick who likes to blow me off. For starters, I'd like to know why it's all so hush-hush."

"Stone, private medical research is always proprietary, for God's sake. Sooner or later he undoubtedly hopes to patent whatever he's doing. A privately held corporation doesn't have to report to anybody, least of all some nosy reporter."

That was true, of course. But Stone Aimes knew that the only way his book would be the blockbuster he needed to get free of the *Sentinel* was to tell the real story of what Gerex was in the process of achieving. And to be first doing it.

For which he needed *access*.

"Make it happen. Because, like it or not, Winston Bartlett is about to be the subject of a major volume of investigative journalism. I've already got a lot of what I need." That wasn't precisely the case, but there was no need to overdo brutal honesty. "The only question is, does he want it to be authorized or unauthorized? It's his choice."

Winston Bartlett, Stone knew all too well, was a man who liked nothing better than to see his name in the papers. In fact, he used the free publicity he always managed to get with his jet-setting lifestyle to popularize his various business ventures. Like Donald Trump, he had made himself a brand name. So what was going on here? Was he just playing his cards close to the chest, waiting to make a dramatic big announcement? Or was he keeping this project secret because he was worried about some competing laboratory beating him to a patent?

Or was he hiding something? Had the clinical trials out in New Jersey gone off the track? Was he keeping the project hush-hush because something was going on he didn't *want* the public to hear about? Had stem cell technology turned out to be an empty promise? Or had there been some horrible side effect they didn't want reported?

"So could you just raise this with his attorneys? Because if he lets Van de Vliet talk with me directly, he can be sure I'll get the story right. We can do this the easy way or the hard way. It's up to him."

"Stone, I hope you have an alternative career track in the advanced stages of planning. Because the minute the Family gets wind of this, that you're writing some tell-all about Bartlett, they're going to freak. Even if you're doing it on your own time, you still work here. At least for the moment. Your name is associated in the public's mind with the *Sentinel*."

He knew that, which was why this was going to be all or nothing.

"Just do me this one itsy-bitsy favor, Jane. It's the last thing I'll ever ask of you." He was turning to walk out. "And look on the bright side. When the Family finally sacks me for good and all, you won't have to write me any more nasty memos telling me to be a good boy."

He walked to the elevator and took it down. The next thing he had to do was make a phone call, and this was one that required a pay phone.

He'd thought about it and decided one possible way to encourage Bartlett to open up was to try to bluff him, to make the man think he knew more about the clinical trials than he actually did. There was only one way he could think to do that.

In premed days Stone Aimes had shared a dorm room at Columbia with Dale Coverton, who was now an M.D. and a deputy director at the National Institutes of Health. His office was at the National Heart, Lung, and Blood Institute.

One of the nice things about having friends who go way back is that sometimes, over all those years, something happens that gives one or the other a few chips to call in. Such was the case with Stone Aimes and Dale Coverton.

Dale's oldest daughter, Samantha, a blond-haired track star and math whiz, had—at age thirteen—developed a rare form of kidney cancer and needed a transplant. She was given six months, tops, to live.

Stone Aimes had done a profile of her in the paper he worked for then, the *New York Globe,* and he'd found a transplant donor, a young girl on Long Island with terminal leukemia, who was able to die knowing she'd saved another person's life. The two had met and cried together, but Samantha was alive today because of Stone Aimes. It was a hell of a chit to call in, and he'd sworn he never would, but now he felt he had no choice. The truth was, Dale Coverton would have walked through fire for him. The question was, would he also violate NIH rules?

Stone hoped he would.

He stopped at the pay phone at the corner of Park and Eighteenth Street, an area where nine people out of ten were wearing at least one item of clothing that was black. It also seemed that six out of ten who passed were talking on cell phones. He took out a prepaid phone card and punched in the access number and then the area code for Bethesda,

Maryland, followed by Dale's private, at-home number. It was, after all, Sunday morning.

"Hey, Atlas, how's it going?" That had been Dale's nickname ever since he lifted two kegs of beer (okay, empty) over his head, one balanced on each hand, at a Sigma frat blast their senior year. It now seemed like an eternity: for Dale, two wives ago, and for Stone, one wife and two live-togethers.

"Hey, Truth and Justice, over and out." It was their all-purpose old code phrase for "I aced the quiz. I hit with the girl. I'm doing great."

"My man, I need some truth," Stone said. "Justice may have to wait."

A big delivery truck was backing up against the sidewalk, its reverse-gear alarm piercing and deafening. The mid-morning sun was playing hide-and-seek with a new bank of clouds in the south.

"That thing you told me about? Is that it?" Dale's voice immediately grew subdued. He was a balding blond guy with just enough hair left for a comb-over. Beyond that, his pale gray eyes showed a special kind of yearning. He *wanted* truth and justice to prevail.

"Don't do anything that won't let you sleep nights. But this situation is very special. I was hoping I wouldn't have to come to you about what we talked about last month, but I'm running out of time and ideas." He paused, listening to the sound of silence. "I suppose it's too much to ask."

"Well, I still haven't seen any data or preliminary reports. The NIH monitor for those particular clinical trials is a woman called Cheryl Gates and she's not returning anybody's phone calls. The truth is, she doesn't have to. But another possibility is, she doesn't actually know beans and she's too embarrassed to admit it. If somebody wants to keep a monitor in the dark for strategic commercial reasons, it's easy enough to do."

"Well, how about the other thing? The thing we talked about. The list?"

He sighed. "I was afraid you might come to that. That's a tough one, Truth and Justice."

"Hey, you know I didn't want to ask. But I'm running out of cards."

He sighed again. There was a long silence and then, "You know you're asking me to give you highly restricted access codes to the NIH Web site. We shouldn't even be talking about it. So officially the answer is no. That's for the record."

"Strictly your decision." But he had his fingers crossed, even as he was ashamed of himself for asking in the first place.

"Maybe this is God's way of letting me even up things a bit. It can't be something easy or it doesn't really count, does it?"

"I could end up knowing more about these trials than the NIH does," Stone said. "Because it doesn't sound like you guys actually know much at all."

"Let me think about it and send you an e-mail tonight. Whatever comes up, it'll be 'scrambled eggs.'"

"Thanks, Atlas."

"Scrambled eggs" was a reference to a made-up code system they'd used in college. A name or number was encoded by interlacing it with their old phone number. This time the interlaced number would be an access code for proprietary NIH data.

"I do not think I'm long for the world here at the *Sentinel*. We're forming a mutual hostility society."

"I sure as hell hope you've got a new career concept ready for the day when they give you the ax." Dale's attempt at a light tone did not quite disguise his concern.

"Funny, but that's the second time I've received that advice in the last half hour. I deem that unlucky."

"Stone, sometimes I think you ought to try not living your life so close to the damned edge. Maybe you ought to start practicing a little prudence, just to see what it feels like."

"I'm that wild ox we used to talk about. I like to scrounge.

But I also like to look around for the biggest story I can find. I'm trying to get an interview with a guy on Bartlett's staff. Maybe our 'scrambled eggs' will flush him out."

"Just take care of yourself and keep in touch."

"You too."

And they both hung up.

Was this going to do the trick? he wondered. As it happened, Stone Aimes already knew plenty about Bartlett's business affairs. He had been a lifelong student of Bartlett the man, and as part of his research into the Gerex Corporation he had pulled together an up-to-date profile of Bartlett's cash-flow situation. If you connected the dots, you discovered his financial picture was getting dicey.

Bartlett was overextended and, like Donald Trump in the early 1990s, he needed to roll over some short-term debt and restructure it. But his traditional lenders were backing away. He had literally bet everything on Van de Vliet. If his research panned out, then there was a whole new day for Bartlett Enterprises. That had to be what he was counting on to save his chestnuts.

The funny thing was, Bartlett didn't really like to spend his time thinking about money. One of his major preoccupations was to be in the company of young, beautiful women, usually leggy models.

Bartlett also had an estranged wife, Eileen, who reportedly occupied the top two floors of his mansion on Gramercy Park. Rumor had it she was a paranoid schizophrenic who refused to separate or give him a divorce. She hadn't been photographed for at least a decade, but there was no reason to think she wasn't still alive and continuing to make his life miserable.

Another tantalizing thing to know about Winston Bartlett was that he had bankrolled a Zen monastery in upstate New York twenty years ago and went there regularly to meditate and recharge. He had once claimed, in a *Forbes* interview, that the monastery was where he honed his nerves of steel and internalized the timing of a master swordsman.

The *Forbes* interview was also where he claimed he had quietly amassed the largest collection of important Japanese samurai swords and armor outside of Japan. For the past five years he had been lobbying the Metropolitan Museum of Art to agree to lend its dignity to an adjunct location for his collection, and to name it after him. The Bartlett Collection. Winston Bartlett lusted for the prestige that an association with the Met would bring him.

At the moment some of his better pieces were housed in a special ground-floor display in the Bartlett Building in TriBeCa. Most of the collection, however, was in storage. He had recently bought a building on upper Park Avenue and some people thought he was planning to turn it into a private museum.

Well, Stone thought, *if the stem cell project works out, he could soon be rich enough to* buy *the Metropolitan.*

He walked back to the lobby of his building and stood for a moment looking at himself in the plate glass. Yes, the older he got, the more the resemblance settled in. Winston Bartlett. Shit. Thank goodness nobody else had ever noticed it.

Chapter 4

Sunday, April 5
9:00 A.M.

When Ally and Knickers walked into her lobby, Alan, the morning doorman, was there, just arrived, tuning his blond acoustic guitar.

Watching over her condominium building was his day job, but writing a musical for Off Broadway (about Billy the Kid) was his dream. He was a tall, gaunt guy with a mane of red hair he kept tied back in a ponytail while he was in uniform and on duty. Everybody in the building was rooting for him to get his show mounted, and he routinely declared that he and his partner were *this* close to getting backers. "We're gonna have the next *Rent,* so you'd better invest now" was how he put it. Alan had the good cheer of a perpetual optimist and he needed it, given the odds he was up against.

Knickers immediately ran to him, her tail wagging.

"Hey, Nicky baby, you look beautiful," he effused. Then he struck a bold E minor chord on his guitar, like a flamenco fanfare, and reached to pat her. "Come here, sweetie."

"Hi, Alan. How's everything?" Seeing him always bucked Ally up. He usually came on duty while she was out for her un, and she looked forward to him as her first human contact of the day. He was younger than she was—early thirties—but she thought him attractive in an East Village, alternative-lifestyle sort of way. He was very proud of the new yin and yang tattoos on his respective biceps. She admired his guts and his willingness to stick to his dream, no matter the degradation of his life in the meantime.

"Doing great, Ms. Hampton. Things are moving along."

"Alan, I've told you a million times to call me Ally." Anything else made her feel like a hundred-year-old matron.

"Hey, right, I keep forgetting." Then he nodded at the manila envelope Grant had just given her. "Pick that up on your run?"

"I was ambushed by my ex-brother. He passed it along."

"What's that mean?" he asked with a funny look. "Brothers are for keeps."

"Unfortunately, you're right, Alan. The whole thing was long ago. And not far away enough." She was urging a reluctant Knickers on through the inner door. "Seeing him just now was sort of like an aftershock. From a big earthquake in another life."

"Sounds like you need a hard hat," he said, and turned back to his guitar, humming. And dreaming.

She took the elevator up to the top floor and let herself into her apartment, as always feeling a tinge of satisfaction at where she lived. Home, sweet home.

Her loft-style apartment was in an idiosyncratic building whose six-year-old renovation had been designed by her old architectural firm, just before she had to leave and take over CitiSpace. It was their first big job in the city. She was the one who had designed the large atrium in the middle and the open glass elevators that let you look out at tall trees as you went up and down.

She loved the building, but at the time she couldn't have begun to afford an apartment there. Later, when she could, none was available. Then she heard through the managing agent that a German owner, after completely gutting his space, had to return to his homeland in a hurry and was throwing it on the market for half what he'd paid.

She'd built a bedroom at one end—walling off an area with glass bricks that let light through—and installed a "country" kitchen at the other, but beyond that it was hardwood floors and open space and air and light, along with a panoramic view of the Hudson River out the north window and a central skylight that kept her in touch with the sky and the seasons. In much of Manhattan it was possible to go for months and not actually walk on soil. You could completely lose the sense memory of the feeling of earth beneath your feet. She didn't want to lose the sky too. Since she couldn't afford a brownstone with a rear garden, the next best thing was to have a giant skylight.

What she really dreamed of was to someday have a vacation home on the Caribbean side of the Yucatan, where she could wake to the sounds of the surf and play Bach partitas to the seabirds in the coconut palms. She felt there was something spiritual in the pure sound of a stringed instrument. It was sweetness and joy crystallized. It went with the sound of surf. They belonged together.

She had actually researched and designed that dream house already. The place itself would be based on the Mayan abodes of a thousand years ago, on stilts with a bamboo floor and a palm-frond roof to provide natural ventilation.

And since this was all a dream, she could fantasize that Steve was alive and was there too. Maybe this was her version of the Muslim Paradise, a land of milk and honey and infinite beauty and pleasure. Sometimes late at night, when the world was too much with her, she would put on headphones and a Bach CD and imagine she was on that beach in the Yucatan, gazing up at the glorious stars.

The other thing she wanted to do someday was memorize the first violin score of all the Beethoven late quartets. But now any intensive playing, which was more tiring than it looked, brought on chest pains after a few minutes. Shit. She felt like she was slowly being robbed of everything she loved. . . .

She decided to stop with the negative thoughts and get ready for the stressful day to come. She just needed a few quiet moments to get mentally prepared for it.

The first thing she did was give Knickers an early morning snack, then a fresh bowl of water and a large rawhide chew to occupy her energy for part of the day. After that, she would shower and change for the trip uptown.

She had to dress for the rest of the day, which eventually might include going down to the office, if she had the time and inclination, so she decided to just throw on jeans and a sweater. She didn't pay any attention to the envelope Grant had given her; she just tossed it onto the burnt-tile breakfast counter.

She told herself there wasn't time to look at it now, but she also realized she had a very serious psychological resistance to opening it. She hadn't anticipated that just seeing him once more would make her this tense and angry. His proposition was surely part of some kind of scam. She'd vowed never to believe him again. It was going to take a lot of persuading to get her to break that resolve.

Look at it later. Whenever.

She gave Knickers a good-bye pat and headed out the door.

In times gone by, she took Knickers with her, since her mother loved to give her sinful sugar treats and fuss over her, but these days Nina's condition was never predictable. Knickers was one confusing element too many.

On the trip uptown she always stopped at Zabar's for some smoked fish that she could pass off as "kippers" and some buttery scones. Nina was born in a little place called Angmering-on-Sea, in southern England, and she was an unreconstructed Brit. She insisted on oatmeal (the nutty, slow-cooked kind) for breakfast on weekdays and kippers and dark tea on weekends.

Now when Ally visited, she never knew what to expect. Some Sundays Nina could be as spunky as Phyllis Diller, and other times she seemed to barely recognize her. (Though she sometimes wondered if her mom just acted that way so she'd leave sooner and let her get back to her Spanish-language soaps. She claimed to be watching them to study Hispanic culture, but Ally suspected the real reason was their racy clothes and plot lines.)

And today, on the anniversary of Arthur's tragic death, would she even remember him? Early-onset Alzheimer's could proceed at a frightening pace.

Nina had been a notable Auntie Mame kind of figure around Greenwich Village for decades. She smoked Woodbine cigarettes fiendishly and was forever giving homeless people food and handouts. She had adopted the garden at St. Luke's and worked there weeding and pruning and planting and nurturing from late spring to early autumn. As soon as after-noon tea was completed, she waited an only moderately decent interval before her first scotch and soda. Room tem-perature. No ice.

"One should have a little something, shouldn't one?"

Arthur joined her to have a cocktail after work once in a while, but mainly he successfully kept his mouth shut about her smoking and drinking. Everyone knew she was destined to live to a hundred. Cancer was surely terrified to go near her. But then the Alzheimer's struck.

One of Nina's greatest gifts was an unerring BS detector. She had been skeptical about Grant since he was in his twen-ties. She deemed him a hollow suit, full of vapid ambition. She also believed his irresponsible behavior was a contribut-ing factor to Arthur's death, though she did not have the same ferocity of feeling about it that Ally did. She had had him pegged as a no-goodnik for so long that she already had zero expectations about his character.

In any case, Grant contributed nothing to the care of Nina and that suited Ally just fine. As part of the posttragedy fi-nancial restructuring, she sold their Greenwich Village

condo, which was too big and too full of memories for Nina
to continue living there. She then found her a rent-regulated
one-bedroom apartment in a wonderful old building on Riverside Drive, and when Nina's early-onset Alzheimer's pro-
gressed to the point where she couldn't really be relied upon
to take proper care of herself, she arranged for a very con-
scientious and sprightly woman from the Dominican Republic
to be her full-time caregiver.

Maria was devoted to Nina, and Ally didn't know anyone
who could have been more nurturing. She had been there for
nine months and she also used Nina's space to baby-sit periodically for her daughter, Natalie, who had a darling five-
year-old son. What would the next stage be, Ally wondered
fearfully, and would her mother's medical insurance pay for
it, whatever it was? She didn't know the answer and she was
terrified.

Aging. It was nature's process to make way for the new,
but why did the last act have to be so cruel? Seeing her mother
this way made her sometimes think that perhaps Arthur was
luckier than anyone knew. He'd managed to miss out on having to watch the woman he loved go into a humiliating decline.

Then she thought about her own mortality, the heart condition that refused to get any better. Dr. Ekelman had never
been more serious. *Slow down, take it easy, watch out for
warning signs.* She'd said everything except start saving up
for a transplant. Or maybe she was just postponing that announcement as long as possible.

Dammit, why couldn't she do something to make her
heart stronger? That was the most frustrating part of all. The
rest of her body could still have run a mile before breakfast.
She could traipse all over lower Manhattan Saturdays, shopping for herbs in Chinatown and shoes in SoHo. Damn. Why
wouldn't her heart get with the program?

Half an hour later, a big Zabar's bag on the seat beside
her, she found a space for her Toyota right on Riverside Drive,
just across from the park. She took a final look at the sky,

which was bright and blue and cheerful, and then, bag in hand, she headed up.

Nina's building was a dark brick prewar and had no doorman, though the super's apartment was right off the lobby, allowing him to receive packages and generally keep an eye on comings and goings. To Ally, the bland, inevitably tan hallways in many old West Side buildings had a musty quality to them that always left her depressed. But her mother's eighth-floor apartment was light and airy—after Ally had had it remodeled and redecorated—and she couldn't have wanted a more cheerful home. The wallpaper was a light floral pattern and the overstuffed furniture was buried in enough pillows to please Martha Stewart. And in the living room there was the piano her mother once played, now covered with photos from happier times, and a stereo system with a turntable.

When she buzzed, Maria came to the door with an unusually bright smile.

Great! Ally could always tell immediately from Maria's face whether her mom was having a good day or bad day. Today, she knew immediately, was going to be good.

"Miss Hampton, she was asking about you, wondering when you'd get here," Maria said. "She remembered this is the day you come."

Maria was half a head shorter than Ally, and her hair was dyed a defiant black. She had an olive complexion and her fine features made her a handsome woman for late fifties. She always wore bold silver jewelry that might have done more for her daughters than for her, but Ally liked the spunky persona that went along with too many accessories. She still had a trace of her Spanish accent even after all the years in New York. On days when her mother was cognizant, Maria was the perfect companion for her.

Ally handed over the Zabar's bag and walked in. "Hi, sweetie."

Nina was on the lounger, where she spent most of her

waking hours. Yes, she was definitely having a good day today. She'd done a full makeup number.

Her face could only be described as youthful, no matter that she was past sixty-five. She had elegant cheekbones and a mouth that was still sensuous. And her blue eyes remained lustrous, though nowadays they often seemed to be searching for something, or someone, no longer there. She had a colorist come in every three weeks to keep her hair the same brunette it had always been, and that had a way of making Ally fantasize she hadn't aged at all. Ally also felt—hoped— she might be looking at a spitting image of herself some decades hence. You could do a lot worse.

The TV was on, sound turned low, and her mother was staring at the multihued screen. Probably the tape of a Spanish-language soap she'd somehow missed. Three cosmetic-heavy women in deeply cut blouses were arguing, all appearing either angry or worried or both.

In times past Nina was always starting some new project, claiming that was how she kept her mind alert. She had taught herself French and had a very good accent, particularly for a Brit. Just before the Alzheimer's hit, she decided to try to learn Spanish, as something to divert her mind and keep it active. She also wanted to be able to chat with the increasingly Hispanic workforce in restaurants and delis.

Now, though, Ally thought her mom was continuing the language study as part of a program of denial. Nina knew her mind was being stripped from her, but she was determined to try to wrestle it back by giving herself mental challenges. The struggle was hopeless, of course, but her spirit refused to admit that.

Ally bent down and kissed her clear white forehead. "Hey, how's it going?"

"Look at those pathetic creatures," she declared, only barely acknowledging Ally's presence. "If boobs were brains, they'd all be Einstein. In my day women knew how to make themselves attractive. Simplicity. Less is more."

Yep, Ally thought, *this is going to be a good day. She's obviously spent an hour on makeup. For all her complaining, she probably watches Maria's soaps at least in part to glean cosmetic tips. Who knew, maybe she was learning Spanish too, like she claimed. Dear God, let her do it.*

Maria was looking into the Zabar's bag. "Oh, she's going to love this. Could you come in the kitchen and help me fix a tray?"

That's strange, Ally thought. *Maria thinks I'm all thumbs around food preparation and she never wants me in the kitchen.*

The apartment was old enough that the kitchen was a separate room with an open doorway. When they stepped inside, Maria set down the bag and turned to her.

"There was a man here yesterday. I never saw him before. He said he was your brother. Is that true?"

Ally felt a chill go through her body.

"Your mother seemed to know him," Maria went on, "but I wasn't sure whether she might have just been pretending. Sometimes you never know what she gets or doesn't get. She's a good faker."

"What . . . what did he want?"

"Well, the first thing seemed to be that he wanted to ask your mother a question about you. Then he started trying to talk her into going to some clinic out in New Jersey, where they might be able to help . . . her mind."

Shit. What is he up to? Is he trying to get to me through Nina?

"You said he asked Mom a question about me? What—"

"What are you two whispering about?" came a voice from the doorway.

"All kinds of secrets." Ally glanced up and smiled. "Maria was just telling me about a visitor you had yesterday, Mom. Do you remember if anyone came to see you?"

"Pish. Of course I remember. Seth. But sometimes I think I'd just as soon not." She stared at Ally, those searching blue eyes boring in. "Do you ever see him anymore?"

Funny you should ask, she thought.

Then she wondered, why not tell the truth? She couldn't think of any reason not to.

"As a matter of fact, Mom, Grant came by my building this very morning. I hadn't seen him in ages. He called and said he wanted to meet me while I was out running. I told him to bug off, but he came anyway. He wanted me to . . . Let's just say he's still wheeling and dealing."

Nina looked at her for a long moment.

"He showed up here yesterday morning, darling, out of the blue. After all those years when he didn't give a shit—excuse my *Français.* I acted like I didn't quite know who he was, but I got every word. He's still spending his salary on clothes. He talked a lot, saying he knew a man—a doctor with some kind of experimental treatment—who could turn back the clock on my . . . or at least stop it. He could give me a chance to take my mind back. And then he left his card. He wanted me to talk to you about it and then call him back."

Grant, you bastard. You didn't say a word about any of this. What're you trying to do?

No need for rocket science. He was using Nina as bait. This was his way to make sure she was dragged into whatever shenanigans he was up to. If he got Nina out to that place in New Jersey, whatever it was, it would be like he had a hostage.

She was so angry she was gasping for air. And she felt that damned tightness in her chest coming on.

"I told Maria to throw the card away," Nina went on, "but then I got to wondering. What if it's true?"

"You don't really think—"

"Of course not," Nina declared, but Ally wasn't sure how much she meant it. "Probably he just needs money. That'll come next. I'd guess he's hoping I'll give him a 'down payment' for this 'treatment,' whatever it is. That's surely what's going on. Trying to take advantage of a senile old woman."

Nina didn't appear to be fooled. Or was she? Sometimes she did her thinking out loud before coming to a conclusion.

"Seth may be barking up the wrong tree with me, Ally," she went on. "I'm not sure I want any of his miracle cures. I've lived my life. I'm tired." She looked away. "When you're young, you never think about what it's like to be old. But then when you do get old, you somehow can't imagine being young again. Having to do it all over . . ." Her voice trailed off.

Yes, Ally thought, *you've had plenty of pain you wouldn't want to relive.*

Nina sat back down on her flowered chaise and closed her eyes. "Do you know what day this is?"

"I was hoping you'd remember." She reached and grasped her hand. "It's been five years today. Exactly."

"I still have nightmares about it, the horror, " Nina said, her eyes still closed, "but he did it for me, you know. He thought the insurance was all that would save me. And then when it didn't . . . So now we've got to hang on with all we've got. For him." She opened her eyes and looked directly at Ally. "One day soon, maybe sooner than we think, I'm going to be mad as a hatter. Time, Ally, time has played a cruel joke. God the Prankster is keeping me in physical health so I can experience every step of my own degradation." Then she glanced back at the Spanish soap and went on. "I hope you know how to enjoy life, while you're still full of it. Don't miss a minute."

"I'm going to try, Mom." Ally squeezed her hand again and for that moment sensed Nina was her old self. She wasn't going to tell her about Dr. Ekelman and the latest heart news. But if she did, the response would probably still be the same. *Just live life for all it's worth. You never know if there's even going to be a tomorrow.*

"Would you put on some Janácek?" she said finally, aiming the remote at the TV and clicking it off. "One of the string quartets. I've had my fill of Hispanic tarts. I've learned a good deal of Spanish from them, but sometimes I think understanding what they're saying just makes it all that much cheaper."

That was when Ally realized with a burst of joy that Nina still had an interior life that she was carefully hoarding. What else was going on in that mind? The sense of the night closing in? *Do not go gentle. Please. Stay awhile with me.*

She got up and went over to the record cabinet. Her mother still had her collection of old 33s, today they were called vinyl, with conductors from decades ago like Bruno Walter and Arturo Toscanini. She found a Janácek String Quartet, No. 2, a rare mono pressing by the old Budapest String Quartet fifty years ago, and put it on the turntable, still loving those first crackling sounds that raise your anticipation. She remembered how Nina would put on a record in the evening, after dinner, with room-temperature scotch in hand, and make the family sit and listen. She suspected that had a lot to do with her own desire to play the violin herself someday. And then, in high school, she started lessons. Better late than never.

Now, though, she sensed there was something Nina wanted to tell her and this was her way of setting the stage.

After the music had played for almost three minutes, Nina listening with eyes closed as though in a rapture as the movement clawed its way toward an initial theme in an elusive minor mode, she turned and looked at Ally.

"He didn't tell you he came to see me, did he? Seth?"

"I guess he forgot," Ally said. It was a lie neither of them believed.

"I've been thinking over all he was trying to say. I didn't get everything at the time, but I guess my feeble mind was recording it. Now it's all coming back. He was talking about Arthur and his suicide—Ally, we both know that's what it was—and how he felt responsible and how he was finally going to be able to make up for all the harm he'd done to me, and to you. But he was worried you might not want to go along with this special treatment for me." She was studying Ally, as though searching for an answer. Maria had discreetly departed for the kitchen. "He kept talking about this doctor he knew. At this clinic. He swore this man could perform a miracle for me. He said I should do it, whether you approved or not."

Ally looked at her, wondering what to say. This was getting too devious for words.

Then Nina went on. "I'll probably not remember anything about this by tomorrow. But I just wanted to tell you. When you get as mentally addled as I am now, you compensate by developing your other senses, I call it your sixth sense. And, Ally, I think he's involved in something that's evil. And he wants to draw me into it, maybe both of us." She stopped, carefully framing her words. "I sensed a kind of desperation about him. I don't know exactly what it was."

As Ally listened, the Janáček quartet swelling in the room, scratches and all, she felt more and more like an utter dunce. She hadn't caught any of this in Grant's come-on, but now . . . Nina was right about that sixth sense.

But what could the real story be? Grant was more a simple con artist than some embodiment of evil. Think the Music Man in designer threads, not Darth Vader. Evil was surely too strong a word. He was just the consummate self-promoting hustler. The troubling part was, he was so damned good at it.

"Mom, you're wonderful today. Why don't we all three go somewhere for brunch now? Right now. There's a new French place just down Columbus that needs checking out."

She had an eerie foreboding it might be their last chance.

"No, honey, you brought some smoked fish, didn't you? That's all I want." Nina dismissed the idea with a wave of her hand. "Besides, no one in this town knows how to brew a proper pot of tea." Then, the next thing Ally knew, she was back to musing out loud about Grant. "I can't stop wondering. He said this doctor he knows might work a miracle for me. What am I supposed to think?"

Ally was trying to decide whether a glimmer of hope, even though it was almost certainly false, might be a healthy tonic for Nina just now.

"Mom, Grant gave me some materials about that doctor. I'll read them tonight, I promise." She was listening to the

Janácek quartet soar, and it was bucking her up. "Let me see what I can find out."

"He wants me to start in right away," Nina pressed. "I think he said there are some studies going on at this clinic, but they're almost over. It's free now, and unless I go soon, I can't get in the program. He said he would take me out there Monday morning if I wanted. But if I go with anybody, I want it to be you."

He's such a bastard, Ally thought.

She glanced at Maria, who'd been watching from the kitchen door and listening to all that had happened. She was looking very upset and she motioned Ally toward the doorway with her eyes.

"Let me get a glass of water, Mom." She headed for the kitchen.

"Did you hear all the things she's talking about?" she asked when they were out of earshot.

Maria nodded. "A lot of what your mother said is true. It was very strange. At the time she acted like she didn't understand him. Now I realize she did. Or maybe it all just came back to her."

"What do you think is really going on?" Ally was studying her, hoping to get at the truth. "She seems a lot better today."

Maria paused a moment. "Miss Hampton, I don't believe your mother is going to be with us much longer. I saw my own go through much the same thing. There's always a glimmer just before . . ." She looked down and stopped.

"You said Grant asked her something about me. What—"

"I don't think she remembers. He was asking her about your blood type. It seemed a very strange question."

Ally couldn't think of any reason why he would be asking that.

"Maria, what was your impression of him? Overall?"

"Just that he seemed very nervous. Very uneasy." She hesitated, as though uncertain how to continue. "He wanted something, Miss Hampton. That much I'm sure about. But this doctor he wants to take her to. It sounded to me like he does things that are against the laws of nature."

"Grant wants me to go out to that clinic too."

"Whatever you do, just stay close to her," Maria said finally, picking up the tray with its smoked fish and teapot covered with a knit cozy. "She may not have that long."

Maria had a seer's mystical bent that sometimes troubled Ally. What if she was right? It was moments like this when Ally truly missed having someone special in her life.

Chapter 5

The afternoon was waning when Ally finally headed back downtown. Days like today she couldn't help coming away buoyed, feeling her mom was going to be cogent forever.

In fact, Ally was more worried about herself just now. About two o'clock she'd started feeling that sensation in her chest again, but she hadn't wanted her mother, or Maria, to know she was using vasodilator medication. She casually said her farewells and got down to the car and was sitting behind the wheel before she popped a nitro tab. She immediately felt okay again, and as she drove down Broadway, heading for her office, she reviewed all that had happened.

After their brunch of smoked fish and onion chutney and soda bread and a pot of double-strength Earl Grey, she'd tried to sell her mother on a trip to the Bahamas, with Maria joining them. Soon, maybe at the beginning of summer. She wanted Nina to spend some time thinking about it, but she didn't want to wait too long. Was this just going to be a distraction at the end of Nina's life? God, she didn't want to think so. She wanted to think of it as a rebonding.

Nina had always liked to revisit the Devonshire country-side of her childhood in midsummer—when Arthur could take time off—always for just a week, but it was as inten-sively planned as a major military campaign. Her favorite thing was to trek among the hedgerows and stone fences, making charcoal sketches on opened-out brown bags. In the evenings they would dine *en famille* at a country inn. They went with local favorites, like kidney pie. Then they would stroll the country lanes in the moonlight as a family. No TV, and she and Grant hated everything about the trips. *Booooring.*

But that was long ago and far away, when she and Grant were still kids. Now her mom would surely want something restful. And some guaranteed sunshine wouldn't hurt either. Already she had an idea: why not rent a house with a private pool, say on Paradise Island, where Nina could spend a cou-ple of hours each afternoon in the casino? She'd always loved casinos, and never missed a chance to hit the blackjack tables if she was anywhere near one. Her loss limit was a hundred dollars, but she actually beat the house more often than not. The teatime scotch hadn't impaired her card-counting skills.

Nina appeared to like the idea, so Ally had started making up a schedule in her head. The beginning of summer would be off-season in the Caribbean and there should be some real bargains to be had. She made a mental note to ask Glenda, her assertive, gum-chewing travel agent at Empress, to start trolling for a package.

What was Ally really thinking, hoping? She was fantasiz-ing she could heal Nina all by herself. She so desperately wanted to, she had a premonition she could *will* it to happen. When she saw her mom on good days, she always found her-self believing she could somehow make all her days good. She was sure of it, against all odds.

What she wasn't sure about was what her mother really thought about Grant's proposal to enroll her in this clinic in New Jersey. Was this doctor's "miracle" stem cell cure based on a real medical advance, or was he some kind of charlatan?

The first thing to do was to find out more about this supposed medical magician, Karl Van de Vliet. The envelope Grant gave her was still lying there on her breakfast bar, unopened. She told herself she'd read it the minute she got home tonight, when the day's work was over and she could concentrate. . . .

The Sunday office. The interior-design job she had on her mind was behind schedule and she was feeling a lot of pressure. It was for a Norwegian couple in their midthirties. He was a software programmer working in New York's restructured Silicon Alley, and she was teaching at the Fashion Institute of Technology. Together they pulled down over 250 thou a year and they'd decided to stop throwing away money on obscene New York rents.

They bought an entire floor, actually three small apartments, of what was formerly a tenement in the West Fifties, an area once known as Hell's Kitchen but now much gentrified and renamed Clinton. They had dreams of an openspace loft of the kind made famous in SoHo when artists took over abandoned factory buildings and gutted the space, taking out all the walls.

Because they had combined three apartments, they had to file their plans with the NYC Department of Buildings and modify the building's Certificate of Occupancy to reflect the change in the number of dwelling units.

So far so good, but then a woman who was the local member of the District Council got wind of the project and sent someone from her office to look over the place. The next day, the Department of Buildings' approval of their plans was abruptly withdrawn.

It turned out that there was an obscure law on the books concerning Clinton, one that even the Department of Buildings was only vaguely aware of. It said that in order to preserve the "family character" of the neighborhood, no renovation could alter the number of rooms in a residential building. Not the number of apartments, mind you, just the number of *rooms*.

That was when they showed up at CitiSpace in despair. They wanted Ally to help them by doing some kind of design that would satisfy the law and also give them the open, airy feeling they had set their hopes on. On the face of it, their two goals seemed mutually contradictory and impossible.

He was short and shy and she was plump and sassy and Ally liked them both a lot. Sometimes in this business she sensed she was helping people realize their dreams and that was a very rewarding feeling. Real estate was an emotional thing. Your home was a part of you. She always tried to get to know people before she did any designs for them. Sometimes design was more psychology than anything else.

But this time she had to solve a problem before she could wax creative. If their plan for open space could be stopped by some obscure local provision that even the Department of Buildings was fuzzy about, then maybe there was some other obscure law in the Housing Code that could be used to fight back. The full code had recently been put on the NYC Web site, so she wanted to go over every page and see what she could come up with. And she wanted to do it in the office, undisturbed, with all the architectural plans close to hand.

The office was deserted when she cruised in and clicked on the lights. She got on the expansive NYC Web site and started poring over the Housing Code, though she was still obsessing about Nina. What if this doctor in New Jersey actually *could* do something for her?

Finish here, she told herself, and then go home and read the guy's CV.

A pot of decaf coffee later, she came across a little-known fact, which she now vaguely remembered from her days as a practicing architect. If you installed a fifteen-inch drop across a ceiling, that was technically a wall in the eyes of the NYC Department of Buildings. The space on each side became a separate "room."

As they say in the movies, bingo.

In fact, why not do a honeycomb ceiling that would actually simulate the industrial look they were seeking, anyway? The ceiling was over eleven feet high; there was plenty of vertical space. Nobody would know it was just a sneaky way to get around a funny local aberration in the Building Code.

I'm brilliant, she thought. Yes! *Dad would be proud.*

She made some sketches, and by that time it was after six. Time to go home.

Knickers was waiting by the door, and she gave Ally a dirty look and some very disapproving barks. By way of penance, Ally took her on an extra long walk, all the way up to Fourteenth Street and back. Then she picked up some tuna salad and steamed veggies from a new deli on West Tenth Street.

As she settled down to eat at the breakfast bar, she felt like a single mom, always eating and doing everything on the run—and all she had to worry about was a friendly dog. How did real working moms do it?

It was just past nine when she poured a glass of Chardonnay and picked up Grant's envelope and took it into the living room, pausing to put some Chopin ballades on the CD player.

The envelope contained a bound folder that was Dr. Karl Van de Vliet's curriculum vitae, his résumé. It was in fact a minibiography that devoted a page to each of his career turns. His life story was presented from a god's-eye view, as though it were a novel.

Karl Van de Vliet had done his undergraduate studies at the prestigious University of Maastricht, after which he'd migrated to the United States and taken a Ph.D. in molecular genetics from the University of Chicago, top of the class. Following that, he went to Yale as a postdoctoral fellow, again studying genetics.

From the beginning he focused his research on the mechanisms that govern human cell reproduction. Along the way he'd become interested in something known as the Hayflick limit—which concerned the number of times a cell could divide before it became senescent and ceased to replicate. This natural life span controlled the aging process of every organism, and it seemed to be nature's device for nipping undesirable (i.e. mutant) cells in the bud, by never letting any cell, unhealthy *or* healthy, just keep on replicating indefinitely.

However, there *were* "immortal cells" buried within us all, so-called stem cells that could replicate forever, unchanged. They were present at the very beginning of life and all our differing body tissue was created from them. Some still lingered on in our body, as though to be available for spare parts. If one could figure out how to transfer the characteristics of *those* cells to other cells, then the possibility existed that we could regenerate damaged or aging tissue in our vital organs. The trick was to figure out the mechanism whereby stem cells managed to cheat time.

His research, which was accompanied by a flurry of scientific papers, was celebrated and encouraging. After three years he was lured away from Yale to become a faculty member at Johns Hopkins, which offered to double his laboratory budget. He was there for six years, during which time he met Camille Buseine, a neurosurgeon finishing her residency.

She had a doctorate from a medical institute near Paris and she was doing research that was similar to his, so the biography said. They married and became a team, and when he was asked by Harvard Medical to found a department for molecular genetics, she was immediately offered a tenured position there too. Harvard considered it a double coup.

His research was zeroing in on the telomerase protein, an enzyme many scientists believed was responsible for suppressing the aging process in stem cells. Could it be used to regenerate tissue?

He was well along on the task of exploring that tantalizing possibility when tragedy struck. Camille, who had worked around the clock during her residency at Johns Hopkins, began feeling weak at Harvard and was diagnosed with acquired aortic stenosis. After a 2½-year struggle, she died during a severe cardiac episode.

My God, Ally thought, *that's what I have.*

After Camille died, he left Harvard and its time-consuming academic obligations and went to work full-time at a research institute affiliated with Stanford University. He even formed a paper company to structure the work, the Gerex Corporation. But then there came a second strike against him. He was doing research using embryonic stem cells obtained from the discarded embryos at fertility clinics. After two years of harassment by right-wing political groups, Stanford decided his research was too controversial and terminated his funding.

Three months later, Karl Van de Vliet merged his company with Bartlett Medical Devices and moved his research staff east to New Jersey, to the Dorian Institute. That was five years past, and now his research using stem cells was in third-stage NIH clinical trials.

The official history ended there, though with a strong hint that the final chapter was yet to be written. Then at the back there was a bibliography of publications that extended for eight pages, and included a summary of the most important papers. His work on stem cells and the telomerase enzyme appeared to be at the forefront of the field.

Oddly, however, some of his writings also were philosophical, an argument with himself whether his work could be misused to alter the natural limitations life imposes. One of those papers, from a conference presentation in Copenhagen, had a summary, and in it he pondered whether the use of stem cells to rejuvenate the body might someday give medical science godlike powers.

The Greeks, he declared, had a myth about the punishment reserved for those who sought to defeat our natural life span. When the goddess of the dawn, Aurora, fell in love with the beautiful youth Tithonus and granted him immortality, it turned out to be a curse, since he still reached the decrepitude of age but had to suffer on forever because he could not have the release of death.

But, Van de Vliet pondered, if we could find a way to arrest the aging process in our body's tissue, might we escape the process of aging? If so, was this a good thing? Or might this be a step too far that would bring on unintended, and as yet unknown, consequences?

Well, Ally thought, *I wouldn't mind having Mom's mind restored. Or my own heart, for that matter.*

All in all, Karl Van de Vliet was clearly a genius. He also was a very complex man. But might he be a very gifted huckster as well?

The inside back cover had a group photo, showing him surrounded by members of his research staff, all in white lab coats. There were two men and two women and each was identified, along with a list of his or her academic credentials. They were standing on the porch of what appeared to be a nineteenth-century mansion, which had large Doric columns in Greek Revival style. The lettering in the marble above their heads read THE DORIAN INSTITUTE.

She put down the folder and went into the kitchen and poured herself another glass of wine, finishing off the bottle. Her mind was churning, but not because of the words on the page. It was that photograph at the back. It was dated less than two years ago.

His Ph.D. at the University of Chicago was granted in 1962. But even if he was a genius and got his first doctorate in his early twenties, he'd still have to be—what? At least sixty years old by now. Probably halfway to seventy.

But in the photo, he looks no more than forty, well, forty-five at most. What the heck is going on?

She went back into the living room and picked up the brochure and stared at it. He had sandy hair that lay like a mane above his elongated brow. He was tall and gaunt, with high cheeks and deep, penetrating eyes. But no matter how you gauged him, the guy hadn't aged a day since his forty-fifth birthday, tops.

So what's going on that isn't in the package?

She checked the digital clock on the side table—the hour was pushing ten—and decided to give Grant a call.

Three chirps, and then, "Yo. Hampton here."

My God, she thought, *he even does it at home.* That synthetic bravado was left over from his trader days: *You're the luckiest person alive, just to have reached me. How can I further make your day?* his tone implied.

"Grant, it's me. I think it's time for that vital chat."

It took him a split second to recover, and then, "Hey, I was beginning to wonder what happened to you. If you were going to stand me up or what. Not call, like you said you would."

"Long day. I was up at Mom's this morning. You knew she was going to tell me, right? About your little surprise visit and proposal?"

"I had a hunch the topic might arise." His voice seemed to shrug nonchalantly. "I thought you should hear it from her instead of from me. So what do you think?"

"What do I think? I think I'm wondering what you're up to."

"I'm not 'up to' anything, Ally, except exactly what I told her. Trouble is, I don't know whether she got it. I wanted to see how she was doing. You know, I'm thinking maybe Dr. Vee can do something for her. But I had to see her first. She seemed pretty distant, but that woman there—what was her name? Marie, Maria, whatever?—said she has lucid moments. So who knows. He might possibly help her. I think I can arrange to get her into his clinic. Bartlett gives me a few perks. It's the least I can do for her, so . . ." His voice trailed off expectantly.

"Grant, I need to talk to you about this man. I read the stuff you gave me and I still don't know the first thing about him." She paused, about to speak words she never thought she would. "If you want to come over, I'll stand you a drink."

"You serious?"

"For my sins."

"I'll grab a cab. See you in fifteen."

It's begun, she thought. *I'm about to let Grant screw up my life one more time.*

No. This round, don't give him the chance. Stay ahead of him.

Sunday, April 5
10:39 P.M.

"I didn't know if I should have brought a bodyguard," he was saying as he strode in the door, a Master of the Universe with a leather jacket slung over his shoulder. He looked stylish, but then he always did. He casually tossed the jacket onto the gray couch, then gazed around. Thankfully, he didn't try the New York cheek kiss. "I guess this is not supposed to seem like old times, but somehow it does. Seeing you again. Hey, we're still blood kin, right?"

"Don't push it, Grant." She'd killed the Chopin and put on a Bach sonata. Clear, precise thinking was required, not sentimentality. Knickers had rushed to give Grant a hello nuzzle, happier to see him than Ally was. "Whatever this is, it is definitely not old times."

He sauntered into her kitchen, looking around—trying to act cool, but clearly ill at ease. "You've done a nice job on this place, sis." He was looking over the rustic counter she'd installed. "You get a deal on the space? A bank repo or something?"

"The people who had it wanted to sell fast and I made them an offer." Not that it was any of his damned business. Why didn't she treat the question with the scorn it deserved?

She had an old fifth of Dewar's in the cabinet. She poured him some, over ice, then gave herself a shot of tequila *anejo,* neat, to sip. She loved the pure agave flavor. The more she thought about the situation, the more she was sure she needed it.

He picked up his scotch, then walked into the living room and helped himself to the couch. "Ally, I know why you're ticked. And I don't blame you. I feel crummy about Dad, I really do. I guess I share some of the blame."

He was trying to sound contrite but the reading did not quite rise to the minimal threshold of credibility.

"You 'share' . . . with whom, you self-centered prick? Nobody else was involved. He mortgaged CitiSpace to the hilt and settled those fraud suits to keep *you* from losing your license. Or worse. You destroyed his business and his life all by yourself."

He looked as contrite as she'd ever seen him.

"Look, I thought the business plan I had would work out. I really did. I was managing discretionary accounts, but the bond market hit a downdraft when I was long. A few of my clients didn't have the balls to ride it out. What do you want me to say? That I feel like a complete cretin over what happened? That a day doesn't go by that I don't hate myself for it?" His eyes went dead and he seemed to shrivel, his body becoming visibly smaller. "Well, I do. More than you'll ever know."

"You didn't seem all that contrite at the time."

"I was operating in a high state of denial back then. But now I want to take a shot at growing up. I want to start trying to make up for all that, if you'll just cut me a little slack and give me a chance."

"Grant, you're working for Bartlett Enterprises, doing whatever it is you do. Fine. That's your job. But now you want me to become a guinea pig when this Dutch doctor needs one in a crunch. Or maybe Mom too, for all I know. Maybe he needs her as well. Two guinea pigs. So don't try to make this about me and her. Let's keep it honest. It's really about you, just like always."

"Ally, a lot of things have gone on since Dad . . . passed away. I've changed, in more ways than you could ever imagine." He was all sincerity now, his demeanor rapidly evolving to fit the current vibes of the scene. "I'm not like I used to be. I really mean that. I've learned . . . learned that I can't always just be thinking about myself."

"So . . . what changed you?" The truth was, he did seem different. In some way she couldn't quite understand. But he was always talking about turning over a new leaf, especially whenever he'd just gotten himself in trouble. That part hadn't changed at all.

"Ally, Dr. Van der Vliet . . . I don't know how much I should tell you, but he's a miracle worker." He paused and looked down at his scotch. One thing about him was definitely different, she thought. There was a lot less bravado and swagger. "The thing is, what he's doing is so powerful. I'm not sure which worries me most—that it's not true, that it's just some placebo effect, or that it *is* true. When I think about the implications . . ." His voice trailed off again.

"Go on." She could tell he was dead serious.

"It's not something I'm sure I should talk about." He reached over and touched her hand. "But it's working, I swear. He's doing things that shouldn't even be possible."

Uh-huh, she thought, pulling her hand away.

"Grant, please tell me exactly what you think he could do for Mom." She wasn't sure she should be having this conversation. "You want her to go out to the Dorian Institute, right? Where he does his 'research.' And I take it that's where you want *me* to go too."

"It's in northern Jersey, about an hour's drive from the city, maybe not even if traffic's light. But I'd only want Mom to go if you say it's okay. I'm not trying to do anything behind your back."

She breathed a long sigh, trying to clear her brain. Every other word he uttered was probably part of some hustle. But what was it?

"Why don't we start at the beginning, Grant? I read his CV, and believe me I've got a lot of questions. For starters, how did he convince Winston Bartlett to bankroll him?" She took another sip of her tequila, then set it down. "You're his flunky now, so you should be able to answer that question."

"You read the materials I left?"

"Just finished them."

"Then you know he lost his federal funding at Stanford a few years back, when he was at a critical stage of his research using stem cells. That's when he came to the Man and persuaded him to put up the money to help him take everything private. The only way Bartlett would play ball was if he could buy the Gerex Corporation and get three-quarter interest in all the patents. Van de Vliet kept the other quarter, but now they're both hoping to sell off forty-nine percent to a big pharmaceutical company. Not American. I can't tell you any more than that."

"Congratulations," she said. "Sounds like your job is secure."

"Yeah, right."

That twitch of nonchalance he had when something really mattered—even as a child, he would attempt (and fail) trying not to gloat over some personal success. It was moments like this when she realized she'd missed seeing him and talking to him. When you cut a family member off from you, you also cut *yourself* off from them. After all, he was her closest blood kin, even though he was an unreconstructed shit. At some level she wished she could get past the bitterness she felt toward him. Could it be he really *had* changed?

He didn't like the way the scene was going. What the hell was her problem? He looked at his scotch longingly, then got up and went to the kitchen and got another ice cube for it. *Go easy.*

How was he going to get through to her? If word of the Beta screwup got out, the buyout was toast and Grant Hampton along with it. But if Ally could be brought in . . .

"Grant," she was saying, "I want to start off by asking you if you've ever taken a really good look at that guy Karl Van de Vliet. Does he look anything like his picture? The one that came with that CV of his."

"Sure, that's him."

"And I assume you've actually read his résumé?"

"Of course." *Here it comes,* he thought. *The thing every-body asks.*

"If those dates are right, then he has to be—what?—at least sixty years old. But in the picture he doesn't look a day over forty-five. So what's going on?"

"Ally, you're finally getting it." He rattled the ice in his Dewar's, then finally took a deep sip. Maybe, he thought, it would help with the courage. "He's a truly amazing human being."

"That's not an answer, Grant. It's a generality." She exhaled in obvious exasperation. "But I want an honest answer about one thing, dammit. Do you actually think he could help Mom's Alzheimer's? Maybe even reverse it? Tell me the truth. Just once."

"Ally, I can't guarantee anything. But it's worth a shot."

Now, he thought hopefully, she was sounding like she was starting to come around. Thank God. As for whether Dr. Vee could cure the old bird, who knew? But he'd overheard the nurses talking about how he and his research staff had had some phenomenal luck with Alzheimer's. . . .

"By the way, what happened when you talked to Mom?" he went on. "Did she seem like she understood anything I told her?"

"Grant, she probably understood a lot more than you wanted her to. The bad part is, she let you give her some hope. Now, what's going to happen if she goes out there and ends up being disappointed?"

It's a real possibility, he told himself. *But it's probably the only way I'll ever get* you *out there, and that's what* really *matters.*

"Ally, we'll never know unless . . . You should go too."

"Look, maybe I'll *talk* to Van de Vliet. But it's purely information-gathering." She was staring at him. "So why not tell me? The whole story. Are you doing this for Mom and me, or are we just being used like lab animals?"

"I'm not sure you're going to believe anything I say." He sipped again at his scotch, then walked over to the skylight and looked up. Finally he turned back. "After Dad . . . and everything, I had trouble sleeping. I know you didn't think it got to me, but it was like some bad force had taken over my mind, haunting me. I became obsessed with death. I took off two months and went to Colorado, camping. Out there, under the stars, I did a lot of thinking. Dad had died suddenly, but maybe that was a blessing in disguise. The rest of us, we all die a little every day. Why does time do the things to us it does? Why do we have to grow old and repulsive?"

He drew on his scotch again, then continued.

"When I came back, I started doing research on aging. That's when Karl Van de Vliet's name popped up on the Internet. Some paper he'd given in Vienna years ago. It was about the physiology of aging. But then Tanya came along and I sort of forgot about him. Then when I went to work for Winston Bartlett, there he was. The very same guy. It was weird, but it was as though God had delivered him."

"Is this shaggy-dog story going to end up being about why he looks so young?"

"I'm getting there." He smiled. "I kept wondering too, and then finally I saw an opening in his schedule and took him to dinner here in the city, down at Chanterelle. A social thing. Eventually, after a couple of bottles of serious wine, it came out that once upon a time he had done an unconventional experiment. On himself. It was sort of an accident, something about melanoma research."

"So he—"

"You asked me why he looks so young. Well, some procedure he did apparently stopped his skin from aging. But then he changed the subject and wouldn't talk about it anymore. So do I think he's a miracle worker? I'd say he's walking proof of something. That you *can* cheat nature."

"And?"

"There *is* no 'and.' That's all I know." He came back and settled onto the couch. His scotch glass was empty and he yearned for another, but that small voice inside was urging discretion. This was the moment that could be make or break.

"But to get back to you, Ally, you really should meet him. I can't talk specifics about the actual clinical trials, but let me just say they've been very positive. There's every reason to think he can help you. And Mom too."

He studied her, trying to read her mind. He wondered if she could detect the anxiety he felt lurking just beneath the surface. Was she seeing through him, the way Nina, for all her mental debility, had seemed to?

"Grant, has this doctor Van de Vliet gotten into some kind of medical experiment that's turned into a Faustian bargain? Is his skin rejuvenation a signal that this research has gone over into *The Twilight Zone*? When a sixty-something man looks forty-something, there's got to be an unnatural act going on. What does it mean?"

"Maybe it means he's found the thing Ponce de León was looking for. The Fountain of Youth or whatever."

"Then he'll probably have to pay for it some other way," she said, getting up. "Mother Nature doesn't give out freebies. Look, I've got to give Knickers her midnight walk. That's your exit cue. I'll call him tomorrow. I'll go that far."

"Don't blow this chance, Ally," he said, setting down his empty scotch glass and getting up. He felt hope and it bucked him up. "It could be the biggest mistake of your life. And Mom's."

He was at the door before he turned back. It was time for the insurance. The hedging of bets. Bartlett had authorized it.

"By the way, I almost forgot. Jesus, I'm going senile myself. W.B. told me to tell you he'd like you to come over to his place on Gramercy Park tomorrow morning around ten, if you can work it into your schedule."

"What for?"

"That job on his place that I told you about this morning, I guess. I do know he's planning to renovate the ground floor. But just between us, he's also got a massive renovation job in the wings, so maybe that's what's really on and this is like an audition. Who knows? He bought an old mansion on upper

Park and he's planning to heavily redo it and turn it into a museum for his incredible collection of Japanese military stuff, swords and armor and shit. He's going to do over the entire interior. It's part architecture and part design, so I gave him your name. Who knows? But I was over at his place this afternoon and he asked about you. He said he wanted to see you as soon as possible. He even gave me one of his personal cards to give to you. Here. It has the Gramercy Park address and his private cell phone."

"Just like that?" She looked skeptical but took the card.

"Winston Bartlett is not a man who dawdles. If he decides he wants to do something, he just moves on it. All he asked was that you bring a portfolio, to show him some of your work."

Come on and do it, he thought as he headed out the door. *Go and see the Man. Just fucking do it. If he can't close this frigging deal, nobody can.*

Chapter 6

Sunday, April 5
11:43 P.M.

Winston Bartlett put the newly glazed *crème brûlée,* still warm from his preparation in the kitchen below stairs, on the bed tray in front of Kristen, next to her untouched champagne flute. She used to love it and he was trying everything he knew to jog her memory. He'd cooked her favorite supper, eggs Florentine, with barely wilted spinach topped by prosciutto, had taken her to bed, and now there was champagne and her favorite dessert.

But she still seemed distracted and distant. Yes, it was a good idea to get her away from the institute, but that was merely relocating the problem, not fixing it. If it *could* be fixed. In the meantime, she had to be kept here, out of the public eye.

"Thank you," she said, and gingerly took a small bite. She had been almost lucid earlier this evening and was leaning against the antique headboard, wearing a soft blue nightgown. Her long blond hair was tousled and down over her breasts. Her memory might now be a sometime thing, but her libido was still going strong.

"Do you remember how much you used to like that?" he asked, trying to make eye contact.

She nodded her head dumbly. Did she actually remember? Increasingly, he had no idea.

He had brought her here to stay in this four-story nineteenth-century mansion on Park Avenue. He'd purchased it a year and a half earlier for 23 million and he was intending to have it renovated and converted into a museum. That renovation, however, had been put on hold awaiting a decision by the Board of Directors of the Metropolitan Museum. He wanted the building to be a Park Avenue adjunct to the Met, and he also wanted his definitive assemblage of Japanese implements of war to be known as the Bartlett Collection.

The tax write-off would be monumental, but that was not nearly so important as the prestige.

It was clear now that this project would not have any momentum until he first got himself appointed to the board of the Met. Unfortunately, money alone wasn't adequate. Major-league politics was involved.

He was working on it, with a lot of Upper East Side lunches and targeted charity events. He was also taking his time and getting designs and estimates for the renovation. The way things were at the moment, he didn't have the cash to actually start construction anyway.

For the moment, the place was furnished but unoccupied except for a security guard, a part of Bartlett's personal staff. Now, with Kristen here, discretion was his uppermost concern.

He had sent the security guy home this evening, so he and Kristen could have privacy. In the morning two nurses would come on duty, one to look after her and another to cook.

Over the past year he'd brought her here most weekends. It was like having their own Shangri-la. Best of all, unlike his official residence on Gramercy Park, he didn't have a wife upstairs, like some mad (in every sense of the word) aunt in the attic.

He had hoped that bringing Kristen back here might do

something for her memory. He still hoped, but he wasn't sure. In bed tonight she had been as lithe and enthusiastic as ever. Possibly even more so. Did she know who he was? He couldn't really tell. But he still loved being with her. The soft skin and the voluptuous curves of her breasts and thighs: it made him feel young again.

Since she had been out at the Dorian Institute and away from him, he had begun to feel older and older.

Winston Bartlett was sixty-seven and—increasingly—felt it. To begin with, his prostate was enlarging itself, in spite of all the special, expensive medicines he used. Surgery was increasingly looking like a possibility. And his memory was nowhere near what it once was. He wolfed down ginkgo and ginseng capsules by the handful but was finding it harder and harder to remember people's names, particularly the new wave of donation-hungry politicians who fawned over him.

And then there was the matter of teeth. He'd just gone through major periodontal surgery, a sign of aging gums. How long before his ivories would be replaced by ceramic choppers? Oh, and the heart. His cardiologist was talking more and more about stents to alleviate the two constricted arteries in the left ventricle. They were already down to 40 percent. Face it, his whole damned body was falling apart.

Probably worst of all, the Johnson was far from what it used to be; not long back, it was a daily triple threat. Soon he might be resorting to Viagra as more than a discretionary recreational drug, something he was still joking about less than a year ago.

The dirty secret about living this long is, after you've seen everything you ever wanted to see, done everything you ever wanted to do, bought everything you ever wanted to buy, you gradually lose the only thing really worth having.

Youth.

To try to hang on to it, he had been through clinics as far-flung as Phoenix and Lucerne. He had undergone regimens of antioxidants and injections of human growth hormone. He'd tried testosterone and dehydroepiandrosterone, better know as DHEA. Maybe it had made a difference, maybe not. Sometimes he thought he had more libido and energy, but other times he wasn't sure. Maybe it was just that he'd begun working out even harder, playing handball an extra half hour every other day. He did know his body was continuing to deteriorate.

Shit, the Beta *had* to be made to work. . . .

"I don't want to stay here alone," Kristen said, putting down her spoon. "I want to go back to work."

"Honey, I can't be here all the time, and you're really not well enough to go to work. There'll be someone here with you. It's just till you get better." He studied her, the face that was so young, and felt the full weight of the tragedy sinking in. "Do you remember what it was you used to do?"

"I don't remember right now. I mean exactly. I used to talk to people. I was in this room with lots of bright lights."

She didn't actually remember, he thought. Her former producer at E!, along with everybody else (including her harridan of a mother, Katherine), had been told she was at a private health spa in New Mexico. It had to be kept that way.

No one must know she was here. All the phones had been removed before the ambulance brought her. Starting at six in the morning, there would be a nurse and a nurse/cook downstairs on a twenty-four-hour basis. Under no conditions could she be allowed to leave, not the way her mind was now.

"Kristy, it wasn't supposed to turn out like this. I'm so sorry. But Karl is doing all he can. We're . . . He has a new idea that he's about to explore. He's going to . . ." His voice trailed off as he stared at her unblinking eyes. "You don't remember what happened, do you?"

But how she looked. My God. The *youth*. How could a true miracle have such a tragic downside?

That was when the cell phone on the stand beside him chirped. It was the only phone in the place, and tomorrow it would be gone. No way could she be allowed to have a phone.

The caller ID advised that it was Grant Hampton.

"Kristy, I've got a feeling this could take a while." He was reaching for his silk robe. "I'll be downstairs on the first floor if you need anything, okay?"

She just stared at him mutely. He shook his head sadly. There wasn't much time left to mend her. How in God's name had it come to this?

As he moved down the spiraling grand staircase, he clicked on the phone.

"Yeah."

"I was just at her place, W.B. I actually got in, which is more than has happened in over four years. I think she's on board, but I'm still not entirely sure. So, just to be safe, I told her you wanted to see her tomorrow."

"Are you saying you couldn't make this happen? With your own fucking sister?"

"It's . . . We're not exactly on the greatest of terms, Ally and me." There was an awkward tone in his voice. "It's hard to explain. Like I told you, I confirmed her blood type on Saturday. It's AB, like I thought. And I played the mother angle. At the very least, I think she's willing to drive the old bird out to the institute and meet Karl. That's a start, at least."

"And what about her medical . . . Karl wanted to see—"

"I'm working on it. I remembered something about her. I've got a guy. He's going to check on it tonight."

"Good," Bartlett growled. "There's no time to screw around on this."

"I've set it up for you to meet her tomorrow, the way you wanted. I think she'll show. I told—"

"The one who really should talk to her is Karl." Bartlett sighed. "He knows how to handle patients."

"Then he could call her tomorrow. After she's talked to you. If we all pull together on this, W.B., I'm sure we can get her out there by day after tomorrow, Tuesday."

Winston Bartlett looked at his watch. It had just turned

Monday, one less day to find something that would stop the Syndrome in its tracks.

"We'd better."

He was clicking off the phone when he heard a wail of despair from the bedroom upstairs and the sound of a champagne flute being thrown against a wall.

Kristen was losing it rapidly now. Was she still conscious enough to know what was happening to her?

Chapter 7

Monday, April 6
7:30 A.M.

The commute from Ally's West Village place to the Citi-Space office in SoHo was normally a twenty-minute brisk stroll, and she brought Knickers with her a lot (the boss's prerogative) since her office was arguably homier than her home. (Knickers loved to wander around and—she thought—guard the computers and drafting tables.) This morning, though, Ally had an appointment for her at Pooch Pros, the dog groomers near her office. A wash and a trim and plenty of pampering. Betty and Misha always fussed over her shamelessly, and she gloried in it.

But now a pounding rain had just come through, which meant no walk for either of them. Knickers would show up looking like a bedraggled mop. Definitely the moment to take the car.

Alexa Hampton liked to say that she wasn't really an auto person. Hers was a four-year-old Toyota, light blue, and its modesty befitted her needs. In New York, hopping around SoHo and the Village, it made a lot more sense to rely on a bike or on cabs, or just plain walk. Garaging a car in New York cost the equivalent of a studio apartment rental in most normal places, and the bottom-line truth was, she resented the Toyota's presence in her life. But there were moments when cabs weren't the answer, and this was one of them. Fortunately, the parking garage she used was just around the corner, so she and Knickers got there before being totally soaked. Knickers loved riding in the Toyota, and she always seemed to know what was coming the minute they turned the corner for the garage. This morning she gave a gleeful "Woof" and started panting, a sure indicator of joy.

As they drove the few blocks downtown, the rain was easing up but the streets were still shiny. Ally reached into her bag and took out the personal card of Winston Bartlett. His private residence was on Gramercy Park. The only reason he could possibly want to meet her there was if he did indeed have a job. She decided she would call him from the office and confirm the appointment, assuming he still remembered it. Then she'd get Jennifer to help her assemble a portfolio of their work and make a color copy to leave with him.

She leaned over and rubbed Knickers's ears. Her thoughts were drifting back to Karl Van de Vliet. At some level his stem cell technology sounded like the ultimate snake oil. Was she about to take leave of her common sense to go to see him, or even to consider letting him perform some experimental procedure on her mother's mind?

On the other hand, what about *him?* What kind of "procedure" could Van de Vliet have done that would stop his own skin from aging? If Grant had merely *told* her that Karl Van de Vliet had finally realized the cosmetician's dream and learned how to make human skin youthful and supple again, she would have passed it off as just more Wall Street IPO hyperbole. But seeing was believing, and it also seemed like there was a lot more going on than just a change in his skin. There was something about him, in his eyes, that felt . . . inconsistent.

She was still puzzling on that point when Knickers jumped up and barked. They were passing a garbage truck and the guys were banging the cans into the back.

"Shhh." She reached to quiet her. "We're almost there, baby." Then she tugged at her leash and settled her back into the seat.

Since the rain was all but over, she decided to park the car where she dropped Knickers off and then walk over to her office, which was only a couple of blocks east. She found a spot right next to the awning of Pooch Pros, and the minute Knickers was liberated from the car, she bounded to the door dragging her leash through the puddles. Misha was already there to meet her.

"Come on, my *kraceve* baby, my beauty." He reached down and gave her a big hug. Misha was a gaunt, balding, blond-haired Russian who had once been the hero of the Soviet Olympic swim team. Now he looked like he could stand a piroshki or two to plump him up. "You be big fluff of cloud after we finishing."

Ally followed them in, and there was Betty. Ally figured "Betty" assumed her made-up but totally American name was easier than whatever she'd used in Russia, but to Ally it just felt weird. Betty had dark hair, a broad smile that wouldn't die, and approximately thirty pounds that would have looked better on Misha. They reminded her of Jack Sprat, et al.

"Honey, there is problem at your office. Woman name Jennifer call. Say she try reach you at home but you leave already. And you don't answer your cell phone."

"Shit, I turned it off. Knickers goes nuts if it rings in the car."

Jennifer was only a couple of years older than Ally, but she'd been with the firm back when Ally's father, Arthur, ran it and she was the mother figure of CitiSpace. She was also Ally's best friend, and had been even before Ally came back to run the firm. Ally felt like she had known her forever. These days Jen spent a lot of effort trying to create a social life for Ally that would include eligible men. She kept nagging her to join some clubs, anything, just *get out there.*

Ally knew she was right, but she was working too hard to take time out. She had the idea, which she wasn't naive enough to actually believe at a rational level, that sooner or later someone who could replace Steve would come along. Yes, she was lonely a lot, but until this last deterioration of her heart she'd spent a lot of evenings and weekends outside, biking and hiking around town, and she knew plenty of people who were interesting and kind. She sometimes thought her problem was that she liked people, all kinds of people, as long as they were kept slightly away, at a psychic distance. Maybe it was the getting close part that never seemed to work out. . . .

It had actually been that way ever since Steve disappeared. She had the premonition that if she got too close to somebody, she was destined to lose them.

Now she stood for a second, puzzling. She'd mentioned taking Knickers to Pooch Pros, so that's how Jen knew where she'd be, but what could have gone wrong at 7:45 in the morning?

Jennifer wasn't usually in this early, but she was finishing a rush job for a marble bathroom for a couple on the Upper East Side. On days when Jennifer did get to the office first, she'd have the coffee going and an extra bagel for Knickers, on the chance Ally might bring her, which she often did. But to phone Betty just to tell her to hurry? That was odd.

"Should I call now?" It seemed pointless. She was no more than ten minutes away. What else could go wrong in ten minutes?

"She sound very hurry," Betty declared.

Ally took her cell phone out of her bag and switched it on. The office rang only once and then Jennifer was there.

"Ally, you're not going to believe who called here ten minutes ago, asking for you. *Winston Bartlett.* My God, it's like Donald Trump called. Well, actually it was some male secretary or something. He said he was calling to confirm your ten o'clock appointment. At an address on Gramercy Park East. *What's* that about? Jesus, Ally, where are you? I don't know what you're up to, but this could be *big.* He owns entire *buildings,* for chrissake."

"Did you say I was coming?"

"I didn't know what to say. He left a number to call if you can't make it. Otherwise, he'll assume you'll be there. It's only two hours from now."

"All right, Jen, let's put together a 'folio of our biggest jobs. Lead with that gut rehab we did on the building down by the South Street Seaport. And put in those two floor-through lofts we did on that conversion in TriBeCa. The ones with the slate bathrooms and the stainless-steel countertops in the kitchen."

"I've already started. Do you know specifically what he has in mind?" She paused. "How did he find out about us, anyway?"

"My creepy kid brother works for him." She sighed. "It's a long story. Be there in a couple of minutes." She clicked off the phone.

"Betty, thanks a lot. I've gotta run." She turned and gave Knickers a last rumple of the ears. "Be good, baby. I'll pick you up by six at the latest."

"What wrong?" Misha was concerned, twisting a white towel he was holding. "Big problem?"

"Nothing's wrong. Actually, something probably *is* wrong. I just don't know what it is yet." She headed out the door.

The design firm her father had started and she'd kept going, now with some architecture thrown in, was on the ground floor of an old industrial loft building whose upper floors had been converted into rental apartments in the early 1980s. The owner was an ex-wrestler named Oskar Jacobi, who had turned Zen master (after a fashion) and had a studio upstairs, on the second floor. He had drifted from wrestling into karate during his thirties and thence into the life of the mind, or rather the life of "no-mind," in his late forties. Now he taught meditation as well as karate and insisted they be learned in that order. He served as his own superintendent, mopping the halls and setting out the garbage on pickup days.

The ground floor was zoned commercial, and CitiSpace had a lease for all of it, which meant she had tons of space. Oskar had given Ally's dad, Arthur, a ten-year lease, which was now a fraction of the going rate. They both knew that, and she'd more than once offered to renegotiate or move, but he said he didn't need any more income and, besides, he liked having her as a tenant because she reminded him of her father. It was a generosity perfectly in keeping with his philosophy that excess money corrupted the spirit.

She'd done the place as a sort of Spanish desert flower, with burnt-orange tile floors and all the natural materials she could cram in. A lot of her clients wanted the hard-edge industrial look in their lofts, which was fine by her, but she found it too cold for a daily working environment. The front was unassuming, with small lettering on the window. CitiSpace was not a walk-in business. And she had no metal gates over the windows. What's to protect?

When she marched through the door, everybody looked up from their coffee and computers, and Jennifer led the applause. Winston Bartlett. Had they finally made the A-list? This could be the start of something big.

Chapter 8

Ally stepped out of the cab, holding the large leather-bound portfolio, and checked the number on the card against the bronze plaque above the door. Winston Bartlett lived like a nineteenth-century robber baron. The building had five stories and was adorned with Italian marble window lintels that glowed like mother-of-pearl.

Already she liked his sense of style. Bartlett was New Money, but this place had the solemn dignity of Old Money. The front door was eight feet tall and solid mahogany. The odd thing was, there were two doorbells. One read W. BARTLETT and the other read E. BARTLETT.

That was when she remembered she had read somewhere that he had a wife named Eileen. But why did she have a separate doorbell? Winston Bartlett had a tabloid reputation as a womanizer. Perhaps they lived apart. If so, there it was, for all the world to see.

She found herself examining the late Greek Revival columns on either side of the door. They were marble and meticulously cleaned of soot, whose ubiquitous presence in

New York meant that eventually everything not regularly scrubbed turned gray. It told her that Winston Bartlett liked things to be immaculate and that he was a stickler when it came to details.

She glanced up and noticed that she was being observed by a security camera. She was reaching out to push the bell for W. BARTLETT when the door magically opened. A tall, trim Japanese man in a crisp black suit was standing in the doorway. But he had a muscular build that would be more appropriate for a bodyguard than a butler.

"Hello," she said. "I have an appointment with—"

"Yes." He nodded, appearing to know exactly who she was. "He's upstairs in the library. Please . . ."

She'd expected a grand central staircase in the Palladian design, but instead there were elevators off to the left of the entryway. But even without an obvious staircase, the ground floor and its fifteen-foot ceiling were palatial in every sense of the term. The marble floors were covered with antique, and expensive, Persian rugs, and the light tan wallpaper was flecked with gold leaf, giving the feeling it could have been meticulously stripped from some palazzo in Venice. The lighting fixtures were a row of chandeliers down the middle of the vast room, and at the back was a dining table that appeared to be large enough to seat thirty dinner guests. The architecture was a showpiece for the extravagant taste of some Victorian "enemy of the people."

But what really set it apart was that the walls were lined with exquisitely severe antique swords and armor from Japan. In a way, the room felt like the foyer of a boutique museum, an adjunct of the Asia Society.

The Japanese man directed her to one of the elevators, and then got in with her. She still couldn't decide whether he was a butler or a bodyguard. He had the polished demeanor of the first, but the strapping body and deft movements of the latter. Maybe he was both. In any case, he looked like he would be quite at ease brandishing one of those long samurai swords.

The elevator had dark paneling and smelled of freshness, partly fresh wood and partly fresh lacquer. It was utterly silent as it glided up to the third floor. When the door opened, she stepped into what appeared to be a large den/library, except that there was a huge four-poster antique bed at the far corner, with its drapes drawn around the side. It was definitely something out of another place and time. Was this Bartlett's bedroom? The space was magisterial.

In the other corner was a wide mahogany desk covered with phones and papers and two computers. From his photos, she recognized the man rising to greet her as Winston Bartlett. Seeing him in the flesh, she first noticed that there was something in his eyes that in another man might be called ruthless, but in him it merely came off as determined. They were eyes that were accustomed to getting what they wanted—be it a company, a building, a woman.

"Fine, Ken, and please have them hold my calls," Bartlett said, nodding to the Japanese man, who tipped his head in acknowledgment and disappeared back into the elevator. Then he turned to her and extended his hand. "Ms. Hampton, I appreciate your making time for me. I'm possibly your newest fan. After Grant told me about you, I had a couple of my people do some research. You've been responsible for some very interesting, even elegant interiors. Grant may have told you I have a big project down the road that you might wish to bid on. But for now, as a way of getting to know each other, I wanted to talk to you about a more modest undertaking."

She thanked him, attempting to take it all in. She was trying not to admit to herself that Winston Bartlett was an attractive man, in the way that power brings charisma. "I'd be happy to hear about what you have in mind. I don't necessarily take every job that comes along. I always look for challenges."

She listened to herself and wondered why she was starting off the meeting in such a confrontational manner. Probably, she thought, it was because she didn't want to seem intimidated. Doing high-end interior design, you come across a lot of wealth and power, but this was a whole new level.

"Well, I guess I'm the same way." He smiled. "A lot of the things I've done over the years have ended up being a challenge. And a risk. But now and then, something is worth it." He gestured toward a couch. "Please, we have a lot to talk about."

He returned to the chair behind his desk and turned off the laptop computer he had been using.

"I brought a portfolio," she began, "with photos. There's also a CD-ROM with virtual walk-throughs of some of our projects. I'm not sure what you have in mind, but this should give you some idea of the kind of thing we—"

"I'll look at it," he said, setting the portfolio aside unopened. "I'm sure you live up to your reputation. Like I said, I have two jobs pending, so first let me outline the smaller one. This building was built just before the prior turn of the century, and it was intended to house a small workforce of cooks and nannies and seamstresses below stairs. The rooms were lit with town gas, and coal was used for heating and cooking. Then in the twenties, everything was gradually switched over to electricity and oil and natural gas. But very little effort was made to accommodate the change aesthetically. It was just retrofitted."

"That's typically how it was done."

"And I haven't really cared until now," he went on. "But lately I've decided I want to redo this place properly. Starting below stairs and moving up. It's mainly the kitchen down there that concerns me now. I want to remove all the outdated fixtures and go state of the art. There's nothing original there anymore; just somebody's idea of a 'modernization' back in the fifties. So nothing of historic value will be lost. I don't want a restaurant kitchen precisely, but I want a range with enough Btu's that it could be. Granite countertops are all the rage these days. . . ." He paused, then grinned sheepishly. "I promise I won't start telling you how to do your job. Work up some ideas without any interference from me, and then we'll see where we go from there."

"Do you have any blueprints of this building? The original plans?"

He smiled, as though to say *you ask good questions*. "As a matter of fact, they were filed downtown, in a little-known cranny of the Department of Buildings and I had an expediter I know track them down." He paused. "Ms. Hampton, there is one little matter I want to clear with you in advance. I know that the newspapers occasionally print things about me that might be termed unsavory. You came to meet me here, so that tells me something about your feelings toward me. But I have discovered that I am a somewhat controversial figure in certain circles. I'd just like to know if *you* think of me as controversial."

She found this unexpected new tack in the conversation puzzling. Was he trying to get a rise out of her?

"I barely know you, Mr. Bartlett," she said. "And, frankly, the private life of a client is none of my business. So that question is entirely unnecessary."

"Very well." He smiled. "Like I said, there's a much larger job now in the planning stage. I have a building on Park Avenue in the Seventies that I'm planning to convert into a museum. It would be a private undertaking at first, but in the long run, who knows? The job will require extensive alterations of the building, and I also plan to have a museum café in the lower level. Anyway, there's a lot of work ahead, and I thought this would be a good way for us to get acquainted. Redoing the first floor here would give us both some idea of whether we could work together on a larger project."

She listened and found herself wondering what he was *really* up to. This conversation felt like he thought he needed to have plenty of bait on the hook.

First Grant and then him, a tycoon who's a perfect stranger. Why?

Monday, April 6
10:38 A.M.

Winston Bartlett was not finding himself entirely satisfied with the way things were going. As he looked her over, he had a lot on his mind. This was the woman who shared his rare blood type and could represent his last hope. So far, she seemed smart and courageous. Given the gravity of what he'd heard about her heart condition from Karl—which you'd never realize by just looking at her—she had to be courageous to continue on with her kind of spirit. But that was not necessarily all to the good. She might not be so easy to manipulate.

Inevitably he found himself comparing her to Kristen. For starters, Alexa Hampton seemed to have a lot more self-assurance. Kristy liked to appear tough on camera, but she was riddled with an aspiring actress's insecurities. Which had played a large part in the current tragedy. But you could say she brought that on herself. Alexa Hampton was struggling with something she had nothing to do with. And to look at her, you'd never know it. *That* was spunk.

In truth, this was the kind of woman he'd often wished he'd married—someone who shared his own gusto for life. God had dealt her a particularly lousy hand, and yet she still had drive. She had more courage in her little finger that that monster upstairs, Eileen. And the fact was, she was more appealing than Kristen. *But don't even think about going there.*

"Coincidentally," he said, beginning a new tack, "there's a totally unrelated matter I wanted to discuss with you. I understand Grant has already told you about the clinical trials currently winding up at the Dorian Institute, which is part of one of my companies. He told me about your heart condition and about your mother's Alzheimer's. We're working on a new procedure that could be very relevant for both of you. The clinical trials are scheduled to conclude in just a few days from now, but I spoke with the lead researcher there, Dr. Van de Vliet, and he said there's still time to get you into the program."

"Yes, Grant came to see me and brought me a brochure."

"Your brother is very concerned about you and your mother, and he specifically asked me to inquire if you had any questions about the procedure that I might be able to answer for you."

He was watching her carefully, all the while trying to keep his tone casual.

"Well, I think my mother is interested. Quite frankly, she doesn't have much to lose, though she may be in denial about that. In my own case, I'm not so sure. I still don't know anything about Karl Van de Vliet."

She's still toying with the bait, Bartlett thought. *I can't yank the line just yet, but she's close. She's so close.*

"Truly, the best thing you could do would be to talk to him," Bartlett said, getting up from his desk and walking over to the window and pulling the curtains aside. The midmorning light streamed in, a momentarily blinding presence. *I've got to shake this up,* he told himself. "As a matter of fact, I'd like for you to meet with Karl before we go any further with this job. We need to get you well first. And your mother. He's had some truly amazing successes with both Alzheimer's and Parkinson's."

"It's just that this is all so experimental. Aren't there any side effects? New drugs or new medical procedures always have side effects."

Well, he thought, *now you've hit on it. But that part is best left to Karl.*

"If you have questions, that's all the more reason to check out the clinic," he declared. Time to close the sale. He came back and sat down behind the mahogany desk. "I've seen a lot of medical innovation over the years, including a good bit in my own companies. But there's never been anything that remotely compares to the promise of stem cell technology. And these stage-three clinical trials have shown how many miracles are in the realm of the doable."

"Grant said Dr. Van de Vliet wanted to include someone with my specific condition in the—"

"Let me be frank with you." He looked across at her and smiled. "You would be a perfect fit. But the trials are going to be over very, very soon, so he's anxious to get started."

"Truthfully, I'm thinking about taking Mom out there," she said. "And since we're all being so frank, let me say I'm getting the impression that my going out to your clinic is really the reason you wanted to see me today. It's—"

"It's the second reason," he said. "The design job is uppermost in my mind, but I see nothing wrong with having two purposes in seeing you. As someone once said, commerce is the mutually beneficial exchange of worth."

Was she agreeing to see Van de Vliet? Playing the mother card may have done the trick.

"Well, why don't we stick to tangible worth," she said. "Let me take a look at the space downstairs. But you'll have to tell me some more about what you have in mind."

"I propose we do it the other way around. You go down and look around, take measurements, make sketches, whatever it is you do, and then get back to me with some ideas. That'll be our starting point." He picked up a walkie-talkie on his desk and punched a button. "Ken, could you please come up. I'd like you to show Ms. Hampton the service floor." He clicked it off without waiting for a reply. "I'm due down at the office. When I get there, I'll have them cut a check for five thousand dollars as a retainer and messenger it over to your shop."

Is this going to work? he wondered. *Maybe I should be pushing harder. . . .*

He examined Alexa Hampton one last time as he rose to leave. *Yes, she's a rare woman. Wouldn't it be ironic if Karl actually* could *do something for her heart?*

As Ally watched Winston Bartlett sweep from the room, she was still trying to take measure of the man. What troubled her was why Grant and Bartlett were both so anxious to get her and her mother out to the clinic. But give Bartlett his due. He could charm the birds off the trees.

She looked around the room, wondering what the old kitchen and staff quarters would be like. Certainly not like this. The library/bedroom had a rich, over-the-top feeling, with a beautifully molded plaster ceiling, a virtual bas-relief of fruits and birds and clouds all meticulously painted. It wasn't the Sistine Chapel but had some of that feeling. The paneling and wainscot were burnished mahogany, and the floor was a mix of hardwoods worked into an isometric design. She decided it was probably the most luxurious private residence she had ever seen.

CitiSpace was mainly known for its creative handling of lofts in the abandoned commercial buildings of SoHo and TriBeCa. These old mansions of the nineteenth-century moguls were an entirely different world. It was intimidating, but she was sure she could do something below stairs that would retain the period flavor of the building while creating the kind of semiprofessional space he said he wanted. Still, it was different from anything else CitiSpace had ever done, so he had no way of knowing whether or not she could pull it off. Again that question: why on earth would he hand her this plum job?

And where was his wife? Although he liked to be photographed with blond starlets, the tabloids always reminded you that he had a wife someplace. The two doorbells were a tip-off that that someplace was here. Best guess: she probably had the top floors.

My God, was Madame Bartlett going to get involved in the renovation? A lot of women with superrich husbands and too much time on their hands come to assume that that happenstance creates in them a natural gift for interior design. Big problem.

But *whatever* happened, this could be a sweetheart job. And maybe she'd get a crack at that museum he'd talked about. That was the kind of thing an architect-turned-interior-designer dreamed about.

She looked up to see the Japanese man—Bartlett had called him Ken—stepping into the room. He was all business.

Monday, April 6
11:08 A.M.

Winston Bartlett was on the phone to Van de Vliet the moment he stepped into his limo to head downtown.

"She said she's thinking about bringing her mother out to the institute, Karl. I believe she's ready to do it. Before she changes her mind, I want you to talk to her and schedule an appointment for tomorrow morning, if you can."

"I'll put in a call to her office."

"Karl, she's not there now. Try her cell. Grant has the number. We need to get moving on this. I've done about all I can at the moment." He was watching the midmorning traffic that was clogging the avenue. He always felt claustrophobic in a limo, even a stretch. The only time he felt free was when he was in the McDonnell Douglas chopper. When he was *flying* the chopper, against all the laws of civil aviation.

"Don't you think that's a little pushy, W.B.? We shouldn't seem too anxious. Believe me, I've had a lot of experience with ambivalent patients."

"All right. She should be back at her office sometime after lunch."

"I'll wait awhile and put in a call there." He paused. "When was the last time you saw . . . Beta One? The situation at Park Avenue?"

"I don't want to discuss it over a cell, Karl." This conversation was definitely a bad idea. "She comes and goes. I think it's getting worse."

"I'll try to get over there late this afternoon and look in on her," Van de Vliet said. "I want to see her every day."

"Karl, we can't give up hope. Never give up hope."

He clicked off the phone and thought about his crapshoot with God. Kristen had wanted to play, to experiment with the Beta. But nobody made her undergo the procedure. She should never—

His cell phone rang.

"Yeah."

"Mr. Bartlett," came a female voice with a Brooklyn accent, "it's Bernd Allen calling."

"Put him on."

Shit, Bartlett thought, *this is news I don't want to hear.*

Bernd was a Brit who was in charge of day-to-day accounting for Bartlett Medical Devices. He was forty-seven and not a risk taker and he was always worried about something. That was his job. These days he had plenty to be worried about.

He had been running a weekly projection of the cash flow at BMD, and the drawdown was now getting perilous.

The flagship product of Bartlett Medical Devices had been the "balloons" used in heart angioplasty that inflate and expand clogged arteries. They were marketed together with stents, miniature metal mesh supports that keep coronary arteries open after angioplasty. The problem was that in 27 percent of the cases, the stents manufactured by BMD caused scar tissue to form, a process called restenosis, and reblock an artery, requiring a repeat of angioplasty or even a bypass operation. Other manufacturers' numbers were not any better. But a few months back, out of the blue, Hemotronics, a competing company near Boston, had introduced stents coated with drugs that prevented scarring. BMD's piece of the $2.6 billion angioplasty market had plummeted from 13 percent to 4 percent and was still dropping like a stone.

Add to that, two titanium joint replacements for arthritis patients that they'd pinned their future on—along with millions in cash—still had at least two years of human trials left before they could hope for FDA approval. Long story short, BMD was in a mature product cycle with its most lucrative hospital hardware, with nothing major in the pipeline for at least two years. They had bet the ranch on the stem cell research at Gerex.

"W.B., I just got last week's numbers back from the green-eyeshade chaps downstairs. As you asked, I had them refine all the assumptions. Remember the union contract. There's going to be a three percent wage increase for all hourly personnel at the end of the month. And we didn't hedge our Euro exposure and now it's going against us. That's my own bloody fault. And since we don't have any pricing flexibility in that territory at the moment, it's like a four percent haircut, right off the bottom line. Remember we ran that in a worst-case scenario a while back. Well, chances are we're about to see it for real."

Bartlett had been watching the rate of cash burn and trying not to let the problem be evident. The logical thing to do, start laying off workers in the fabrication divisions, was out of the question. If you had a make-or-break deal cooking, you couldn't afford to look like you were on the ropes.

"Give me some parameters," Bartlett said.

"You know we've already hit our credit lines at Chase about as hard as we dare without them calling for a review. So unless we try to refinance some real property, say the flagship building downtown—and in this interest-rate environment any rational lender would put a gun to our head—we've got to ink this deal with Cambridge Pharmaceuticals in two months max. Right now we're living on borrowed money and it's about to be borrowed time too."

You don't know the half of it, Bartlett thought. *I'm already living on borrowed time.*

What's more, if word of the Beta gets out, we can kiss the buyout adios. The adverse publicity and legal problems . . . Nobody's going to buy into that kind of liability. Not Cambridge, not anybody. Bernd doesn't know about it yet. If he did, then he'd really be worried.

"Bernd, take a deep breath. We're on schedule and we've got to make sure we stay that way. Get hold of Grant and tell him I want him to double-check the regulatory situation for the Cambridge deal. I know he already has, but I want a memo from our attorneys by noon tomorrow. If there are going to be any roadblocks cropping up, we need to know about them *now*. We can't afford to be blindsided."

He clicked off the phone and tried to think. In the confines of a limousine, it was hard.

What's it all for?

Unknown to the world—but, unfortunately, known to his wife, Eileen—Winston Bartlett had a natural son. And that son, now in his own career, despised Bartlett. It was one of many sorrows he had long since learned to bear.

All the same, he increasingly regretted that he had made such a botch of their relationship. The man who was his natural son had done very well for himself professionally, had plenty of drive. And in fact Bartlett believed he himself deserved some of the credit for that. What he had done was let the boy fend for himself, which was exactly how Bartlett was raised. *Make it with your own two hands. How else are you supposed to develop any character?*

And it had worked. The pity was, he now hated Winston Bartlett's guts.

But Bartlett had begun thinking more and more about a legacy. What if he could make peace with that son and bring him into the business? Right now the closest thing he had to a son was Grant Hampton, and Hampton was a little too slick and expedient. Bartlett knew a gold-standard hustler when he saw one.

The more he thought about it, the more he was convincing himself to make his natural son his sole heir.

Assuming there was anything left to pass on.

Monday, April 6
11:20 A.M.

"Mr. Bartlett asked me to give you this," Kenji Noda said, handing her a large manila envelope as they stepped off the elevator. "It's a copy of the original plans. And also, there's a blueprint for the current layout, along with measurements."

She took it, looking him over again as she did. There was something very fluid about his motions. He could have been a dancer. There was a softness about him, and yet you got an unmistakable sense of inner strength. She suspected he had something to do with Bartlett's incredible collection of Japanese katana. He looked like he could have a connoisseur's eye.

She walked into the below-stairs service space and looked around. The back part, which was the kitchen, had stone walls that had been whitewashed. There also were two massive fireplaces, which, she assumed, had once housed coal-burning stoves. Large grease-and-soot-covered gas ranges were there now.

But the space was fabulous. Massive load-bearing columns went down the center, and a partition separated the front half of the space from the back. The front traditionally would have been the nursery and sewing room, in short, the maids' working quarters.

She turned to the man Bartlett had called Ken.

"Does Mr. Bartlett have a cook?" she asked. "This kitchen doesn't look used."

"No," he said. "Actually, he almost never dines here, and Mrs. Bartlett has her meals delivered from various restaurants. Though she does go out sometimes as well."

This was the first time she had heard any mention of Eileen Bartlett.

"She resides on the top two floors," he went on. "She has her own dining room up there, where she takes her meals, along with an efficiency kitchen."

So the Bartletts did live completely separate lives. That explained a lot.

"Okay," she said, "I want to look around and get a feeling for the space and start putting together some ideas." She was starting to focus on the job. The ceiling was lower than upstairs, but still the space had enormous possibilities. "Off the top, I'd probably suggest we open this out. Remove that dividing wall and make a great room. With the right kind of kitchen, this could be a marvelous contemporary space for semiformal dining and entertaining." Assuming, she thought, Winston Bartlett actually wanted a renovated space to entertain. She still had the nagging suspicion that he just wanted *her.* "I'd use materials that have a really warm tone."

Mix different materials for the different parts of the kitchen and the room, she thought. The cabinets could be mahogany, to echo the extensive use of that wood upstairs, and the walls around the stove area and the fireplaces could be an earth-colored slate. And that look could be accented with polished granite countertops in a slightly darker hue. There would need to be a high-Btu stove, probably a big Viking, with a slate backsplash all around. A couple of stainless-steel Sub-Zero refrigerators and a large Bosch dishwasher could be spaced along in the slate and granite. And if Bartlett wanted it, there could be a place for a temperature-controlled wine cellar. High-end design.

There also would need to be a large stone island—say a Brandy Craig—with a couple of sinks and—depending on what he wanted—maybe another high Btu stovetop there.

She turned to Ken. "If you have something else to do . . . I just need to walk around and live in this space a little. Then I want to make some notes on the plans. Possibly take a few digital photos."

"Take your time," he said. "I'll be upstairs."

He disappeared into the elevator, with his curious catlike gait, and was gone in an instant.

As she looked around, she realized the thing that was missing was light.

Wait a minute, she thought, *there must be a garden at the rear of this building. There are windows in the front, so why aren't there any at the back?*

She turned to examine the back wall. It was, in fact, clearly of recent origin, and there was a door at one side. She walked over to the door, which was locked with a thumb latch, and opened it.

And sure enough, behind the building was an unkempt space the width of the building that ran back for a good thirty or thirty-five feet. When she stepped out into the late-morning sunshine and looked at the back of the building, she realized there also was a row of windows facing the garden that had been bricked shut. What a travesty.

The whole design would depend on whether those windows could be reopened. But if Bartlett would allow it, then there were tremendous possibilities. *With all this light, you could—*

"Who the *hell* are you?" came a raspy, oversmoked voice from behind her. "Are you his new tart? We agreed he would never bring his whores here."

Ally turned to see a tall, willowy woman, who appeared to be in her midsixties. She had shoulder-length blond hair, clearly out of a bottle, and a layer of pancake makeup that looked as though it had been applied by a mortician.

"Perhaps it would be helpful if I introduced myself." She squeezed past the woman in the doorway and walked over to the counter, where she had left her bag. She extracted a business card and presented it.

The woman squinted at it, obviously having trouble making out the print.

"I work with the design firm CitiSpace, and I was asked by Mr. Bartlett to give him an estimate for some renovations." She had quickly acquired the sense that the less said to this woman, the better.

"I'm his wife and I still don't know who the hell *you* are." She squinted at Ally a moment, then glanced back at the card. "What is . . . CitiSpace?"

"It's an interior-design firm."

"What are you, then? Some kind of decorator?" She grasped the door to steady herself and Ally suddenly wondered if she was slightly tipsy.

"Actually, what we do is probably closer to architecture."

Ally was collecting her belongings, hoping to get out before Eileen Bartlett decided to do something crazy.

"This is the first I've heard about all this." She turned and slammed the rear door.

"Mind if I ask you a question?" Ally said. "Do you have any idea why those back windows were bricked over?"

"It's for security," she said. "No one is ever down here."

That's obvious, Ally thought, *which is why this job is so odd. This space clearly isn't being used now, and the social dynamic here doesn't bode well for a lot of cozy entertaining and dinner parties in the foreseeable future. So why is he spending money to renovate? And in this big hurry? And he just happened to pick* me *to do this as an audition for designing an entire museum. No, this whole thing definitely does not compute.*

But of course it does. The job is a blatant bribe. To butter me up for something.

"Look, Miss Whoever-you-are, I want you to leave. I don't appreciate strange women walking around unescorted in my house."

"I'm going right now. Perhaps you should speak to Mr. Bartlett and decide together what you want to do about this space."

"I'll tell you right now what *I* want to do. Nothing. For all I know, he's fixing this up so he can move in some tart. We've lived here for twenty-eight years and he's never done anything down here. So why is that tightfisted SOB suddenly deciding to renovate?"

"That would be an excellent question to ask him."

"You're screwing him, aren't you?" she demanded, wrinkled brow furrowed and dim eyes seething. "Like that other little whore of his. That's why he hired you. Well, let me tell you something. I'll outlive you both."

Without another word she turned and got into the elevator.

Chapter 9

"Hey, how did it go?" Jennifer asked the minute Ally came in the door.

She wasn't sure she knew the answer to that. Initially the job looked like a lot of fun, but now she felt the interpersonal dynamics of working in Bartlett's home were already a problem even before she started.

Also, maybe it was just paranoia, but as she took the cab downtown from the mansion on Gramercy Park, she got the impression that somebody was following her in a black SUV. And the stress of that brought on a tightness in her chest. But as she neared their office in SoHo, the vehicle abruptly veered east. She had a nitro tab at the ready, but she didn't have to pop it.

"There's good news and bad news. The good news is he's practically handing us a sweetheart of a job, and dangling another—designing a whole museum—in our face. The bad news is, I don't know why he suddenly thinks we're so terrific. I mean, you and I know that, but how did *he* figure it out?"

Jennifer looked puzzled. "You mean he—"

"Oh, did I mention that his crazy wife showed up after he left and essentially accused me of being a hooker? I suppose that comes under the heading of bad news."

"Great. Does that mean she's going to start second-guessing whatever we do?"

"The communication channels between Mr. Bartlett and Mrs. Bartlett don't appear to be all that great. They live on different floors in his place—which really *is* a huge old mansion on Gramercy Park, by the way—and the job would be in his part, the lower level." She explained the Bartletts' living arrangements. "He wants to redo the garden-level floor. It was originally the servants' quarters. Like *Upstairs, Downstairs.*"

"So he's upstairs and she's *way* upstairs."

"And let's hope she stays there."

Ally fetched herself a cup of coffee, checked in with everybody to see how they were doing, and then settled herself at her computer. She had the latest program in computer-aided-design (CAD) and she wanted to program in the dimensions and layout of the space. And since she had a copy of the blueprints, the first thing she would do would be to run them through her flatbed scanner and incorporate them into the program. She didn't get a chance to take any digital photos with CitiSpace's snazzy (and expensive) new Nikon. But if the job went forward, there'd be plenty of time later.

Everybody's computers were connected to the Net via a broadband DSL hookup and they were never turned off. Because of that, the computers were vulnerable to being hacked, so Jen had installed a firewall program to keep out snoops.

She sat down and stared at the screen saver, which was an ever-changing series of tropical beaches at sunset. She sipped at her coffee—this was the one cup she allowed herself each day, always saved for the moment when she felt she needed to be most alert—and reached to turn on the scanner. The tightness in her chest that she had momentarily experienced in the cab had completely disappeared and she felt perfectly normal.

What was she going to do about her mother and the clinic in New Jersey? Nina certainly appeared to want to go. And with the inevitability of what lay in store for someone with early-onset Alzheimer's, taking her out there was surely worth doing. But as for her own heart, she wasn't so sure she thought the reward was worth the risk. But she'd decided to hold off on a decision till she could have a firsthand look at the institute.

She took another sip of coffee and then tapped the keyboard. When she did that, the screen would normally bring up the "desktop."

But not this time. A file was open, and she was certain she hadn't left it open. *What's* this?

"Jen, could you come here a minute? There's something funny."

The first page of the file that had been pulled up and opened was an ID photo of herself.

"This is what was running. Has somebody been fooling around with this computer?"

Jennifer looked puzzled when she saw it. "Not that I know of."

"Then how did this get . . . ?" She just sat, staring. "I didn't open this file. Does this thing have a mind of its own?"

About eight years ago, Kate Gillis at Manhattan Properties—with whom Ally had an occasional after-work drink—told her she'd scanned all her vital personal documents into her computer at home. She'd said it was an easy way to make a safety backup.

Seemed like a good idea, so Ally had stored a copy of her birth certificate, her driver's license, all her credit cards, her passport, a set of medical records, even the mortgage on her apartment. She'd even scanned in an ID photo, just for the heck of it. She also suggested to Grant that he do the same.

Brilliant, right? Well, maybe not.

The reason was, she'd routinely made an updated copy on a ZIP disk and then copied it onto this computer here in the office. Like a second backup.

"I had everything ready for you for your meeting with Bartlett, so nobody here has touched your computer this morning." Jennifer furrowed her brow. "Could somebody have picked the locks and come in last night and done this, like a prank or something?"

"Come on. That's totally far-fetched." She was trying to imagine how somebody could have gotten in and out and left no trace. Impossible. "This must just be something stupid I did when I came down yesterday after seeing Mom. I don't remember it, but I guess I was pretty tired."

"I've never seen you *that* tired."

Jen's right, she thought. *I was on the city's Web site checking the Department of Buildings' Housing Code, but I certainly didn't pull up my personal data. Computers do strange things, but to open a data file for no reason? That would require a higher intelligence.*

Right?

"Jen, you're our resident computer expert. We leave these things hooked up all the time. I know we have a firewall, but what are the chances that somebody could defeat it somehow and hack into our computers?"

Jennifer was a software whiz and she had all the designs for all the clients on their CAD system, which they used to create a virtual-reality space and allow clients to "walk" through.

"Well, that's entirely possible. Our firewall software is over a year old. Let me take a look. Maybe I can reverse-engineer what happened. If somebody went through pulling up files, I might be able to figure it out."

Ally relinquished her chair and stood staring as Jennifer started checking the firewall.

It was scary to think that some stranger could know everything about you. But on the other hand, what difference could it make? She had nothing to hide. Still, it was creepy. Her

Social Security and credit card information was in that file. Could that be—

"*Shit.* Ally, you're not going to believe this. Whoever did this was damned good. We've been seriously hacked."

"How do you know?" She bent over to look.

"Our firewall software has been disabled. In fact, the actual program was *uninstalled.* Jesus, that's cool. I think we'd better shut down everybody's Internet connection right this minute, till we can get some new software."

"That's incredible. You mean somebody—"

"Honey, hackers have gotten into Microsoft's own site. Even the Pentagon, so I've heard. Anything is possible."

"This is not good."

"What are you thinking?" Jen was still staring at the screen and tapping at the keyboard.

"I'm thinking what a jerk I was. I keep all my personal information in that file, like a safety backup in case my apartment burned down or something. Scanned it in. My passport, driver's license, credit cards, medical records, everything."

Jennifer looked puzzled. "You can just cancel the credit cards. As for the rest of the stuff, what could anybody possibly want with it?"

"I don't know, Jen. I don't even know if we were hacked by somebody who wants to find out about me, or just look at our designs."

She was reflecting that when somebody goes through your files, they want the information for a purpose. And that purpose couldn't be positive for you, or they wouldn't have started their undertaking with a surreptitious act.

"Well, I'm going to check around and download a new firewall program. *Right now.*"

"Shit, I don't need this. I've got enough on my mind already. Mom wants to go out to a clinic in the wilds of northern New Jersey and see a doctor there. And the whole thing makes me nervous."

"Oh Jesus, is the place called the Dorian Institute by any chance?"

"How did—"

"I'm such a scatterbrain. I took a message for you while you were gone. From a Dr. Van de Something. I think that's the name of the place he's with. He wants you to call him back as soon as possible."

*Monday, April 6
11:43 A.M.*

Would she call back? Karl Van de Vliet had to believe she would, but nothing in this world was sure.

On the nineteen-inch screen of his office IBM, he was scrolling the medical file that he'd downloaded earlier that morning. How Grant Hampton got his hands on it, he didn't know and didn't want to know.

Yes, Alexa Hampton would be perfect. She had aortic valve stenosis, well along, the same condition that had precipitated the coronary destruction that took Camille from him. It was the great tragedy of his life.

He studied the charts carefully, trying to assure himself he was making the right choice. What if the stem cell procedure on her heart didn't work? To fail would mean he couldn't have saved Camille after all. That was actually the main reason he'd kept putting it off. He didn't want to know if he couldn't have rescued her.

But Alexa Hampton was the obvious candidate. Her clinical condition had deteriorated to the point that, at some level, you might even say she had nothing to lose by undergoing an experimental procedure.

And she was perfect in another way as well. Other than her heart condition, which she could do nothing about, she was in excellent physical shape. Her last blood pressure was 110 over 80 and her pulse was 67. She clearly had been exercising, which had been both good and bad for her heart, though on balance probably a plus. In fact, it was indicative of a strong fighting spirit, which was often the best prognosticator of all.

He looked up to see Dr. Debra Connolly walking in. He had just paged her. She was an M.D. who had been his personal research assistant during her grad school days at Stanford. Now she was a full and valued member of the research team. Just turned thirty, she also was a smashing blonde, five-nine, with a figure that would stop traffic, even in her white lab smock. She held Van de Vliet in the reverence always bestowed on a brilliant, beloved mentor.

"Hi, Deb, I wanted you to take a look at this." He indicated the screen. She knew all about the Beta and what had happened to Kristen, the Syndrome, but she didn't know about the plan to subject Alexa Hampton to two procedures at once: one for her aortic valve stenosis and another to develop antibodies to combat the looming side effects of the Beta in Winston Bartlett.

"This is the patient I was telling you about. I wanted you to see this. Let's pray she signs on for the trials, because she looks like she could be perfect, in a lot of ways."

But if she doesn't call back, he told himself, *what am I going to do?*

"What am I looking at?" Debra asked, scrolling the page. "Is this what I think it is?"

"It's her medical history."

"How did you get it?" She turned back. "Did she send it?"

"No, Deb, and I don't think you really want to know."

"Somehow, I think I probably should." She looked again at the screen. "We're in this together."

"All I know is, I got an e-mail from Grant Hampton, and this was an attachment. She must have been keeping it on a computer somewhere. I understand he's her brother, but how he got it, I have no idea. He said we're not supposed to let her know we have it."

"How recent—"

"This final battery of tests is less than two weeks old," he said, pointing to the date on the corner of the page. Then he scrolled. "Take a look at her high-speed CT scan. See that degenerative calcification there. Now look at the same test last year." He scrolled past a number of pages. "See." He tapped the screen, then scrolled back to the first image. "Over the past year there's been a significant buildup. She's made-to-order for the clinical trials."

And there was another reason he wanted her, which he was reluctant to admit to himself. There was a photo of Alexa Hampton in her medical files and something about her reminded him of Camille. Her eyes had a lot of spirit. They made you want to root for her. It was nothing short of ironic that this woman had the exact same medical condition that took the life of Camille, who had been at his side during the early stages of the research that now might provide a cure. But for Camille it had come too late. It was more than ironic; it was heartbreaking. Now, though, to save Alexa Hampton would be a kind of circular recompense. He took a last look, then closed the file.

"Does she want to be in the clinical trials? There's not much time left. We'd have to get her—"

"I just left a message at her office," he said, revolving around in his chair. "Grant has talked to her, and so has W.B. This very morning. She's aware that time is of the essence. But there's no guarantee she'll do it."

He glanced at his mute phone. If she didn't call back today, he had a feeling that Winston Bartlett might just have her seized and brought to the institute by force.

"I see that her blood type is AB," Debra said. "Extremely rare."

Funny she should notice, he thought. *Is she going to put it together?*

"That's the same as Bartlett's blood type," she continued. "Interesting coincidence, huh?"

"Right."

"You're already fond of her, aren't you?" Deb asked finally. He detected the usual tinge of rivalry seeping into her voice. "Without even meeting her."

Dear God, he thought, *don't start that. It's the same with every attractive female patient under the age of fifty. I don't have time for games now.*

The truth was, Karl Van de Vliet was turned on by Debra Connolly. What red-blooded primate wouldn't be? But she was half his age and to act on that attraction would be to guarantee trouble. He had enough to worry about without a lab romance. Besides, he was still thinking about Camille. They'd had the kind of long-lasting, thick-and-thin love Debra would never understand.

However, she did sufficiently understand the problems with the Beta procedure and the Syndrome, so he had to flirt back. She had to be kept on the reservation. Feign an interest but not enough for it to go anywhere.

"Deb, she's just an ideal fit for the study, that's all. Nothing more."

The stem cell procedure for her stenosis should go forward with only minimal risk. There was every reason to hope he could rejuvenate the tissue in Alexa's left ventricle. It was merely an extrapolation of the kind of heart procedure that had worked such a wonder for Emma Rosen.

The real challenge was simultaneously attempting the Beta-related procedure. The trick was to stimulate the development of antibodies through a moderate dosage of the special Beta enzyme, tempering it enough that it didn't go critical and begin replicating uncontrollably, the way it had in Kristen, and (probably) very soon in W.B. Not so low as to be inoperative but not so high that it would go out of control. The "Goldilocks dosage," not too much, not too little. The problem was, he wasn't absolutely sure what that dosage was.

Should he tell Alexa Hampton the full story about what he was doing? About the Beta? *That* ethical question, he had decided, he would leave to Grant Hampton, Bartlett's hustler of a CFO. It was *his* sister, after all. Presumably, he'd tell her whatever she needed to know to make an informed decision. Let the responsibility be on *his* head.

The phone on his desk finally rang.

Chapter 10

Monday, April 6
12:57 P.M.

Stone Aimes was floating through cyberspace, through the massive data pages of the National Institutes of Health. Since the Gerex Corporation had a complete clampdown on their clinical-trial results, he was attempting an end run. By going to the source, he was hoping he could find out whether or not Karl Van de Vliet's experiments with stem cell technology were succeeding.

He needed that information to finish his book, and he hoped that the remainder of the advance could be used to pay for his daughter Amy's private school in New York, if he got it in time. He was dreaming of a life in which she could come back to live with him at least part of the year. Sometimes, particularly days like this—Monday was his official day off—he couldn't avoid the fact he was incredibly lonely.

But first things first. He had gone to the section that described the many and varied clinical trials the NIH had under way. Then he used "scrambled eggs," the entry protocol given to him by Dale Coverton, to circumvent security on the site and get him into the second-level NIH data files.

He was hoping to find the names of patients who had gone through the Gerex stem cell procedure and could be interviewed.

It really wasn't all that difficult, or even—he told himself—unethical to get in this far. No big deal. Entry protocols were available to any high-level NIH employee who had the right security grade. Now he was poking through the reams of proprietary data that the Gerex Corporation had submitted to initiate the clinical trials.

It was one of the more ambitious studies he'd ever seen, not in numbers of patients necessarily but certainly in scope. They were indeed running stage-three clinical trials of their stem cell procedure on a variety of maladies. There was no double-blind placebo. You either were cured or you were not.

Jesus, it was incredible. They were shooting for nothing less than the unified field theory of medicine, aiming not just to patch some failing element of the human body but to regenerate entire organs. Among their stated objectives were building pancreatic islets, reconstructing the ventricles of the heart, reconstituting the damaged livers of individuals with advanced cirrhosis. They were also accepting patients with Alzheimer's and Parkinson's.

"Christ," he said, scrolling past page after page, "how come they're suddenly so secretive about this?"

If Van de Vliet had achieved results in just a fraction of those trials, it would herald the beginning of a new age in medicine.

The NIH monitor for the Gerex trials was Cheryl Gates, just as Dale had said. Her photo was featured along with the introductory description of the trials. Nice-looking, he thought, probably late thirties, dark hair, dark-rimmed glasses. She wasn't wearing much makeup in the photo, probably to emphasize how serious she was. Sooner or later, he told himself, he had to find a way to meet her. . . .

He stared at his IBM Aptiva screen a moment longer, overwhelmed at what he was seeing, then got up and walked into the kitchen and made a peanut butter sandwich, whole wheat. It was a rehearsal for the possibly hard times to come. Then he retrieved a Brooklyn Lager from the fridge. It was his day off and the sun was over the yardarm.

He lived on the fourth floor of a brownstone in Yorkville, in New York's East Eighties. The apartment was small, but it was rent stabilized, which meant he was paying well under market value—$1,128 a month on a place that probably could go for close to twice that on the open market. He'd lucked into it after he and Jane split—even though they weren't married, they'd bought a condo in the West Fifties, and at the breakup they'd switched the mortgage to her name—but the problem now was, how was he going to pay even this piddling rent (not to mention child support for Amy) after he got fired from the *Sentinel*? That day, he sensed, was fast approaching. And if it happened before the book was finished, he was just three months away from going back to freelancing. That was how long his "nest egg" would last.

Carrying the sandwich and beer, he walked back to his "office," a corner of the cramped living room that had an Early American desk, and sat down at the frayed chair in front of his IBM.

So here he was, past the first level of security of the NIH site, zeroed in on the Gerex clinical trials. Somewhere here had to be all the data about the patients who had been, and currently were, participating.

He moved on to the results section and opened the first page. *Yes.*

Then he looked more closely.

Hello, we've got a problem. The patient data he was looking at had only code numbers for names. The categories of trials also were just numbers. Without a key, there was no way to get a single patient name or differentiate Alzheimer's from fallen arches. Then he saw the notice at the top of the page: *As part of the NIH policy on privacy, all patient data are aggregated and anonymous.*

Shit.

This was as far as "scrambled eggs" would take him. He needed a higher security protocol to get into individual-case data. Dale either didn't have it or didn't dare give it out.

Well, he thought, *at least I've got information on the structure of the clinical trials. I should print that before the system realizes it's been hacked.* He clicked on the print icon. *Let the games begin.*

His real objective was to try to wangle an interview with Karl Van de Vliet, an interview that would have to be approved by Winston Bartlett. Maybe what could be gleaned from this level of the NIH site would be enough to bluff Bartlett into thinking he knew more than he really did. In truth, interviewing discharged patients would have meant anecdotal information, probably not rigorous enough for use in a definitive book. But at the moment, that would have been a start.

He lifted the first printed page and studied it.

Stone Aimes had seen enough clinical trials over the years to know that the data were reported according to an established schedule. Obviously, the schedule was always adapted to fit the nature of the trials under way, but studies that produce the kind of short-term results Gerex hinted at in their early press releases—before they clammed up—would probably have a tight reporting schedule, possibly even weekly.

He stared at the page for a moment, then lifted out another. He wasn't sure just yet what it all meant, but he might be able to infer something. He was still puzzling over the columns of numbers as the data finished printing.

What was it telling him?

He went back and clicked on STUDY PROCEDURES. This section explained how the reporting was structured. He still held out hope that the names of the discharged patients in the clinical trials could be accessed somehow. In the past, when the FDA tested drugs, it often happened that the names of the participants were not revealed to the monitor, or to anybody. The policy was intended to preserve the privacy of study participants. But lately it had been under review. All that

secrecy and nonaccountability had permitted some spectacular fabrication of test data.

Surely the NIH had taken this into consideration by now
and come up with a system whereby the identities of the participants could be checked and verified. That information
had to be stored somewhere.

No such luck. It appeared the NIH had begun using a
modified version of the new FDA sunshine policy. NIH clinical trials had a "one week of sunshine" provision, during
which the suitability of test subjects could be evaluated by a
review procedure. During that time, their real identity was in
the database. But after that, the identity information of any
patient actually selected for inclusion in the clinical trials
was encoded—where thenceforth it could only be accessed
through a lengthy legal process.

Screwed again.

At this late date, the Gerex Corporation surely was not
going to be adding any new names and giving them that
week of sunshine. According to press releases at the beginning of the clinical trials, when Gerex was a lot more com-
municative, at this date the entire study should be just days
away from being wrapped up.

He went back to the patient files one last time, out of frustration. As he continued to scroll, he noticed that although
the identities of patients and crucial personal data were encrypted, the *dates* on which they entered and finished the trials were all supplied.

Hmmm. It was actually more detailed than that. There
were dates for when a patient entered each stage of the procedure: Screening, Initial Evaluation, Admitted into Program,
Procedure Under Way, Procedure Monitoring, Results Evaluation, Patient Release, Patient Follow-up.

The time between screening and patient release averaged
around five weeks, six weeks at most.

Looking at the time-sequenced data, you couldn't avoid
the conclusion that the clinical trials had been a spectacular
success. No doubt the specific data would reveal whether

there had been any adverse reactions, but as clinical trials go, these seemed to have been without major incident. He had a nose for trouble, and these looked as rigorous as clockwork. . . .

Hold on a second. . . . That's odd.

What the data structure did not have was a category for Termination. Yet one of the patients had been listed with dates leading up to and including Procedure Under Way, but after that the patient was noted parenthetically as having been "terminated." That was all the information given.

What could *that* mean?

He leaned back with a sigh and pulled on his Brooklyn Lager. Okay, patients frequently got dropped from clinical trials because some underlying condition suddenly manifested itself and made them unsuitable trial subjects. In fact, that was preferable to keeping them in a study when they were no longer appropriate. But the thing about clinical trials was, there always had to be a compelling, fully explained reason for terminating a test subject. Otherwise you could just "terminate" nonresponsive participants and skew the results. No reason was given here.

He thought again about the "one week of sunshine," and as a long shot checked to see if anyone had been admitted this week.

Nada, but again that was reasonable. The entire study was wrapping up.

Which meant, in short, that he had nothing to work with in terms of people. All he had were dates and encrypted names.

What now?

He finished the beer and was preparing to go off-line when a drop-down screen flickered NEW DATA.

He was being directed to the new applicants' "sunshine" page.

He clicked back, then stared at the screen.

A name had appeared.

He couldn't believe his luck. For some unknown reason,

they must still be adding new test subjects at this late date in the trials.

NINA HAMPTON.

Finally he had a name. This was an incredible stroke of . . .

Wait. A second name was appearing now, the letters popping up one by one as they were being typed in.

He rolled the mouse to print, and felt his hopes surge.

Then his heart skipped a beat. The second name was . . .

ALEXA HAMPTON.

Jesus, could it be?

No way. Too big a coincidence. But wait, the other was Nina Hampton. Isn't that the name of her Brit mum? That unredeemable piece of work.

Impossible.

If it *was* the Ally Hampton he knew, she was a woman he still thought of every day. It went back to when they were both undergraduates. She was taking a degree in architecture at Columbia and he had just switched from premed to the Columbia School of Journalism.

Wasn't there a Cole Porter lyric about an affair being too hot not to cool down? They undoubtedly were in love, but they both were too strong-willed to cede an inch of personal turf. It was a combustible situation.

When they decided to go their own way, it was done under the agreement that they would make a clean break and never see each other again. *Be adult and hold your head high and look to the future.* No recriminations and no second thoughts. In respecting that agreement, he had gone out of his way not to keep track of her. He particularly didn't want to know if she'd gotten married, had a family, any of it.

Thinking back now, he remembered that she had had some kind of heart condition. She refused to talk about it, and now he couldn't remember exactly what it was. But that could possibly explain her entry into the clinical trials, though it didn't clarify why she was only being added now, at the last minute.

If it was actually her.

And if so, how would he feel talking to her? He hoped time had mellowed her, though he somehow doubted it. Not Ally.

What an irony. If it was the same Alexa Hampton, she could end up being his entrée into the secretive world of Winston Bartlett's Gerex Corporation. The trouble was, he wasn't sure he actually wanted to see her again. Even after all the years, the wounds still felt fresh.

He closed out the NIH file and opened People Search, which he often used to look up phone numbers. He started with New York State as a criterion. The names Alexa and Nina undoubtedly belonged to women, so they might be listed merely by their initials. *But start with Alexa and be optimistic.*

He got lucky. Three names and phone numbers popped up.

One was in Manhattan, and Ally was a dyed-in-the-wool New Yorker, but he wasn't sure he was psychologically prepared to speak to her. That number he decided to save for last, though it was by far the most plausible.

The next Alexa Hampton lived in Syracuse, with area code 315. He was still shook up as he dialed the number.

"Yeah, who's this?"

Sure didn't sound like Ally. But he was playing this straight. As a reporter he always started a conversation by identifying himself, so naturally he answered, "Stone Aimes, *New York Sentinel.*"

"The fuck you want?" came the voice. It was female but it definitely was not ladylike. "I don't need any newspapers."

Whoa, that *definitely* didn't sound like Ally. She was direct, but she didn't talk like a sailor.

"Sorry, ma'am. I have a few questions about your participation in some clinical trials. Sorry to bother you, but I have a deadline. Shouldn't take a minute."

"You a fucking reporter?"

"I'm doing a story on the Gerex Corporation. Are you—"

"The *what* corporation? The fuck you talking about?"

"Seems like I'm calling the wrong number. I'm very sorry and I apologize."

"Listen, if you're some kind of weirdo, I'm going to call the cops and have this call traced."

"I said I apologize." He hung up and thought about another beer. This was beginning to feel like the moment.

But he resisted the urge and called the next number. *Come on. Be the right one and don't be Ally.*

This one had a 516 area code. That meant Long Island.

"Hello," came a rusty old voice that had to be in its seventies. It sounded oversmoked and just hanging on. Again definitely not the Ally he knew.

"Hello, ma'am," he said, "I'm sorry to bother you, but—"

"Are you trying to sell me something, young man," the woman asked. "It's not going to do you much good. I live on a Social Security check, and it's all I can do to make ends meet as is. You sound nice, but—"

"No, ma'am, I'm a newspaper reporter. I'm doing a story on . . . I just wanted to follow up on your admission to the clinical trials for the Gerex Corporation." He felt a surge of hope. It wasn't Ally, but she did sound like a woman who might well be a candidate for medical treatment. "Do you know what day you plan to start?"

"What on *earth* are you talking about?" she asked. "Young man, it's ill manners to start asking a body silly questions, no matter how nice you might be otherwise. I've never heard of this, whatever you called it, corporation." *Click.*

She sure didn't sound like a patient. Or maybe she was too far gone to even know if she was a patient or not. In any case, this was not a promising lead.

Okay, he thought, *go with the one you should have in the first place.*

Blast. He wanted this to be the one, but he just didn't want it to be Ally. Or maybe he did.

He took a deep breath and punched in the last number, which had a Manhattan area code, 212. The phone at the other end rang five times and then an answering machine came on. At this hour, she would most likely be at work.

"Hello, this is Alexa Hampton. I'm sorry I can't come to the phone now, but if you'll leave your name and number, I'll get back to you as soon as possible. If you're calling about design work, the number of CitiSpace is 212-555-8597."

He felt his heart flip, then sink. It *was* Ally. It was a voice he had heard for years in his reveries—or were they the nightmares of roads not taken?

She still might not be the new patient in the clinical trials, but at least he knew he could reach her.

The sound of her voice. After all this time he didn't realize it would still affect him the way it did.

So, he thought, clearing his head, *she's running a design business now.* He wondered how that had happened. The last time he saw her, she was a single-minded student of architecture. Intensely focused.

No message. Don't leave a message. It probably would freak her out. Actually, it might freak them both out.

Assuming she was the new patient, *how the hell* did Ally get involved with Winston Bartlett? It probably would have something to do with that heart condition she didn't like to talk about.

He clicked off the phone and settled it onto the desk. Then he glanced again at the computer screen and decided to go back to the NIH files. The other woman, Nina, he would look up later. Ally's Brit mum must be getting on by now, but still it was hard to imagine anything being wrong with her; as he remembered Nina, the woman was well nigh indestructible. . . .

When he got back to the NIH Web site and went to the "sunshine" page, it was again blank. The two new names, Nina Hampton and Alexa Hampton, were not there anymore. They must have been entered immediately into the clinical trials. But why now? If Van de Vliet kept to the original schedule, the trials would be over in a matter of days.

Maybe, he thought, *this was a momentary screwup. I just happened to be at the right place at the right fleeting mo-*

ment, when somebody, somewhere, was entering those names. Maybe some NIH bureaucrat hit the wrong key on a keyboard someplace in Maryland.

But it was the break he'd been waiting for.

He turned off the IBM and headed for the fridge and another Brooklyn Lager. *Ally, Ally, Ally. Can it be you? This is so weird.*

Worse than that, it was painful. There was that immortal line from *Casablanca:* "Of all the gin joints in all . . . she walks into mine."

Why you, dear God?

Coming back, he sat down, took a long hit on the icy bottle, and reached for the phone.

Chapter 11

Monday, April 6
1:29 P.M.

As she hung up, Ally wondered again what she was getting into. But she did want to meet this miracle worker. The kind of thing Van de Vliet was talking about sounded as much like science fiction as anything she'd ever heard. Still, his voice was reassuring, even mesmerizing, and there seemed no reason not to at least check out the Dorian Institute firsthand. But then what? *Help!*

She looked at her coffee cup and wished she dared have a refill. But that much caffeine always made her heart start to act up. And maybe she didn't need it. The conversation with Karl Van de Vliet had energized her and sharpened her senses quite enough.

She was still thinking about that when the phone rang again. There was an electronic voice directory, but her own phone was the default if a caller did not care to use it.

"CitiSpace."

"Hi, Ally. Tell me if you recognize the voice. Just please don't hang up."

Who was it? The intonations were bouncing around somewhere in the back of her brain, as though they were a computer file looking for a match. The one her unconscious mind was making was being rejected by her conscious mind. Then finally the match came through and stuck.

My God, it couldn't be. The last time she'd talked to him was . . . what? Almost two decades ago.

The irony was, she'd been thinking about him some lately, as part of taking stock of her life. She'd been meditating over all the roads not taken, and he'd been the last man she'd actually loved, or thought she loved, before Steve.

"What . . . How did . . . ?" She found she was at a loss for words. She figured he'd have been the same way if she'd called *him* out of the blue.

"Hey, this isn't easy for me either. But I have a pretty good reason for breaking our vow of silence."

She was immediately flooded with mixed emotions. Stone Aimes. She already knew he wrote for the *Sentinel*. Or at least she assumed the irreverent reporter by that name who did their medical column was him. The tone sounded so much like the way she remembered him. There was a lot of passion and he was always editorializing against "Big Medicine." He had plenty of raw courage, but sometimes he had too much edge. That was one quality he had that had eventually gotten to be nerve-racking back when they were together.

Now, in hindsight, she remembered their breakup with both anger and regret. She was angry that, even though she tried like hell, she could never really connect with him at the level she yearned for. He always seemed to be holding something back, some secret he was afraid to divulge. Truthfully, they both were grand masters at never allowing vulnerability. In short, they were overly alike. They shared the same flaws.

Still, after Steve was taken away, it was hard not to think of Stone now and then. Before Steve, Stone was the only sane lover she'd ever been close to.

But she also knew the bit about letting sleeping dogs lie. Sometimes that was the better part of wisdom. This conversation, she finally decided, was just going to open old wounds. Better to nip it right now.

And add to that, she didn't actually know if he was free now or not or what.

But he'd said he had a good reason for calling—what could that be?

"Stone, I read your columns in the *Sentinel*. So I sort of feel like I've kept in contact. I can almost hear your voice sometimes."

"That makes me think you were cheating a little on our deal."

"Well," she heard herself say, "some of them were pretty good. Sometimes you sounded like you knew as much as a doctor."

"Don't flatter me excessively, or I might want to start believing you." He laughed. "But speaking of doctors, didn't you used to have some kind of heart issue? How is that these days?"

"You really want to know?"

"Maybe it might have something to do with why I'm calling. Best I recall, you never actually told me, even back when."

"Thank you for asking," she said. "I guess it's not much of a secret anymore, with me popping nitro every other day. I have a scarred valve, coronary stenosis, and it's not getting any better. I don't know what to do about it, short of going to Lourdes for a miracle."

"I see," he said. Then he fell silent. Mercifully, he didn't come up with false bravado about revolutionary treatments and you never can tell, blah, blah, blah. Then he said, "So is that why you've enrolled in the clinical trials at the Dorian Institute? To be part of their work using stem cells?"

What! "How the *hell* do you know about—"

"Hey, Ally, you know I can't divulge my sources. After I knew you, I grew up to be a real reporter. That was my grand plan, remember?"

"Then this may turn out to be a very short conversation. I have nothing to—"

"Okay, okay, let's start over." He paused and cleared his throat. "Ahem. Are you the Alexa Hampton who was formally entered about half an hour ago into the stage-three clinical trials for the National Institutes of Health being held by the Gerex Corporation? Or maybe I should play dumb and begin by asking if you've ever heard of them."

"Stone, why . . . why are you asking me this?"

It was bizarre. How could he know? And, wait a *minute*, what did he mean about enrolling? She hadn't *enrolled* in anything.

"Ally, I'm finishing a major—I hope—book about stem cell technology, and right now the world leader is the Gerex Corporation. I think, but I can't yet prove, that their Dorian Institute out in New Jersey is the site of some pretty incredible stuff. I was . . . fooling around on the Internet, on the NIH Web site, looking for information about them, and—it must have been some momentary computer glitch—someone with your name popped up for a second. Along with a Nina Hampton. Which made me suspect it was you."

She was incredulous. She was being entered into the clinical trials before she had even seen the place? Somebody was pushing the pace. Winston Bartlett or Van de Vliet had taken it for granted that she and her mother would enter the trials. Worst of all, it took a former lover she hadn't talked to in x-zillion years to give her this unnerving information.

"Nina *is* your mom, right?" he went on. "I still remember her fondly. I don't think she thought much of me, however. By the way, how is she?"

"She's . . . she's not doing all that great." Ally was still trying to get her mind around what she'd just heard. "But why are you calling *me*, Stone?"

"If anything I've said rings a vague bell, then could we meet someplace and talk? I don't think it would be a great idea to do it over the phone. That's all I really can say now."

Maybe, she thought, Stone Aimes might have uncovered a few things of which she ought to be aware. His pieces in the *Sentinel* showed he was a damned good reporter.

"I don't think what little I know about Gerex would be any help to you." She was attempting to get her mind back together. "I actually have a lot of questions about the stem cell procedure myself. I spoke on the phone just now with Dr. Van de Vliet and he described their technology to me in general terms. But maybe I should interview *you*. Maybe you could explain it to me using that wonderful gift you have for simplification in your columns."

"Ally, I don't know anything except what's in the public domain. They're privately held, so they don't have to tell anybody zilch. I assume you've actually been out to the Dorian Institute, which is more than *I* can say."

"Never."

"But you're enrolled—"

"I'm not *enrolled* in anything." To say the least. "And it bothers me that anybody thinks so. But I *am* thinking about taking Mom out there tomorrow, if she still wants to go. When I talked to him on the phone, Dr. Van de Vliet wanted me to start the procedure immediately. That's scary, but he does seem to know what he's doing."

"I take it, then, that you're leaning toward going through with it."

She hated the way he'd just made her sound so gullible.

"The truth is, I'm more concerned for Mom. He claims he can help her early-onset Alzheimer's, and that would mean a lot." Why was she telling him all this stuff? She found herself wondering if he'd ever married.

"I'm so sorry to hear that. But the chances are he can."

"What are you thinking?" she asked finally. "And why did you call me? Really? *What's* going on?"

"I don't know yet. There's a lot I don't know." He seemed to hesitate. "Ally, is there any chance whatsoever that—while you're out there—you could get me the names of some of the people who've been through the clinical trials? The Dorian Institute is entirely off-limits to the press. I tried several times to schedule an interview with Karl Van de Vliet, the guy you talked to, but no luck. I can't get past the corporate people. My only hope is to try and find some patients who've been treated and released, who've completed the clinical trials. But Gerex has been ruthless about keeping their identities secret. You are literally the first person I've found who has any connection with the institute and is willing to talk about it. That is, *if* you're willing."

"Stone, it would be like the blind leading the blind. I don't know the first thing about the place."

"Well, let me ask you this—when you were talking with him, did Van de Vliet happen to mention any occasion where a subject had been terminated from the trials?"

"It never came up. Why do you—"

"Never mind. But when and if you go out there, you might inquire about that." He paused. "Don't get me wrong. I'm actually Gerex's biggest fan. I mean, considering merely what you told me, that they're claiming to have a procedure that treats early-onset Alzheimer's. Think about it. I'm rooting for your mom, sure, but that's a Nobel Prize in itself, right there. We're talking major medical history in the making."

"And?"

"And I want to publish the first book about it." He paused. "Also, a little birdie tells me that something not entirely kosher may be going on out there. No proof, just a reporter's hunch. There's a little too much sudden secrecy."

Ally was having a strange feeling come over her. She was actually enjoying talking to him.

"Shit, Stone, I'm glad you called. I lost two men I loved very much since I knew you and I'm feeling very alone at the moment. I could use some moral support. I've got a lot of people bugging me to enter those clinical trials. Even people I'd never met before, like Winston Bartlett, the New

York big shot. He's suddenly very concerned about my health. I have no idea what that's about. But it makes me uneasy."

There was an awkward lull, then, "Ally, all I'm asking is that you just take the measure of the Dorian Institute when you're out there and tell me what you think about the place. Are they performing the miracles they announced as their objective?"

"Look, I'll help you when and if I actually can. So give me your number, okay?"

He did.

"I can tell when I'm being blown off," he went on. "I have a very sensitive blow-off detector. But why don't you try a test? When you're out at the institute, ask Van de Vliet or somebody why that mystery patient was terminated from the clinical trials. See if the question makes them uncomfortable."

"Why does that matter so much to you?"

"If a patient is dropped for no good reason about the same time they clamp down on information, I think it could be fishy. Beyond that, I cannot speculate. And while you're at it, I'd love the names of some other ex-patients. *Anybody.* I found a list on the NIH Web site but they're all encoded, so it doesn't do me any good. I just want to ask them if the procedure worked or not. It's information that's going to be made public eventually, no matter what. Come on, Ally, don't you want some testimonials?"

"Okay, look, I'll try to see if anybody there will give me any info."

She was realizing she was in a comfort zone when she was talking to him. Still, so much about him remained a mystery. He had always said his mother and father were both dead, but it was still suspiciously hard to get him to speak about them. She'd gotten the impression that he didn't actually remember his father. That was the part of his life that he'd always been the most closed off about. Either that or he was repressing some horrible memories.

"Thanks a lot, Ally." A pause, then, "Interested in getting together sometime?"

"Let me think about it."

She put down the phone with her mind in turmoil. She realized she hadn't asked him if he was "attached," but the next time they spoke, she was going to try to ease it into the conversation.

Chapter 12

Tuesday, April 7
9:50 A.M.

Ally steered her Toyota onto the ramp leading to the George Washington Bridge, the entryway to northern New Jersey. She was just finishing a phone call to Jennifer. She wanted her to take a look at the notes and blueprints for Bartlett's Gramercy Park project and scan them into their CAD program. After all the phone calls yesterday, she'd been too sidetracked to do it. Although Bartlett had declared he wasn't in any hurry, he had messengered a certified check to her office Monday afternoon. The project was a go. She wanted to get moving while everything was fresh in her mind.

Before leaving her apartment this morning, she'd downloaded a map from MapQuest and from it she had estimated that the drive up to the Dorian Institute would be approximately an hour—give or take. She had begun the trip early because her mother's mind had been lucid the previous evening and she was hoping that interlude might last into this morning.

Unfortunately, it had not.

Nina was sitting next to her now, in full makeup but completely unresponsive, seemingly in another world. When Ally arrived at the Riverside Drive apartment to pick her up, Maria—now silent and uneasy in the backseat, reading a Spanish novel—met her at the door with a troubled look and shook her head sadly.

"Miss Hampton, I know she was all right when you were here last night, but this morning . . . she may not recognize you. She'll most likely snap out of it and be okay later on, but right now she's just in a fog. It was all I could do to get her ready."

When Ally walked in, Nina was sitting in her favorite chair, dressed in her favorite black suit. Her makeup was perfect. *Thank you, Maria.*

"Hey, sweetie, you look great."

Nina stared at her as though trying to place the face and said nothing. She just looked confused and very, very sad.

Dear God, Ally thought, *this is the first time she's completely failed to recognize me.*

It was so disheartening. Last night, when Ally had come up to discuss whether or not she still wanted to explore Dr. Van de Vliet's experimental treatment, Nina had been completely cognizant. Ally had tried to explain the concept of neural tissue regeneration using stem cells, which was difficult since she barely understood it herself.

"Mom," she had said, "this might be something that could reverse some of the damage to your . . . memory. At least keep it from getting worse. I know it sounds scary but everybody says the conventional treatments for what you have don't work very well or very long."

"Then let's go out there and talk to him, honey. Just come in the morning and take me. By then I'll probably forget everything you've said tonight."

How prescient, Ally thought sadly. Now Nina was just gazing blankly ahead, silent. *Does she remember anything from last night?*

For that matter, what *was* Nina thinking now? Was she conscious of the fact she was losing her mind? And what about the ultimate question: do we want to live longer merely to be alive, or do we want to stay alive in order to do things? To be or to do? In her mother's case, she knew it was the latter. Nina had always been full of life, ambition, and projects. Would she want to go on living if none of those things were possible? You never know for sure about other people, even your own mother, but Ally suspected she would rather not live to see that day.

Now, though, was she even aware it was coming?

Ally thought back about the first signs. Nina hadn't yet turned sixty-five when she abruptly started having trouble remembering little things. She began forgetting where she'd put items, and she gave up on remembering phone numbers and dates. Initially it had just seemed like a lot of "senior moments" run together, very puzzling.

But then it got worse. She'd always loved music, and she'd always played the piano. She loved Chopin, especially the nocturnes. By the time she was sixty-six, however, she was having trouble remembering the names of her favorite composers. She also completely gave up trying to play, either from memory or with the music. When getting dressed one day, she put on her blouse completely backwards. It was bad.

Ally had taken her to see four different specialists and they all had concluded that Nina Hampton suffered from what was known as familial early-onset Alzheimer's. It was caused by a mutated gene and was extremely rare, representing only some 5 percent of all Alzheimer's cases.

There were two major drugs currently on the market, Exelon and Reminyl, that could relieve some of the symptoms of Alzheimer's by boosting the action of the brain chemical acetylcholine. However, Nina had not yet declined to the stage where doctors would prescribe those drugs. To resort to them was an admission you were at endgame, since they usually were effective only for a few months.

So the Dorian Institute might well be a long shot worth taking. *Frankly, what's to lose?*

This morning, she knew, was going to be difficult. If Nina

wanted to stay and checked in, there would surely be a pile of paperwork. Ally had had the foresight to acquire power of attorney for her mother three months earlier, and she'd brought along that document in case it might be needed. And Maria, the wonderful, ultimate caregiver, was there to help. The real challenge, however, might well be trying to help Nina understand what was going on and participate in the decision. This was the moment every child dreads, when you have to face, really face, a parent's mortality.

As the green forests of northern New Jersey began to envelop them, she slipped a CD of Bach partitas for unaccompanied violin into the CD player. She had loved to play them all her life, but now Dr. Ekelman had urged her to put her violin into storage. Hearing the violin now reminded her of the other purpose of the trip, the treatment decision she needed to make for *herself*.

In that regard, one of the things that kept running through her mind was what Stone Aimes had said about the Gerex Corporation instituting a news blackout simultaneously with a patient being mysteriously dropped from the trials. Those concurrent facts did not need to be ominous, but they also could use an explanation.

What was she going to do? Was Van de Vliet's stem cell procedure on her heart really worth the risk? She honestly didn't know. Even though the violin had temporarily been taken away from her, she had hopes she could gradually get it back. There were other ways to try to strengthen a dysfunctional heart.

Well, she thought, *wait and hear him out.*

From the George Washington Bridge she had taken I-4, which turned into I-208 and now the green forest held sway. It felt like she'd gone through a time warp, from the beginning of the twenty-first century to the end of the eighteenth. Then finally, as the second partita was ending, the icy-cold Greenwood Lake came into view. It was associated with those long Finger Lakes gouged out by glaciers.

Driving past remnants of the last Ice Age, she reflected on how insignificant humans are in the scheme of things. Suddenly she thought of Aldous Huxley's novel *After Many a Summer Dies the Swan,* about a wealthy madman who'd discovered a way to prolong life by eating the entrails of prehistoric fish. Maybe it was seeing the lake that made her flash on that.

She was now on Greenwood Lake Road, which passed around the west side, and there were numbers on several gated driveways as she passed along. She suspected the place would be somewhere along the middle of the lakeshore, and she was right.

After a few miles she came to a discreet sign announcing the Dorian Institute, and a large iron gate that protected a paved roadway leading into a forest of trees. That was it: just forest, no hint of a building, though she saw signs of some kind of industrial park farther down the road. When she drove up to the gate, she realized there was a video camera and a two-way intercom.

When she reached out of the window and pushed the talk button, she heard "Good morning." And then the gates parted in the middle and slid back.

They must be expecting us, she thought, and drove through.

The road was cobblestone, or rough paving brick. It wound among the trees for approximately half a mile and then widened.

There, framed by the lake in the background, was a magnificent three-story building with eight Doric columns across the front in perfect Greek Revival style. There were windows at ground level, but they were heavily curtained.

Built of red brick, the building probably dated from the late nineteenth century, and it looked every bit like an Ivy League dormitory.

"Miss Hampton, I don't like the feeling I'm getting about this place," Maria said quietly. "It is very cold and formal from the outside, but inside I sense a place where there is bad magic.

In the Dominican Republic, we call it Santeria. I can always tell these things."

Ally knew and respected Maria's sixth sense. But then Maria sometimes still acted like a freshly minted citizen just off a green card, and she had an innate suspicion of authority-evoking buildings. Her aversion to the Dorian Institute might be nothing more than that.

On the other hand, Ally was having a bit of the same feeling. There was something formidable and foreboding about the place that seemed out of keeping with its supposedly benign purpose. She felt a moment of tightness in her chest.

There was a parking area off to the left, and she drove into the nearest slot and turned off her engine. This was the moment she'd been both anticipating and dreading. The clock on the dash read eleven-fifteen; she was fifteen minutes ahead of the appointed hour.

"Okay, Mom, how do you feel?"

Nina turned and stared at her, uncertainty in her eyes. "Where are we, Ally? I don't recognize anything."

"This is the institute I told you about last night. Can you remember anything we talked about then?"

"This is the place you were . . . Didn't you say there's a doctor here who can do something for my . . . memory?"

"We're both here now to just talk to him." She turned to the backseat. "Maria, can you get Mom's purse?"

She nodded, then reached hesitantly for the door. She was clearly reluctant to get out.

Ally walked around and opened the door for her mother. "Okay, Mom, time to stretch your legs."

Ally held her hand and together they headed across the oval brick driveway. Birds were chirping around them and she could smell the scent of the lake, borne up the hill by a fresh wind. Then, through the trees, she saw two women walking up the trail that led down to the lake. They were, she assumed, some of the patients.

They both looked to be in their early sixties, but also athletic and nimble. One was wearing Nikes and a pale green pantsuit. The other had on a blue dress and a white cap and Ally realized she must be a nurse. She'd been taking the other woman out for a stroll.

They were engrossed in conversation, but as they approached, the woman Ally had decided was on staff looked up and smiled a greeting.

"Can I help you?"

She introduced herself and Nina and Maria. The woman smiled again but didn't introduce herself in turn.

"We're here to see Dr. Van de Vliet," Ally went on, "about the trials. But we're a couple of minutes early and I was wondering if we could look around a bit first? I'm trying to understand what the institute is really like."

"Well, dear," the woman said, "even those of us who work here aren't allowed everywhere. You know, into the research lab in the basement. Some places here have to be completely hygienic. Of course, for patients who are in the recovery phase, strolling around outside is definitely recommended, as long as they're able. But that's getting way ahead of ourselves. First we'll have to check you in. There's a lot of paperwork for the clinical trials." She seemed puzzled. "They're almost over, you know. But come along and I'll let him know you're here. He's always down in the lab at this time of the morning. It's well after his rounds. They're so busy now."

Then she turned to the other woman. "Sophie, do you think you can find your way back to your room? It's number two-eighteen, on the second floor, remember?"

Sophie appeared to be pondering the question for a long moment before she huffed, "Don't be silly. I know exactly where it is."

As she strode on ahead, the nurse watched her carefully, as though unsure what she might do next. She pushed a buzzer at the door and then a man in a white uniform opened it and let her in. Only after Sophie had disappeared through the doorway did the nurse turn back.

"I'm Elise Baker. Please forgive Sophie if she seems a little . . . confused. Her procedure is still under way."

"Her 'procedure'? What—"

"She was diagnosed with Parkinson's before she came here. She's improved an enormous amount, but we're not allowed to say so."

"Why is that?"

"We're in clinical trials. No one is allowed to discuss our results. Everyone here had to sign a secrecy agreement."

Now Maria was helping Nina up the steps. The porch, with its soaring white Doric columns, was definitely magisterial. The front door, however, was not wooden or decorative. It was solid steel, albeit painted white to blend in.

Elise walked to the door, which had a video camera mounted above it, and a split second later, it buzzed, signaling it was unlocked.

This is a lot of security, Ally thought, *for a clinic doing research on cells. Are they worried about spies getting in, or patients getting* out?

But the locked steel door was just the beginning of the security. Next they entered a small room just inside the door with an X-ray machine to see into purses and parcels.

"The first floor is reception and dining," Elise explained as she swept through the metal detector. "There are rooms— we call them suites—upstairs for patients, and the research lab and offices are in the . . . lower area."

"What . . . what is all this security for?" Ally asked.

"The work here is highly proprietary. No one is allowed to bring in any kind of camera or recording equipment."

The guard dressed in white looked like a retired policeman, with perhaps a few too many jelly doughnuts over his career. He had a beefy red face and a hefty spare tire. But he was certainly alert to his responsibilities, eyeing the three newcomers with scarcely disguised suspicion.

In fact, Ally sensed a palpable paranoia in the air. *Well,* she told herself, *medical research is a high-stakes game. It's understandable they would be concerned about industrial espionage.*

After the security check, they went through another steel

door and entered the actual lobby. The first thing she noticed was a grand staircase leading up to the second floor, and then to the third. Off to the right was a modern elevator with a shiny steel door.

A number of patients were coming down the stairs and heading for a hallway leading to the back. They were mostly women, whose ages ranged anywhere from forty-five to well beyond seventy.

Who are these people? Ally wondered. They must have been sufferers of various kinds of debilitating afflictions, but now they were certainly ambulatory, if not downright sprightly. She wanted to talk to some of them, watching them moving along chatting and smiling, but this was not the moment.

"At eleven-thirty we have meditation in the dining hall," Elise was saying as she led them through the lobby, "for those who care to participate, and after that a vegetarian lunch is served at twelve-thirty sharp." Then she glanced back. "After you see Dr. Van de Vliet—and assuming you're admitted—there'll be an orientation and then you're welcome to begin participating fully in our activities."

"Actually," Ally said, "if people are well enough to be in 'activities,' why can't they be outpatients?"

"These clinical trials require twenty-four-hour supervision," Elise explained, heading for the wide desk in the center of the room. "Now, if you would all sign in here at the desk, Ellen can take you downstairs to the medical reception."

A dark-haired woman smiled from behind the desk, then got up and came around. A sign-in book was there on a steel stand. Ally finally noticed that light classical music was wafting through the room, Tchaikovsky's *Swan Lake* suite.

"You must be Ms. Hampton," the woman said. "And this must be your mother. We were told to expect you."

She nodded a farewell to Elise, who said, "It was so nice to meet you. Good luck."

She then turned and headed for the back.

Ally signed all three of them in.

"Good," the woman said as she checked the information.

"My name is Ellen O'Hara, by the way. I'm in charge of the nursing staff here. We're ready to go downstairs now."

Ellen O'Hara had a knowing, earnest face that fairly lit up when she smiled. She had short brown hair streaked with gray and was pleasantly full-figured.

When they reached the elevator, she zipped a small plastic card through the reader on the wall and the doors slid open. As they emerged on the lower level, Ally realized they were in the precincts of a very sophisticated medical laboratory. Occupying most of the floor was a glassed-in area, inside of which she could see three men and two women, all dressed in white. She also noticed rows of steel containers that seemed to be ovens or incubators of some kind, as well as racks and racks of vials. At the far end of the laboratory, there was a blackboard on which one of the men was drawing something that looked like hexagonal molecules, linking them together.

"That's Dr. Van de Vliet," Ellen said, pointing. "I'll let him know you're here. The laboratory is a special environment. The entrance there is actually an air lock. The air inside is filtered and kept under positive pressure."

She walked over to a communications module, buzzed, then announced into the microphone, "Dr. Vee, your eleven-thirty appointment is here."

He turned and stared in their direction, then smiled and waved. Next he walked to a microphone near the center of the room and clicked it on.

"I'll be with you in a minute. Can you please wait in the receiving room? And, Ellen, can you start getting them ready?"

"Of course." She nodded, then clicked off the microphone and turned. "Receiving is just down at the end of the hall. Next to his office. Please come with me."

She led them through a large wooden door, into a room with a retractable metal table covered in white paper and several chairs. It was a typical examination room, with a device on the wall to monitor blood pressure, a stethoscope, and other examination paraphernalia.

"If you'll kindly take a seat," Ellen said, "I'm sure he'll be here as soon as he can, in a few minutes at most. But while we wait, I need to take your temperature and blood pressure, and start a chart."

"Ally, where are we?" Nina asked. Her face was becoming alarmed, and Maria reached to comfort her. "Are we in a hospital somewhere?"

"Yes, Mom, it's actually the institute I told you about last night. The doctor here wants to see if he can do anything to . . . help you."

"Oh," she said, "is he the one you told me about? I thought that was just a dream."

"No, he's real. Whether he can help you or not, that part is what's still a dream. But we're all praying."

She looked around at the pure white walls and wondered again what she was getting into. Meeting a new specialist, in the sterile white cold of an examination room, could be frightening in itself. God, how many times before had she done this as she trudged through HMO hell? Maria was so unsettled she was deathly pale.

Ellen took their blood pressure and temperature, including Maria's, even though she protested mildly, half in Spanish—a sign of how unsettling it was to her. Ellen had only just finished putting all the numbers on clipboard charts for each of them when Karl Van de Vliet opened the door and strode in.

Chapter 13

Tuesday, April 7
11:39 A.M.

He had a high forehead and prominent cheekbones, just like in the photo. And just as in his photo, there was a genuine dichotomy between his face, which looked to be early forties and unwrinkled, and his gray eyes, which were much older. That was it. That was what seemed odd. He was *different* ages.

Underneath his white lab coat he was wearing a black suit and an open-necked blue shirt. Ally noticed that his fingers were long and delicate, like those of a concert pianist, and overall he had a kind of ghostly presence, as though he were more spirit than man. Although he looked exactly as he did in the photograph in the Gerex Corporation brochure, in person there was an added dimension, a kind of raw magnetism about him. It was more than simply a physician's bedside manner; it was the allure of a pied piper. The first thing you wanted to ask him was *How old are you, really?* Maybe the next thing you'd want to do was ask him to dinner.

What had she expected? Maybe a self-absorbed nerd researcher in wrinkled, stained lab attire, anxious to scurry back to his test tubes. But in person Karl Van de Vliet was debonair and youthful, living proof that his photo wasn't re-touched and was recent. He had to be twenty years older than she was, easily, but to look at him you'd guess he was close to the same age. She was dying to ask him about that but she couldn't think of a polite way to raise the subject.

She introduced herself. "We spoke yesterday." Then she introduced her mother and Maria. "Mom and I talked last night about the clinical trials, and she said she's interested. This morning, unfortunately, I'm not sure she remembers what we discussed."

He placed a hand on Nina's shoulder and studied her face as he smiled at her, embracing her with his eyes. "Well, we're going to see what we can do about that, aren't we, Mrs. Hampton?"

"I've got a question right up front," Ally said. "Have we already been entered into the National Institutes of Health clinical trials?"

He seemed taken aback for a moment, caught off guard, but then he stepped up to the question.

"As a matter of fact, I did take the liberty of authorizing the preliminary NIH paperwork for both of you. Of course it doesn't obligate you in any way. The thing is, there's a lot of red tape, so if you do decide to participate, the sooner we get that part started the better. On the other hand, if you decide not to, we can just terminate everything at this preliminary stage and you won't even be part of the official record."

Well, Ally thought, *that undoubtedly explains why Stone saw our names on the NIH Web site. But why did Van de Vliet look so funny when I brought it up?*

He focused on Nina. "Mrs. Hampton, I'm Dr. Van de Vliet. You're a pretty lady, and we've had some luck helping other ladies like you."

"Honey, if I had you in my bedroom, then maybe you could help me."

Oh my God, Ally thought, *she's about to go ribald on us. But that's a sign she's coming out of her funk.*

But then she had another thought. Maybe Nina sensed he was older than he looked. Like that paranormal perception that told her Grant was involved in something evil. So far, however, *that* particular perception hadn't panned out (though Grant clearly was up to *something*).

Maria was mortified. She blushed and made a disapproving animal noise low in her throat and turned her face away, but Van de Vliet simply smiled even more broadly.

"Mrs. Hampton, I don't think you should be talking that way in front of your daughter." He gave her a wink. "What you and I do together is none of these people's business. But I do think we should consider keeping them informed, if only a couple of hints."

Ally found herself wanting just to listen to his voice. There was an intelligent warmth about it that reminded her of a kindly professor at Columbia, a truly gifted architect who also could quote Keats and make you cry. You wanted to give yourself to him. *My God,* she thought, *how am I going to stand up to this man?*

"There're some issues you and I need to discuss," he said, turning back to Ally. "The first thing I need to do is take a look at Mrs. Hampton's records. But whatever they say, it won't do any harm to run what we call a 'mental state examination' for her, to establish a general baseline of cognitive impairment as of now."

"How long will that take?"

"Actually, Ellen can start in just a few minutes," he said. "Of course, we'll need to hear about the usual danger signs everybody knows. Does Mrs. Hampton have recent-memory loss? Does she get confused about places and people? Does she have trouble handling money and paying her bills?"

"The short answer is yes."

All of those things, Ally knew, had accelerated in the last six months. It was the tragic, recognizable onset of the latter stages of Alzheimer's. Already more than once Maria had said there were times when she didn't think Nina recognized her. More and more she seemed to be confused, unable some days to find her way around the apartment, and she'd started repeating herself. She often had trouble finding the right words, and she was increasingly paranoid and suspicious. Maria, who had worked with other Alzheimer's patients, feared she might begin hallucinating soon, seeing things that weren't there.

Ally turned to her. It felt obscene to talk about her when she was sitting right there with them.

"Mom, sweetie, do you understand what Dr. Van de Vliet is asking? Do you think you have trouble doing everyday things?"

She knew the answer but she was determined that her mother not be treated like a potted plant.

"Ally, you know that half the time I can't remember a blessed thing. I'm getting crazy as a bloody coot."

Then Nina turned and looked Van de Vliet in the eye.

"I don't want to lose my mind, Doctor. I don't want to see the shade closing in. I can't do crosswords anymore. I used to do them all the time. And all the music I used to know. It was my love and now . . . now I can't tell Scriabin from Strauss half the time. It wasn't supposed to happen that way. I thought my mind would go on forever."

"Mrs. Hampton, if you'll let me, what I want to do is try to work on your recollection. I don't know how much I can help you with crosswords, but then I've never been much good at them myself either. Your memory of music should improve, though. There are no guarantees, but—"

"Then I'm ready to try it, Doctor," she cut in. "You're all that stands between me and losing the only thing I have left, my past." Next came a burst of rationality. "Now, I hate to be a pest, but could you explain what *exactly* it is you're going to do. I want Ally to hear this too and then maybe she can go over it with me later and help me understand it."

He smiled and reached over and stroked her slightly thinning hair. "I'd be happy to try, Mrs. Hampton. It's actually pretty simple."

Then he turned to Ally. "We touched on some of this on the phone. Do you want to hear it again?"

"Yes, I'm still trying to get it all into my simple mind."

"Well," he began, "to go back to the very beginning of my interest in stem cells the focus of our research has been directed toward challenging the notorious Hayflick limit. Back in the 1960s, Professor Leonard Hayflick discovered that when tissue cells are taken from the body and cultured in a laboratory dish, those cells grow and divide about fifty times, give or take, and then they stop. They have reached old age, senescence. The physical basis of the Hayflick limit is a section of DNA known as telomere, which gets shorter each time the cell divides. Eventually the telomeres become so short that all cell division stops. It's like an internal clock telling them the game is over. They've had their innings."

"And you're saying you've found a way to beat the clock, to stop the telomeres from getting shorter?"

"All cells possess a gene known as the telomerase gene, which can restore the telomeres to their youthful length. But in most cells the gene is permanently repressed and inactive. It is only found in egg and sperm cells, and in cancer cells." He gazed away for a moment as though collecting his thoughts. Then he turned back. "However, we've found that by isolating and inserting an active copy of the telomerase enzyme into adult stem cells, which can be found in minute quantities throughout the body, we can set their clock back to zero. We extract cells, 'immortalize' them with telomerase, and then return them to the body as a youthful infusion."

"And is that what you'd be doing for Mom?"

"There'd be a series of injections, but given what appears to be her level of mental awareness right now, the procedure probably can be accelerated." He patted Nina on the shoulder.

"All right," Ally said, "but can you use the same procedure for someone's heart?"

"Well, yes and no," he said. "Did you bring your medical records? I should have a look at them before making any pronouncements."

To prepare for this moment, she'd printed off a copy of the medical files she'd scanned into her computer.

"There're a lot of files," she said, opening her bag. "I've got copies of my EKGs over the past eleven years. Dr. Ekelman, my cardiologist, says my condition is getting progressively worse."

She took the folder out of her bag and handed it to him. He flipped through the files with what seemed an absent manner, almost as though he already knew what was in them and was just going through the motions. Then he looked up.

"Well, your physical condition looks pretty good. You clearly exercise. And I don't see anything here that would suggest a complication. As to how your procedure might differ from your mother's, I guess the main area of concern is simply the scale." He laid her files on the steel table. "Your heart has reached the stage of aortic valve stenosis where cardiac output no longer can keep up proportionately with vigorous exercise. And that has put an even larger strain on an already weakened condition. What we are about to undertake here corresponds to what might almost be considered an aortic valve replacement, though it is done at the cellular level. We call it regenerative medicine. Millions of cells will be involved. We'll attempt to reverse the calcification and also to develop new blood vessels that supply the heart muscle."

"You know, this is so risky. I remember that not long ago they tried to use fetal cell injections into the brain for treating Parkinson's disease. And it turned out that the side effects were horrendous. Why should I assume that this is any safer?"

He looked pained. "I assure you we don't do anything here that is remotely like that particular, unfortunate procedure."

She stared at the ceiling trying to grasp what he'd just said. "So how risky do you think this is?" she asked finally. "Truth time."

He looked away again and sighed. There was a long silence in which he seemed to be pondering some extremely troubling thoughts. Finally he turned back.

"In medicine there's always something that can go wrong. Even the most innocuous procedure can end up being lethal if that's what the gods want that day." He looked at her intently and seemed to try to measure his words. "But I wouldn't recommend we proceed if I didn't feel that the potential benefits far outweigh the risks."

She listened, wondering. *Something in his voice is sounding cagey. What is he leaving out?*

"I still want to think about it."

"Of course, but we can make some preparations in the meantime," Van de Vliet said, turning back to Nina. "Mrs. Hampton, do you understand anything of what I've said? Nothing is risk free."

"Young man, if you'd lived as long as I have, and then felt it all slipping away, you'd be willing to take a chance with anything."

"Mrs. Hampton, Alzheimer's is one of the more promising areas of stem cell research. We've already had successes here. I truly think we can help you. In fact, Ellen can start your preliminaries right now, if you like. A lot of it you may have done before. For example, there's a game where you have to memorize the names of three unrelated objects, and you have to count backwards from one hundred by sevens. Finally there's a test where you copy sentences and symbols." He chuckled, and there was a warmth but also a distant sadness. "Some days I'm not sure I could even do it all myself. In any case, it's not something you pass or fail. But if we do enter you into the trials, you'll have to stay here for the duration. That's absolutely essential. We'd also like a caregiver to be here with you, as long as it's necessary."

Ally looked at Maria. "Do you think you want to stay here with Mom?"

Maria's eyes were very sad. "I could stay for a day or two. But . . . maybe we should talk."

"We can arrange for someone," Van de Vliet interjected. "We routinely provide caregivers from our staff when called for. And because we're still in clinical trials, there is no charge."

Ally watched Nina brighten and turn to Maria. "You can bring some things from my closet when you go back. I want to start right away. I just know he can help me. I've got a feeling and you know my feelings are always right."

Ellen reached and took Nina's hand. "Come, dear, we have a special office where we handle all the paperwork for admissions. We can do the tests there."

Ally leaned over and kissed her mother. "I love you, Mom. And I love your spirit. You taught me how to be a fighter a long time ago. And I guess you're still teaching me."

Tuesday, April 7
12:03 P.M.

Karl Van de Vliet watched the three women leave. Now he was alone with Alexa. *So far, so good,* he thought. *With her mother checked in, we're partway there. Now what is it going to take to get* her *with the program? I'm not sensing commitment. She's asking too damned many questions.*

It looks like we may have to go to Plan B tomorrow. Too bad.

After the door was closed, he turned back.

"Your mother is quite an inspiration," he said with a smile. "I'll need those tests to create a baseline, but already I can tell she'll almost certainly respond to the treatment. She fits our success profile. I'd say the odds are heavily on her side." Then he darkened his look, for effect. *Better let her know I don't* have *to do this,* he reasoned.

"The truth is, we already have enough data on Alzheimer's that I don't really need any further clinical trials. I know the parameters of what the procedure can do and what it can't. But when Grant told me about his mother's condition, I saw no reason not to work her into the trials. We're winding down now and we have some empty beds."

"Don't think I'm not grateful," she said, "even though I may ask a lot of questions."

She got the message, he thought. *Good.*

"Alexa, I'm now going to tell you something I've never told anyone else," he went on, feeling a tinge of sadness arise in his chest. He hadn't planned to say this, but for some reason he now wanted to. Perhaps because it was true. "My late wife, Camille, was a brilliant medical researcher. We worked together for many years, first at Johns Hopkins and then at Harvard. What took her from me was a heart condition very similar to your own. That was over a decade ago and I vowed I would dedicate my work to her. I wanted the final clinical trial in this program to be on a young person with advanced valvular stenosis, but I could never find a patient who matched that profile. But you would be perfect." He looked carefully at her. It was all so true, which made this whole scene especially poignant.

"I'm sorry about your wife," Ally said. "I read in your—"

"You see, if I can succeed with you, it would almost seem as though I'd had a second chance to save her life. You bear such a striking likeness to her in several ways. You look something like her, but more importantly I sense that you share her indomitable will."

"So I'm not just another statistic to you?" She seemed to be trying to gauge the depth of his sincerity.

"No one here is a statistic, but you would definitely be someone special."

"I see," she said, still sounding noncommittal.

Am I getting anywhere? he wondered. *Just press on. You've got to make this happen.*

"All right, whatever you decide, we need to get some preliminaries out of the way. For one thing, we must have a complete new cardiology exam. Nothing in the file you brought presents an obvious red flag, but still, it's essential that we have an up-to-the-minute stress test. Toward that end, I've taken the liberty of arranging for a checkup at the New York University Faculty Practice Radiology on East Thirty-fourth

Street. Among other things, they can run a high-speed computed tomography screening using ultrafast X rays. Also, I'd like to see a phonocardiogram. A sonic analysis of 'murmurs' can tell us a lot about valve abnormalities. Regardless of what you decide to do here, it's a good idea for you to have this done regularly anyway."

"You've already scheduled tests?" Her tone of voice told him she was mildly taken aback at the presumption.

"It's just that the NYU Faculty Practice is sometimes difficult to get into on short notice. They can be booked for weeks in advance. But a cardiologist I know there, Lev Amram, has agreed to make room for you this afternoon. It's a professional courtesy. There'll be no charge. After that, and assuming you want to proceed, you should get a good night's rest and then come back here as early as possible tomorrow morning. You should pack for a three-week stay, though we'll provide you with pretty much everything you'll need here."

Just get *her here.*

"You know," she said, "I was actually hoping we could do this on an outpatient basis. I know you like to have your patients here for constant observation, but I run a business that needs me there every day."

"Alexa," he said, putting every last ounce of authority he had into his voice, "this is not a conventional procedure, and it's possible you might suddenly need special care of some kind. This is an experimental clinical trial, so we don't know *what* can happen. That's why I really must insist that you be here twenty-four hours a day." He looked at her with great tenderness. "We're talking about the possibility of completely repairing your heart. Surely you don't expect just to drop by now and then for that."

"All right, point taken," she said, "but—if we go forward with this—I'll need to hire at least one temp to be at the office while I'm gone. Somebody to at least handle the phone. That could take time."

"Surely someone there could manage to handle that," he said. *She's getting resistant again,* he told himself. *Don't let that happen.* "And there's also the matter of your mother. I think it would be wise for you to be nearby during the early stages of her procedure. When her mind starts climbing out of the abyss, it's important for a close family member to be there to provide a visual and emotional anchor. It truly can make all the difference. I fully expect that her functions of attention and recall will return to those normal for a woman her age, or quite possibly even better, but it will happen a lot quicker if you're here to help her, to remind her of things."

"This is a lot to digest." Ally turned and sat down in a chair. "All right, I might as well get the exam. It doesn't mean I've agreed to anything here."

He heard the ambivalence and knew he had no choice but to do what he was going to have to do tomorrow.

"I will proceed on the assumption that you'll be entering the program. Truthfully, if you don't, a week from now your mother is going to be asking you why." He smiled. "In any case, we need to have those tests done in the city. Also some blood work here. We're affiliated with a lab. I want to check your T cells and certain other markers, like C-reactive protein and homocystine. It's something you should do regularly anyway."

"All right, then," she said finally. "But after that, let me go see how Mom's doing. Then I'll arrange things with Maria somehow and drive back to the city."

"By the way, before I forget, we have to complete a formal application for your mother to admit her into the clinical trials, and we also need a signed liability waiver. I assume you have power of attorney for her by now. If you don't, then we may not legally be able to proceed."

"I have it."

"Then let's get started," he declared, almost certain he had her.

Chapter 14

Stone Aimes was in his cubicle, staring at the phone when it rang.

He prayed this was the call he'd been waiting for. As a gamble, a long shot, he'd requested that Jane Tully, his former live-in lover and the *Sentinel*'s part-time corporate counsel, do him a small favor. After he hacked the NIH Web site, he'd asked her to pass along just one question concerning Gerex to Winston Bartlett's corporate attorneys: Why had a patient been abruptly and mysteriously terminated, without explanation, from the clinical trials now under way by the Gerex Corporation? If that wouldn't get a rise out of Bartlett, he didn't know what would. It was the only part of the corporation's encrypted NIH file that seemed irregular. But would Bartlett take the bait?

He reached for the phone.

"Aimes here." Around him came the clatter of computer keys and muted laughter from the direction of the water cooler. Everybody had watched a rerun of *The Sopranos* Sunday night and they were still critiquing the show. Mondays were everybody's day off, so Tuesdays were the first chance to catch up. The staff was also starting to rev up again for the coming week's edition, everybody with the hope that *their* particular assignment would have legs and make its author a household name. Stone, however, felt like this was either the first day of the rest of his life or the last day of a career built on dealing to inside straights. *This cannot go on much longer,* he kept telling himself; it was an unstable condition. His soul was already over the fence, keeping company with that wild, free ox he liked to muse about.

"Stone," came a husky female voice, strained and yet strong. Just as he'd hoped, it was Jane, whose office was down on the third floor. "Can you come down? Right now."

"Did you hear back from—"

"Stone," she admonished, her voice growing urgent, "just come down. Do it *now,* all right?"

"Sure." He paused a moment, wondering. Why did she sound so upset? Had his plan somehow backfired? "I'm on my way."

He glanced up at the fluorescent light over his head, like a pitiless hovering spaceship, and wondered if this was going to be the break he had been praying for. There was a nervousness in Jane's voice that indicated something major was afoot. *Something* was about to change.

He switched off his Compaq laptop and reached for his brown corduroy jacket, which was hanging from a hook on the side of the glass-walled cubicle. He straightened his brown knit tie as he stepped on the elevator, and for some reason he found himself thinking of his daughter, Amy.

He mimed a toast. *Here's looking at you, kid.*

She was in the fifth grade and lived with her mother, Joyce, in a small condominium nestled in the hills near El Cerrito, where his ex-wife grew up. Joyce was a television producer who had left him to go back out there, where she got work as a garden designer. When he got over the shock, he finally concluded she loved California more than she loved him.

Maybe not an unreasonable choice. But then she got custody of Amy, based solely on the fact that his income was inadequate to send her to private school in New York and the public schools were out of the question. But Joyce had agreed that if he ever had the money, she could live with him some of the time. This book, he hoped, would make that happen.

He still didn't know why he and Joyce couldn't have made a go of it. It had occurred to him that there was the real possibility she had fallen in love with the *idea* of a dashing investigative reporter, not the grueling reality. These days she had Amy all the time except for three weeks in July, and he had so many things to regret he scarcely knew where to start.

He kept a year-old photograph of Amy on his desk, in a frame far too expensive for a snapshot of a young girl on a black horse named Zena. But it was Zena that his $1,500 a month in child support had helped to pay for, and he felt it somehow bonded them.

Hi, Dad, from me and Zena, went the inscription.

Why was he thinking about her now? he wondered. The answer was, because he wanted her world to be different from the one he had known as a child. He hadn't had a father around, and that had left him with a lot of anger. He didn't want the same fate for her.

Amy's world, he knew, was going to be very different, no matter what he did. To be young like her and starting out was a daunting prospect these days. He wanted to make everything easier for her, but the only thing he could give her now was a measly $1,500 every month and his unshakable love.

Even so, that was more than *his* mother, Karen, got for child support—from a natural father he had never actually seen in the flesh until he was eleven. And that was a chance encounter. . . .

So, if this book got some traction and he got some recognition, along with some economic security, he might be able to have Amy come back and live with him. It was something she'd said she wanted to do, though he wasn't sure where he would keep Zena.

But all in good time. Now everything depended on the book. . . .

The elevator door opened and he stepped out on the third floor. The receptionist, Rhonda, a dark-haired resident of Avenue A who usually tried to flirt, looked at him as though he'd just been convicted of a crime and nodded with her head toward the corridor leading to Jane's office.

"Stone, you've *really* screwed up this time. You'll never guess who's in there and after your scalp. *What* on earth did you do?"

"You mean—"

"This is a guy I've only seen in newspaper pictures, though, needless to say, not in *this* upstanding rag." In her dismay, she unthinkingly reached for the pack of Virginia Slims lying next to the phone, momentarily forgetting that smoking had long-since been forbidden in the building. "You'd better get your ass in there. Jesus, he came in with a bunch of lawyers, but then he told them to split. 'I'm going to handle the fucker myself.' Quote, unquote. Right here by my desk."

Stone didn't know, with absolute certainty, who she was talking about, but surely it had to be . . . *My God,* he thought with a thrill, *maybe it worked. Maybe I've smoked him out.*

"Truth tellers have nothing to fear, Rhonda." He winked at her. "I'm protected by the sword of the Lord. 'He is my rod and my staff. He leadeth me beside still waters.'"

"You're crazy, you know that?" She'd remembered where she was and began putting the cigarette back into the pack. Then she smoothed her short black hair. "He leadeth you into the shit, handsome. That's where He 'leadeth' you. You're adorable, but you're also a sane person's nightmare."

"Thanks," he said, giving a thumbs-up as he walked past her desk. "I appreciate your unstinting praise."

He headed on down the hall, the plush gray carpet soft against his feet. Could this be the break? he wondered, feeling his hopes cautiously rising. Had the Big Man himself shown up? Could it be that there *was* something funny going on with that patient who got dropped?

But what? He still didn't have a clue.

As he walked into the room, he felt as though time just stopped. He had fantasized about this moment more and more as the years went by. Now here it was. What next? He thought he had been emotionally prepared, but now he realized he wasn't. Were they going to acknowledge the past, or were they just going to act as though nothing existed between them?

That first chance meeting, when Stone was eleven, had been when his mother threatened to sue Bartlett for formal child support. The threat of publicity caused the matter to be immediately settled, as she'd hoped it would be. Stone had been sitting in the law firm's reception area when Bartlett walked through. Each knew who the other was, but Bartlett just stopped and glared at him for a moment before moving on. Stone had sized up the man who had abandoned his mother and only barely managed to suppress an urge to leap up and lash out at him, if only to say, *Look at me. I'm here.*

He had not been in the same room with his father since, but this time around he was definitely noticed.

Winston Bartlett looked just as he did in news photos. He was in his late sixties, with thinning blond hair that was cut too long and shaggy in the back. Stone's first thought was that the tightfisted old roué should spring for a better barber.

But it was Bartlett's eyes that really caught him. They were strong and filled with anger, but they also contained a hint of desperation. They were very different eyes from the haughty dismissal he remembered from a lifetime ago.

Good, Stone thought. *I've finally made you squirm, Daddy dearest. Nothing else I've done has ever gotten the slightest notice from you.*

For a moment they stood sizing up each other.

"Stone," Jane said, "this is—"

"I know," he said.

Even though they had been practically married, he had never

told her that he was the unacknowledged son of Winston Bartlett. He had never told anyone. To him, his father had died before he was born and that was the story he stuck to.

He naturally had a lot of complex feelings about that. He had seen his mother struggling to give them a decent life, hoofing in the chorus line of Broadway shows long after she should have, and a lot of his anger remained. Now, though, Stone Aimes wanted nothing from the old man. Except the truth.

"Miss Tully," Bartlett barked, glowering at her, "I think you'd better leave us alone."

"Of course," Jane said with a wry look, and in a tactful instant she had slipped past them and out, gently closing the office door behind her.

"I don't believe it," Bartlett said, turning back after he watched her leave. "You're trying to blackmail me, you little prick. Which tells me you're not half as smart as I thought you were."

Wait a minute! Did that mean Winston Bartlett has *been following my career?* Stone felt a thrill in spite of himself.

"I never knew you thought about me, one way or the other."

He was experiencing a curious sensation. Although he was in the same room with his father for only the second time in his life, it felt natural. They were having one of those age-old arguments. The younger generation had just challenged the older generation, and because of that, sparks were set to fly.

This was the kind of thing that was supposed to happen between fathers and sons all the time. In fact, it felt good. It felt normal. More than that, he was finally being acknowledged.

My God, he thought, *I share DNA with this man and yet we have so little in common.*

Then he had a more scary thought: *Maybe we have a lot in common.*

"I think it's time you told me what the *hell* you're up to," Bartlett declared, ignoring the jibe. "How did you—"

"I'm trying to do us both a favor, but you're not cooperating. If the Gerex clinical trials are going half as well as I think they are, then it seems to me you've got everything to gain by publicity. I'm trying to write the first book that tells the Gerex story. So why the *hell* won't your legal flunkies let me interview Karl Van de Vliet?"

"That's actually none of your business." Bartlett's eyes abruptly turned cloudy. "I want you to stay the hell away from—"

"Right now I'm the best friend you've got in this world. Believe me." Stone couldn't believe he was saying this. For how many years had he loathed and despised this man? But now, for the first time, he actually needed something from him. "I want to tell the real story of what Van de Vliet has accomplished. What Gerex has accomplished. It'll be the latest word on stem cell technology. But your office keeps giving me the runaround."

"We have a damned good reason to keep our work proprietary just now," Bartlett declared. "This is like the Manhattan Project." His eyes bored in. "The results of the clinical trials are going to cause a press feeding frenzy, and I want to be in a position to control that when the time comes."

This is incredible, Stone told himself. *We're talking as though we have no history. You have a granddaughter by me whom you've never even seen. Don't you at least care about* her?

"I've got a pretty good idea of what Gerex is doing and I think it's going to be a milestone in medical history." Stone looked at him, trying to figure him out after all these years. For all his bluster, Winston Bartlett seemed like a man with a lot of vulnerabilities and insecurities. He hadn't expected it. "It so happens I'm a damned good medical reporter and all I'm asking is to be the Boswell to Van de Vliet's Johnson. I want to be the one to chronicle this historic moment. There's no one who can do it better, believe me. I'll even agree to embargo everything until I get a green light from Gerex. But I want to start now and get it right."

"You can't ethically know any details of the work," Bartlett declared. "So the question I'm waiting to hear answered is, how did you find out . . . ?"

"I can't reveal my source." *Because,* he told himself, *I still don't have one. All I have is guesswork.* "But I know that Karl Van de Vliet is running the first successful clinical trials using stem cell procedures. And I'm going to report on it whether you want me to or not. So are you going to help make sure my facts are accurate?"

"I'm going to help make sure there's no reporting at all till I say so," Bartlett went on. "Anything you print will be— by definition—irresponsible speculation and you can expect enough legal action to—"

"The original schedule was that they'll be finished in less than a month. I'm not going to publish anything before that. I just want to have the manuscript I've been working on ready when the Gerex story finally can be told. It'll be the final chapter, the payoff. I'm going to describe your clinical trials, and it would be better for all concerned if it could be the 'authorized' version. If you force me to publish without your cooperation, it's not going to do either one of us as much good."

Again he wondered why Bartlett was so upset. What was it about that one terminated patient that made him freak when he found out somebody knew? So freaked he charged up here personally, all the way from his fancy corporate building in TriBeCa, to breathe fire and brimstone and yell threats?

"Do I have to get a court injunction to put a stop to this corporate espionage?" Bartlett demanded.

"Everything I know is in the public domain somewhere." *Actually,* Stone thought, *that's a serious out-and-out lie. Nobody knows that a patient got mysteriously terminated from the trials.* "I just want to work together with you."

Even as he was saying it, Stone Aimes realized that it was not in the cards, now or ever. He watched Winston Bartlett's eyes narrow.

"What kind of contract do you have with this paper?"

"Quite frankly, the terms of the contracts for employees of this paper are confidential."

"I knew I should have kept those fucking lawyers here. It takes a shark to deal with a shark." Then he seemed to catch himself. "So if you're planning on writing anything about this, you'd be well advised to get yourself an attorney, because you're sure as hell going to need one."

"Thanks, Dad." It just came out. Maybe he'd been wanting to say it all his life.

Bartlett's look was shock for a moment, and then it turned pensive.

"You don't think I take an interest in you, but I do."

"Yeah, you've really been around through thick and thin." He felt the old anger of abandonment welling up.

"I took care of your mother. Whatever *she* did was beyond my control." The eyes were switching to chagrin. "Do you have the slightest idea what I could do for you? I've . . . I'm not getting any younger and I've been thinking about . . . with your medical background you could easily have a place . . . I mean, if you've got a head for business, then someday . . . So why do you fucking want to do this *now?"*

Stone listened, trying to internalize what he was hearing. Not only did Winston Bartlett know about him, he was finally thinking about acknowledging him. Sort of.

Or was this just a bribe to hush him up?

Either way, it was too little, too late.

"You've never given me anything and I've sure as hell never asked. I'd just like for you to get out of my way so I can do my job."

Bartlett stalked toward the door. Then he turned back.

"You'd better think long and hard about what you're getting into. You can ask some of the two-bit reporters I've dealt with in the past. They're fucking roadkill."

With that pronouncement, he slammed the door and was gone.

Stone stared after him, feeling his heart pump. It wasn't the threat; it was the mixed emotions. For a moment, in spite of his better judgment, he'd felt like he had a father, but then Bartlett became the enemy again.

Then the door cracked open and Jane appeared, dismay in her eyes.

"What was *that* about?"

"What was *what* about?"

"I've gotta tell you, that man doesn't know how to keep his voice down. What was that about helping your mother? Karen. You never talked about her much, but I sure don't remember you ever saying anything about her and Winston Bartlett."

"That's because I didn't. Jane, there are parts of my past life that I try not to think about any more than I have to."

"After the fact, it's nice to know that there were parts of your life that you didn't see fit to share with me." She sniffed.

"Maybe someday."

"It's a little late for that," she declared, hurt lingering in her voice. "Look, Stone, I don't know what you know that's got Bartlett so upset, but he's not the best guy in the world to piss off. He stormed in here, fit to be tied, personally demanding to know how the hell did you have proprietary information about the Gerex Corporation's clinical trials. He already seemed to know who you were. Now I realize there's more to the story, somewhere back there in time."

"And what did you tell him?"

"I was completely blindsided, for which I thank you. I told him I didn't know anything about your sources, but I wouldn't reveal them even if I did. He's our landlord, but that doesn't give him subpoena power. He doesn't have the right to barge in here and try to intimidate the *Sentinel*'s staff. We're current on the rent."

Stone felt a tinge of nostalgia. Sometimes her gold-plated bitchiness was the very thing he admired most about her.

"Well, thanks for sticking up for me. Maybe I've got him upset enough that he'll come around eventually and decide it's better to have me *inside* the tent, where I can be monitored."

She snorted at the improbability of that.

"No, Stone, as usual you're an idiot idealist and dreamer. I'll tell you exactly what's going to happen. Bartlett is most likely on his cell phone right now, as we speak, threatening the Family, trying to get you fired. He's saying you're stealing proprietary information somehow and he's going to sue the *Sentinel* for our last dime if we print a syllable of anything you write about him. That's his next move, Stone. I expect my phone to ring in approximately fourteen and a half minutes. Their attorneys are going to tell me to tell Jay to get you under control. That's what's going to happen. The Family does not want Winston Bartlett pissed off. Especially by the likes of you, somebody who's always writing muckraking articles that make them *real* nervous. Does anything I've said have the ring of logic to you? Or are you living in some never-never land where the facts don't fucking penetrate?"

Hey, he thought, *that's pretty good. Jane is in DEFCON 1 mode today.*

"Depends on what you look at, the doughnut or the hole. That is, the stick approach or the carrot. I'm betting he's going to split the difference and try a little of both. He's going to cool off and then offer me a few crumbs as an inducement to go away."

"God, you're so naive." She laughed in derision. "Winston Bartlett is not accustomed to having to ask anybody for *anything*. So the fact he came up here this morning to try to get you to back off on whatever it is you're doing must mean you've really got him psyched." She stared at him. "What is it, Stone? Tell me. What do you have on him?"

"Right now I'm more interested in what he *thinks* I might

have. And the truth is, I don't really know. But it must be something pretty big."

"Stone, why is it so hard to hate you? You can make a person's life miserable and that stupid person will *still* root for you. God, I don't know what it was about you." She paused a moment as though thinking. "Maybe you're just too honest. Or just too sincere. Maybe that's what it was."

"Don't try to butter me up. I know my weaknesses. But dammit, Jane, I'm this close to the story of the century. And the paranoid zillionaire who was in here just now yelling at me is trying to freeze me out."

"Well, please don't involve me in this anymore, Stone. You've just provided me with a week's worth of unnecessary shit. From now on, any communicating you want to do with Gerex's attorneys is going to have to be done by someone else. Trust me when I tell you *I do not need this in my life.*"

"Sweetie, wait till you see what I'm on the track of. What the Gerex Corporation is doing at a small clinic out in New Jersey is going to change everything we know about medicine. And it's going to blow wide open the second they finally let the press in on what's happening at the clinical trials they're now winding up for the NIH. When they finally hold that big press briefing, I want to have a manuscript already in copyediting. I want to be *first.*"

"Then why is he so worked up over your question?" she mused. "About somebody being dropped from the clinical trials?" She paused. "Incidentally, I can do without being called 'sweetie' by a man I'm no longer screwing."

"Sorry about that." He winced. It did just sort of slip out in this orgy of intimacy. "But what I think Bartlett desperately doesn't want me to find out is the *reason* that patient was dropped. And he's afraid I'm getting close. Unfortunately, I'm not, and I just took my best shot at prying the information out of him and—you're probably right—blew it." He was turning to leave. "But I'm, by God, going to find out somehow. Just see if you can keep me from getting fired for a little while longer. If I'm still working for the *Sentinel* three months from now, you may get honorable mention in my Pulitzer acceptance."

It was bluff talk. But he believed it with every fiber of his body. *You've gotta believe, right?*

Come on, Ally, get lucky. Find out who that mystery patient was. The way things look now, you're the only shot I've got left.

Chapter 15

What a day! When Ally finally settled onto her couch, after giving Knickers a long walk, she was exhausted. She leaned back and kicked off her shoes. There had been a few moments of tightness in her chest—maybe it was psychological, anxiety-induced—but that was gone now. She thought about calling New Jersey to ask how Nina was doing, but she doubted they would tell her anything.

She'd spent the latter part of the afternoon getting yet another heart exam. After driving to northern New Jersey and back, she'd had a formal (and exhausting) stress test for her heart at the New York University Faculty Practice. God, she was sick of examining rooms and those blue paper shifts you put on backwards, as though it was okay for doctors and nurses to see your bare ass. Then she put on shorts and sneakers and an Israeli physician stuck wired suction cups all over her chest and put her on a treadmill for seventeen minutes, boosting her pulse to over 150, which was as high as he dared to go. Then he called Van de Vliet, faxed him the charts, and they reviewed the squiggly lines for another ten minutes.

Finally she had a high-speed CT scan, whose results were then sent directly to Karl Van de Vliet's lab computer.

The bottom line was, the damaged valve in her aortic ventricle was deteriorating even more rapidly than her regular physician, Dr. Ekelman, had thought, but her heart was still strong enough for the procedure.

She wondered if she had gone this far because she was letting hope outweigh a sober evaluation of the risks. Was this the sign of complete desperation? Whatever she decided, tomorrow was the day, D day, decision day.

She thought again about her mom, who had been bubbling with hope when she looked in on her. Nina hadn't even been formally checked in, but already she seemed transformed. It was enough for her just to entertain the possibility that her mind could be renewed. That in itself was sufficient to convince Ally to sign the consent agreement for Van de Vliet to go forward with her procedure. He even offered to provide a car service to take Maria home to the Bronx after Nina was settled and resting.

In her own case, the special injections for her heart, she was far less sure what she thought. The part that bothered her most was having to give herself entirely over to a person she scarcely knew. It was the kind of ultimate surrender that she abhorred.

While Knickers rummaged behind the couch for the remnants of her rawhide chew toy, Ally momentarily considered calling Grant. She couldn't think of a reason why except that he was the only coherent immediate family she had left and this felt like a moment for pulling together. God, she missed Steve. Sometimes she felt so *alone*.

Then she considered calling Stone Aimes, but she decided that would seem pushy. The truth was, she'd enjoyed talking to him and she'd been surprised at how comfortable she'd felt. Looking back over the elapsed years, she couldn't remember exactly why they split up. There must have been a good reason, but now she could only recall the good times. A picnic in Central Park, or the time they took the

Staten Island ferry at night just to see the inspiring down-town skyline.

With those jumbled thoughts cluttering her mind, she fi-nally got around to remembering she hadn't checked her phone machine. She got up off the couch and went into the bedroom.

There were three calls and at first she thought she was too exhausted to check them.

But no, that was irresponsible. She was running a business. . . .

"Hi, Ally, it's me." The voice was Jennifer's. "No emer-gency, but call when you get in and let me know how it went, okay?"

Not tonight. There was too much to explain and she was too tired. She went to the second message.

"Hi, it's me again. I need you to look over the Jameson design, that Italian-marble bath. They're having trouble get-ting the ocher. Some kind of strike at the quarry. What can they substitute? But remember, it's got to be absurdly over-priced or they'll assume it's crap. If I don't hear back from you, I'll fax you some stuff in the morning."

Okay, she thought, *these rich clients love to show off. I'll get them what they should have ordered in the first place, knowing them. Stone from the quarry near Agra, where they got the marble for the Taj Mahal. That ought to be ostenta-tious enough. It'll take an extra couple of months, but that will impress them even more. . . .*

As she considered going to the third message, she had a feeling of misgiving, though in truth there were several peo-ple she wouldn't mind hearing from.

Or maybe the Dorian Institute had called about Nina. Maybe she'd freaked. This whole thing was happening way too fast. In any case, she didn't really want to talk to anybody right now. What she really wanted to do was sit and think, maybe run the whole thing by Stone and get his take. . . .

She decided to check out the third message.

"Hi, it's your intrepid reporter, just checking in to see

how it went today. It's just after eight, and I'm at home. I may not be able to afford this place much longer, given all the excitement I've had today, so call me while I still have an apartment and a phone."

She felt a ripple of excitement and the feeling pleased her. Maybe she *did* have someone stable and rational in her corner, someone who understood the risks and possible rewards of going forward with the procedure.

She'd put his number in her Palm, which was in her bag, and she went back to the living room, poured herself a glass of wine, and then retrieved it.

She heard him pick up on the second ring.

"Hi, it's Ally. Thanks for checking on me. I'm really not in the greatest shape at the moment."

"Oh yeah? So how'd it go?"

"Well, I met Dr. Miracle. . . ." She paused. "I don't know quite how to handle you, Stone. Are we having some kind of reunion? The affair redux. Are we friends all over again? Two days ago, all we had were memories. Then I start getting phone calls from you. I still don't know what I'm supposed to think."

"I'll tell you what *I* think. I think we're playing this by ear. I don't know what you've been doing for the years that I haven't seen you. I don't know what you know about me. So this is kind of like a blind date with a lot of baggage."

"I agree," she said, then hesitated. Her resolve was melting. "I might as well say this. Is it too late to come down and talk? I thought I was tough enough to handle this on my own, but I definitely could use psychological support."

"Give me the address. I could use a little support myself. I got threatened today, I think, by somebody who would like to crush me like a bug. And easily could. I'll spare you the ironies, but you and I may have more in common than you think. My interest in the Gerex Corporation has just gotten extremely personal."

After she hung up, she felt energized and she decided to give Jennifer a call after all. In truth, she wanted to tell her about Stone and to get her take on whether seeing him was a good idea. Aren't these second-time-around things always doomed?

"Hi, Jen. I'm home and I'm making all kinds of fateful decisions."

"So what happened? Are you going to be a guinea pig for that clinic?"

"Is that what you think it amounts to?" She couldn't tell how serious Jennifer intended to be. "I'm still debating it. Mom loved the place."

"Well, good. Good for her. But you're still not sure about *you?*"

"I'm leaning . . ." She paused. "Jen, somebody I used to see in college is on his way down here right now. He's a medical reporter, but the truth is, I don't know why I asked him."

"I guess if I were your shrink, I'd ask, 'How do you *feel* about that?' "

"If I knew the answer to *that,* I wouldn't need you to be a one-woman support group." She bit her lip. "He's doing a book about stem cell procedures. So in a way it's a lucky break that he appeared exactly when he did."

"Yeah, Ally, if you ask me, it sounds like it was a lucky break in more than one way. An old flame reappearing can be a positive sign. It's high time something happened in your life."

You're righter than you know, she thought. *I'm ready for this, whether I admit it to myself or not. But is there going to be any chemistry when we actually see each other? There used to be a lot.*

The embarrassing thing was, her first thought was to wonder if he was still terrific in bed. She remembered thinking he was very adroit back then, but back then she didn't have much experience to compare him with. Mainly, thinking about him now made her painfully aware she was overdue for some closeness.

Tuesday, April 7
10:22 P.M.

What's she going to think of me? Stone wondered as he knocked gently on the door. She'd buzzed him up from the lobby without a word.

More to the point, he thought, *what am I going to say if she wants an opinion about whether she should undergo the procedure or not? So far, the only evidence I have that the clinical trials are working is circumstantial, the patients who've been through the sequence and discharged. So how can I, in good faith, advise her one way or the other?*

But, he then concluded, *I'm getting way ahead of myself. She may take one look at me and decide she was right to dump me the first time.*

Nice building, though. Housing for grown-ups, not like the one-bedroom starter setup I've *been reduced to.*

He knocked—he always hated the idea of ringing a bell on an apartment door—and a second later, it opened.

Alexa Hampton and Stone Aimes just stood awkwardly for a moment and stared, taking each other in. Finally . . .

"*You look . . . great.*" They both said it simultaneously, and that served to make the moment even more awkward.

"Well," he said finally, into the silence, "you do." And he meant it. There was, however, a lot of strain on her face, in her eyes. The mark the years had left seemed more psychic than physical.

"You don't look so bad yourself."

"God, it seems like a lifetime ago when we went to our separate corners," he said after another long, contemplative pause. Then he stepped in and she closed the door. He didn't try to peck her cheek, for which she looked relieved. "Tell me how you're doing, really."

"You really want to know? Okay, this afternoon I had a heavy-duty heart checkup. Nobody wants to put odds on this thing, but my condition is getting worse." She led him through to the living room.

"Then we should talk," he said, looking around. "I love your loft, by the way. You make me envy you. You should see the makeshift quarters I live in. I'm sort of waiting for my ship to come in."

"The truth is, Stone, that I no longer know the first thing about you or your life. And I think I'd like to."

"'Had we but world enough, and time.'" He smiled. "We'll get around to the catching up, but I don't flatter myself that you asked me down at this hour to reminisce about our respective pasts."

"You've already got me figured out." She made a face. "I don't know whether I like that or not. By the way, would you care for something? You used to like scotch, right?"

"The operative part of that statement is 'used to.' These days I try to avoid anything harder than beer. I was starting to have an ethanol dependency problem. I think it's a common occupational hazard for a reporter."

"I don't keep beer around. It's fattening. How about some diet cranberry juice?"

"Maybe I'll have that scotch after all." He laughed. "I have a feeling it might be more suited to the occasion."

"Know what, I think I'll join you." She walked into the kitchen and started making the drinks. "On the rocks, right?"

"Good memory."

"Stone, I asked you down because I've got to make a big decision." She was bringing the drinks into the living room. "Tonight. You're the closest thing I've got to a knowledgeable sounding board. You have some idea of the risks and rewards here. So do I check into the Dorian Institute and let them start injecting doctored-up stem cells into me or not? Turns out that's what Van de Vliet wants to do."

"We're in worse trouble than we thought." He took a scotch. "You've at least seen the place. I don't have a shred of actual physical evidence that those clinical trials are producing results. I can make inferences from what I see on the

NIH Web site, but it's nothing you can take to the bank." He ventured a sip, then looked up. "By the way, did you get a chance to ask about the patient who got dropped?"

"Oh shit, I forgot." She sighed. "There was so much going on, with Mom and all the rest, that it completely slipped my—"

"Don't worry about it," he said.

Come on, Ally, this could be really important. You've got to get focused, she thought.

"I'll try to remember tomorrow."

"I do think it's kind of vital. But be careful not to mention my name. I've . . . I've just acquired some problems of my own with the Gerex Corporation."

"What kind of 'problems'?"

"Let me take a rain check on answering that. Suffice to say, they're not thrilled about the idea that I'm doing a book in which they're prominently featured." He paused. "Look, Ally, there's a lot going on here. Including that patient who was dropped for some reason that nobody wants to disclose. But if you do decide to do it, you couldn't have a better physician. Karl Van de Vliet is quite possibly the world's leading researcher in stem cell technology. On the other hand, this is the first time there've been actual human trials. If anybody tells you there's no risk, then they're not behaving ethically."

"Well, the way things stand now, I'm due out there at the institute at ten A.M. tomorrow. If I want to, I can be formally entered into the clinical trials on the spot. I've passed my qualifying exam."

"You know the trials are almost over. It's like they're taking you at the last minute."

"That's what he said. I'm going to be the last . . . whatever. My friend Jennifer just called me a guinea pig. Van de Vliet also said I'd have to stay out there for at least a couple of weeks, probably longer. That's going to be a bloody drag, since things are really busy down at CitiSpace now."

"Ally, given what I know, or don't know, I don't have an

entirely good feeling about this. It could be they're hiding something, but I don't have a clue what it is. It's quite possibly connected to that patient who got terminated. And when I tried to raise this with Gerex's attorneys, no less person than Winston Bartlett himself went ballistic."

"What are you saying? That I shouldn't do it?"

"Hey, I can't make that decision for you. But one possibility would be to just play along for a day or two and see if you can't find out a little more about what went wrong with the patient who was dropped."

"Stone, that's maybe a little paranoid. Couldn't a single patient have been dropped for a whole bunch of different reasons?"

"Of course, but it's not that simple. A patient was dropped from the Gerex clinical trials, and there was no official reason given in the data file. It made me curious enough that I had our paper's attorney pass along a question about it to their attorneys. That motivated Winston Bartlett to come personally to threaten me. So why is a guy who runs a huge conglomerate suddenly afraid of one tiny question? Is there some problem, some reaction to the procedure that they're terrified will come to light? Ultimately millions and millions of dollars are at stake. I want the book I'm writing to tell the whole story, not just the part they'll want to have told. That's why God put reporters on earth."

"Shit, Stone, I'm glad you're here. I think I told you on the phone, I had someone I loved very much disappear on me some years ago, and I'm feeling very alone at the moment." She looked him over. "Okay, I'll ask. We're adults. Are you married, divorced, attached, unattached, seeing someone, alone and suicidal, what? I mean, where do things stand here?"

"Where things stand is that I'm very happy that I stumbled into you after all the years. And, yeah, I've got a little history. At least I'd like to think so. But nothing is going on at the moment." Then he told her about Joyce, the divorce, Amy. "And what was that you said about having somebody disappear on you?" He studied her, reaching back for the feelings that were still buried. Seeing her *was* bringing it back. "What did you mean by that? Disappear like a missing person, or disappear as in up and split, or—"

"He was my husband, Steve, and he was a political consultant. He was in a single-engine Cessna that went down in the rain forest in Belize and I miss him terribly."

"I'm so sorry, Ally. Nothing that's happened to me comes close to that tragedy."

"It gets worse. A few months before that, my dad had an accident with a Browning shotgun that was no accident."

"Jesus. What's that line about how the troubles tread on one another's heels. Was he depressed? I guess that's a stupid question."

"He thought he was going to lose his business. After a lifetime of work. What do you think?"

"Ally, I'm really sorry about all that."

"Well, I suppose it could be worse. As I recall, you never knew *your* dad, did you?"

When am I going to tell her the truth? he asked himself.

"Let's get off the history topic tonight, what do you say. We'll both get ourselves depressed."

"Agreed." She sipped at her scotch. "So . . . you're saying I should play along and see if I can find out something about this discharged patient, the mere mention of whom causes grown millionaires to become unhinged?"

"It's what *I* would do," he said, finishing off his scotch and settling the glass on a coaster on a side table. Then he got up. "I have to tell you, Ally, you look awfully tired. I'd love to be responsible for keeping you up all night, but I doubt that would be a humane act."

"It might remind me of a time long ago and not so far away," she said with a faint smile. "But you're right. When I get this tired, I can precipitate an episode."

"I'd offer to drive you out there tomorrow, but that would just get you in trouble. They probably have orders to shoot me on sight. I'm the number one persona non grata with the top management of the Gerex Corporation at the moment. So I'm the last person you want to be seen with. Right now the only way you're going to find out what they're hiding is if nobody suspects anything. Which means you've got to show up alone."

Maybe that's true, she thought. *But you're a person I'd like to be with tonight.*

"Thanks for coming over." She walked over and pecked him on the cheek.

You're vulnerable tonight, she told herself, wanting to ask him to stay. *Don't start making any big life decisions.*

Chapter 16

Winston Bartlett looked at the white phone on the oak end table beside his chair and argued with himself about picking it up and calling the Dutchman. When Van de Vliet was at his office at the institute, they communicated by encrypted videophone. By this time, though, he was usually home, but he still hadn't called to say what had happened with Alexa Hampton. Now they would have to talk over an open line. Damn him.

After his explosive run-in with Stone Aimes—damn him too—Bartlett had gone up to the Park Avenue place to check on Kristen firsthand and try to console her. But he wasn't actually sure she recognized him; at times she seemed to and then at other times she would just stare at him blankly. Her mind increasingly had an in-and-out relationship with reality, and today was an out day.

The time had come to be deeply concerned about her. She couldn't be kept under wraps forever. He had checked her into the Dorian Institute under an assumed name, Kirby Parker, to try to avoid any publicity. Now that was the only name she could remember. How had the Syndrome done *that* to her?

Kristen Starr, whose identity was known to several million watchers of cable TV, could no longer remember her own name. Karl had worked with her every day, but no medication he had tried had even minimally slowed the Syndrome's progress.

The Beta had seemed so promising. Kristen's body had been rejuvenated—her face was looking like she'd had perfect plastic surgery, and there'd been no discernible side effects. It was everything they'd all hoped for. Kristen was elated, and even the normally cautious Van de Vliet was buoyed.

Yes, the Beta was so close. Karl *had* to find a way to make it work.

In spite of all Winston Bartlett's entrepreneurial derring-do, he always knew he was at the mercy of time. He was getting ever closer to that final dance with destiny. But . . . *but* what if the Beta could be made to work the way Van de Vliet theorized it might? Was there the possibility the music would never stop?

Nursing a second Glenfiddich, he looked around the room, the third-floor study/bedroom, finding it pleased him as always. This room of his five-story mansion was a handmade gem from New York's turn-of-the-century Gilded Age, with molded plasterwork ceilings and brass doorknobs and mahogany paneling. Favorites from his superlative Japanese sword collection lined the walls, giving him constant joy. He wanted to live to enjoy it for another three score and ten.

The only galling thing about the place was that he had to share it with Eileen, who had the top two floors. They had been living in marital purgatory for the past twenty-eight years, ever since she found out about the existence of his natural son. Because of that humiliation, she had refused to give him the one thing he most wanted from her, his freedom. She let it be known that as long as he flaunted a string of mistresses in the cheap tabloid press, she was determined to stay in his face.

He sighed and took a last sip of his scotch, then set it down and clicked on the phone. Van de Vliet had rented a small villa half a mile down the lakeshore, south from the institute, and he lived alone. Until recently he'd been sleeping in the lab. There was no encrypted phone where he lived, so this had damned well better be brief.

"Karl, it's me. How did it go today with the new Beta prospect? I contracted her to do some work here, hoping to do my part to get her with the program. I was expecting to hear from you by now."

"I've met with her and she had a stress test this afternoon in the city. Other than the aortic stenosis, she seems to be in superb shape, which is important. I'm assuming—make that hoping—that she'll come back in the morning and formally enter the clinical trials. I'll let you know if she does. Till that happens, I have no progress to report."

"All right, but how soon after that do you think you could get started with the Beta matter?"

There was a pregnant pause, and then . . .

"W.B., we truly need to talk, and maybe not on this line. Just before I left the lab, I ran another simulation on the Mothership to try to figure out what dosage level of Beta enzyme would be safe. But it's like trying to extrapolate backwards, and I just don't have enough data. I'm beginning to wonder if using her to try to create telomerase antibodies is actually such a good idea. It's just so risky. . . ." His voice trailed off.

"Karl, everything in life is a goddam risk. I know I'm supposed to be the beneficiary here, but if the antibody concept works out, we might still be able to do something for . . . Beta One."

"I'm already doing everything I know how for her. That's a tragedy we're all still in denial about. And now we're talking about risking yet another woman. Yes, maybe it's the answer, but for now I *don't know* what a safe dosage of enzyme should be. It has to be enough to generate the antibodies, but not so great that . . . You know what I'm talking about."

I sure as hell do, Bartlett thought. *I'm looking at the Syndrome myself.*

"Karl, just think of what it could mean if you could get the Beta to work the way the other procedures do. What great medical discovery didn't have a few missteps at the beginning? This is experimental medicine that could change the world. So, dammit, we've *got* to take risks."

"Why are we having this conversation at this time of night? Over an unsecure phone?"

"Because we don't have a lot of time," Bartlett growled.

"We've got nineteen days left on the clinical trials. That's certainly enough time to conclude the procedure on her heart. But if we also try to—"

"Karl," Bartlett said, "it's the Beta we should be focusing on. I'm looking at the Syndrome myself now, though I think I've got the strength of will to handle it. My mind is a lot stronger than Kris . . . Beta One's. But I don't want to have to find out. You've *got* to get this fucking problem fixed."

"If we do use her, I can't begin to tell you how unethical this is about to become."

Bartlett wanted to remind Van de Vliet that ethics were the least of their problems at the moment, but that wasn't the kind of thing you aired over an unsecure phone connection.

"Karl, just fucking do it," he said finally. "If she's not under way with the Beta before the end of this week, ethics are not going to be your primary concern. I may have to revisit some of our agreements. Cross me and you forfeit a lot."

"All right." He sighed. "I know what I can do to make sure she's in."

"Good. Do it, whatever it is." He now had to warn Van de Vliet about Stone Aimes, but how much information should he provide? He quickly decided to keep it simple. "Oh, and as though we didn't already have enough problems, there's something else I need to alert you about. There's a smart-ass reporter from the *New York Sentinel* nosing around. Yesterday he got to my legal department and asked about Beta One, though he doesn't know her name yet. He somehow found out she was terminated from the clinical trials. Please tell me you haven't been talking to the press behind my back."

"My God, I've been waiting for this to happen." Van de Vliet sounded like someone who had just had the wind knocked out of him. "You know, Grant once mentioned that a reporter had been pestering him about getting an interview with me."

"When?"

"Maybe two months ago, possibly three."

"First I've heard about it," Bartlett said. "I wish he'd told me. I could have taken steps."

"It might be the same person. Now that I think about it, I do remember he mentioned the *Sentinel*. How much do you think he knows?"

"I'm not sure. The question in my mind is, how did he find out about her in the first place? He's supposedly doing a book about us, Karl, a book about this project."

"Well, that's the first I've heard about *that*. Christ! A *book!*"

"I think he's just fishing at the moment. But this should be a warning. We've got to keep security tight."

"What do you know about him? Is he good?"

Yes, Bartlett thought, *he's damned good. The truth is, I'm almost proud of him sometimes.*

"He's the medical columnist for the paper. So happens, I own the building where their editorial offices are."

"I don't have time to read newspapers."

"Well, he's good enough that we may have to handle him somehow."

"What are you trying to say?" Van de Vliet asked, though he sounded like he already knew.

"What I'm saying is, he's a pro, and I get the strong impression he's hungry."

"Hungry for money or for fame?"

"If I knew that, I'd know what to do next," Bartlett said. *Probably some of both,* he thought, *if the kid is anything like his old man.*

"Then why don't we give him an interview? Meet the whole matter head-on. I've always found it better to shape the news yourself rather than trying to stonewall, which usually means a lot of speculation ends up getting published and then you have to correct it after the fact. It's also the best way to find out how much a reporter already knows."

Idiot, Bartlett thought, *that's the worst possible thing we could do. This kid would have your balls for a bow tie.*

"Karl, you've just provided a perfect illustration of why I have my own people handling the press. Some amateur like you starts talking to a guy like that, and the next thing you know, you might as well be on sodium pentathol. Again, his name is Stone Aimes. Remember it. And don't *ever* even *think* about exchanging a single word with him."

"W.B., my experience is that you can only stonewall the press for so long, if they're any good at all. Sooner or later, they're going to find out more than you want them to. The only way to forestall that is to parcel them carefully controlled information to work with. Trust me. I've had a little experience with reporters too. You can't treat them like they're complete dolts. You have to co-opt them, bring them into your confidence, and then convince them that it's in everybody's interest for them to help you rather than harm you. So why don't you let me talk to this guy? We could always start off with the carrot and then move on to the stick."

"This conversation is making me very nervous, Karl. I don't want you or any of your people within a mile of him. I mean it, goddamit."

With which Winston Bartlett slammed down the phone. "Shit."

What are *we going to do? So far, Van de Vliet hadn't helped Kristen in the slightest. Okay, she wanted to try the Beta, but still . . . What happened was a tragedy.*

And who are we kidding—Stone wasn't going to back off.

Seeing his natural (and only) son again after a lot of years had shaken him up more than he had expected. At some level he wanted to feel proud of his own flesh and blood.

But now . . . if anything got published about the Syndrome, the financial consequences could be devastating. Stone Aimes had to be kept at bay long enough to complete the buyout. Unfortunately, it might come to involve force.

He smiled to think that Kenji Noda would be ready for that challenge.

But overt violence really wasn't Winston Bartlett's style. At least it hadn't been his style up to now. But he was staring at the horrific possibility of the Syndrome. Starting very soon, a lot of things might have to be handled differently.

Chapter 17

Wednesday, April 8
10:15 A.M.

Ally was walking down the second-floor marble hallway of the Dorian Institute, feeling a mixture of hope and dread. She'd parked her blue Toyota in the same slot she'd done the day before, and then she'd gone through the security check at the front entrance, which included verifying (again) a solid ID and a check for any kind of camera or recording equipment. Maria did not come along; she was using this as an occasion to have some well-deserved time off with her grandchild. The caregiver was giving herself some care.

The downstairs foyer had been empty except for security and staff, and she'd paused just long enough to sign in and ask the receptionist at the central desk which room Nina Hampton was in. Was her mother going to be as enthusiastic about being here today as she'd been yesterday? Truthfully, just to see her spirits immediately improve yesterday was a high in itself. But who knew? Maybe she *could* be helped.

"I think she's . . . Let me check." She'd pulled up a computer screen. "Right. Mrs. Hampton is in room two-thirteen, second floor." She'd looked up and smiled. "Your mother, I assume. She's quite a card. I hear she's doing very well. You can use the elevator over there."

"I'll take the stairs," Ally had said. They were wide and blue marble and had a kind of splendor as they seemed to literally flow down from the upstairs landing. "I didn't have my run this morning."

The marble hallway upstairs showed no signs of use. The place felt more like a grandiose palace from another time than a hospital doing cutting-edge research. There was a nurse's station at the far end of the hall and two women were there in blue uniforms. Other than that, however, there was nothing to suggest the Dorian Institute was a medical facility. It could easily have been an exclusive resort hotel. It didn't feel medical or aseptic in any way.

Stone should see this, she thought. *He'd definitely be impressed.*

Driving out this morning, alone, she'd been thinking about him a lot. There was something about him that was different from what she'd remembered over all the years. He was as serious as ever about his work, but she suspected he might possibly be more fun now that he seemed to have lightened up some. He used to be wound extremely tight. In any case, she was finding herself surprisingly happy to talk to him again, whether or not it went any further.

But was his concern about the mysterious terminated patient justified? And what, if anything, did that have to do with her?

She was still musing about that when she heard the Spanish-language TV going in room 213, even before she touched the doorknob. *That's a good sign,* she thought.

She pushed open the door and strode in. The room was decorated in earth tones, including a lovely brown hand-woven carpet, which had Indian symbols in it, probably Navajo. The bed was a single, but it was faux Early American, not a hospital bed. Again the place felt more like a resort than a research institute.

Nina was sitting up, leaning against the headboard, and wearing blue silk pajamas underneath a white bed coat.

"Mom, how're you feeling? You look great."

It was true. She was wearing a full complement of makeup and her hair looked like it'd been newly washed. Whatever else was going on, the Dorian Institute was making sure patients looked their best. *Do they have a beautician on staff?* she wondered. Also, there was a sparkle in her mother's eyes that she hadn't seen since before her father died.

"How does it look like I'm feeling?" Nina reached for the remote and muted the sound from the TV.

Yes, that old twinkle is definitely there.

"Gee, I have to say that you seem a lot better than you did yesterday." It was true, thank goodness. She was having one of those supercogent days.

She laughed, deep and resonant. "Ally, you have no idea. He started in with the injections yesterday evening, after you left. When I woke up this morning, I could remember everything that happened yesterday. I even remembered why I was in this strange place. Try me. Ask me something and see if I can remember it. Go ahead. Ask me anything."

"Okay." She thought a moment. It should be something easy. "When was Dad's birthday?"

"March twelfth." She didn't even hesitate. "You'll have to do better than that."

"How about *my* birthday? You couldn't remember it last week."

Nina paused and looked disoriented for a moment. *Uh-oh,* Ally thought, *I pushed her too hard.*

"It was October third." A smile abruptly took over her face, as though she was experiencing a live breakthrough. "You were born at Roosevelt Hospital, at three-forty in the afternoon."

"Mom, this is incredible." She was joyously stunned, though it felt like something resembling shock. "It's a miracle."

"Your mother's responsiveness *is* impressive," Karl Van de Vliet said as he strode through the open door, startling her. "Ellen will run the first battery of monitoring tests later this morning. Short-term memory and the like. But from all appearances, there's been a lot of tissue regeneration under way overnight."

"Is . . . is this permanent?" Ally asked, not wanting to let herself get her hopes up too soon. *And what* is *he doing?*

"No one can answer that question." He looked at Nina and smiled. "But this is not some drug regimen to trick the brain's chemistry, Mrs. Hampton, you have my word. In Alzheimer's, tissue responsible for the production of certain neurotransmitters dies. What we're doing here is enabling your brain to regrow healthy, long-lived tissue to replace what has become damaged and destroyed by an excess of the wrong . . . Let's just say we're not trying to salvage damaged tissue. We're actually *replacing* the dysfunctional tissue in the cortical and hippocampal regions of the brain, so we're working *with* the body. And you're responding wonderfully." He turned back to Ally. "I've got to get back to the lab now. Come on down when you're ready, and we'll finish the paperwork."

She started to say she wanted to ask him to linger a moment and answer a few questions, but before she could, he'd disappeared into the hallway.

"Ally, I haven't felt this alive in months," Nina bubbled on. "Dr. Vee did a minor procedure late yesterday afternoon, using local anesthesia. Then he did something in his laboratory and came back and gave me an injection. Then there was another one this morning. It's supposed to continue for a week or two. Ellen said she'll be giving me one of those little memory tests every day to see if I'm improving, but you know, I already know I can tell a difference. It's just been overnight, but I swear some of the haze is already gone."

"I'm so happy for you." Ally felt a surge of joy. Already she was thinking about some new trips they could take together.

"Come over here and sit by me," she said, patting the bed. "I was thinking about Arthur again this morning. If Doctor

Vee can do something for your heart, it would be a miracle that would have meant so much to him. It's just so sad he can't be here to see this."

As Ally settled next to her, Nina reached over and took her hand. "I want to ask you something, darling. Just between us. Why do you think Seth . . . Grant is doing this for me, for us?"

"What do you mean?" Ally was trying to read her thoughts, wondering where the topic was headed. Nina had declared on Sunday that she thought there was something evil about Grant. Now this.

"I hate to say it about my own son, but caring is not his first nature."

"Mom, we see him so seldom, do you really think either one of us still understands him?"

Nina and Grant had never been all that close. In fact, he'd always been something of a secretive loner within the family, even though he was very much an extrovert with his friends, of which he had many, or at least used to. Ally had left for college just as he reached high school, which meant she wasn't around during his impressionable teen years. And when she came back to take over CitiSpace, he was virtually a fugitive from the family.

"I remember plenty about him. You think I don't know my own son, Lord help me."

"Well, Mom, I'm not really prepared to talk about him. It was so upsetting just to see him, I couldn't really take everything in." She smiled and touched Nina's brow, which felt warm and flush. "But I'll tell you something I *am* taking in. You're really looking great. I don't know what he's doing, but—"

"Hope, darling. It's the greatest tonic in the world, even if there's no good reason for it." She squeezed Ally's hand. "And I do so wish Arthur could be here now. I miss him so much."

"I know, Mom. He was as much a friend to me as he was a dad." She thought back fondly over her father's many passions and how she'd shared a lot of them with him. One had been the nineteenth-century Romantic poets, particularly Wordsworth and Shelley. Then he'd had his astronomy period and they'd spent a lot of time together at the planetarium. But he took an interest in her passions as well. When at age eight she decided to collect coins, he went to the bank and brought back rolls and rolls of dimes and nickels for her to go through. And during the summertime he'd take her and Grant on the LIRR to Long Beach, every other Sunday, all summer long.

That was why the pain, the personal loss, of his horrible death had never fully subsided. Perhaps it never would. But the difference between them was that he had finally lost his will to live, whereas Ally found her own will growing all the more with every new adversity she faced. The weaker her heart got, the more determined she was to exercise, whatever it took, to make it strong again.

"He would be so proud of the way you pulled CitiSpace back from the brink." She let a tear slide down her left cheek, smearing her makeup. "And I'll tell you something else, young lady. You take after us both when it comes to guts. My memory may be slipping, but I remember you were always willing to take chances. And I guess that's what we're doing here now. Both of us. We're gambling on life. In your case, you've got a lot to lose."

Ally looked at her. Nina was having one of her moments of incredible lucidity, but how did she know so much about what was really going on.

"Mom, did the doctor tell you what I—"

"The head nurse, Ellen, told me that you're going to undergo a procedure for your heart. That you're going to start today." Her eyes darkened. "She also admitted he'd never used the procedure on a condition like yours. It's completely experimental."

"You talked to her this morning?"

"She took me downstairs, where they did my hair. She said Dr. Vee thinks it's important for everyone here to have a positive attitude. They ask you what you'd like and then they try to do it. Now I'm ready for whatever comes next." She stared directly into Ally's eyes. "But that doesn't mean I still can't be nervous about all this untried stuff."

"Mom, don't worry about me. I'm going to get through this. If you'll be strong for me, I promise I'll be strong for you."

She got up and walked to the window. From this vantage she could just see the lake down through the trees. They were starting to put out leaves, but it was still early spring and nippy here, so they mostly had just buds. All the same, there was a sense of renewal about them, which made her think of her own body.

"Life is so bittersweet." Nina sighed. "But you still want to go on living, even when it's a daily struggle. Either I'm an optimist or I'm pigheaded."

"You're just wonderful," Ally said. "That's what you are."

She glanced down at her watch. She was scheduled to meet Ellen O'Hara downstairs at ten forty-five, to fill out the paperwork that formally entered her into the clinical trials. If she decided to go ahead and enroll, this would be her last day of freedom. Tomorrow she would have to begin the intense phase of the therapy. Did she *really* want to do that? She wanted to talk to Van de Vliet one last time. "Look, Mom, I'm going to be downstairs for a while now, but I'll come back up later."

"All right. Ellen said there's a little library here somewhere, so I may go down and look. I might even get something in Spanish, to try and keep my mind alert." She sighed. "Oh, Ally, I so want to be the way I was again. Pray for me."

Ally knew prayer wasn't something her mother engaged in a lot. In fact, she'd always been a fervent agnostic. What had brought about the change? Was it that she'd finally discovered that both her body and mind had limits and wouldn't do what she wanted forever?

"I'll pray for us both, Mom. But we're going to be okay. I have faith."

"Good for you." She looked away. "I'll try to have it too."

Ally walked over and kissed her, then turned and headed out the door. Where was this all going to end? She had absolutely no idea. But with Nina's miracle change overnight, the concern she'd heard in the voice of Stone Aimes seemed a million miles away.

As she walked down the marble stairs, she tried to take the measure of the place. The Dorian Institute did inspire you with its look of utter perfection. It was an appropriate setting for miracles.

When she got to the lobby, she saw Ellen stepping off the elevator, coming up from the basement.

"All set to get going?" she asked, walking over. "Before we start any procedures, anything at all, we've got to fill out the forms for the NIH. Technically, what is going on here is a clinical trial, a very detailed study in which we constantly monitor the patients and try to measure their progress objectively. So we'll have to take some time and establish a very thorough baseline. We began that yesterday when you went to the clinic in New York for a stress test. Among other things, we'll be running an EKG on you here on a daily basis."

"And all this goes into my NIH files?" Ally asked. They were getting on the elevator to go down.

"Not the raw data. It's our job to structure our patients' files in ways that will permit the NIH monitor, or other third parties, to assess our results quickly."

They were getting off now, entering the starkly lit hallway that connected the laboratory and Dr. Van de Vliet's office with the examination rooms.

"Dr. Vee is working in the lab this morning, so we can use his office to fill out all the forms."

Ally could see Dr. Van de Vliet and three other people, members of his research team, all dressed in white, clustered around a blackboard, where he was drawing some kind of flowchart. Again she was struck by his youthful appearance. He surely did not look a day older than forty, or forty-five tops.

This was the first time she had been in his office, and she paused to look around. As was usual, he had a wall of framed diplomas and certificates. From her cursory check-out, they seemed to correspond to the educational history she remembered from his CV. It was a spacious room, with an executive feeling, and he had an expensive flat-screen nineteen-inch monitor sitting on the left-hand side of his desk. Next to it was a wooden table and chairs. A pile of NIH forms was there, along with a green raku mug, filled with ballpoint pens.

"He likes to let people use his office whenever possible," Ellen explained. "It's a lot less institutional than the conference room."

Ally settled at the table and picked up the form.

"They want a lot of personal information," Ellen went on, "but your mother and I filled out her items yesterday and it wasn't too hard. Needless to say, all personal information is completely confidential. Even your name. After the first week, we only identify you with a coding system."

As Ally was reaching for a pen, a petite blond woman with a smashing figure strode through the door. She was wearing a lab coat, not a nurse's uniform, but it still showed off her curves. She was carrying a stainless-steel tray containing a hypodermic needle and three glass vials.

"Hi," she said with a smile, "I'm Dr. Connolly. Welcome to the Dorian Institute. We're all very excited about having you here."

"Deb, come in," Ellen said, seeming slightly startled. "Is there something we forgot to—"

"No, I just need to take one hundred fifty milliliters of blood. We've got to get started on the cultures we'll be using ASAP."

"Hang on a second," Ally said. "I was hoping to talk this over a bit more with Dr. Van de Vliet before I take the final leap."

"You're free to dither as much as you like," Dr. Debra

Connolly said, her smile vanishing, "but our programs are on a schedule."

"I'd still—"

"I'll just be taking a small amount of blood. We can then get started on the cultures while you talk." She was already swabbing Ally's arm and feeling for a vein. "Now make a fist."

Ally hated giving blood and to distract herself she glanced around the office, trying to construct a life story for Dr. Karl Van de Vliet. Then she noticed a photo of him and a woman standing together on a bridge, next to a sign that said CHARLES RIVER, which meant Boston, and they were holding hands and smiling.

The odd thing was, the cars behind them were models at least fifteen years old, yet he looked just the same as he did today.

Whoa. There it is again. That odd age thing. There is something very strange about this man. She finally got up her courage to ask.

"Dr. Connolly, do you know how old Dr. Van de Vliet is? He looks so young."

"There are some things it's not polite to ask." She was capping off the vial and reaching for a second. Her voice had grown genuinely frosty.

"Frankly, I don't see why. He knows everything there is to know about me. He has all my files."

"You could ask at the front desk for one of our brochures. I'm sure it would clear up any questions you have." She attached the second vial to the needle.

"I've seen it. I know when he went to school and all that. But still—"

"If you really want to know personal things, you might just ask him yourself. You two seem to get along so well."

What is with *her?* Ally puzzled. *Why is she being so hostile and negative? And why that little jab about "getting along"?* The truth was, Debra Connolly could have been a runway model, but in a lab coat her blondness and figure just intensified her bitchiness.

Okay, maybe the question about his age wasn't overly relevant, more a matter of idle curiosity. But how *did* he do it? Every woman alive would like to know. Maybe the story Grant had told about Van de Vliet and his experimental skin treatment was actually true. She hadn't put much stock in it at the time, but seeing him out here in the flesh . . ."

"There's actually something else I was curious about. Was a patient dropped from the trials a few months back? I was wondering if you could tell me anything about that."

"What have you heard that would make you ask such a question?" Debra Connolly's face went blank, but her blue eyes registered alarm. "No one here is allowed to discuss specific cases. That would be a violation of NIH rules and highly unethical. What made you ask that question?"

Hey, why so defensive? Could it be Stone is on to something that needs more daylight?

"I did a little research on the Gerex Corporation and . . ." Then she had an inspired hunch. "You know, the NIH has a Web site where they post all the clinical trials they have under way." This was actually something she knew to be true. She had used the site to look up information about possible clinical trials for Alzheimer's patients that might accept her mother. But she never could find any in the New York area that seemed to offer any hope. "So naturally, your study was there. I like to know as much as I can about what I'm getting into."

"I've been to that Web site many times. The public part doesn't include—"

"So, *has* a patient ever been terminated?" Ally cut her off, hoping to avoid being caught in a lie. "If so, I'd really like to know why."

"No one is allowed to discuss any details of the clinical studies." She was capping off the last vial of blood, the three cylinders of red against the steel.

"I think I'm going to have a talk with Dr. Van de Vliet before I go any further with this program," Ally said, feeling her temper and her warning instincts both ratchet up. "I feel like I'm being stonewalled."

"You're free to think what you like." Debra Connolly had turned and was brusquely heading for the doorway when it was blocked by another blonde this one in her late fifties, who was standing in the threshold and brandishing a black automatic pistol. Her eyes were wild. The security guard from the entrance and the nurse from the front desk upstairs were both cowering behind her.

"Where's Kristen?" she demanded. "Where's my daughter? I know she's alive, goddam you. I've come to take her home."

Chapter 18

"Who are you and how did you get in here?" Debra Connolly demanded, backing away from the door and quickly settling her steel tray onto a table. Ally got the instant impression that Deb knew *exactly* who she was.

The woman's hair was an ash blond tint above dark roots and was clipped short in a curt style. Her troubled face had stress lines, and her heavy makeup reminded Ally of a younger Sylvia Miles or perhaps a particularly intense real estate agent, except that real estate agents don't charge in on you brandishing a Beretta.

"It's all been a lie," the woman declared, her cigarette-fogged voice shrill. If she recognized Debra, it wasn't apparent.

Ellen hit a button on the desk and spoke into the intercom. "Dr. Vee, could you please come to your office immediately. It's an emergency. There's someone here who—"

"You're damned right it's an emergency," the woman barked at her.

"Hadn't you better give me the gun?" Debra asked, holding out her hand and stepping toward her.

The woman turned and trained the pistol on her. "Just back off, sister. And keep out of this. I know you work for him but you're just a flunky."

"Then could you at least keep your voice down," Debra Connolly said, her composure hard as ice. The jab had bounced right off. Underneath the beauty pageant exterior she was all steel and sinew. "There are patients upstairs. . . ."

The hapless security man who'd been trailing behind the woman had gone over to the positive-pressure door of the laboratory and was desperately banging on the glass and waving for Dr. Van de Vliet. A moment later, he strode out, still wearing his white lab jacket.

"You," the woman hissed, turning to meet him. "You're the one who has her. You and that bastard Bartlett."

"Madam, I must ask you to leave," he said warily as he came up to her. "Immediately." He glanced down at the pistol. "Otherwise I'll have to call the police."

Although he was giving the impression that the woman was just an anonymous annoyance, Ally was sure she caught a glimmer of recognition, and a patina of poorly disguised panic, in his eyes.

"I want to see Kristen, damn you. I want to know what you've done with her. *To* her. You and that bastard Winston Bartlett who got her into—"

"Kristen?" He seemed puzzled. Then he appeared to remember. "There was a patient here briefly a while back, who I believe was named—"

"Kristen Starr. That's right, you fucker. And you damned well do remember her. And me. She's my daughter. Where is she?"

My God, Ally thought, *could she mean that Kristen Starr, the one who had an interview show on cable. The world around this institute just keeps getting smaller.*

Ally had actually done an interior-design project for Kristen

Starr back when she was first getting up to speed at Citi-Space. It was one of her first jobs. At that time Kristen had just signed a two-year contract with E! and she wanted to renovate her co-op in Chelsea. But then just as the job was completed, she sold the place and moved to a brownstone in the West Village, or so she'd said. Ally didn't know why she had done it or where precisely she had moved to, but she got the impression some very rich new sugar daddy was setting her up and he wanted the privacy of a town house.

Could it be that *Kristen* was the mysterious missing patient Stone was trying to locate and interview? Ally hadn't seen her on TV for a while, so maybe she had moved on to other things.

"I really don't know where she is now," Van de Vliet said. "She became emotionally unstable in the middle of her treatment. It's a rarity but it has happened. She checked out. After that, I don't—"

"That's a damned lie," the woman declared. "I know it now. That's what your receptionists have been telling everybody. It sounded a little like her at first, but now I realize it's preposterous. She didn't just up and run off. You're keeping her somewhere. Where is she? Where's my only child?"

"Wherever she is, I can assure you she's most assuredly not *here*," Van de Vliet intoned smoothly, even as his eyes struggled to stay calm. "Would that she were. She wanted . . . a procedure done and I think we were having some success. But then she became traumatized for some reason best known to her and insisted on leaving. No one is forced to complete the regimen here against their will. As best I recall, someone said she went to a spa in New Mexico."

"I know that's what your flunkies have been telling me over the phone. That she went to New Mexico to hide out. But now I know everybody lied to me. For the last three years she's been sleeping with that bastard Winston Bartlett, but now his office won't even return my phone calls. You all think you're so smart, but I could smuggle a gun past your guards. In my bra!" Her eyes had acquired a further kind of wildness now as she awkwardly began opening her purse, hanging from a shoulder strap, with her left hand while still holding the pistol in her right. "And I got a letter from her just this morning. The postmark is New York City. So—"

"What—" Van de Vliet's eyes began to blink rapidly.

"She's not in New Mexico now. If she *ever* was." The woman waved a small tan envelope at him. There was large, loopy writing on the outside.

"Could . . . could I see that?" He started to reach for it, but she waved the black Beretta at him and shoved the letter back into her purse.

"No you can't. What you can do is tell me where the *hell* you're keeping her. *Now.*"

"Before we proceed any further, that gun really isn't necessary," Van der Vliet said as he reached and deftly seized her wrist. He was quick, and his quickness seemed to spook her, because just as he turned the pistol away, it discharged.

The round went astray, ricocheting off a metal lighting fixture at the end of the hallway and into the wall. The hapless, unarmed guard who'd followed her downstairs yelled and dived behind a large potted corn plant near the office door. Both Ellen O'Hara and Debra Connolly just stared, momentarily too stunned to move.

Ally stepped toward the woman, wanting to help Van de Vliet disarm her. She was feeling her heart race dangerously upward.

Van de Vliet was still struggling with the woman when the Beretta discharged again. This time it was aimed downward, at the hard tile floor, and the ricochet was not so harmless. The round bounced back and caught the woman in the chest, knocking her sideways. Van de Vliet unsuccessfully grabbed for her as she crumpled. Ally reached for her too, but by that time she was already on the floor. Ally pulled the hot pistol from her fingers, then turned and handed it to Ellen.

"Here. For God's sake, do something with this." She realized she had never actually held a real pistol before.

Blood was flowing across the floor as Van der Vliet and Debra Connolly began tearing open the woman's blouse. The bullet appeared to have entered her chest just below the rib cage, a jagged wound caused by the projectile's tumble and splattered shape, and then exited a few inches away, at her side. She had passed out.

"Get a gurney *now*," he yelled to Ellen. "We've got to get her into OR one and try to do something about the bleeding."

My God, Ally marveled, *what desperation drove her to threaten him with a gun when she obviously didn't know the first thing about how to use it?*

The woman's open purse was lying no more than two feet from where she had fallen. With the hallway rapidly filling as nurses from upstairs poured off the elevator, no one was paying any attention to anything but the prostrate woman.

Get the letter, Ally!

She gingerly moved over to where the purse was resting and peeked in. There was a jumble of the usual things: cosmetics, a ballpoint, a change purse, an address book, and a billfold. There also was the tan envelope. *Yes!*

The scene in the hallway was increasingly chaotic. Two of the researchers from the laboratory had come out, in their sterile whites, with disinfectant and a roll of bandages. As they began to bind her wound, to stanch the bleeding, her eyelids fluttered and she groaned.

"She's just in shock," Van de Vliet said with relief. "Ellen, page Michael and tell him to bring the ambulance around front. Just in case. But I think we can handle this here."

Now two nurses were rolling a gurney off the elevator. While Van de Vliet and the two lab researchers lifted her onto it, Ally realized that nobody seemed to think that calling the police—about any of this—would be a constructive step.

She pulled out the letter and examined it. The oversize script on the front read *Katherine Starr, 169 East 81st St.* There was no return address.

Katherine Starr. She was repeating the name and address, trying to lodge them in her memory, while she was pulling the letter out of the tan envelope.

It was in the same rotund script as the address:

Dear Whoever You Are,
  I think you're my mother but I'm not sure. Please help me. I don't know where I am or what my name is. But I found a bracelet with Starr on it and I looked in the phone book. Your name sounded kind of familiar. I think I'm . . .

"I'd better take that," Van de Vliet said, lifting the letter out of Ally's hands. "All her personal effects should be kept with her."

"Dr. Vee, OR one is open," Ellen was saying as she marched down the hall toward them. "Debra has the IV and oxygen ready."

"Good," he said, glancing at her for a second.

As he did, Ally reached into Katherine Starr's purse and palmed the small black address book.

Then Van de Vliet turned back to her. "Let me see about her bleeding and then I'll try to explain. I now remember this woman all too well. It's all coming back like a bad dream I'd repressed. I pegged her as schizophrenic the minute I saw her, when she came here and tried to talk her daughter into leaving. She's paranoid and—"

"What was Kristen Starr here for?" Ally asked. "I actually did an interior-design job for her a few years back and she never mentioned any health issues."

"Actually nothing," he declared quickly. "She was having an early midlife crisis. I gather she'd had some kind of television program and her contract wasn't renewed. She'd decided it was because of her appearance." He shrugged and gestured with empty palms, like, *How absurd but that's the way some women are.* "It turned out we had a . . . mutual acquaintance who told her about the stem cell procedure here at the institute. When he brought her in, I wasn't in a position to turn her away."

"That wouldn't be Winston Bartlett, by any chance?"

He nodded. "As a matter of fact. He writes the checks, so he has a certain amount of influence around here. As it happened, I had experimented with a procedure some years ago involving stem cells and the epidermis. There seemed to be a regenerative effect. And I thought there was a reasonable chance she might respond to it. Since we had clinical trials for other stem cell procedures already under way, it was easy to fit her in. But I had a lot more important things going on at the time than her cosmetic work, so I didn't pay much attention to her. Then she abruptly left, and since then I've had so much else happening, I just haven't thought about her."

"Was it not working? Is that why she left?"

"Some of the staff swore it was having results. The truth is, I wasn't following her very closely. In my honest opinion, stem cell technology shouldn't be used for cosmetic purposes. It borders on the obscene."

Whoa, Ally thought, *according to Grant, you "experimented" with a procedure for the skin on* yourself. *And you've got the youthful-looking skin to prove it. Let's not have the pot calling the kettle black here.*

"But if it was working, then why did she decide to stop?"

This story sounds way too pat, she thought.

"You'll have to ask someone closer to her. Maybe she didn't think it was."

"How about Winston Bartlett. I gather he's pretty close."

"Well, she's a touchy subject with him. Good luck." Van de Vliet hesitated and his face flushed. "But now I really have to get in there. I'm responsible for whatever happens around here. Particularly whatever *bad* that happens."

He was heading down the hall.

"One last thing. If Kristen is here in New York, then how could I contact her?"

"I have absolutely no idea," he said over his shoulder. "If her own mother couldn't find . . . Actually, you might check with the front desk. All clinical trial participants are here under a confidentiality agreement, which means that giving out any information about her would be a liability issue, but now . . . See if they have a prior address they can give you. After she left, it never occurred to me to pursue her."

He was going through a door marked OR 1, but then he revolved back. There was a darkness in his eyes she hadn't seen before. "I guess I'm wondering why, exactly, you're so interested in this deranged girl. It has no bearing whatsoever on your own treatment."

"It's just something I'm curious about." She stopped, her emotions in a jumble. What *is going on?* "You know, I'm wondering if maybe we shouldn't start my procedure later in the week. All this . . . guns and shooting . . . is a bit much for me to take in." She looked at him. "I guess I can't remember ever seeing anyone pull a pistol on their doctor before."

"I can understand your disquiet," he said, his eyes dimming even more, "but I'd really hoped we could get started today. I should be free in an hour or so and we can—"

"I've given the blood sample you wanted, but I've just had the fright of my life. I want to go up and see Mom again and then I want a day to recharge."

Get hold of Stone, she was thinking, *and then try to find Kristen.* Something *feels very nonkosher here.*

"Just be aware," he went on, "that this procedure can't wait forever. I told you that we have less than three weeks left. At the end of the month, the clinical trials will be completed and this facility could be temporarily closed because of corporate restructuring."

What is he talking about, "corporate restructuring"? You're pressuring me again, she thought. *I really don't like that.*

"It can wait for a day."

"All right. If you must. But that's it. We have to start tomorrow. Seriously." He came back and reached and took her hand. "This means a lot to me, Alexa. I really want to help you. And I truly think we can."

With that, he turned and walked into the OR.

She stood watching for a moment, and when he was definitely gone, she took the small black leather volume out of her waistband.

On a hunch she opened it to the first page and . . . sure enough, there it was, penciled in down one side: *Kristy 555-1224.* No last name and no address.

The rest of the book had only a dozen entries, so few that Ally wondered why Katherine Starr bothered carrying it. Compulsive, maybe.

She couldn't wait to get to her car and get on the phone to Stone.

Kristen Starr could well be the mystery patient he was looking for. In any event, she was missing, freaked out, unsure who she was, and probably in a *lot* of trouble.

But now they had a phone number.

Chapter 19

Wednesday, April 8
12:32 P.M.

"You think you've got *what?*" Stone Aimes sounded like he'd just won the lottery. "For the patient who was 'terminated'? My God, Ally, you're incredible."

"Possibly. But what I *know* I am is very worried. For one thing, if this is the person you're looking for, the one who got dropped from the trials, it's somebody you've probably heard of, and for another, I've just had a series of very disturbing experiences. . . ."

She'd called him on her cell phone the minute she cranked up her Toyota to return to the city. She couldn't get away from the Dorian Institute fast enough.

After leaving Karl Van de Vliet, she'd taken the elevator up to the second floor to check in on Nina.

"What's all the excitement?" her mother had asked. "One of the nurses just told me that a deranged woman with a gun barged into the lobby looking for Dr. Vee. Then she shot herself."

"It's nothing, Mom. Everything is all right now." She hadn't wanted to upset Nina, but she was convinced Karl Van de Vliet had just done some major lying. His uneasy body language told her he knew a lot more about Kristen Starr than he was admitting; for that matter, Debra Connolly probably did too.

"Well, thank goodness," Nina had said. "Are you going to start the procedure for your heart today?"

"Not yet. I want another day to think about it. But tell me how you're doing, really. I mean, are you comfortable with how everything's going here? You can still stop if things don't feel right."

Ally half wanted to get her out of the Dorian Institute immediately. She didn't know what either of them had stumbled into. She just knew now that, along with the possibility of miracles, the Dorian Institute had a lot of questions that needed straight answers. She no longer trusted Karl Van de Vliet. She had seen his facade crack momentarily and what lay beneath it made her very uncomfortable.

Furthermore, she thought he realized she knew he was lying. And it seemed to make him even more desperate to keep her there.

"Ally, what a silly thing to say. Of course I want to stay." She'd fluffed up her pillow and reached for the TV remote. "Some of the smoke has already been blown out of my mind. I'm feeling clearer by the minute."

There's surely got to be some "placebo effect" at work here, Ally thought. *But still, she does seem more aware.*

"Okay, Mom, I'm going back into the city now. But I'll be here tomorrow and every day to check on you. Just don't . . . don't let them do anything to you that seems strange."

With that, she had given Nina a kiss on the forehead and taken the marble stairs down to the first-floor reception.

It was now time to find Kristen Starr.

The nurse at the desk was a woman named May Gooden. The main floor had returned to normal after all the excitement, with patients passing through as they came back from the cafeteria.

Ally had decided to try a long shot and see if she could pry out any information about Kristen from the patient files. She asked point-blank.

"I guess Dr. Van de Vliet was not aware of the legal strictures in our NIH agreement," May had said. "No personal information can be released without a patient's signed authorization."

"You do remember her being here, though? Kristen Starr."

"My Lord, that's not something that goes unnoticed. She had an assumed name but everybody knew who she was. A nice girl. Nicer than you'd expect from seeing her on television."

"So when, exactly, did she leave? Surely you can tell me that harmless piece of information? It was several months ago, right?"

May got a strange look in her eyes. "Who told you that?"

"I . . . I was downstairs when her mother showed up. I just got the impression that it was—"

May glanced furtively around. "I shouldn't be telling you this, but the truth is, I think she was still here until just a few days ago. She was down in intensive care. No nursing staff is allowed down there, just those medical-research people he has working for him, what some of the nurses call the Gang of Four. But they brought her up in the elevator and then an ambulance took her away."

"When, precisely, was—"

"I've said too much already." She glanced around again. "And I can assure you that Kristen didn't sign an authorization to give out her personal information." She abruptly turned frosty and officious, as though rethinking how open she'd just been. What was she afraid of? "Now, if you'll excuse me, I've got some things I need to do."

Ally had nodded and thanked her and split.

Thus the search had already produced an interesting factoid. Karl Van de Vliet was most assuredly engaged in the practice of a big lie about Kristen. . . .

"Maybe you should start by telling me about the disturbing experience," Stone was saying.

As the shadows of the trees that lined the leafy driveway glided past the Toyota's windshield, she told him about Katherine Starr and Kristen Starr. She also told him the disparate versions of Kristen's departure as recounted by Van de Vliet and May Gooden.

"Sounds like they've got a situation," Stone declared. "They're trying to hide somebody who's well known. But you've got a number?"

"Like I said, I palmed Katherine's little black book and it's got what could be the last known phone number for Kristen. Since she probably left the institute in an ambulance a few days ago, I doubt if she's at that number now, but it's someplace to start. I assume the area code is two-one-two. There're reverse directories where you can find the address for a phone number, right? In fact, I think there's a site on the Web that—"

"Leave that part to me. If the number's still good, I'll have it in five minutes. Then I'll call you back and maybe you could meet me there, assuming it's somewhere in the city. Just give me your cell number."

She did and then clicked off the handset.

My God, she thought, *that's the first time I've "given my number" to a man—not a business acquaintance—since Steve died.* Okay, there were dinners with a couple of bachelor clients that turned out to be more than dinner. But neither relationship had lasted past a month. Both the men, nice guys, had complained she wasn't there for them—she wasn't—and had broken it off.

She meditated on that as she went through the iron gates (which opened automatically) and headed down the leafy, twisting roadway leading to the expressway.

She also found herself wondering what Stone Aimes was *really* like. There was an openness now that made her feel comfortable—though maybe that was just his deceptive reporter's manner, his calculating way of getting below her radar. He'd definitely picked up a few social skills over the past years. God knows he needed them.

Whatever was going on, it was good to have him around again. There was something different about talking to him than talking to Jennifer, though Ally wasn't quite sure what it was—and she was afraid to think too hard about it. But whatever that difference, it was one of the million reasons she so missed having Steve around.

Because if there ever was a time when she needed somebody to talk to . . .

Why am I thinking all this? she chided herself. *I'm trying to psychoanalyze him and put him in a category when I don't know the first thing about what he's actually turned into after all this time. Is all the warmth and sincerity for real?* Back in the old days he'd make nice whenever the stakes were low, but then when he had something on the line, he'd push as hard as he needed to get what he wanted.

Well, she reminded herself, *I'm that way too. That was part of our problem.*

The phone beeped.

"Voilà," Stone's voice announced. "I got an address in the West Village. It's Two-Seventeen West Eleventh Street. The phone is unlisted but it's billed to her name, so you were right about the number. And get this, it hadn't been turned off. So I thought, idiot, why don't you do the obvious and just try calling?"

"But her mother said she'd disappeared. . . ."

"Well, that's highly plausible. There's an answering machine there with a very strange message. It doesn't give a name, but it's a woman's voice and it's like a cri de coeur. She's away but she—quote—can't say where. You should listen to it."

Greenwood Lake Road had now become Skyline Drive,

for no discernible reason, and the traffic was picking up. Ally put on some speed and passed a truck.

"I'll do that. But we don't actually know for sure if it's the same Kristen Starr, though it surely has to be. Did you recognize her voice?"

"I've never watched her cable show. I just sort of know who she is. But you'd better listen to her announcement. How could there be two screwed-up young women named Kristen Starr in the same town, even if it is New York?"

"I'll listen. It's got to be her, though. Give me the address." She hesitated a moment after he did, then, "Would you like to meet me there? I think I could probably make it in an hour, or an hour and a quarter to be safe. We could ask around, see if anybody in her building or the neighborhood has any idea what's going on with her. Maybe somebody's seen her."

"I was supposed to head into the office, but nothing could keep me away," he declared with enthusiasm.

A patrol car was speeding by in the opposite direction, siren blaring. She waited for the noise to subside.

"Great. I'll try for an hour. Unless the traffic really gets crazy. You never know what to expect at the GW Bridge, even in the middle of the day."

She clicked off the phone, then checked the number in the front of the black address book and punched it in.

The phone rang twice and then an answering machine started. The voice making the announcement sounded thin, tiny, and fragile. Just hanging on. It was the verbal equivalent of the loopy handwriting on the letter, a transparent attempt to bolster nonexistent courage.

"Hi. I'm away for now—I can't say where—and I'm not sure when I'll be back. But you can leave a message or whatever, in case I get a chance to pick them up at some point. Or you don't have to. That's okay too."

What an odd thing to say, Ally thought. *It's like she's trying not to sound too needful.*

But it was definitely *the* Kristen Starr. The slightly ditzy tone was right there.

Next came a long series of beeps as the machine proceeded to rewind.

This is surreal, she thought. *I'm about to leave a message for a person who's God-knows-where.*

While the machine beeped, she tried to rehearse what she wanted to say, to make it as nonthreatening as possible. Finally the machine stopped rewinding.

"Kristen, hi, my name is Ally Hampton. You may remember I did an interior-design job for you when you lived in Chelsea. CitiSpace? I just met your mother. She got your letter." *Should I tell her about the gun accident?* Ally wondered. *No, she's weirded-out enough already.* "Your real name is Kristen Starr. You seemed a little confused about that in your letter to her, which I read part of. You'd been at the Dorian Institute in New Jersey. Listen, it's really important to me, and to your mother, that you get in touch. I'd like to help you if I can, because from what I saw of your letter . . . Anyway, let me give you my cell phone number. If you pick this up, you can call me anytime, night or day. It's—"

"How did you get this number?" a frightened voice burst through. Ally recognized it, though it was nothing like the one she remembered from the confident, brassy TV personality that Kristen used to be. "I just got away and came here. And right after I got here, someone called my machine and then hung up. Are you tracking me? Who *are* you?"

"I . . ." Ally was so startled she couldn't think of anything to say immediately. "Kristen, is that you? I just saw your mother. I . . . I got this number from *her.* She came out to the Dorian Institute looking for you. She's very worried about—"

"You're lying to me. You're trying to trick me and get me back." She was breathing heavily, as though she'd just run a set of stairs. *This is a person just barely holding it together,* Ally thought. "Anyway, Kristen is not my name. My name is Kirby. They wrote it down for me and . . . I'm very confused.

I found a bracelet in my suitcase that had 'Starr' on it. Maybe that's my last name. It sounds right, but I can't remember—"

"You don't remember having a show on cable?"

"I . . . I think I knew someone who had a TV show, but I don't think it was me."

"Kirby . . . or whatever your . . . listen carefully. I think you were undergoing an experimental procedure for your skin. At a place in New Jersey called the Dorian Institute. The doctor was Karl Van de Vliet. You were in clinical trials for the National Institutes of Health. Then something happened and you left. Do you remember *why* you left? Or when?"

"No." She stifled a sob. "I can't remember anything."

Ally took a deep breath, not liking the vibes she was getting. "Do you want to talk about it?"

"No. I don't want to talk to you or to anybody. I got out of that place and—"

" 'That place'?" Ally asked. She was being passed by a huge bus and she could barely hear. "You mean the institute?"

"You know where I mean. And don't come looking for me down here either, because I'm not going to be here."

Jesus, Ally thought, *what's with her?*

"Kris—Kirby, I'm not connected with anybody at the Dorian Institute. I'm supposed to become a patient there myself. I'm just trying to find out what happened to you when you underwent your treatment there."

"I can only remember little things." She was moaning. "There was this man. He said I could have anything I wanted. I trusted him. And now . . . I see faces but I can't remember who—"

"Kristen—that's your real name, by the way—can we meet? I promise you won't be harmed. I just—"

"You don't understand, do you? You don't know what's happening to me." Her voice had begun to break. "It's the Beta. I don't know how long it's going to be before—"

"Before what? What beta? What are you—Kristen, we've

really got to meet. I mean it. I desperately need to talk to you. Maybe we could find another doctor, if that's what you need. Could I come down—"

"I have no idea who you are. You could be . . . He says they're trying to help me, but I'm not getting any better."

Ally was pulling onto the interstate, heading south. It was hard to concentrate on driving, but at the same time she wanted to push the speed limit. Kristen sounded like she was getting ready to disintegrate or flee.

Then she had another thought.

"Kristen, it's okay if you don't trust me. But could you tell me more about your . . . side effects? Are they—"

"I think that's why he moved me. To that place. But then he . . ." She was growing even more agitated and impatient. "Look, I really can't talk anymore."

I'm losing her, Ally thought. *Try to make her hang on.*

"Kristen, would you please take my phone number? You sound like you could use a friend."

"Oh Christ, I'm so scared. I don't—"

"Just take it. No harm. Then if something happens and you want to—"

"All right," she said finally. "Tell me and I'll write it down."

Ally gave it to her, then added, "I run an interior-design firm. I actually did some work for you once, so we've met. You can call my office, so let me give you that number too. No way am I connected to the institute where you were."

She said she was writing it down.

"You know," Kristen went on, "I think this is God's way of punishing me for wanting something nobody should have." Then she began to sob again.

"How exactly—"

"I found a door that wasn't locked and I just came here. I don't know what guided me. And when I got to this street, I knew exactly which building it was. There was no name on my bell or anything, but I knew. I even knew who had my emergency key. It's like I have a sense memory of this apartment but I can't remember ever actually living here."

"Your name is Kristen Starr," Ally said again. "Try to remember that. And will you please stay there till I can get there and talk to you?" Then she made what she immediately realized was a fatal mistake. "There's a reporter, a sweet guy who's doing a book about . . . a medical procedure at the clinic where you were. And he's dying to talk to anybody who's been part of the clinical trials there. Could he talk to you too? It sounds like you've got quite a story to tell."

"You've got to be kidding. If they find me, I don't know what they'll do." And the connection was severed.

"Shit, don't do this." She quickly tried the cell phone number for Stone Aimes.

"It's me again. Listen, she's actually *there*. Kristen's in the apartment on West Eleventh Street. I just got off the phone with her. She's the one you want. But she's like a frightened rabbit. She said she was about to leave, but if you get there soon, you might be able to catch her."

"Damn, we're stuck in traffic at Fifty-ninth Street. There was a fender bender on Lex. But I'll get there as soon as I can."

"Okay, maybe get your driver to try Fifth."

"Good idea."

She clicked off and stared at the road. The George Washington Bridge was just ahead. If she broke the speed limit once she hit the West Side Highway, and caught the lights right, she might even beat Stone there.

Chapter 20

"W.B., we've got a problem," Karl Van de Vliet said into the microphone. He was in his private office, on the scrambled videophone. "Kristen's mother showed up just before noon with a pistol, demanding to know where she was. When I tried to take the gun away from her, she accidentally shot herself through the side. Fortunately, it was only a flesh wound, but it took us almost an hour to stabilize her."

"Christ! Even Kristy thinks that woman is crazy. Why did she—"

"Kristen smuggled her a letter somehow. And she came looking for her." He thought about how they shouldn't be having this conversation on any kind of phone, even one that was supposedly scrambled. But there was no choice. "It gets worse. I just called Eight-Eighty Park and they checked her room and Kristen's not there. She was there when Roxanne brought up her breakfast at nine, but nobody's seen her since. They assumed she'd gone back to sleep. Nobody there has any idea where she went."

"Shit. What am I paying them for? The staff is there for

the sole purpose of making sure something like this didn't happen."

"Well, W.B., that's your part of the show. I'm just trying to practice medicine. In any case, she slipped out somehow. So the thing now is, where did she go?"

"Well, she didn't come here. Or at least she hasn't yet. Depending on how much she can still remember, she might have gone to her old place down in the Village. Maybe she still has a homing instinct. That's probably the first location we ought to check. Jesus, if she gets recognized and starts acting crazy and then Cambridge Pharmaceuticals finds out—"

"W.B., the bigger problem now could be her mother, Katherine. You know her. She's unbalanced but she also still remembers how it all started. She was actually here a couple of times. If she sees Kristen, then God help us."

"Karl, I've got everything—and I do mean *everything*—riding on this. What happened with that Hampton woman? You've got to get started with her. Is she on board yet or what?"

"She was here this morning, but she got temporarily spooked by the gun and the craziness. She'll be back, though."

"When?"

"I took care of it, trust me," Van de Vliet declared. "In the meantime, I'll try to maintain Kristen's mother under sedation as long as possible. But we can't keep her out of touch forever. That would be flirting with kidnapping."

"I'll send Ken over to West Eleventh Street to check out her place," Bartlett said. "If she's there, he'll get her."

And he signed off, the image on the computer going dark.

Van de Vliet felt a wave of apprehension. Every day it got worse. Would any of the other patients develop the Syndrome? Or was its development unique to the Beta?

Kristen had agreed of her own free will to undergo the Beta, and she'd been warned that any experimental procedure involved significant risk. She'd signed release documents absolving Gerex of any liability. But when treatments go awry, patients tend not to recall the releases they signed. Undoubtedly, she'd now conveniently forgotten that fact. Assuming she still remembered anything.

Time to go back to the OR and see how Katherine was doing. If she seemed completely stabilized and coherent, she could be moved down to the intensive-care area in the floor below, the subbasement. That way absolutely nobody could get to her. He clicked off the computer and walked back to the OR.

"Karl, she's awake," David said as he walked in. He'd been monitoring her. "It's probably okay to move her."

Thank God, Van de Vliet thought. *Maybe there's some way to reason with her rationally.* He moved over and looked down. Her hair was soaked with sweat and she looked very, very tired.

"Mrs. Starr, can you understand me? I'm Dr. Van de Vliet. I need to talk to you about your daughter, Kristen."

"Who . . . who are you?" she mumbled, her eyes trying to focus.

"I'm Kristen's physician. She came to see me some months back. Do you recall? About her . . . skin problem. I seem to remember you came here with her at one point."

She stared at him mutely for a moment, then closed her eyes and nodded.

"At that time, Mrs. Starr, we discussed some radical treatment options. Things that hadn't been tried before. Do you have any recollection of that?"

She opened her eyes again and stared at him, trying to focus.

"You said she'd be all right," she mumbled, slurring the words. "Then your receptionist told me she'd gone to New Mexico. But I got a letter—"

"That story was to protect her professionally," he lied. "She was afraid the press might find out she was here and start speculating about her health. But now she's in the post-procedure phase of treatment. It may be a while longer before she's able to return to the normal life she's used to."

"She's okay, isn't she?" came a plaintive, slurred mumble. "In her letter it sounded like she'd lost her memory or something. She didn't sound right."

It was a question that cut him to the core.

"Mrs. Starr, I think we should focus on *you* right now. You've had a traumatic episode and you've injured yourself pretty seriously. You may have to stay here at the institute for a few days so we can take care of you." He took her hand, which felt deathly cold. "Tell me, is there anyone we should notify of your whereabouts so they won't be alarmed?"

"There's an address book in my purse." Her eyelids flickered. "Those are all people I'm close to. I just want to sleep. I can't think now."

Good, he thought, *the sedative is finally kicking in.*

"All right. You need your rest. We'll talk about this later." He turned and picked up the purse at the foot of the bed. But when he searched inside, he didn't see an address book.

Where was it? he wondered.

Alexa Hampton had started reading Kristen's letter, which probably was part of the reason she got uneasy. *Did she make off with the address book? But why?*

It didn't matter. She would be back.

If Debra had done what she was supposed to do.

"David, have Mrs. Starr taken downstairs. I need to see Deb."

"You've got it."

Van de Vliet went down the hall and then through the heavy steel air lock and into the laboratory.

"Deb, can I have a word with you?" He motioned for her to follow him to the computer cubicle in the back, past the head-high racks of solvent vials and the giant autoclave.

"Is she going to be okay?" Debra asked.

"I think so. It's in her interest that we keep her here and away from a hospital. Gunshot wounds raise a lot of questions. I seriously doubt that that pistol was licensed in her name, given how little she seemed to know about its operation." He settled into a chair and began stroking his brow.

"Did you manage to take care of that matter with Alexa Hampton?"

She nodded. "You know, she's not yet entirely with the program."

"Yes, but she will be. Putting her mother in the clinical trials was probably crucial." He grimaced. "God, what a nightmare. A medical experiment that got away from us has turned into guns and virtual kidnapping and God knows what manner of felonies. If this thing gets completely off the track, we could all go to prison. But the real tragedy is that all the successful research we've done here will be buried in infamy."

"It's not going to turn out that way. The results here have been so spectacular." She was gazing at him with eyes that seemed too worshipful. More and more, she made him self-conscious. She needed a father, but he did not need a daughter. He still lived on the memory of Camille.

"This has all got to be resolved soon, Deb. There's a reporter who found out that we had to drop a patient from the program—which would be Kristen—and W.B. thinks he's a little too close for comfort. Now Kristen's mother shows up. It's all starting to unravel."

"Don't worry," she said, getting up. "This Hampton woman is going to be back today. So I've got to get started on her blood."

Chapter 21

Ally was very fond of Kristen's West Village neighborhood, since she herself had once had an apartment on West Eleventh Street, just west of Seventh Avenue. The street was tree-lined and many of its nineteenth-century town houses were home to single families, though sometimes the ground floor, with the entry "under the stoop," i.e., beneath the stairs, was rented out to provide a little side income. She had rented one of those "garden apartments"—the upstairs owners were two gay bankers—and had loved it. However, it also was entirely possible that Kristen had the whole town house to herself—that was the kind of thing that a lot of celebrities who lived, or even just spent time, in New York did. There was privacy and there also was the sense of living in an actual house instead of in some cookie-cutter apartment. Then again she could have a downstairs neighbor.

A solitary town house seemed somewhat at odds with the extroverted personality Kristen displayed on TV, but the privacy was probably intended more for her sugar daddy, Winston Bartlett, than for her.

Ally had been pushing the pace ever since she got off the phone with Stone. At Twenty-third Street she had peeled off the West Side Highway and gone over to Seventh Avenue, where she had a straight shot downtown. She passed St. Vincent's Hospital, and the notorious six-way intersection that caused so many accidents, and hung a right on West Eleventh.

She was approaching the corner at Bleecker Street when a huge black Lincoln Navigator lumbered in front of her, at an angle that cut her off and blocked the street. Then the vehicle abruptly slammed to a halt.

"What—"

She hit her own brakes and managed to slide to a stop just before she collided with the Lincoln's rear bumper. At first she thought they'd deliberately cut her off, but then she realized the move had nothing to do with her. A man and a woman were piling out. He was muscular and balding, with dark hair and sunglasses, and he was dressed in black. She had red hair streaked with white and was dressed in a nurse's whites. They were in a major hurry.

That was when she recognized the man she'd met at Gramercy Park, the Japanese sidekick Bartlett had called Ken.

Oh shit.

Then she realized that a thirtyish woman was running down West Eleventh Street toward them, carrying a dark green backpack in her left hand. They were gesturing for her to come to them and get into the vehicle, though she didn't appear to see them yet. Halfway down the block behind her, a man in a tan flight jacket was running, calling out.

"Kristen, wait. I just want to talk—"

The running woman glanced over her shoulder at him and, at that moment, collided with Bartlett's flunky. As she recoiled from the impact, the red-haired woman seized her left arm.

"Kirby, come," the woman said. "You're not well. We'll take you back."

"No!" she yelled, and twisted free of the woman's grasp. But now the Japanese guy had grabbed her other arm.

"It's going to be all right," he said as he caught the top of her head and started shoving her through the open door of the Navigator. "You shouldn't go out alone."

At that moment the man in the tan flight jacket reached the scene. It was Stone, but he'd been moments too late.

He stretched his arm into the Lincoln and tried to take the girl's hand. "Kristen, don't go with them. I just need to talk—"

"You don't need to do anything, pal," the man called Ken declared. "Except get out of the way."

He chopped the side of Stone's neck with an open hand, sending him sprawling backwards onto the pavement, flight jacket askew.

Now something odd was going on. Another girl was running down the sidewalk. "Kristy, wait. Don't . . ."

But the redheaded woman had already gotten into the back-seat of the SUV, beside the girl, and the Japanese man was heading around the front. Three seconds later, he was behind the wheel and peeling out. They were gone.

Ally sat watching, stunned. But now a Chevy sedan was departing a parking space three cars down from where she was and she quickly pulled in.

By then Stone Aimes had picked himself up off the side-walk and was gazing wistfully in the direction of the vanishing Lincoln. The girl who'd been behind him stopped and was talking to him.

Ally quickly locked the Toyota and went over.

"But why did she run?" Stone Aimes was asking. He was disheveled, but then being slugged and knocked to the sidewalk takes a toll on anybody's poise.

"She didn't know who you were," the girl replied. She looked like she would have been more at home in the East Village than here: late twenties, tattoo on one bicep, eyebrows pierced, blue jeans, hair needing a better day. She had serious acne scars on her cheeks. "I think she thought you were *them,* whoever they were."

Ally looked Stone over and felt a surge of admiration. In

spite of the fact he just got decked, there was an athletic feeling about the way he carried his body, as though he was ready to pounce on a news source. Only he just didn't pounce quite fast enough this time.

She walked up and gave him a hug. For a lot of reasons.

"Hey, we can't go on meeting like this."

"My God, how humiliating." He winced.

"What in heaven's name just happened? That was Kristen, all right. But why was she running from you?"

"I saw this woman walking very fast up the street carrying a backpack and I just took a shot and called out 'Kristen.' She glanced back at me, then took off like a rabbit. All I accomplished was to drive her directly into the grasp of those goons."

"You scared her," the girl with the pierced eyebrows shouted, gazing angrily at Stone. "Who *are* you? Why did you—"

"I'm a newspaper reporter," he said. "Who are *you?*"

"I sublet the garden apartment from her. I met her when I was doing her makeup at the E! channel. I mentioned I was looking for a place and she said she liked me and wanted somebody she liked to be her subtenant. The rent is really low. Then they canceled her show and she had a mental meltdown and went to a spa somewhere to regroup. Or at least that's what everybody at E! says."

"So that's definitely Kristen Starr?" Ally asked.

"I hadn't seen her in over five months, not even to pay the rent, and I couldn't believe it was her when she rang my bell and asked if she could borrow my copy of her key. At first I almost didn't recognize her. She looked . . . different somehow. The odd part was, I got the impression that she didn't recognize me either, at least for a minute or two. When I asked her if she wanted the rent, she just looked at me funny. A few minutes later, she brought the key back and she had a half-open backpack stuffed with clothes and papers. She seemed nervous and disoriented. I was going to try and help her get a cab. But then you showed up."

"Hey, look, I had no idea I was going to freak her out like that," Stone said.

"What's your name?" Ally asked, and then she introduced herself.

"My named is Cindy Dobbs. And you know something? Kristen didn't seem like the same person, in a lot of ways. She looked really different. I don't know how to explain it. But something was really, really wrong with her. And she kept saying her name wasn't Kristen, that it's something else—I can't remember what now. All I know is, she was totally spooked."

"Talk about bad timing," Stone said.

"She was so paranoid. She kept babbling about how 'they' knew she was here in her apartment and were coming to get her and she had to get away real quick. I don't know who she was talking about. Some guy used to come by and his white stretch limo would be double-parked for a couple of hours while he went in. But other than him, nobody ever came here."

"Cindy, the truth is, I was talking to her this very morning on the phone," Ally said. "I'm the one who called her. I also met her mother today, who just got a crazy letter from her and was walking around with a pistol because of it. I'm getting to be deeply invested in Kristen Starr. Something bizarre seems to have happened to her and I need to find out what it is."

Ally didn't want to confess that she felt indirectly responsible for what had just occurred. If she hadn't phoned . . . She stood thinking a minute, then, "Did you say you had a key to her place?"

Cindy shrugged. "I've had it since I moved in. We had copies of each other's keys. Just in case, you know." She reached into her ragged jeans and pulled it out and stared at it. It was attached to a blue plastic tab, GREENWICH LOCK-SMITHS.

"Then could we borrow it long enough to go in and take a

look around? Maybe we could find some clue to what's going on."

"Hey, if you want the key, and you think it can help you find her, you can just have it." She was holding it out. "I don't want to go in there, ever. With my luck, those people would show up again and take *me* away. But let me know if you find out anything, okay? I really thought of her as a friend, even though we actually didn't know each other that well. She didn't ever introduce me to that older guy who came around. Probably because he was married, at least that's my guess."

"I think she knows those people who grabbed her just now," Ally said, taking the key. "Cindy, can we exchange phone numbers?"

"Sure. I meant it about letting me know if you find out what's going on with her. Everybody at work is going to be really bummed when they hear about this."

Moments later, Ally and Stone were alone on the street, with Stone still appearing dazed. Now, taking measure of him in the daylight, she noticed a bit more of the mileage in his face and body. Still, it was good mileage and it had left him seasoned and lean. Also, she sensed that he really cared about things. This was more like the man she remembered, a mensch in wolf's clothing.

"Are you sure you're okay?" she asked.

"I'm going to be fine," he said. "Jesus, I never dreamed I'd spook her the way I did. By the way, did you get the license number of that Lincoln? I sure as hell didn't."

"I didn't need it. That guy is Winston Bartlett's personal bodyguard. He called him Ken. I was at Bartlett's place on Gramercy Park a couple of days ago and I saw him there."

"You're not kidding, are you?"

"I wish." She paused. "You know, Kristen and Bartlett were being talked about as an item back when. 'Page Six.' "

"The *Sentinel* would never touch it, but that was more than a rumor. Over the years I've had occasion to take more than a passing interest in his affairs." He grinned. "And for the past several days, he's been taking a lot more interest in *my* affairs, ever since he found out about the book."

"Incidentally," she declared, "I didn't have a chance to tell you on the phone, but Kristen seems to have no memory of who she is. Somebody told her that her name is Kirby, and that's what she insists on being called. All in all, she sounded deeply screwed up." She dangled the key. "So why don't we go up and see if we can learn anything?"

"Did it seem odd to you that, what's her name, Cindy didn't want to go in with us," he mused as they headed up the steps.

"Well, maybe she's already seen it. God only knows what we're going to find. Though the place she had in Chelsea was pretty well maintained. After I redid it, it was a knock-out, of course, but she'd already moved down here by then."

The building dated from the middle of the nineteenth century and the entryway, painted white, was a slight nod to the fashion for the Greek Revival style that made its way into the New York town houses of that period.

She shoved the key into the new lock, a Medico, and pushed open the door. Stone moved past her and switched on the light.

What awaited them was a minimally furnished but elegant living room, with a small couch and table. The downstairs "parlor floor" had been "opened up"; a lot of walls had been taken out and a staircase was on one side of the front room. It felt like a modern loft.

Memorabilia from E! was all over, the logo on throw pillows and two empty mugs on the table. The main decoration, however, consisted of publicity photos of Kristen around the walls, a smiling blonde with flowing tresses down over her shoulders. In all of them she was wearing heavy makeup and the photos appeared to have been airbrushed.

They were both trying to absorb what they were actually seeing. Each photo, and there were at least sixteen, was pinned to the walls with a steak knife, all with matching white bone handles.

"Jesus, who do you think did this?" Stone asked. "Could it be that ditzy girl downstairs?"

"I'd say she did it herself. Supposedly the reason she went to the Dorian Institute was because she was having some kind of personal crisis over starting to look older. She was consumed with terminal self-hate. That's what this has to be about."

"I've never caught her on TV," Stone said, walking over to study one of the photos, "but from what little I saw of her on the street just now, she sure seemed different from these head shots."

"Well, this is exactly how she looked on the tube." She told him the alleged story of how Kristen had ended up at the Dorian Institute. Then she gazed around the room, still having trouble taking it in. "Jesus, this is really sick."

"Ally, I'm absolutely convinced that whatever happened or didn't happen—keep that possibility in mind—to Kristen is connected somehow to the reason Gerex's clinical trials have been put under ironclad security."

"Which is why, no matter what, they've got to get her back on the reservation." Ally thought a moment. "Van de Vliet told me she'd left the clinic of her own accord. Which clearly was BS. Winston Bartlett has her stashed somewhere. Probably in an apartment in one of the buildings he owns." She looked over. "What do you think it all means?"

"How's this for a guess? Kristen is experiencing some kind of side effect that's truly horrendous. Losing your memory is bad enough, but there's probably something more too. I can't imagine what it is, but if the truth about it ever gets out, their entire program of stem cell research would be jeopardized."

"Well, I don't see much here to help us find her," she declared, looking around. "The knives in the walls don't speak well for her grip on sanity. Who knows? Maybe nothing's physically wrong with her. Maybe it's just all in her crazy head. Look at this place, for goodness' sake. Except for the knives, it looks pretty normal. Maybe she's just a nutcase and imagining that her memory is going."

As she gazed around the room one last time, she noticed an answering machine on the floor next to the couch. The message light on it was blinking, and she walked over and pushed the play button. She remembered that Stone had said he hadn't left a message, and Kristen had picked up when she called her, short-circuiting the voice mail.

The phone machine announced in an electronic voice, "You have one message, at two-eleven P.M."

Then an unctuous male voice came on. "Kirby, we know you're there. You're still in treatment. You shouldn't be wandering around unsupervised. It's a lot better, a lot safer, for you to stay with us now. This is Ken. I'm coming with Delores to pick you up. I know you're upset, but you shouldn't be. We're going to take care of you and help you."

Then the phone machine clicked off.

"My God," Stone said, glancing at his watch, "that's almost exactly when I got here. That's why she thought I was with them."

"That's the guy who slugged you. I recognize his voice. Guess they suspected she was here and that phone call was intended to flush her out. It worked."

"And I ended up right in the middle of it. Damn."

She walked around the empty room, checking it out. Except for the head shots stabbed to the wall, there was not a scrap of paper to be seen.

So how do we find Kristen without a clue? she wondered. *Should the kidnapping, if that's what it was, be reported to the police? But what proof do we have that any of it actually happened? They're not going to third-degree Winston Bartlett.*

"You know," Stone said, staring closely at one of the photos, "I didn't actually get a really good look at the woman running down the street. She glanced back at me when I called out her name, but the truth is, I'm not a hundred percent sure this is her."

"Come on," Ally said, "that had to be Kristen. The girl

downstairs recognized her. Though she did say she looked different somehow."

"You're going to think I'm crazy," he went on, still staring around at the walls, "but it seems to me the girl on the street was a lot younger than this one." He bit a fingernail contemplatively. "Christ, this is some sick material."

"Stone, I'm going down to my office, to take care of some things and think about this. Come along if you like. Maybe we've overlooked something obvious. Something that—"

That was when the beeper on his belt went off. He looked down at the number.

"Whoops. It's my managing editor."

"Where you work?"

"Right. Only I've got a feeling this call could be about how I *used* to work there."

Chapter 22

Ellen O'Hara, R.N., who was in charge of the nursing staff at the Dorian Institute and chair of the union committee for the Gerex Corporation, looked around the room, which was a conference space just off the laboratory in the first level of the basement. Each of the three other nurses present reported directly to her and they had filed in casually one by one, in order not to draw the attention of the research staff as they passed the laboratory. They all sensed the imminence of crisis and this was a clandestine emergency meeting.

The appearance of Katherine Starr and the shooting that transpired had left the entire nursing staff in dismay. Of course they all remembered Kristen Starr, the outgoing and scatterbrained TV personality, who had arrived in the throes of a mental meltdown. Some also remembered her mother, Katherine, who had made a nuisance of herself till she was refused further admittance (on the orders, everyone suspected, of the owner, Winston Bartlett, who was widely reported to have a romantic relationship with the girl).

They also suspected that something had started going terribly wrong with Kristen's cosmetic procedure. After seeming okay, her behavior had suddenly become erratic and she had been immediately whisked into intensive care in the subbasement and quarantined before anybody on the regular nursing staff could learn what the problem was. She was attended by the research team he had brought from California, and the information officer at the registration desk in the lobby, May Gooden, was instructed to say she had voluntarily left the program. (Well, maybe she had, but she hadn't left the institute.) Then less than a week ago, she was rolled out on a gurney and loaded into the ambulance, which was driven by Winston Bartlett's Japanese thug, and taken God knows where.

Ellen had checked and was dismayed, though not entirely surprised, to discover that none of this had been included in the weekly clinical-trial reports being forwarded to the National Institutes of Health. (Which in itself was a flagrant violation of procedural requirements.)

And now this. Kristen's own mother showed up deranged and carrying a pistol, looking for her. How much longer would it be before the NIH, or the police, found out that something funny had gone on?

Right now the first thing to do was to get the three senior nurses in the room to put a lid on the rumors. They were her lieutenants; it was their job.

Elise Baker, single and sharp and acerbic, was in charge of the second floor; Mary Hinds, a kindly mother of two, had responsibility for the third floor, and May Gooden, the queen of communication skills, handled the reception and oversaw the staff responsible for the dining room. All three were in their forties and they reported to Ellen O'Hara, who reported to Karl Van de Vliet.

"Elise, could you please close the door."

"Sure." She was getting up. "Is this the quorum? You don't want anybody else here?"

"We have to decide what to do about Katherine Starr," Ellen began. "In my opinion, the absolute first thing we have to do is make sure the story of what just happened never leaves this building."

"Well, I think Dr. Vee should call the police and have her arrested," Elise said as she quietly shut the door. "The very idea. Barging in here with a loaded gun."

"I don't feel safe in the lobby anymore," May Gooden declared. Her face was lined and she had streaks of premature gray. "We're all exposed out here in the middle of nowhere. I think Charles should have a pistol. What good is it having a 'security guard' if you're still not secure."

"Mary, what do you think?" Ellen asked. She knew Mary would always try to split the difference and reconcile differing opinions.

"I don't know. Maybe it was just the case of one crazy person. It's probably not going to happen again."

Okay, Ellen thought, *that's three different votes. Call the cops, beef up security, or put our collective heads in the sand.*

She worried about the others, but she was also worried about her own situation. Her husband, Harold, left her eight years ago for a younger woman, and after reclaiming her maiden name, she'd raised their two young sons on her own. Now the oldest, Eric, was ready to start college and she had no idea how she was going to pay for it if she lost this job.

The Gerex Corporation paid her almost twice what she would be earning as an R.N. at an ordinary hospital. With her current salary, she had a shot at providing the boys with an education. Without it—if Gerex got embroiled in some horrible scandal and was put out of business—she had no hope whatsoever.

Even worse, she might be named as being complicit in some unethical shenanigans, knowingly putting a patient at risk in a human trial. That would certainly drive a stake into the heart of her nursing career.

"Elise, we'd better think long and hard about bringing in the police. They would talk to Katherine and she'd tell them Kristen was missing and we simply have no idea where it would end." She paused. "I'm about to say something I shouldn't, but I guess this is the moment. You all deserve to know an important fact. The NIH has not been told the reason Kristen Starr was terminated from the stem cell program."

"How do you know that?" Elise asked.

"I just checked the reporting records. Call it a hunch. We all know that, for a formal clinical trial, that's a flagrant violation of NIH rules."

"What are you saying?" Mary asked, her voice filling with alarm.

"I'm saying we have no choice but to keep this whole matter of Kristen and her mother under cover. If the Dorian Institute gets caught tampering with the data from a clinical trial, it could be the end of everybody's career. Dr. Van de Vliet's certainly, but most probably ours as well."

"My God," Elise blurted out. "Did we have to wait till some crazy person with a gun barged in here before you got around to telling us that clinical-trial data had been fiddled with?"

"Maybe Dr. Vee still intends to provide a full report to the NIH. Whatever he intends, if this whole matter blows up, the less any of us knows about what may have gone on, the better."

"Well," Elise declared, "I think they all should be confronted. The clinical trials aren't over yet. There'll be a final report, so he can still give the NIH whatever data had been left out. We should confront him and demand that he give a full accounting in the final report. Otherwise we all could end up being part of some conspiracy."

"Maybe we ought to think this over for a few days before we do anything drastic," Mary said. "We don't know what he intends to do and there's still time. If we start giving Dr. Vee ultimatums, it's just going to upset him even more. He could have been killed taking the gun away from her. He's got enough to worry about just now. Maybe he's going to handle her special case some other way that we don't know about."

"My concern right now," Ellen said, "is the people who

work under us. I don't think pulling an ostrich number is going to protect anybody. We've got to get out of denial and face up to how serious this might get. And I'll tell you our number one priority right now. If Katherine Starr walks out of here before the Kristen problem is cleared up and gets the ear of someone in the media, then everybody who works here . . . Let's just say we mustn't allow that to happen. That's why we're having this meeting."

"Are you suggesting we should keep her . . . sedated?" Mary asked. "All her medications have to be approved by—"

"No sedative should be listed on her chart and I'm not telling you what to do, but use your imagination."

There was a moment of silence as the implications of the unspoken order settled in.

"And starting immediately, we need to hold a meeting of the staff on each floor and impress on them that the story of Katherine Starr must *never* leave this building. *Ever.* Remind everybody that that would be a serious violation of a staffer's original security agreement and would subject them to legal action the likes of which they can't even *begin* to imagine. And if somebody comes around asking questions about Kristen Starr, nobody here knows anything. We can say she was here because that's part of the record, and she is no longer here. End of statement. Beyond that, nobody knows zip."

This problem is far from over, Ellen told herself. *God only knows how it's going to end.*

Chapter 23

Wednesday, April 8
3:22 P.M.

As Stone Aimes stepped off the elevator on the sixth floor, his mind was running through his options. This phone call had to be about Winston Bartlett. He was going to step up the pressure. First there was the hellfire meeting in Jane's office, and now he'd seen a kidnapping. Maybe this was about *that*. Was Jane going to pass along a threat of legal action if that crime got reported?

The managing editor, Jay, had left a message with the third-floor receptionist, Rhonda, to be forwarded to Stone. Gist: he was urgently required in the office of their corporate counsel.

What does this tell me? he wondered. *That they're going to try to do something to me that could have legal ramifications?*

No, more likely it means that I'm going to be given an ultimatum, maybe an injunction. And Jane gets to deliver it with all the legal trimmings.

Still, he was determined to go on. *"You shall know the truth, and the truth shall make you free."* Right? Well, not *necessarily. But at the least, the truth could make a hell of a book. And with that came financial freedom, at least for a while. . . .*

The hallway felt desolate and ominous as he walked through the doorway that opened onto the cubicles. Jane Tully was down on the third floor, but he wanted to stop by his desk first and see if there'd been any further communications from Winston Bartlett. Possibly there still could be a deal in the making. . . .

The room itself was silent, no one meeting his eye. *Maybe,* he thought, *it's the middle of the afternoon and everybody's dozing off from a late lunch.* But when he got to his cubicle, he realized why he had suddenly become invisible. The top of his desk was bare, and there were three large cardboard boxes sitting on the gray carpet next to it.

"I think I get the picture," he said to the empty space.

It looked like Winston Bartlett had just provided him with a career decision. For a moment he felt his life passing before his eyes, but then all he could think about was the future. This was not just the end of a wage-slave era; it was the beginning of the next phase of his life.

He saw everyone still avoiding his eyes as he turned around and walked back to the elevator. How much did Jane know about this? She had to know everything, which was why Jay sent him to see her. She would have no qualms about giving someone the ax, including a former lover.

When he stepped off the elevator on the third floor, Rhonda looked at him as though he were a corpse.

"She's—"

"I know she's here. Don't bother buzzing her."

He strode purposefully down the hallway, realizing it was probably the last time he'd ever walk it, and pushed open Jane's door. She was on the phone and looked up startled, putting her hand over the mouthpiece.

"What—"

"Just came to say farewell. Jay told me to come see you. I

guess he was sure you'd want to be part of this important life moment."

"Stone, for God's sake"—she turned back to the phone—"let me . . . I'll call you tomorrow." She slammed down the receiver. "You have to know I had nothing to do with this. Bartlett got to the Family. I think it was one of those noblesse oblige kind of things. Old Money meets New Money and needs to placate it. The *Sentinel* is only marginally a profit-making enterprise and the last thing they need is a lot of shit from their landlord. He wanted you gone. And since your job was a small price for them to pay to ensure domestic tranquillity, do the math. Sorry, but that's how it had to be. For God's sake, Stone, why did you drive him to this?"

The ironic thing was, she was managing to look vaguely contrite—tugging at a lock of short hair. He wasn't sure how she had the brass. Apologies from the executioner are traditionally a tough sell.

"Let me tell you something, Jane. I already know more about Winston Bartlett than he wants. He had somebody kidnapped today before my very eyes. I even got slugged trying to stop it. So you can tell his lawyers to tell him he'd better back off. The people who did it were recognized and they work for him. If he wants to play tough, I could have a heartfelt exchange with somebody I know very well at the Sixth Precinct, and also with the tabloids, where I know a shitload of hungry columnists. Winston Bartlett could get real famous, real fast."

"Stone, you brought this on yourself. I tried to warn you, but you're hell-bent on your own destruction. You're your own worst enemy." She picked up her HP Jornada PDA and switched it off and sighed. "You never listened to me before and I don't expect you to do it now, but take some free advice anyway: try not to piss off important people. It's frequently a negative career move."

"Jane, you know John Kennedy once said, 'Sometimes party loyalty asks too much,' and I think that moment, for me, is now. From here on, I'm going to be doing what I need to do, not what Bartlett or Jay or whoever tells me to do. I guess that includes you too. There comes a time when I have to do what's in my heart."

She was finally focusing, looking at him strangely. "Stone, what did you just say? Bartlett had somebody *kidnapped?* Today? What on earth are you talking about?"

"Did I secure your vagrant attention? Good. Actually, it was less than an hour ago. There's no point in going into details, but I'm pretty sure she was the patient terminated from the clinical trials at the Dorian Institute that I had you ask Bartlett's lawyers about. I think there's the possibility that something really weird began happening to her out there in New Jersey. But I didn't get a chance to talk to her because they grabbed her and took off."

"Well, what do you *think* happened to her out there?"

"The only thing I've heard, and that's secondhand, is that she lost some part of her memory. She's even having trouble remembering her name."

"How do you know all this?" she asked, staring at him. "Were you—"

"I . . . know somebody who talked with her this morning. Just a few short exchanges on the phone. That's all I can tell you. They're doing something very powerful there at the institute, but in her case it seems to have gone horribly wrong. That's my best guess. So they dropped her from the clinical trials and gave her a new identity and stashed her someplace incommunicado. But she got away for a couple of hours, somehow, and managed to go back to her old apartment. In her case, it's a Village town house. But Bartlett nabbed her back."

"If you really believe all that, Stone, shouldn't you be worried for your own safety?" It was clear she was finally taking him seriously.

"Bartlett got me fired. That's probably enough for now. I don't know enough to be a threat to him. Yet."

"But what if you find out . . . whatever it is you're looking for? Then—"

"Then I'll know if medical miracles sometimes come with a strange price."

She was looking at him, pity entering her dark eyes. "What are you going to do for money? The child support you send to Amy?" She hesitated. "I'm so sorry about this, Stone. If you need a little help for the short term, I could—"

"*Don't* go there. I can take cash out on a couple of credit cards. And when I turn in the manuscript for the book, I'll get the other two-thirds of the advance. After that, I'm hoping I might get an actual career."

"Oh, Stone, I'm really sorry about this," she said with feeling. "Truly I am. I . . . I guess I still enjoy seeing you. Having you around. You're a mensch, you know that? Whatever your other failings, and God knows they're plenty, you were always kind. You're even kind to people who don't necessarily wish you well."

"Well, tell that to Amy if you ever get the chance. Sometimes she thinks her dad is the meanest guy alive. Particularly when I don't honor her every whim."

"You're a good father too." She sighed.

For Stone, this was always the moment that he wanted her back—when she let her guard down.

"Dammit, Stone, why couldn't we make a go of it?"

"We stopped having fun, Jane. That's all that happened. I started to bore you. Back then I didn't provide enough excitement, enough Sturm und Drang in your life."

"You weren't dull, Stone, but sometimes you could be maddeningly smug."

"That may be about to change. Now that I'm an unemployed freelancer. And I just ran into a blast from the past. Who knows what my life is about to be like?" He turned to leave. "By the way, give my best to Jay. Hopefully, he'll be the last managing editor I'll ever have to suck up to."

"Take care, Stone." She was getting up. "You can fight

this, you know. They had me write up some kind of bullshit breach-of-contract brief, in case you wouldn't go quietly. But it's full of holes. I know, since I deliberately wrote it that way."

"Hey, thanks anyway. It's not worth it. I'm not going to fight to keep a job I never liked all that much in the first place. Every time I wanted to do some serious journalism—like that piece about using the Internet to store everybody's medical records—Jay always found a reason not to run it. I've only got so much dignity to lose."

He turned and strode out of the office, deciding to forego any more farewells. Besides, he had better things to do. Get somebody from the mail room to carry the boxes—the shards of his erstwhile, so-called career—to the lobby, where he could get a cab. Take the files home, stash them, and then *get going*.

Chapter 24

"Hi," he said, walking through the door of Ally's downtown studio, CitiSpace. Jennifer had the desk at the front and she served as a makeshift receptionist. She looked up as he continued, "I don't have an appointment, but I'd love to see Ally Hampton. Any chance?"

"And you're . . . ?"

Just as he started to tell her, Ally emerged from her office/cubicle in the back and spotted him.

"Stone! What—"

"Bet you didn't think you'd see me again quite so soon."

She felt her pulse jump. No, she hadn't. She'd told him she was going down to the office, but she'd certainly had no idea (or hope) he'd just show up a couple of hours later.

Since she got back to the office she'd been in a struggle with her conscience over what to do about Kristen. Was there any good to be served by bringing in the police? At the time it had seemed pointless and it still felt that way. The whole matter was awfully anecdotal.

Worse, she didn't really feel she should talk it over with

Jennifer, which she would have loved to do. They supported each other in a lot of things, but this crazy story would just freak her out. Why do that?

The more troubling thing was, she'd started feeling tired and slightly dizzy. Now she was just hoping to stay focused long enough to last out the day. What, she wondered, was happening to her? It wasn't like a chest-tightening spell of angina—which, thankfully, she hadn't had for a couple of days now. No, this just felt like something was sapping her energy. She couldn't help the suspicion that this queasy condition was somehow related to her encounter with Dr. Van de Vliet's testy blond colleague Debra. While she was supposedly taking that blood sample, was she also doing something else?

"Welcome to my home away from home. You're right, I didn't expect—"

"CitiSpace," he interjected, seeming to try out the word as he looked around. She noticed that Jennifer and the others automatically assumed he was a new client of hers and were trying to look preoccupied. Jen, however, was giving him a furtive appraisal, running the numbers. He was a decent looker, actually kind of cute, and he seemed pleasant and outgoing. Not a bad start. That was what she would say the moment he was out of earshot.

"You like the name?"

"Not bad. Sort of a takeoff on Citibank?"

"My dad came up with it back before they copyrighted that name. Maybe they stole the idea from *us*." She was feeling cheered by the sight of him. Yes, it was good to have him back for a while, maybe longer. "But come on, let me introduce you around."

Which she did. Jennifer gave her a telepathic glance that said, *This guy looks like he might be worth the effort. What's the deal?*

Then they went to Ally's office, a high-walled cubicle in the back with a computer and a drafting table. She had a CAD program running.

"Sorry to just invite myself down like this," he said, "but I got off work early. Matter of fact, I just became a free-lancer. My office now consists of three cardboard boxes in my walk-up apartment."

"What do you mean? That phone page? Did—"

"Winston Bartlett owns the building where the *Sentinel*'s offices are. Seems he convinced the management that it would be in their interest if I were no longer employed there. I gather he thinks I know more than I actually do about what's going on out at the Dorian Institute, and I guess he thought getting me fired would slow me down. What it has done, however, is to give me even *more* incentive to surpass his most paranoid assumptions. Now I'm going to take him on full-time. I want to know *everything*."

"Oh, Stone, I'm so sorry." She wasn't buying his bravado. He didn't look like a guy who could last very long without a paycheck.

"I have to say he gave me fair warning. That meeting where he yelled at me. This little turn of the screw is not a total shock."

"But that whole thing with Kristen . . . I'll bet that's what sent him over the edge. I shouldn't have gotten you involved in that."

"This had nothing to do with you, believe me." He shrugged. "Besides, it gives me even more motivation to finish the book fast. And I'm also looking forward to spending some of my newfound quality time with you again, if you'll let me. In your favor, you've actually been inside the Dorian Institute, which is more than I can say."

She wasn't a big believer in the magic of a second time around—that would have to await further evidence—but having Stone back in her life was definitely helping on the psychological-support front.

"I'm thinking," he went on, "that maybe we should go back to Kristen's apartment and turn the place inside out. Do it right. We both let ourselves get distracted by the little matter of our other lives."

"Stone, I'm not sure"—she lowered her voice and sat down at her desk—"but I may be having a reaction to something one of Van de Vliet's research assistants did to me out at the institute this morning. I don't know. I'm just feeling sort of weak and . . . funny. I'm thinking maybe I should call out there and talk to him." She took a deep breath and seemed to be mounting her courage. "Or if he needs to see me, could you possibly drive for me? I'm not sure I'm up to it."

"Hey, I'd love a chance to get inside that place." Then his eyes grew uncertain. "But are you sure you want to go back, after what seems to have happened to Kristen? You might consider waiting till we find her and—"

"Ally, are you all right?" Jennifer was walking in, carrying a manila folder. "You look kind of queasy. Can I make you some tea or something?"

"Thanks but not now," she said. "I'm feeling weird, but maybe I should call out to the institute and see what Van de Vliet says."

"Just don't agree to do anything until we talk," Stone said.

"Don't worry," she said, reaching for the phone. The number for the Dorian Institute was now newly entered on her Palm Pilot and she called it. When the receptionist answered, she gave her name and asked for Dr. Van de Vliet.

"I was there this morning and gave a blood sample to Dr. Debra Connolly. I don't know if there's any connection, but I'm really feeling strange right now."

"What do you mean by 'strange'?" the woman asked. "Can you describe how you feel *exactly?* He's in the lab downstairs."

"That's just it. I'm not sure I need to actually see him. I'd just like to talk to him."

"He doesn't like to be disturbed. Unless it's something very important."

"It's important enough for me to try to call him," she declared, feeling herself abruptly seething. "I'm weak and dizzy. And my stomach is not in such great shape either."

"What did you have for lunch?"

My God, she realized she hadn't actually had any. After the disaster with Kristen, she'd been in such turmoil that she hadn't even thought about food.

On the other hand, she knew what food deprivation felt like. This was something else.

"I didn't have all that much lunch, but that's not the problem. Now will you please put me through?"

"Let me see what I can do," she said. "I'll call down and ask him. He might be able to see you."

Ally listened as the line went blank.

That was when she remembered she had some smoked turkey in the office fridge. Maybe a quick sandwich was called for.

While she waited, Stone was looking around the offices, taking everything in. Carrying the phone, she walked out and followed him. What, she wondered, was the place telling him about her? The meager furniture was low-slung and utilitarian, with lots of beige and dark brown. And there were several huge storage files for blueprints and designs. There also was a comfortable easy chair and lamp near a bookcase in the corner. On the table next to the chair were two British mysteries and a thick, recently written history of New York City.

He walked over and picked it up. It was 760 pages long.

"This your idea of reading for relaxation?" he asked, waving it at her. "I tried to get through it, but I only got up to the 1930s and then I started having a bout of acute sleeping sickness every time I picked it up."

"Hey, the history of this city is a mental hobby of mine. It's always renewing itself." She smiled. "Think about it. When developers convert industrial space to residential, we end up getting a lot of work."

Then she heard the phone crackle alive. It was Van de Vliet. "Alexa, what seems to be the problem?"

She told him.

"Then I think it's important that you come back out here as soon as you can. I can't say anything until I've seen you. This could be something that could affect your procedure."

"But what do you think—"

"I don't diagnose over the phone. I was about to go home, but I'll wait for you."

She listened as he clicked off.

"Shit."

"What did he say?" Stone asked.

"He said I've got to come out."

"Do you really want to do that?"

"I don't know. But what's the point of going to a doctor here? They wouldn't know—"

"Then at least let me drive you," Stone declared. "And I'll make damned sure they don't pull something funny."

"Ally," Jennifer said, "you look absolutely wiped out. Before you do anything, at least let me fix you a sandwich. I think there's some turkey in the fridge."

"I was thinking about that." She glanced at Stone. "You want something?"

"Sure. I'll have whatever you're having."

"Don't be so sure. Jen can tell you I take mayo and mustard both. I know it's weird, but that's the way I am."

"Then I'll give it a try. I want to get to know you all over again."

"Also, I hate to say it, but I think maybe I ought to swing by the apartment and get some things. Just in case."

She listened to her own voice and wondered, *Would whatever happened to Kristen happen to me too?*

Maybe, she thought, *what I really ought to take with me is a gun. Maybe Katherine Starr had the right idea.*

Jennifer finished the sandwiches and was wrapping them. "Ally, I'll go with you to your place and pick up Knickers. She can stay with me till you know what's going on."

"Thanks, Jen. I was hoping you'd volunteer." She knew she could have dropped a hint and made it happen anyway, but this was nicer.

She then went around and had a few last words. It felt like a good-bye and she didn't want it to. But it did.

Ten minutes later, while Stone waited in her double-parked car, she and Jennifer took the elevator up to her Barrow Street apartment.

"Where did you find that man?" Jennifer asked as soon as they got on. "He seems nice. Interesting. He's not a client, is he? And, pardon me for noticing, no wedding ring."

"He actually found me," Ally declared, punching her floor. "It's a long story, but he was a guy I was deeply in love with for about fifteen minutes back around college. The old flame I told you about, remember? Then we started getting on each other's nerves. We're both going easy on the personal details right now, but I've got a hunch he's got nobody else percolating. Which, incidentally, goes for me too, or hadn't you noticed."

They stepped off the elevator and she unlocked the door to her apartment. Knickers exploded with delight.

"Hi, baby." She reached down and ruffled the sheepdog's ears.

"I really love her," Jennifer said as she reached down to pet her too.

Knickers began a dance of joy, then ran to search for her rubber ball behind the couch, hoping for a game of fetch with Jennifer.

"By the way, I can't tell you how I appreciate your taking her. She's going to love being at your place awhile. I'm sure she gets bored crazy being here all the time. I probably should get a puppy or something to keep her company, but then she'd be jealous. And I'm not about to get a stupid cat."

"She loves me because she knows I love her," Jennifer said. "I always play with her when you bring her into the office. At least I think she loves me. This may turn out to be the test."

Ally headed into the bedroom, opened a drawer, and took out some black sweatshirts. Those and black jeans were her favorite things to wear around the house. She slept in a T-shirt and panties, so it wasn't hard to put together her evening ensemble. Besides, if something went wrong with the experimental stem cell procedure, it wouldn't matter a damn *what* she was wearing.

She threw the clothes into a blue gym bag and headed for the bathroom to fetch some toiletries. By the time she got back to the living room, Jennifer had a measuring cup and was shoveling Science Diet into a large plastic bag. . . .

They delivered Jen and Knickers back to the office. After she gave them both a farewell hug, she came around and slipped into the Toyota's driver's seat, moving Stone across.

"I'm actually feeling better now, so I'll drive as long as I can. And by the way, I'm famished. How about that turkey sandwich?"

"Thought you'd never remember."

Five minutes later, they were headed up the West Side, with Ally at the wheel. She checked the gas and was relieved to see that she still had two-thirds of a tank. Stone was leaning back in the seat looking at her.

"You know, it's easy for me to say, but trying the stem cell procedure on your heart is probably the right thing for you to do. Still, though, it makes me nervous. If there's a medical glitch of some kind, then . . . I mean, what the hell is going on with Kristen?"

"I'm going to confront him about that," she said. "I damned well want some answers *before* I just turn myself over to him."

After they crossed the George Washington Bridge, she began feeling slightly better. *Maybe,* she thought, *whatever it is is going to pass.* As they headed north up the tree-shrouded highway, she decided to ask him a question that had been nagging at her mind.

"Stone, I know you hate to have these talks, but something about you doesn't quite compute for me right now. There's a kind of unnatural intensity about your pursuit of Winston Bartlett and his stem cell work. And the same goes for his reaction to you. Way back when, I never really thought

I knew you, and it's still true. I mean, is this all just about a book on stem cell technology? Or is it something more?"

The question was followed by a long moment of silence as he looked away, into the forest, and appeared to wrestle with his thoughts.

"You're very intuitive, Ally," he said at last. "Maybe I didn't consciously set out to write about stem cells just because I knew Bartlett's Gerex Corporation was a leader in the field. But writing about stem cells automatically meant that I'd have to get close to him at some point. So was it an unconscious choice? If it was, then I wouldn't be aware of it, would I?"

"But why would you want to get close to Winston Bartlett?"

"I guess that was your original question, right?"

"Pretty much."

"There are things about my past that I never told you. I could never decide exactly how to go about it. And truthfully, right now doesn't seem exactly the right moment either. You've got enough on your mind."

"Want to give me a hint?" What could he mean? she wondered. It was clear that Stone Aimes and Winston Bartlett had some kind of holy war going on between them.

"I'll tell you someday soon. But I want us both sitting down in a safe place when I do. It's going to be hard." He looked away again. "Someday soon I've got to tell my daughter, Amy, too. Maybe telling you would be a practice drill."

"So what I'm learning is that I'm not crazy. This is about more than it's about?" She sighed. "Nobody's leveling with me. With Van de Vliet, I have to worry whether he's telling me the truth every time he opens his mouth. And now you're holding out. It's like that joke about feeling like a mushroom. Everybody keeps me in the dark and feeds me bullshit." She was slowing down, pulling into an open space by the roadside. "Stone, I'm feeling a little dizzy. Maybe it's this conversation, but I think it's time you took the wheel for a while."

"Hey, don't pass out on me now," he said, snapping into the moment. "I'm not sure I could actually find this place without your help."

"Don't worry," she said, bringing the car to a stop. "I'm all right. I'm just a little worried about my reflexes."

He got out and walked around, while she hoisted herself over into the other side.

The evening commute had begun in earnest, so there was a lot more traffic than there had been that morning. But Stone turned out to be an aggressive driver, right on the edge, as though he were racing the clock. She gave him directions and then closed her eyes, hoping to rest. But all she could think about was Stone's refusal to tell her about something that loomed very large in his life.

"Tell me if I'm bothering you and I'll shut up," he interjected after a few minutes, "but—not to change the subject— did you actually give anybody permission to stick a needle in you this morning? I mean, are you sure you understood what was going on at the time?"

She shifted and opened her eyes, looking straight ahead.

"Truthfully, I assumed I was just giving a blood sample. That's what his assistant said and I took her at her word. I hate needles and I never actually watch when I give blood. This morning I just sort of went along with what was happening. And nothing seemed particularly ominous till Katherine Starr showed up and started blasting away."

"Well," he said, "do your best to get some rest and I'll try to get you there as soon as legally possible."

She stared out the window a moment before closing her eyes again. Around them the encroaching greenery of northern New Jersey felt like an ancient forest where magical things could happen. Out here in the forest, was there a magician who had the power literally to save her life?

And what about Stone? Setting aside the troubling fact that he was harboring some mysterious connection to Winston Bartlett—and that was hard to set aside—she was feeling a sense of togetherness with him that brought back a lot of positive memories. Which was bizarre, because she knew so little about what kind of man he'd become. If people are worth their salt, they change a lot in their late twenties and early thirties. So what was he really like now? What did he love? What did he hate? What were his priorities? Did he believe in the Golden Rule?

Mulling over all this, she slowly drifted away. . . .

Dusk was approaching by the time he pulled to a stop at the gated entrance of the Dorian Institute. Along the way he'd begun getting a sense that they were being followed by a dark-colored Lincoln Town Car, but it could have been his imagination. And he hadn't seen it for the past fifteen minutes, after he pulled onto the leafy lakeside drive leading to the institute.

"Hey, we're here, Ally. Rise and shine. How're you feeling?"

There was no response when he touched her.

Chapter 25

"Jesus, Ally, are you all right?" He leaned over and shook her.

Finally she jumped, and then her eyelids fluttered open.

"Where . . . ?" She looked around.

"The sign says this is it. The institute."

"Oh shit, Stone, I'm feeling really strange," she said after a moment of getting her bearings. "Everything around me seems like it's moving. It's as though the space I'm in has an extra dimension. I don't know . . . maybe it was totally stupid to come back out here. Maybe I should have just gone to my doctor in the city."

"Hey, you've got a seriously deficient sense of timing. We're here now. I've been breaking the speed limit for the last half hour."

"I know. Shit. I really don't know what to do. I don't trust anybody."

"Well, you could start by trusting me. I'm along to try to make sure nothing bad happens." He paused. "So what do we do?"

A brass plaque on a redbrick pillar beside the gate bore a two-inch-high inscription, THE DORIAN INSTITUTE, and just below it was an intercom. She stared at it for a moment, then said, "There, give it a buzz. I think there's a video camera around here somewhere. Last time I was here, they knew I'd arrived."

He reached out and touched a black button.

"Yes," came back a quick voice. She recognized it as belonging to the woman she'd spoken to on the phone.

"It's Alexa Hampton." She leaned over. "We talked—"

"Yes, I know, Ms. Hampton. He's been waiting for you."

A buzzer sounded and the two wrought-iron gates slid back, welcoming them. As they drove down the tree-lined road, an elegant three-story redbrick structure with white Doric columns across the front slowly came into view.

"From here, it's pretty classy-looking," Stone declared, sizing it up. "I know his big manufacturing-and-research campus is right down the road. But still, it sure feels godforsaken and lost out here in the middle of these pines. It's like the place is hiding from the world."

"Where better to do secret medical research," she said. "If you want to keep everything proprietary, then the isolation gives you a big jump on security."

She directed him to the side parking lot, where she'd left her car that morning.

"Stone, here's what we'll tell them. You're next of kin, a cousin on my mother's side."

"Works for me," he declared. "I'm beginning to feel part of the family anyway." He pocketed the car keys and helped her out of the Toyota.

As they headed up the wide steps, past the white columns, Ally felt a wave of nausea sweep through her. She reached out and took Stone's arm and sank against him.

"I'm . . . I'm not feeling at all well. Please let me hold—"

No sooner had she said it than the front door opened and two nurses appeared, their hair backlit from the glow of the reception area. She recognized one as Ellen O'Hara.

"Here, dear, let us help you," she said as she strode toward them. She was dressed in white and her eyes were flooded with concern. Ally looked through the doorway to see a waiting wheelchair.

"That's fast," Stone said. "Looks like they were ready for you."

My God, she thought, *did they already know what kind of shape I'd be in? What else do they know? Surely Van de Vliet has heard by now that I'm aware of Kristen.*

Then she saw him standing behind the nurses.

"Alexa, we need to get you downstairs as soon as possible." He was coming forward to help her settle into the wheelchair. He appeared to take no notice of Stone Aimes.

"I'm just feeling a little dizzy."

He smiled reassuringly. "There's always a small percentage chance that there may be side effects from the initial inoculation."

Huh?

"What 'initial inoculation'?" She bolted upright in the wheelchair. "I was just supposed to be giving blood."

"I thought Debra explained," he said, appearing confused. "There's always an initial . . . antibiotic dosage, just as a prophylactic." He shook his head in self-blame. "I should have insisted you stay here, but after that . . . incident this morning I was so disoriented I let you talk me out of it. You may be having a reaction to the antibiotic, but it can't be all that serious. I didn't see anything about side effects in your file. We just have to get you horizontal for a while. Everything's going to be all right. In fact, this might be a positive development. With you here now, we can begin fine-tuning your procedure immediately."

"Dr. Van de Vliet, this is my cousin Stone. He drove me here and I'd—"

"I'd really like to stay," Stone said, reaching to shake Van de Vliet's hand. "It would mean a lot to both of us. To the whole family."

"Family?" Van de Vliet declared. Ally noticed that he was

examining Stone with narrowed eyes and seemed to be debating something with himself. "Well, we'll see." Then he turned back to her. "The first thing is to make sure your . . . situation is stabilized. I actually think a good night's rest might do the trick. But I need to run a quick blood test downstairs."

She felt her dizziness coming and going, but she was determined to stay awake and in control of what was being done to her.

"By the way, I was wondering how is Katherine Starr doing?"

His eyes grew somber.

"She's a very lucky woman, considering. We've given her some coagulants and stitched her up."

"Are you going to press charges?"

He looked at her strangely. "Do you think we should?"

"I guess it's none of my business." *Of course you won't,* she told herself. *The Kristen matter will not stand the ordinary light of day, let alone a police investigation.*

"Maybe it's time to let her daughter come and see her."

"I looked at that letter," he said with a matter-of-fact tone. "I suspect it's a hoax. And a very cruel one at that."

"I don't think so. I talked to her today. The woman formerly known as Kristen. On the phone." She stared at him. "I really think it's time I learned more about what happened to her here at the institute. All I could really find out was that she thinks she's experienced some pretty dramatic memory loss."

He looked as though this information was new to him. He also looked startled. "You *spoke* to her? What . . . did she say? Is she all right?"

"No, she's not all right." *Don't mention the kidnapping,* she told herself. *Play dumb and see how he behaves.* "I want to know what happened to her when she was here."

He paused, then took a deep breath. "I told you everything I know this morning. She was a very troubled young person. Her treatment seemed to be going well, but she couldn't accept that. She began to believe there was some kind of conspiracy against her. In a word, she became completely paranoid."

Well, Ally thought, *there's "paranoid" and then there are times when somebody really is out to get you. So which was it in Kristen's case?*

She glanced over at Stone, who appeared to be trying to act as though he didn't know what on earth she was talking about. But she could see him efficiently taking mental notes.

"When you can't remember who you are," she said, turning back to Van de Vliet, "and then someone who *does* know who you are gives you a new, fake identity, I think it's enough to justify paranoia."

He was rolling the wheelchair toward the elevator but abruptly paused.

"Is that what she's claiming? Good God. I told you she was paranoid and that should demonstrate it better than anything. Letting her discharge herself and leave the program, to go off unsupervised, was a truly bad idea, but nothing short of physical restraint could have stopped her."

"And do you have any idea where she is now?" Ally asked.

"I told you . . . Look, if I knew her whereabouts, don't you think I'd do everything I could to contact her, find out how she is?"

"Right."

She reached out and took Stone's hand as they all moved onto the elevator. She could sense his excitement at finally being inside the Dorian Institute, but at that moment her concentration was drifting and she felt as though she were slowly beginning to drown in a sea of white.

"Stone, please don't leave me. Don't let me out of your sight. Something funny is happening and I don't know what it is."

Van de Vliet bent over. "Alexa, look at me. I want to see your eyes. I think they may be dilating." He waved a hand across her face. "Can you see me?"

"It's the fluorescent lights," she mumbled. "There's too

much glare. Could someone please turn them down? I think that's what's wrong. They're giving me a headache."

"Ally," Stone said, "the lights are not very bright in here. We're going down in an elevator. There aren't any fluorescents."

Then the elevator chimed and the door opened. They were in the basement now, where the research lab and the office and the examination rooms were. Debra, wearing a white lab coat, was standing there silently looking at her.

Now there really were fluorescent lights, and she turned away and tried to shield her eyes.

"God, turn them off. It's so painful. It's like they're shining into the back of my skull."

"She's started hallucinating," Van de Vliet whispered to Debra. "I've got to draw blood for a test and give her an injection. We need a gurney now. We've got to take her down to the IC. Her condition is progressing much more rapidly than I expected."

"Ally, is this what you want?" Stone demanded. "You don't have to do this."

Her breath was coming in rapid pulses now and she was cringing from the light even as she struggled to rise out of the wheelchair.

"I want . . . to get . . . "

She managed to pull herself onto her feet, but then she sagged and collapsed against Stone as he pulled her to him.

As one of the nurses grabbed the newly arrived gurney and pulled it over, Van de Vliet and Ellen O'Hara seized her out of Stone's arms and lifted her onto it.

"You'll have to leave now," Van de Vliet said to Stone. "I'm sorry."

"I'm not going anywhere. I promised her I'd stay by her side and, by God, I intend to do just that."

"I'll determine what's best for her," he replied. "Please go up to the reception area. I'll let you know how she is."

"I'm not leaving."

"Then I'll call our security and have you removed from the premises."

"Stone," Ally said, her eyelids flickering, "it's okay. I want you to tell my mother I'm here. She's in room two-thirteen, upstairs, the last time I saw her."

"You've got it. Don't worry. I'll take care of everything."

She heard him saying that, but then she thought she heard another voice inside her head begging him not to leave. It was the last thought she had before the world went entirely white.

Wednesday, April 8
7:39 P.M.

Ellen O'Hara watched the scene with mounting dismay. She'd overheard Dr. Van de Vliet talking to Debbie about the procedure scheduled for Alexa Hampton. Then she'd checked the schedule that had been put into the database. It turned out that Alexa Hampton had *two* procedures scheduled.

The troubling part was, one was identical to the procedure that had been performed on Kristen Starr several months back, or at least so it seemed. And *that* had resulted in what she'd just overheard Debra call "the Syndrome." By whatever name, it had produced some horrible side effects. Why on earth were they now repeating that with this new patient? Hadn't they learned *anything?*

Karl Van de Vliet—or whoever ordered this idiotic travesty—was about to put the job of every person at the Dorian Institute at risk. If whatever happened to Kristen was replicated, and the word got out, it was going to be the end for everyone who worked here.

Most troubling of all, what about Ms. Hampton, who seemed like such a nice person? Did she agree to that experimental procedure? If she knew what had happened to Kristen Starr, surely she wouldn't have.

Ellen O'Hara didn't know how she could stop Dr. Vee from doing what he appeared to be planning to do. The procedure was going to be performed *in* the laboratory.

The only way she could think of to stop it was to try to warn Ms. Hampton that what they were about to do was extremely dangerous. But how? Her chart in the database said they were going to keep her quarantined down in the subbasement. That was specified.

On top of all this, Kenji Noda had brought in some unidentified patient this afternoon, wheeled in while strapped to a gurney, and they had taken that patient to the subbasement. Noda was still down there, and Winston Bartlett had come in and gone down also. The unholy pair. And now they'd be holding Alexa Hampton down there too.

Was it possible to get past them and warn her?

She was determined to find a way.

Chapter 26

Stone was deeply troubled as he entered the elevator to return to the lobby. He had promised Ally he'd stay by her side and now he'd let her down. Was this the best he could do? He felt like he had to earn the right to be back in her life, but he seemed to be making a slow start.

But he wasn't about to leave the premises until he knew she was okay.

Hoping for the best, he reminded himself that although Van de Vliet was wound pretty tight, he clearly was more than competent. The problem was, he'd just offered a transparent song and dance when Ally asked him about Kristen. Now it was easy to understand why she'd said she didn't know whether to believe a word he said. But that didn't necessarily preclude him being a Nobel Prize–quality medical genius.

In any case, to finally be inside the Dorian Institute was a major coup in his own quest. Up until now, Bartlett's press heavies at BMD had turned back his every attempt to get a firsthand look at the institute or an interview with Karl Van de Vliet. Now, at last, he'd actually seen the man.

So . . . after he visited with Ally's mother upstairs—which ought to be interesting, an actual patient interview—he was going to try to keep a low profile and scout the place. Maybe he could finally talk his way into an interview with the celebrated Van de Vliet himself, or at least with some of his research staff. This was definitely the break he'd been waiting for. Finally he'd have some actual reporting to put in the book.

When he stepped off the elevator, he noticed that the uniformed security guard looked him over suspiciously. He and Alexa had been waved through the metal detector when they came in, owing to the urgency of her condition. Now he felt as though the guard, a tall, middle-aged black guy with thinning hair, was trying to frisk him with his penetrating eyes.

Stone smiled and nodded toward him and headed for the desk in the middle of the reception area. Around him a number of patients were ambling through the lobby, returning from a room in the back that was identified as DINING HALL. Some were wearing blue gowns, and most appeared to be in their sixties and seventies. But they all were sprightly and animated as they walked along chatting. Somehow the place felt more like a vacation spa than a clinic. He'd like nothing better than to sit them all down right this minute for an interview. "How has the Gerex stem cell procedure affected your condition? Have you had any side effects?" But to do that without official permission would undoubtedly get him evicted on the spot.

He took a deep breath and walked over to the reception desk.

"Hi."

The woman looked up. She was the same middle-aged Hispanic nurse with bold eye makeup who was there when they came in. "Hi. How's your friend feeling?"

"Actually, she's my cousin, and I don't know how she's

doing because they kicked . . . sent me up here. But she gave me a mission to keep me occupied."

"Well," the woman declared with a smile, "I'm sure she'll be fine. Dr. Van de Vliet is a miracle worker."

"So everyone says." He smiled back. "My cousin asked me to look in on her mother. Nina Hampton. She is, or was, in two-thirteen."

"Mrs. Hampton is your aunt?"

"Uh, yeah, right." *Whoops. Get this act together.* "Funny, but I always just think of her as my cousin Ally's mother. My own weird way to look at it, I guess. I don't really know her all that well."

Things are not getting off to a great start, he told himself. *I don't even believe me.*

"Visits to patients, except by those on a preestablished list, require a photo ID."

"Well, let's get started." He reached for his wallet and withdrew a driver's license. He made sure his press card was well out of sight.

Keep this dumb and innocent as long as possible, he told himself.

She glanced at the driver's license, then pointed to the sign-in sheet. "Just sign your name and print it and then also print your relationship to the patient. I have to say this is unusual. There are regular visiting hours and guests are normally approved in advance by Mrs. Young, who's in charge of security. But you came in under extraordinary circumstances, with Ms. Hampton, and you're already here, so I don't see the harm."

He signed himself in as quickly as possible.

"Mrs. Hampton is still in room two-thirteen."

"I'll show myself up."

"Please keep it under fifteen minutes. We don't want to tire her out. You understand."

"Thanks. I really appreciate this. My cousin Ally likes to get an update on"—he realized he had momentarily blocked her mother's name—"her mom as often as possible."

He headed for the elevator, trying to contain his excitement. The idea was to keep this as below the radar as possible. Was he about to crack the wall of secrecy that Winston Bartlett had erected around Karl Van de Vliet and the Gerex Corporation?

Just as the elevator door was closing, he saw a figure emerge through the security entryway. The man clicked a memory-moment from somewhere in the far-distant past, but he couldn't place him. As best he could tell, the guy didn't see him.

Just keep moving. Don't look back.

As he stepped off the elevator onto the second floor, the pale marble floors were lit by small bulbs along the walls. This was a place where medical miracles were supposedly being made to happen and yet it was lit only with a ghostly half-light. The sounds of televisions emanated from several of the rooms.

The nurse's station at the end of the hall was empty, which added to the sense of a surreptitious undertaking.

He walked quickly to room 213 and tapped lightly on the door. When he heard a bold "Yes?" from inside, he opened it and entered.

He hadn't seen Nina Hampton in almost two decades, but she looked pretty much the way he remembered her. Her hair was surely dyed now, but her face was as square and strong as ever. She was reading a paperback book with a title that appeared to be Spanish. She looked up and stared at him for a moment, adjusting her glasses.

"Hello, Stone. That is you, isn't it? You're older but you're still a hell of a looker. How did you get in here? Is Ally here too? I haven't seen her since this morning."

"Mrs. Hampton, don't tell me you recognize me."

"Of course I do. When you and Ally were . . . going out, I confess I didn't hold out much hope that you'd ever amount to anything, but I've been a fan of your columns for a long time. Though it took me a while to put it together that that newspaper writer I liked so much was *you,* the man I didn't think was ambitious enough for my daughter." She appraised him a moment. "Does this mean you two are together again?"

Good question, he thought. *And I don't have a clue about the answer.*

"I wish I knew. Why don't you ask *her* the next time you see her?" He smiled and walked over. "She wanted me to come up and see how you're doing."

"Come up? Is she here now? When she came to say good-bye this morning, I got the impression that she wanted both of us just to get out of here. But I told her that was silly. I'm already feeling so much better."

"Really. Well, she's downstairs now and she'll be happy to hear that." He walked over and smiled. "Mrs. Hampton, I came along with her this time to keep an eye on her. Hope you don't mind."

"Of course not."

"And there's another reason I'm here. I want to warn you. I'm writing a book about stem cell procedures and anything you say to me about your treatment could well end up in it. So don't tell me anything you don't want everybody to hear about."

"Are you really writing a book about Dr. Vee?" She beamed. "That's wonderful! He's a saint. Everyone here says so. He deserves a special place in heaven."

This is great, Stone thought. *I've got my own Deep Throat.*

"Then could I ask you what you know about what he did and how you think you've improved."

"I don't really understand what he's doing, but I do know what is happening to me. It's as though my mind was full of fog a lot of the time, but now there's a wind that's blowing it away."

"And how—"

A shaft of light from the hallway pierced across the room as the door opened. Stone turned to see the man he'd first noticed in the lobby. The man walked past him and marched over to the bed.

"Hi, how're you feeling?"

"I'm touched." Her visage immediately hardened. "It's thoughtful of you to finally come by and favor your mother with a visit."

That's *who he is,* Stone finally realized. *Ally's kid brother.*

In his few dealings with the wiseass brat that Ally used to rant about—what was the kid's name . . . right, Grant—he'd found him devious and pompous. He was particularly deft at cutting ethical corners and using other people any way he could.

"Stone," Nina Hampton said, gesturing toward Grant, "this is—"

"I know exactly who he is," Grant said, turning around to face Stone. "W.B. has put out an all-points alert for you, pal. You've got a hell of a nerve weaseling your way in here. But not to worry. You won't be here long."

"I won't have you talking that way in my presence, young man," Nina declared. "Whatever else you may be, I thought I'd raised you to have a civil tongue in your head."

Grant replied without taking his eyes off Stone. "He lied to the front desk, Nina. He signed in as Ally's cousin. And that twit-brain down there let him get away with it. He got up here by using a lie. Now what does that tell you about him?"

"It tells me he's creative. This man came with your sister. He's helping take care of her, which is more than can be said about her own brother."

"This creep is a newspaper reporter, Nina. He's here to spy. He's planning to do a hatchet job on the Gerex Corporation, and Mr. Bartlett has expressly forbidden anyone to speak to him."

"I'm not in your corporation, Son, so I guess it's all right for me then."

"You signed a secrecy agreement with Gerex when you entered the clinical trials. Now maybe you don't remember it, but you did." He turned to Stone. "Nice try, amigo. Now come on, let's go."

"You know, Grant, I remember you," Stone said. "Not very nice recollections."

"And I remember you too, pal. You were that screwed-up journalism student Ally dated for a while. Thank God she got rid of you."

"Sounds like we were awash in mutual admiration," Stone said.

"Tell you what. Are we gonna continue this touching reunion outside, or do I have to call for security and take your trespassing ass out of here in handcuffs? It's entirely up to you."

"Grant, I see no reason why I can't talk to him if I want," Nina interjected. "Who I talk to or what I say is nobody's business but mine."

"You wouldn't be here if it weren't for me," Grant declared. "So I have a little say-so too." He turned back. "Come on, pal. We're gone."

I'm screwed, Stone told himself. *But what about Ally? If I get kicked out, I'll really be leaving her completely defenseless.*

"Mrs. Hampton, thank you for letting me check up on you," he said quietly. "Alexa is downstairs. I think her procedure is starting whether she's ready for it or not. You seem very alert, and if I were you, I'd try to monitor her . . . progress as closely as you can."

"Don't worry," Grant said. *"I'll* be keeping close tabs on her. And now let's go."

With no option short of killing him on the spot, Stone followed along, seething. *This little creep obviously works for Winston Bartlett*—he wished Ally had warned him about that. Grant was bound to have shown up at some point.

They went down the marble staircase and Grant signaled the security man, who leaped up and opened the front door for them. *He probably got a tongue-lashing from Grant,* Stone told himself.

As they stepped onto the wide porch, dusk all around them, Grant turned and headed toward the south end and a long wooden bench.

"Want to tell me what the hell's going on?" he said, gesturing toward the bench and then sitting down. "W.B. said you claimed to be writing a book about this project. If that's true, then it's a seriously bad idea. You have no idea what he's capable of if he gets pissed."

"Oh, I think I'm getting a rough idea, but I'm a little pissed too," Stone said, remaining standing. "For example, there's the matter of Kristen Starr. You see, she was terminated from the clinical trials approximately three months back. So I was wondering, when is Van de Vliet planning to report her current condition to the NIH?"

"I don't know what you're talking about." His startled voice said otherwise.

"Oh, I think you do. I saw her today." Then he decided to bluff. "She had an interesting tale to tell. She—"

"Shit, you interviewed Kristy? Aw, man, don't believe anything she . . ." He hesitated. "What did she say about W.B.?"

"Tell you what. We'll play twenty questions. You tell me what you think she said and I'll tell you if you're right or not."

"Hey," Grant declared, his eyes intense, "she *wanted* to do it, man. Nobody put a gun to her head or anything. She was freaking out after she got sacked. She thought Dr. Vee could fix her skin and she couldn't wait to try it."

"You mean—"

"The Beta. Take a look at Van de Vliet. He's a walking testimonial. No side effects for him, so why not? The worst thing that could happen would be nothing, right? So she figured, what did she have to lose? Well, now we all know."

"The Beta? That's . . . ?"

"You fucker." Grant bounded to his feet. "You don't know the first thing about what I'm talking about, do you? How the fuck did you find out about Kristen anyway?"

"I told you I spoke to her." Well, it was almost true. He'd yelled at her. "She's very . . . unsettled just now. But I guess you know that."

"Hey, she was always fucked-up, but W.B. liked all the energy behind that. He looked right past the eating disorders and the coke and the late-night clubs she went to all the time. But, man, if you think *she's* spaced, try her mother. That crazy—"

"Grant, why not level with me? There's something very wrong going on here. I'm in the business of telling the truth, and I've got a keen nose for medical horse-pucky. So how about coming clean? If it's good, why not, and if it's bad, it's going to come out eventually anyway. Hasn't Winston Bartlett learned anything from all the screwups in Washington? It's not the situation—it's the *cover-up.*"

"Well, I don't know what Kristy did or didn't tell you, so we're not going in that direction. I heard about her little trip downtown this morning. I assume that's probably when you saw her, if in fact you actually did. Right now she's being taken care of, for her own good."

" 'Being taken care of'? So happens I had a close encounter with a couple of her caregivers today. They're taking care of her, all right."

"Look, she used to be W.B.'s girlfriend, okay? He's still very concerned about her. Everybody's really sorry about her situation, but nobody saw it coming. And now he's got some problems of his own."

"You seem to be pretty heavily involved with Winston Bartlett's personal problems."

"Yeah, well, the man's been like a father to me. And I think he feels that way too, since he doesn't have a son of his own."

Stone let the taunt just hang in the air for a moment. He mainly just wanted to slug the smug little bastard.

"You don't know how little you know, about him or about anything. Someday I may take the trouble to straighten you out. But right now you're not worth the effort. All I care about at the moment is what's going to happen to Ally."

"Everybody cares what happens to her. A lot depends on it. Dr. Vee thinks she's our best shot."

"What . . . what the *hell* are you talking about?" Stone stared at him through the twilight. *"What* depends on it?"

"Guess you're not as smart as you think you are." He was up and heading for the parking lot. "Come on, pal. Time to hit the road. I'm gonna tuck you in. This conversation is terminated. And it never happened anyway. I'll have them unlock the gates for you."

Chapter 27

Wednesday, April 8
8:25 P.M.

Alexa watches as the prow of their forty-one-foot Morgan, two-masted, cuts silently through a placid sea. She vaguely remembers the vessel. It was teak and magnificent. Steve had chartered it, bare-boat, for two weeks and taken them cruising through the Bahamas. By the end of that time, she felt they could have sailed it around the world.

But that was six years ago, when he was still very much alive. Now the boat feels like a magical carpet taking them someplace together, effortlessly. The genoa, the mainsail, and the mizzen are all full and blossoming outward even though there's no wind. She's at the helm, holding a course toward something white on the horizon, and Steve is with her. He's alive again and he's with her. She feels her body suffused with joy. Then she looks at the reflection of herself in his sunglasses and realizes she's a little girl, still a child. This is all a dream, she realizes, a cruel dream. Then she looks again at the horizon, the blazing white light, and senses that it represents the future. Their destiny.

Now the sea around them, which had been placid, starts

to roil. The wheel is becoming harder to control, and the sun is starting to burn her. In its pitiless glare she feels herself beginning to age rapidly. She glances at Steve and she can see his skin starting to shrivel. She senses he is dying, right there before her eyes, but her hands feel glued to the wheel and she can't let go to try to help him.

Now the sea is growing ever more choppy and the white symbol on the horizon has begun to bob in and out of view. Sometimes she can see the "future" and sometimes she can't. Waves are crashing over the sides, inundating the deck, and she feels anxious about what lies up ahead. Will they ever get there, and if they do, will she want what she finds? Even more important now, will Steve still be with her?

As the waves pound against them both, oddly she doesn't feel wet. Instead, what she feels is a stab of muted pain in her upper chest, pain she knows would be searing if she were to experience its full impact. She looks down to see that the wheel she thought she was holding is gone, and her chest is pierced by the steel mechanism to which it was attached. It has gone all the way through her.

Next a huge wave comes straight over the bow and slams against her and Steve. Her body convulses with pain and she senses that he is being swept overboard, directly off the stern. She screams at him to hold on, but then he is gone, lost in the dark sea.

Now the boat itself is starting to disintegrate, as both masts tip backwards, then come crashing down. Up ahead, the white light that is the future is growing ever more flame-like. It is part of a shoreline she is trying to reach, but now she doesn't think she's going to get there. Around her, the boat's lines and cleats are being swept into the pounding sea.

In moments the boat has disappeared, but she continues on, propelled by some force she cannot see, until she finally crashes onto the rocky shore.

It is a chiaroscuro landscape of blacks and whites. Oddly, Stone Aimes has appeared and is holding her hand as they make their way along the barren seascape, where everything

is hazy and trapped in fog. She thinks she sees figures lurking in the mist around them but can't make out who they are.
Everything is static and frozen in place, like the images of
motion on the Grecian urn caught for eternity.

She reaches out to touch Stone and her hand passes
right through. That's when she realizes the white light and
this rocky shoreline represent the other side. *Is this what
death feels like?* she wonders. *Like the white tunnel drawing you in?*

But then she has another thought. Maybe she isn't dead at
all. Maybe she is in a third place, somewhere suspended between life and death. She looks again at Stone and tells herself they're not dead, they're in some kind of time machine.
This voyage is about time.

Now time has begun to flow around her like a river. Days,
weeks, months, years, they all course by. But she knows it is
a chimera. Nothing can make time go faster or slower.

Then the bright lights are gone and she feels alone. Very
alone.

But she isn't. She hears voices around her, drifting, echoing, and she tries to understand what they are saying.

"She's stabilized. We're past the critical phase."

"Do you want to bring her up now?"

"Not yet. We still don't know how it's going to go."

There was a pause, and then a male voice.

"This was the Beta too, wasn't it, Karl?" Another pause.
"Well, wasn't it? The injections. That's the first time since . . ."

Again the voices drift off. She listens, not sure what she
is hearing. She tries to process the word "beta" but makes no
headway. In computer slang, "beta" means a program that is
still being tested. Then she remembers hearing the word just
hours earlier. She had been talking to some woman. But she
can't remember who. . . .

"I changed the procedure this time," comes a voice. "I injected the special Beta enzyme separately from the activated
stem cells. Whatever happens will happen at the enzyme's
own pace now. And I kept the dosage as low as I could. We'll

be monitoring her telomerase levels throughout the day. If there's no rejection, we will be past the first phase."

"Is the dosage the only difference from before?" comes the other, accusing voice.

"At this point, David, manipulating the Beta is an art, not a science. I'm just attempting to create antigens, the way a smallpox vaccination does. Then we'll try to harvest them. This is not really a full-scale Beta procedure. I don't plan to do that ever again."

There was another long silence.

"That man who was here with her. Her cousin, did he say? I saw no family resemblance, but he seemed very upset."

"That's why I had him sent upstairs. I think he's the reporter W.B. was so concerned about. Anyway, he's gone."

Stone. She realizes that's who they're talking about. And now he's gone. She's on her own.

Next the voices drift away for a time, into some echo space that mutes them. Finally, though, they come back.

"This should be adequate for another four hours. After that, you'll need a glucose IV to keep her hydrated."

"I've already put it on her chart. By then we should have some idea of which way this is going. I'm thinking, I'm praying, that this time is going to be the charm. That I've learned how to modulate the enzyme."

"Is she ready for transfer to IC?"

"Anytime."

The voices start drifting away. A fuzziness is enveloping her senses, leaving everything soft and muted.

The pain is gone from her body now, and the bright lights around her seem to be dimming. The figures in the white haze on the perimeter are now disappearing, one by one, as though filing out of a room. And now she feels like she's floating, with things moving past her.

Then, finally, one lone voice is talking to her, is really talking *to* her, in a private and unmistakable way. And as she drifts back into the gulf of anesthesia, she listens to words that do not make a lot of sense.

"The Fountain. Through all the ages, we've been looking in the wrong place. It's *within* us. Together, Alexa, we have this chance."

She listens as the voice begins to drift away. Yet she feels a genuine sense of closeness to it. She realizes she no longer has control of her destiny. But still she wants to be where she is.

Now the sea is coming back, flowing around her, and she tries to remember where she is and why, but all she is aware of is the sea rising, until she is engulfed.

Chapter 28

Thursday, April 9
8:00 A.M.

Stone awoke in his Yorkville apartment nursing a hangover and a lot of regrets. He'd inhaled a triple scotch after driving Ally's Toyota back and parking it on the street the night before. He'd needed it. Yesterday had been a day where, in sequential order, he'd seen a woman who'd lost her memory get kidnapped (probably); he'd been fired from his day job; he'd finally gotten inside the Dorian Institute, only to blow the opportunity completely. But the most important thing that happened was, he'd rediscovered a woman he'd once been in love with and he currently didn't have the slightest idea what was happening to her. Thinking back over their last few moments together, when she was being checked in by Van de Vliet and his research team and he was being hastily sent up to the lobby, Stone suspected that Ally was about to be subjected to something they didn't want anybody to know about.

Now he was determined to get back inside the institute and look out for her.

As he pulled himself out of bed and shakily made his way

into the kitchen to start the coffee, he was trying to decide where to begin. As it happened, he now had all the time in the world.

He didn't mind all that much losing his position at the *Sentinel*—come on, that was writ across the sky—but he particularly regretted being denied the pleasure of quitting on his own terms, complete with a flamboyant fuck-you-very-much farewell speech to the managing editor, Jay. He'd actually been rehearsing it for weeks.

The dream of just showing up at the Dorian Institute and walking in was no longer even a fantasy. There was a special "not welcome" mat out for him. Even more than the first time, he'd need a calling card.

That had to be Kristen Starr. She clearly held the key to whatever it was Winston Bartlett and Karl Van de Vliet were trying to cover up. But how to find her? The only real lead he had was the apartment she'd come back to, apparently returning like a genetically programmed salmon going back upstream but not really knowing why.

Okay, why not go back down there and look around again, only do it thoroughly? He and Ally hadn't had time to do much more than a cursory look-around. The specter of the knives in the walls still haunted him.

But how to get in?

Then he remembered that Ally had been given the key by Kristen's spacey subtenant, Cindy, the one who was renting the ground-floor apartment. Did she leave that key at her CitiSpace office or did she put it on her key ring?

Her car keys were lying on the table by the door, where he'd tossed them last night. He walked over and checked them out. There were several house keys on the ring in addition to her Toyota keys. Could she have put Kristen's key on the ring too? Or did she stash it in her desk at CitiSpace?

Swing by the apartment and try these, he decided. *Maybe I'll get lucky.*

As he headed for the shower, a cup of black Jamaican

coffee in hand, he thought again about the last thing Alexa's good-for-nothing brother, Grant, had said, something about how Alexa was their "best shot." Whatever that meant, it couldn't be good.

By nine o'clock he had showered, shaved, and was in Ally's Toyota headed for West Eleventh Street. As he turned right on Fourteenth, he had a fresh idea.

Kristen's phone was still working, at least as of yesterday. So did she have speed dial, a memory bank of numbers? That could be a gold mine of the people closest to her. But if not, there were other tricks, ways of getting phone information. There might even be information in the phone itself: who do you get on "redial" and who do you get with *69, the last number that dialed in?

The last number that dialed in would probably be the Japanese guy who left a message and then kidnapped her. But the last call out could be interesting.

He had a nagging feeling that this wasn't the best way to be spending his morning, but he couldn't immediately think of anything else.

West Eleventh Street was comparatively empty, so he had no trouble securing a parking space. After he'd turned off the engine, he looked at Ally's key set again. Well, there were four other keys on it besides the Toyota keys. Give it a shot.

He got out and locked the car and walked up the steps. It was a perfect spring morning, cool and crisp, and this part of the Village was quiet and residential. He found himself envying the owners of these beautiful nineteenth-century town houses. There was something so dignified and secure about them.

Then he saw a man emerge from the apartment below the stoop, just a few feet from where he was standing.

"Hi. How's Cindy?" he called down, hoping the social gesture would let the guy know he wasn't about to do a second-story number on Kristen's town house.

The man, who looked to be in his late twenties, was dressed

in a black suit, with long blond hair tied back in a ponytail, and carried a shoulder bag that appeared to be serving as a briefcase. He stared at Stone with a puzzled look.

"Who?"

"I was here yesterday and . . . a woman named Cindy, friend of Kristen's, said she was leasing the garden apartment. I was just wondering—"

"I'm sorry. Maybe you have the wrong address. I've had this place for almost a year and a half now." He was moving on down the street as he called back over his shoulder. "Good luck."

What the hell is going on?

He looked up and checked the number. *Yep, it's 217.* Cindy had definitely gone into that apartment yesterday and talked convincingly about living there and working at the E! station. She even had keys to Kristen's place.

So who the hell *was that guy?* He looked back, but now he had disappeared.

Did I just imagine that? he puzzled.

He moved up the steps to the heavy white wood door and started trying keys.

The first one wouldn't enter the lock, nor would the second. The third key entered but would not turn.

Okay, last chance.

He inserted the fourth and it seemed to stick. But he gave it a wiggle and, voilà, he was in.

Thanks, Ally.

But when he stepped through the door and switched on the light, he could only stare in disbelief. The apartment had been completely cleared out. The white walls, which had been covered with knifed photos of Kristen only yesterday, were now blank. Even the few pieces of furniture were gone.

"Jesus, I don't believe this." His voice echoed off the empty marble mantelpiece and bounced across the room.

He looked around. Since late yesterday, somebody had come in and cleaned out the place. Thoroughly. Any hopes of finding old letters, an address book, anything personal, were gone. He knew immediately that he had been out-smarted. Kristen Starr, and now her friend Cindy, had officially ceased to exist. Cindy might still be at E!, but she was going to be terrified and subject to massive memory loss on the subject of Kristen.

But wait a second. They left the phone. The answering machine is gone, but maybe they didn't realize that phones can have memories and can sometimes tell tales. That might be worth a try, but check out the place first.

He walked into the kitchen alcove and gazed around, not entirely sure what he was looking for. The main thing would be some phone numbers and addresses.

He opened the refrigerator and peered in. It was still running and contained two unopened jars of British marmalade and an empty quart jar with traces of orange juice bordered by mold. The freezer compartment was entirely bare.

The two kitchen cabinets above the stove had been similarly emptied. He gave them a cursory look, then came back and followed a hallway to a bathroom in the back.

When he opened the medicine chest above the sink and peered in, he initially thought it was empty, with a pile of wadded-up Kleenex on the bottom shelf. He was pulling that out when he realized that the tissue had been wadded around an empty prescription drug vial.

Kristen Starr had prescription number 378030. It was for Libinol—whatever that was, probably some kind of screwed-up diet pill—and it had been filled five months ago. It had been delivered from Grove Pharmacy on Seventh Avenue to here, 217 West Eleventh Street. The address was pasted on a sticker on the back.

Hmmm, he thought. *After she left, rather than transfering the prescription, what if they just had subsequent refills delivered to some other address? There's a long shot that Grove Pharmacy might have a new address for the prescription number. Okay, it would be a* very *long shot, but still . . .*

Unless, of course, her new address had been the Dorian Institute. In that case, the prescription would undoubtedly have been discontinued once she became a patient. He reached for his cell phone to call the drugstore.

Shit, I forgot it! Damn hangover.

He walked back into the living room and stared at Kristen's phone. If it was still working, he could call Grove Pharmacy and—

No, idiot, that would wipe out any number stored in the redial function. Without a cell, the best thing to do is just go over there and check with the pharmacist in person.

He settled yoga-style onto the hardwood floor next to the phone and stared at it. *What if the line is already disconnected? Why did whoever cleaned this place out leave it here? The phone, of all things. It's—*

It *rang.*

He jumped, a foot off the floor, and then stared at it.

A series of reasons flashed through his mind:

1) *They know I'm here and they're going to warn me again to back off.*

2) *They know I'm here and the last incoming call here was from a number they don't want me to know about. I pick this up and I wipe out any chance of ever finding out what it was.*

Don't answer it. This phone call is not intended to be helpful.

Not picking up the phone was the hardest thing he'd ever done, but he was determined to be disciplined.

He counted eleven rings and then he couldn't take it anymore and reached for the receiver.

It stopped.

"Thank God." His hand froze in midair. The timing had been a split-second salvation.

All right, he thought, *time to find out if I just totally screwed up. Time to dial.*

He got his pen and notebook poised and then lifted the black receiver. He knew from the message on her machine yesterday that somebody had called her just before he got there. Or maybe whoever came and cleaned out her apartment had received a phone call while they were here. Possibly from whoever sent them. A checkup call.

Who knew? But give it a shot. He hit the code.

A mechanical voice came on immediately: "Your last call was from area code 212, number 555-3935. If you would like for me to connect you, please push—"

"Go for it," he said aloud, scribbling down the number and then following the instruction.

At that moment somebody's cell phone began to ring just outside the front door.

"Oh shit." It was just too big a coincidence.

After two rings it stopped and he heard the voice of Winston Bartlett, both outside the front door and in his ear. "Yes."

He was too startled to respond, but he didn't need to, because an instant later he also heard the sound of a key and then the front door opened.

A shaft of daylight shot across the room as Bartlett took one look and exploded.

"Damn, so it's true. How the *hell* did—"

"Hey, come on in," Stone said, trying to recover some poise and take marginal control of the situation. "I'm here by permission. The downstairs tenant, who you just evicted, or kidnapped too, gave me her key."

"You don't get it, do you? I told you to keep—"

"But we have signs of progress. I know all about Kristen." Well, that was hardly the case, but it never hurt to start off with a bluff to see how far you could get. "That's why I'm here. The question is, when are *we* going to start talking to each other? Because I'm putting together a hell of a story."

"I don't fucking believe this." Bartlett slammed the door.

"By the way, a special thanks for getting me sacked at the *Sentinel*. Now I'll have the leisure to concentrate full-time on the stem cell book. And Gerex."

"I warned you, but you wouldn't fucking listen." He was

peering around the living room as though searching for clues to explain why nothing was going right.

"Like I said, I talked to Kristen yesterday." Stone stood his ground. "She's not a happy person."

"If you bring her into this . . ." Bartlett glared at him. "I can't imagine what makes you think you can just run roughshod through my business and my life."

"Here's how it is. You can abuse me, or you can *use* me. Keep in mind I'm accustomed to working for people who buy ink by the barrel. As I tried to explain before, if you won't let me get at the whole truth, I may end up spreading half-truths."

Bartlett walked across the room and ran his fingers along the marble mantelpiece above the fireplace. "You know," he said, turning back, "up until now you've never asked me for anything. I have to say I've always admired that, but I'm curious why."

"Maybe I thought it was your place to come to me," Stone said, puzzled by the left turn the conversation had suddenly taken. "You know, I have a life of my own. I have an eleven-year-old daughter you've never seen or—apparently—care to see. I'm wondering what that says about *you*. Your granddaughter's name, by the way, is—"

"I *know* her name. I know quite a bit about our blood ties, or lack of."

"Well, I'd bet she'd be just thrilled by that. Incidentally, she doesn't know a goddam thing about you and I'd just as soon keep it that way."

"I knew having this conversation was a fucking mistake. This is why I never had it. Any real son of mine has got to have some of my character, my stature. You're a bean counter."

"If *you* had any character, you wouldn't be hiding behind all this secrecy. I try to tell the truth, as much and as often as I can. That's my take on character."

"What we're doing at Gerex is going to change the history of the world. We're at the brink of things mankind has only dreamed about. And I've taken all the risks. In fact, I took the biggest risk of all personally. There's a lot going on that you don't know a damned thing about. We're on the edge of—"

"All the more reason you should want the whole story told," Stone interjected. "Yes, stem cell technology is going to change everything, but you can't just tell half the story. I want it to work, but I'm a truth seeker. I want to find out what, if anything, can go wrong too. You've been using people, first Kristen and now—I'm beginning to fear—Ally, to take your risks *for* you. I mean, what's going on? Why did you send somebody down to obliterate all evidence of Kristen? And now Cindy, that girl downstairs? My God, she's somehow vanished too. Whatever happened to Kristen to make it come to this?"

"What may or may not have gone wrong is nothing that can't be made right. No great medical advance ever succeeded in a direct line."

"I don't need the sales pitch," Stone said. "I agree it's going to revolutionize medicine. But you can't—"

"That's why you'll never be a son of mine. You always think small. This is about more than mere medicine. It's about doing the one thing mankind has never been able to do. I am *this* close. Nothing is going to be allowed to destroy this chance. Not even you, my own flesh and blood."

"Am I that?" Stone asked, feeling an unexpected satisfaction. "Your own 'flesh and blood'?"

"*That* is something," Bartlett said, "we are about to discover. Whether we are made of the same thing. The best way for you to understand what's going on here is to do what I've done. Have the Beta procedure. Show me you've got the balls."

"The 'Beta procedure'? It might help if I knew what it is."

"Why don't I just show you," Bartlett said. "You want to be on the inside, see everything up close? Fine. I think the time has come. You seem determined to stick your nose into what I'm doing. You weaseled your way into the institute, and now you show up here. So I guess it's time you were an insider all the way."

"Good, maybe then I can start getting some answers. For example, was changing Kristen's name part of the NIH study?" Stone turned to face him. "Or is it your way to hide one of your mistakes?"

"Quite frankly, that's none of your goddam business."

"Well, let me tell you what *is* my business. Ally Hampton is a particular friend of mine. I damned well want to know whether she's scheduled to undergo the same procedure as Kristen. I don't know what you and Van de Vliet did to Kristen, but if you turn Ally into a zombie too, I'll personally—"

"I think we'll continue this discussion later." He pulled his cell phone out of a jacket pocket, flipped it open, and punched a memory number.

"Ken, could you and Jake please come in. We have the problem I was afraid we had." He flipped the phone shut and turned back to Stone. "Karl entered Ms. Hampton and her mother into the clinical trials at the last minute, as a special favor. She's in no danger."

Now Stone saw two men come through the front door. One was the tall Japanese man who had slugged him the day before.

Shit. I need this? Is he going to work me over again?

The other guy was dressed in white, as though he were an orderly or nurse. Stone noticed he had a plastic syringe in his right hand.

"Ken, could you and Jake please take care of this. He'll be going with us."

Stone examined the three of them. *Well,* he thought, *I guess I'm going to be back inside the Dorian Institute after all.*

"Look, there's no need for excessive violence here. We could just set some ground rules for this situation."

The Japanese man named Ken walked over and seized him around the neck, while at the same time pulling his right arm around behind him, a decisive hammerlock.

"You fucker," Stone choked out. "Let—"

The man Bartlett had called Jake, the one in white, shoved a needle into his arm.

"This could be the experience you've been looking for," Bartlett said. "You've been pursuing me like a dog chasing a car. Now we're about to see if you're man enough to handle the consequences when you've caught it."

You're damned right I'll handle it, he tried to say. But he wasn't sure if he actually got it said, the void was closing in so fast.

Chapter 29

"Grant, is that you?"

Ally squinted in the semidark of the room, finally making out the silhouette. He was sitting in a chair beside her bed, and his face was troubled, reminding her of when he'd had a bad day in high school.

Am I dreaming again? she puzzled. The clock on the wall told her that this was a late hour for whatever he was up to now.

"It's me," he said, his voice low, just above a whisper. The door behind him, she noticed, was shut. "Welcome back to the world. They moved you upstairs just for tonight. This is the first chance I've had to get near you."

She was still wondering where she was, what day it was. The walls were an icy blue, illuminated only by the silver-and-green glow of the bank of CRT screens that now monitored her heart and her respiration. She lifted her head off the pillow and, for a moment, looked past Grant, examining the screen of the heart monitor. It was a phonocardiogram. She knew what to look for. Over the years she'd learned to interpret every irregular pulse, every errant amplitude, but now the sonic abnormalities that typically characterized her stenosis, the struggle of her heart's scarred valve to maintain adequate coronary output, were significantly damped.

There'd always been murmurs, abnormal heart sounds, as long as she could remember, so what did this mean? Had the damaged valve already begun restoring and strengthening itself? While she slept?

Or was this just more of some dream?

Why was she in this hospital anyway, hooked up to monitors? She still couldn't remember exactly.

"What . . ?" She tried to rise up out of the bed. Again she wondered, was Grant real or some chimera?

Then she realized she was strapped in, though the straps were held only with black Velcro.

As she started to pull them open, she noticed she had an IV needle in her arm, with a plastic tube that led to a bag of liquid suspended from a hook above her head. More annoying, however, was the checkerboard of taped-on sensors on her upper body, for the ongoing phonocardiogram. She looked at all the tubes and connected wires and felt like a laboratory animal in the middle of an experiment.

"Ally, you're at the Dorian Institute, remember? Dr. Van de Vliet's stem cell clinical trials. Nina's here too."

"Oh." That rang a bell, sort of. "What . . . what day is it?"

He told her. "You've been under sedation since late yesterday, Ally. But Dr. Vee says your test data show you're responding—"

"Mom's here, right?" Now things were starting to come back. "How's she doing? Is she—"

"He's talking about discharging her by the end of next week, even before the NIH clinical trials are officially over." Grant tried a smile. "By then, he thinks the procedure will have replaced enough tissue in her brain that she might not even need a caregiver. She's doing crosswords again. Need I say more."

"My God." Now she remembered how on-again, off-again Nina's mind had been when she brought her out to the institute. Had she really been given a second chance? And so quickly? If so, it was truly astonishing.

But now she found herself staring at Grant, mesmerized. Something about him seemed oddly off.

"Grant, what . . . what's going on with you?"

"I've . . ." He was hesitating. "I've been thinking about everything. Now I really wish I hadn't done what I did."

"What are you talking about?" This kind of revisionist remorse didn't sound like the Grant she knew.

"Have you seen Kristen? They said you know about her, were asking about her." Then he stepped back. *"Do* you know about her?"

Kristen. She tried to remember. *Is that the woman everybody . . . Her mother had come to the institute with a pistol trying to find her? Then she was kidnapped. . . .*

"It's the Syndrome," Grant went on. "She wanted the Beta procedure, and Dr. Vee finally agreed. But nobody expected anything to happen like what eventually did. That's why W.B. went ahead and had it too."

Beta. Now she remembered that Kristen had mumbled something about that word.

"Ally, I got you into . . . When I told W. B. that I thought you and he had the same rare blood type, AB, he wanted to bring you into the program."

"You mean for my heart?"

He looked away and his eyes grew pained. "Well, that's part of it. There's another part they haven't told you about."

"What's that?"

"Antibodies. They think there's a chance you could be made to develop them and then they could use them to help W.B. He doesn't have the Syndrome yet, but it's probably just a matter of time."

What, she puzzled, *is he talking about? What "antibodies"? What "syndrome"?* She was weak and she wasn't sure her mind was fully functional. But after what appeared to be the miracle of her heart, she was willing to forsake a certain amount of momentary rationality.

Then more memory started returning. "Kristen. What *about* her? I saw—"

"Ally, the Syndrome started with her over four months ago. At first they didn't fully realize how serious . . . but now it's getting worse every day." He paused and turned away. "Look, I've been thinking. I'm really sorry that I brought you into this. What if something goes wrong?"

"What do you mean?"

"If you could see Kristen now, you'd understand."

"Where is she? Is she still wherever they're hiding her?"

"No." He turned back. "Kristen . . . After what happened yesterday, she had to be brought back out here. There's a ward downstairs, on the floor below the offices and lab, that's kind of like an intensive-care unit. That's where you were until tonight. But you can't go back down there on your own. Not even the nurses can go without a special authorization, which is never given."

"But if Kristen is—"

"Ally, *you're* the one I'm worried about. I thought what they were going to do to you was safe. But last night I . . . I heard them all talking and I think you could be in serious danger. They don't actually know *what* the consequences of what they're doing will be. You need to get out of here and at least get the real story. I don't want this on my hands. Truthfully, there could be some deep legal shit coming out of all this. I can think of at least three felonies. I don't want any part of that liability, and I want you to testify that I got you out of here if it ever comes to that."

Finally *the straight story,* she thought. *He's afraid he's about to be an accomplice in a criminal conspiracy. He's getting cold feet.*

"Grant, do something for me. Get me unplugged. All these sensors. I want to go see her for myself."

"Ally, forget it. To begin with, I can't unplug you. Only a

nurse can do that. And I don't want to. You've got catheters in places I—"

"Then I'll get a nurse to come and do it. I'll say I need to go to the bathroom. That should get me unhooked."

Annoyed, she looked around. *Where's the buzzer? There has to be one somewhere.* Then she spotted a set of controls attached to the bed and, sure enough, there was a red button. *What else could it be?*

She pushed it and a light came on above her door. Moments later, a short blue-haired woman with the name MARION sewn into her white uniform opened the door and came striding in, flicking on the fluorescent overheads.

"My, my, we're looking well," she declared, ignoring Grant. "I'm glad you're finally awake. He told us to call him the minute . . . They're all saying you and your mother must have special genes. You've both been such terrific patients. He'd been keeping you sedated, but he discontinued that medication this afternoon. He wanted you to wake up with your mind clear."

"Well, I'd really like to get up and go to the bathroom and get something to eat," Ally said. "Mainly, I just want to get out of this bed for a stretch before I start developing bedsores. I'm feeling strong, for now at least. Can you unhook some of these wires and suction cups? And I certainly don't need that IV. I'm so hungry I could inhale a quart of ice cream in one gulp."

"Yes, of course," Marion said, and began dismantling the intravenous tubes. "We only monitor you and hydrate you when you're not conscious. The standard procedure is to let you get up and start getting some exercise as soon as possible. You should be careful, though, because at this point you're not as strong as you think. Changes are taking place in your body that require a lot of your energy. If you feel up to it, you could walk around for a couple of minutes, but you shouldn't let yourself get tired."

As Marion continued, now removing the taped-on sensors, Ally looked up and saw another uniformed nurse standing in the doorway. She also was middle-aged, with prematurely gray hair, and she was holding a syringe.

"May I come in?" she asked. "At this stage he needs a blood sample every three hours. Just twenty cc's."

Ally watched as the new nurse quickly and deftly took a small sample of blood. Then she capped it off and turned to leave.

"I need to centrifuge this immediately."

And she was gone.

Then Marion finished removing the IV tube and catheter and all the taped-on electrodes.

"If you want to get up and use the bathroom and walk around a little, I'm sure it would be all right. I'll come back in a few minutes and bring you a tray with a nice healthy bowl of broth."

The moment she was out the door, Ally turned to Grant.

"I want to see Kristen. Now."

"I thought the first thing you wanted was to go to the bathroom."

"I'll get to that. You said she was downstairs somewhere. How do I get there?"

"It's in the security zone," he said. "You're not authorized—"

"You're a big shot around here. Winston Bartlett's right-hand flunky. So why don't you authorize me yourself."

"Ally, you know I can't do that."

"Then *take* me there."

"I don't want to see Kristen anymore," he declared, biting his lip. "She's completely lost . . . everything. I could deal with it until I saw her this morning. It's just too much."

"Has he let her mother see her?"

"Are you kidding? Letting that psycho anywhere near her is the last thing anybody's going to do."

"Then get *me* in, dammit."

"Ally, forget about it."

"Why?"

He hesitated, as though marshaling his thoughts.

"Sis," he said finally, "there're only so many risks I can take for you, and they have to be about something that matters. Forget about Kristen. Nothing can save her now. But I'm offering to help *you* get out of here before they go any further. I can't be seen helping you, but they've started you down a road that you don't want to go, believe me. I got you into this, but if there's still time, I want to try to help get you out."

She didn't know what was going on, but if Grant of all people was freaked about what Karl Van de Vliet had in store for her, then maybe she'd better take it seriously.

But she was through relying on him for anything.

"Okay, but I want to call somebody to come and get me."

"Are you referring to that reporter, by any chance?" he asked. "The guy who drove you here? W.B. hates him."

"Yes." She was puzzled that he would know about Stone. "How do you—"

"Bartlett has him."

"What do you mean?"

"He's radioactive now. I actually kicked him out of here myself yesterday. This is not a moment for press freedom. He could screw up everything. W.B. said he's doing a book. No way is that guy going to be allowed human contact with *anybody* till the sale of Gerex is in the bank. He had a run-in with Bartlett in the city and they took him somewhere. I don't know the location. And I don't want to know."

"Oh my God."

"He's most likely okay. It's just temporary safekeeping."

"All the more reason I'm not leaving till I see Kristen."

"There's no way you're going to get into where they're keeping her, Ally."

"All right." There was no arguing with him when he was this freaked. "What do you want me to do?"

He pulled a plastic card out of his jacket pocket. It was white, with THE GEREX CORPORATION embossed on one side and a magnetic strip on the other.

"This is a master key to this place. Because of security, you can't just go out the front, through the lobby. But if you take the elevator down to the first floor of the basement, where the lab is, there's a fire exit there, in the back, that opens onto a path down to the lake. If you'll go out that door and wait right there, I'll come around and get you to the parking lot. I know a way that will miss their surveillance cameras. I'm scheduled to go back to the city now and I'll take you with me."

"But if I wanted to see Kristen?"

"You'd have to go into the laboratory and then take the elevator that's inside there. Don't even think about it. It's way too risky."

She looked at him, trying to gauge his sincerity. Had he become a new man, finally caring about somebody other than himself? Or had a glimpse of whatever had happened to Kristen scared the hell out him and awakened the specter of being part of a felonious enterprise?

"Why are you doing this?"

"To make up for a few things," he said, turning to leave. With that, he walked out and quietly closed the door. *That remains to be seen,* she told herself.

She went to the bathroom, then put on a bathrobe and headed out into the hallway. The nurse's station was not occupied. Marion was still in the kitchen on the first floor, presumably.

Good.

She was feeling shaky, not nearly as strong as she'd initially thought she was, but she pressed on, taking the elevator, her first use of Grant's Gerex master key. She bypassed the first floor and an instant later she was stepping into the basement's laboratory area.

At the moment it appeared to be entirely deserted, though the fluorescent lights bathed the space in a stark, pitiless light.

Down the hall was Dr. Van de Vliet's office and the examining room, where she and her mother had gone when they were being admitted. At this time of night, everything was closed and probably locked.

She turned and looked at the forbidding entryway to the glass-enclosed laboratory. Through the transparent walls she could see the dim glow of CRT screens and incubators filled with petri dishes. And there at the back was—could her eyes be trusted?—the outline of an elevator door. She hadn't noticed it until this minute. It seemed to be built with a nod toward camouflage.

It could lead to Kristen, she told herself. *Find out what Grant is so freaked about. He can wait a couple of minutes.*

She was starting to feel even weaker, but she pressed on. Next to the heavy steel, high-security air lock leading into the laboratory was a card reader and she swiped the white card through the slot.

The air lock opened, silent and perfunctory. When she went through, the door behind her automatically closed and then the hermetically sealed door in front of her opened. She was in.

Next a bright fluorescent light clicked on, all by itself. "Jesus!"

Maybe it was connected to a motion sensor. Or on a timer.

Then she looked around. *This,* she thought, *is the place where the Gerex Corporation has supposedly changed medical history.* What was created in this very room had, if Grant was telling the truth, saved her mother's sanity. And if she could believe the monitors she had looked at in her room, her own heart condition had begun to be reversed after a lifetime of progressive decline.

Yet something about it had been pushed too far. Somewhere in the midst of this miracle, the Gerex Corporation had done something so obscene no one could even talk about it.

She looked around the laboratory, wishing she could understand what she was seeing. It smelled like solvent, acetone, with a mingling of more pungent fumes. The black slate laboratory workbenches were spotlessly hygienic and equipped with several large microscopes that featured flat-panel screens. She noticed a heavy server computer at the back, presumably networked to all the terminals in the building, and then she remembered that Van de Vliet had once spoken of computer simulations.

Someday soon, she told herself, she was going to understand what really was going on here, but for now she headed for the elevator.

Another zip of Grant's white card and the door opened. There was indeed a floor below the laboratory, and she pushed the button. The Dorian Institute was all about security, but this subbasement area was doubly secure.

After a quick trip down, the elevator door opened onto another air lock chamber, this an exit from the pressurized environment of the laboratory.

Why, she wondered, had no one spotted her yet? Perhaps this part of the clinic was such a lockdown that nurses and guards weren't necessary.

As she stepped from the air lock, she was in a hallway. She walked down and tried the first unmarked door. It was locked, but then she saw the slot for her card. She slipped it in and the door opened automatically.

The room she entered had a row of beds, each shrouded in a curtain. As she walked down the center aisle, she realized that only one of the beds was occupied.

And, yes, it was Kristen. She was lying there and when Ally slid back the curtain, her eyes clicked open, startled.

"Hi, don't be afraid. I'm a friend." She quietly finished drawing the curtain aside.

Now the once-breezy Kristen Starr was staring at her with angry eyes, the false bravado of a frightened child. And she looked much younger than she had in the head shot she'd attached to the walls of her town house with steak knives. She said nothing for a moment; then she mouthed, "Who are you?"

"I talked to you on the phone a couple of days ago," Ally said, not sure herself exactly when it was, "when you went down to your place on West Eleventh Street."

"I don't know you," she mouthed again, this time with a slight whisper.

"My name is Ally Hampton." She moved next to her so she could keep her voice down. "I'm an interior designer. I once did an apartment for you in Chelsea."

"I'm about to go on a journey," she whispered. "I don't remember you, but maybe you're the one who's going with me."

There was something otherworldly and chilling about her voice.

"What journey do you—"

"We were going to go away. That's what he promised. Just us two. Well, I'm ready. I want to go out and play. But he doesn't care anymore. He just wants me to disappear. So that's what I'll do. Only we'll do it together, you and me." She reached up from her bed and ran a finger across Ally's face. "Will you take me out of here? He promised me everything, that I could get it all back. But now I know he didn't care. He was just using me." She stopped, then gave a cruel laugh from the back of her throat. "But now it's going to happen to him too. I can tell. That's why he doesn't want to see me anymore. He doesn't want to see what's in store for *him*."

What has happened? Ally wondered. *It sounds like some kind of bizarre experiment gone wrong.*

"Won't you come with me?" Kristen went on. "We'll go to a place nobody has ever been to before. It'll be just us."

Her seductive eyes, at once plaintive and demanding, would have lured anyone toward wherever she wanted to go. For a careless moment Ally found herself wanting to follow them.

No, this is madness.

Or, Ally thought with horror, *is she seeing something in me that I can't see?*

"Kristen, listen to me. Please. I think it's very possible I've just had a stem cell procedure. For my heart. I don't know if it's like what you had, but I want to know what happened to you."

"Don't do it," she mumbled, seeming to come back to a kind of reality. "Just get out of here now. After . . . it starts, he gives you shots and things, but nothing works."

Ally felt her consciousness start to wobble. She reached out and seized the edge of the bed for support.

"Kristen, talk to me."

Her eyes went blank again, and Ally could just barely make out what she mumbled next. In fact, all she could catch were random words, words that only drifted through her consciousness and failed to stick or make any sense. It was as though Kristen were in a séance and sleepwalking among the words of some alien language.

"Young," Kristen seemed to say. "You want to be . . . to stay. Old is so horrible. Time. You're young and then suddenly you're old and it turns out you can't . . ."

Ally heard the words, but they didn't make any sense.

"I'm sorry, Kristen. I'm feeling a little dizzy."

"It's started," she said, abruptly coherent again and focusing in on Ally. "That's how it began with me. At first they said everything was okay and then it wasn't."

"What are you talking about?"

"It's happening throughout my body." She sobbed. "I've stopped having periods and I'm getting acne. Everything is . . . changing."

The words drifted through space, and Ally felt like she was hallucinating, in a place where time was sliding sideways. The images were all retro, things from her past that floated through her vision in reverse chronological order.

That was it. In her mind, time was going backwards. But was it just in her mind? She looked again at Kristen and gasped. Finally, *finally* she understood the horror of what was really happening. . . .

Oh my God.

"I got here as soon as I could after they called me," came a voice from the doorway. She turned and saw Karl Van de Vliet, together with the nurse Marion. "You really shouldn't be down here. I don't know who gave you a card. But we've brought a wheelchair. You really should be resting."

Marion rolled the chair through the door and expertly plucked the card from the reader.

"Now, please sit down," she said. "We all just want to be on the safe side, don't we? I'll need to give you a sedative."

Ally looked at Van de Vliet, wanting to strangle him.

"No, you're not giving me a damned sedative. I don't want to be on the 'safe side.' I want the truth. And I want it *now.*"

Chapter 30

"Let's go into the lab to talk," Van de Vliet said. "I'm very sorry I wasn't here when you came out of sedation. But Marion called me at home, as I'd told her to do, and I came in as quickly as I could. I've got a place on the lake, just down the road, so I'm never far away."

He was rolling her through the air lock door, Marion behind them. Then they took the elevator up. She was furious that Kristen was being left behind like an abandoned casualty of war.

Ally also was reminding herself about her appointment with Grant to get the hell out. But her mind was having trouble holding a lot of thoughts at once.

He pushed her wheelchair into the section of the laboratory where a line of computer terminals was stationed. After he'd fluffed a pillow behind her head and turned off some of the glaring fluorescents, he began.

"Alexa, this is a delicate time for you. We need to get you upstairs as quickly as possible and feed you some broth and put you back to bed. However, I want very much to give you an update on the status of your treatment. The headline is, it's going very well. We fused some of the telomerase enzyme with your existing stem cells and your response was immediate. In fact, it appears the new heart tissue has reached critical mass and has already begun replicating itself. We've learned to expect the unexpected around here, but your response has significantly exceeded our simulations."

He turned to Marion and asked her to go up and make sure Alexa's bedding had been changed. "We'll be up in a second. And please make sure that bowl of broth is ready and waiting."

After she departed through the air lock, he walked over to a lab bench and checked the numbers that were scrolling on a CRT screen.

"All right," Ally said, "talk to me. I just saw Kristen. I'm still not sure if I believe what I think is happening, but I want the real story and I want it now."

"That's part of what I need to discuss with you." He glanced away for a long moment, a pained expression on his face, seeming to collect his thoughts. Finally he turned back. "You see, the clinical trials have demonstrated that we can use the telomerase enzyme to 'immortalize' a patient's own stem cells and then rejuvenate their brain or liver or even their heart. So the *next* question that's hanging out there in space is obvious. What would happen if we could find a way to generalize the enzyme and disperse it throughout someone's entire body, not restricting it to just one organ? And not just rejuvenate—*regenerate.*"

This question had actually passed fleetingly through her consciousness, though not fully articulated. It had taken the form of wondering where the use of these "immortal" cells could eventually lead.

"The trick would be to have just enough enzyme in your bloodstream to replace senescent cells as they are about to die, but not so much that *healthy* cells are replaced." He paused, searching for a metaphor. "If we thought of the process of cell senescence as something inexorable and steady, like a treadmill, then what we want to do is run just fast enough to stay in one place."

"This whole thing does sound like *Alice in Wonderland*."

"Yes, well . . . if we could do that, then it's possible, just possible, that one's entire body would simply begin regenerating itself instead of aging. Not just your skin. All of you. That's the theory behind what we've called the Beta procedure."

"But is that something you ethically ought to be doing?" she said, feeling a sense of dismay, of playing God. "Isn't that going too far?"

"Frankly, I'm beginning to agree with you, but there are others who ask, *how far is too far?* Half the medicines we now have are intended to trick the body's responses somehow—or to meddle in some other way, turning off stop-and-go signals at the cellular level. For example, some birth control pills make your body *think* you're already pregnant. They trick our natural mechanisms. That kind of thing is commonplace in medicine today. But our research is poised for the next level, to answer the question of how long we can *actually* live. So here's the argument. There's no reason the human life span has to be what it is. In some unhealthy nations the average citizen doesn't even reach sixty. Whereas in others, like the United States and Japan, the mean is already well past three score and ten. So what is right? What is reasonable? A hundred? Two hundred? It's entirely possible to believe we could live productive lives at least twice as long as we do now."

"And you think we should do this? The world would be thrown into chaos."

"But look at the incredible cure rate we've already effected here using the telomerase enzyme. When our clinical trials for the NIH are announced, it will be the medical equivalent of the shot heard round the world. Nothing we know will ever be the same again."

"That's where you should leave it. To go further is obscene."

"I fear recent events may have proved you right. Against my better judgment, I went ahead and experimented with the Beta procedure. And the results thus far have turned out to be disastrous."

"I guess you're referring to Kristen."

"One day I casually mentioned the Beta to Winston Bartlett and, without telling me, he brought it up with Kristen. She insisted on trying it." His expression grew increasingly pained. "I want you to know I was against it. I warned her that it was highly experimental, that I could not guarantee what the side effects might be, but she begged me to do it anyway. Then Bartlett essentially ordered me to do it."

"So what happened?"

He grimaced. "I got the dosage wrong. That's my best guess. After I performed the Beta on Kristen, the enzyme was stable in her for over two months and appeared to be having an effect. All signs of aging abruptly stopped. It gave me a false sense of confidence. Also, there were no side effects. That was when Bartlett wanted to try it too. So I went ahead with him. But then, to my horror, she started evincing side effects. I now believe the dosage I gave her was badly calibrated. It was too high—by how much I think I've finally determined—and the enzyme eventually began replicating too rapidly. It got away from me." He paused. "What happened to Kristen, we now call the Syndrome, for lack of a better name. And it's about to happen to Bartlett."

"But what does all this have to do with me? Why was I brought out here with all kinds of bribes and pressure and—"

"Do you want a simple answer? Of excruciating honesty?"

"It would be helpful."

"The simple answer is, Winston Bartlett has an extremely rare blood type. It's AB. You have the same."

"How did you know—"

"Your brother. You see, I need to try to develop antibodies to the telomerase enzyme that won't be rejected by his immune system. I think there's an outside chance that I could culture antibodies taken from someone with the same blood type and use them to arrest the rampant multiplying of telomerase enzyme about to begin in Bartlett's blood."

"I'm here because you're *using* me!" She couldn't believe her ears. And Grant had set it up. No wonder he was finally feeling guilty.

"I just need to borrow your immune system for a few days. It's very safe."

"I *don't* think so. I'm out of here."

"Actually, the procedure is already under way. While Debra was taking your last blood sample, she also injected a minuscule amount of the telomerase enzyme in active form, the proprietary version used in the Beta, into your bloodstream. Don't worry. It's perfectly safe. The dosage was so minute that there's no way it could have any effect on you."

"You have *got* to be kidding!" *My God,* she thought, *I could sue the hell out of—*

"Don't worry, think of it like a smallpox vaccination." He paused. "Now, though, I have to tell you that I just learned the initial dosage probably didn't do the trick. The amount of antibodies created was, unfortunately, minuscule. Which means we need to go to a slightly higher infusion. But again, don't worry. It's still safe."

"I can't believe I'm hearing this," she said finally, gasping for air in her fury. "You didn't ask—"

"Alexa," he cut in, "right now I have something like two weeks left to try to head off the Syndrome in Winston Bartlett. If we achieve that, then I'm hopeful the antibodies *he* creates can be successfully used to start reversing the Syndrome in Kristen. We will know how to manage the Beta. Who knows where that could lead? But it all begins with you. You're the clean slate we need to start."

"Before we go one step further, I want to know what, exactly, happens with the Syndrome. I think I know, but I'd like to hear—"

"Something that's too bizarre to believe. It literally defies every natural law we've ever known."

He couldn't bring himself to put it in words, she thought, but she knew she'd guessed right the first time. *The Syndrome.*

Kristen Starr was *growing younger.* That was the horrible development and nobody could deal with it.

And *they couldn't stop it.*

Karl Van de Vliet had created a monstrosity.

"I am *so* out of here," she said, struggling to rise from the wheelchair. "If you try to keep me here, that's kidnapping. We're talking a capital crime."

"Alexa, I understand you're upset, but you're in no condition to be discharged. I'm very sorry." He pushed a red button on a radio device on his belt. There was genuine agony in his eyes. "I've never in my life coerced a patient in any way. But you have to understand that so much is dependent on you now. There are no easy choices left."

He's lost control of the situation here now, she told herself. *He's truly terrified of Winston Bartlett. That's who's really got control of my fate.*

Moments later, the security guard from the lobby, accompanied by Marion, came through the door of the laboratory.

"No, I'm not going to let you do this," Ally declared. "I'm not letting you do any more medical experiments on me."

As she struggled again to get out of the wheelchair, she felt a prick in her arm and saw the glint of a needle in the dim light.

"I'm sorry, Alexa. It should all be over in just a couple of days. And I swear no harm will come to you."

She was feeling her consciousness swirl as Marion began rolling her through the steel air lock.

The last thing she heard was Van de Vliet saying, "Don't worry. A week from now, all this will seem like a dream."

Chapter 31

Friday, April 10
7:04 A.M.

Stone felt his consciousness returning as the blast of an engine cut through his sedative-induced reverie. Where was he? There were vibrations all around him and a deafening roar that was slowly spiraling upward in frequency and volume.

As the haze that engulfed his mind slowly began to dissipate, he wondered if this wasn't more of the fantasy he'd been having, of flying through some kind of multicolored space-time continuum. Or was he waking up to something spectacularly real?

As he opened his eyes and looked around, he realized it was no dream. He was in a cramped airline seat, strapped in with a black seat belt. His head was gently secured to a headrest by a soft cotton scarf, but his hands were free, lying in his lap.

Somebody had lifted him into the seat and strapped him down.

On his left was a Plexiglas window, and when he looked out, he saw the earth beneath him begin falling away.

My God.

Then he realized he was in a white-and-gray helicopter that had just lifted off from a rooftop helo pad. He watched spellbound, quickly coming awake, as the craft quickly began a flight path that circled around and past the lower end of Manhattan.

Then he heard the pilot speaking curtly to an air controller somewhere and he looked up and realized it was the same samurai bastard who'd slugged him on the street and then aided in his kidnapping.

But that had to be yesterday, or God knows how many days ago. He was realizing he'd just lost a chunk of his life.

And now he was being taken somewhere. In a very big hurry.

"Being up here always seems like being closer to God," came a voice from behind him. He recognized it with a jolt. It was the man who thought he *was* God.

Shakily he removed the scarf that had been holding his head and turned around. Winston Bartlett was gazing down through his own plastic window, seemingly talking to himself.

"What . . . what the hell is going on?" He could barely get the words out.

"Oh," Bartlett said, turning to look at him. "Good. I particularly wanted you to see this. It should help make my point."

Stone struggled to comprehend what was happening. He was with the man he had wanted to call *Father* for nearly four decades, whether he could admit that to himself or not. It could be the beginning of the kind of bonding he had always hungered for, but he didn't want it like this. They finally had a relationship, and it was completely antagonistic. He had just been drugged and kidnapped by his own father, this after being threatened and fired. Again, Daddy dearest.

So what was *this* evolving chapter about? Winston Bartlett, he knew, could be ruthless, but he also was a visionary in his own way.

Then he remembered what had happened. He'd been trying to track down Kristen.

"Where . . . where are we going?"

"We're going to the place you seem to find so interesting," Bartlett declared over the din of the engine. "But I was hoping that we could have a rational discourse along the way. What's been happening thus far doesn't serve either of us. I'm hoping things have cooled down a bit and we can call a truce."

Stone was still trying to clear his head, get the cobwebs away. It was difficult. He'd lost consciousness in a town house in the Village, on solid ground, and regained it here, where the earth itself seemed in motion. And now Bartlett was trying out another bargaining style, so even the rules appeared to be in flux.

"Look, down there." Bartlett was projecting through the din around them and pointing toward the wide expanse of New York Harbor. "This McDonnell Douglas is my Zendo, my monastery, and the world below is my contemplative garden. I come up here to find peace. This is an intersection of the great forces of nature, one of a finite number on earth, where a mighty river returns to the salt sea from which it came. These waters have flowed in the same cycle for millions, billions of years, mingling, evaporating, separating again—just as life on this planet continually replicates itself, growing and aging and dying, but not before producing the seeds of its replacement. How can something be at once both timeless and constantly changing? I ponder that a lot and I always end up thinking of this river meeting the sea. Down there, nature is a force unto itself, oblivious to good or evil, to human desires or human laws."

Bartlett was doing a riff on some obsession of his own, Stone decided. Or maybe it was some of the Zen philosophy that went along with acquiring a world-class collection of samurai swords (if you believed the published profiles).

All the same, looking down at the sprawling city and the harbor full of ships, it was hard not to feel omnipotent and humble at the same time. The thing Bartlett seemed to be getting at, though, was that nature could not be told what to do. And he seemed to be on the verge of declaring himself a part of that unbridled natural force, also powerful enough to do whatever he pleased.

Now they were heading up the Hudson, teeming with early bird tourist cruises and small single-masted sailboats. Bartlett paused to take in the view with satisfaction. Finally he continued his monologue.

"I know we've had our differences, but I'm prepared to try to get past that. I want to talk to you about something I always think of when I fly across this river. Time. I call my obsession Time and the River. Physicists will tell you that time should be thought of as a kind of fourth dimension. Things are always at a certain place in three dimensions, but when you describe the location of a subatomic particle, for example, you also have to say *when* it was there. To locate it accurately, you need four dimensions. We think of them all as rigid, but what if one of them could be made fluid? What if you could alter the character of time?"

In spite of himself, Stone took the bait. "I don't know what this has to do with anything. Nobody can alter the pace of time." He found himself recalling a snippet of verse by John Donne:

> *O how feeble is man's power,*
> *That if good fortune fall,*
> *Cannot add another hour,*
> *Nor a lost hour recall!*

"Strictly speaking, that's true," Bartlett said gravely, turning away again to stare out the Plexiglas window, down into the morning space below them. The Hudson was now a giant ribbon of blue heading north into the mist. "But what if we could alter the clocks in our body to make them run slower?" He smiled, then pointed off to his left. "All this below us has happened in a couple of hundred years. What will it look like down there in another hundred years? Will we still need these puny machines to fly, or will there be teleportation? Whatever it is, what would you give to be around to see that? To have your own time slow down while the world around you went on?"

Stone was looking out into space, wondering . . . not *whether* Winston Bartlett was an egomaniacal madman but rather how truly mad he really was.

Flying in the helicopter, he felt like Faust being shown the world by Mephistopheles. Except here Satan was his own father, offering him a teasing prospect of what it would be like to live on and on.

It would make a hell of a story. The problem was, miracles always came with some kind of terrible price. What was the price this time?

Then he had another thought. Was that what had happened to Kristen? Was she paying the price for some kind of hubris that pushed nature too far? Nobody had claimed she had any kind of medical condition that necessitated a stem cell intervention. So had she been experimenting with some other procedure? Had Mephistopheles now called in his marker?

He wanted to ask but the vibration and the noise made his brain feel like it was in a blender.

"Do you understand what I'm saying?" Bartlett went on. "Do you want to be part of the most exciting development in the history of medicine? Well, this is your chance. There is a majestic experiment under way. But now we know it's not for the fainthearted. The question is, do you want to live life or just write about it?"

"I think it's time I heard the whole story," Stone said finally, forcing out the words. "What's your part in this 'experiment'?"

"I've put everything at risk, but now I'm *this* close to controlling the clock. So . . . are you my son? My flesh and blood? Do you have the balls to try it too?"

Stone suspected the question was rhetorical. He was already up to his neck in whatever was going on. He just didn't yet know how *big* a part of it he was. While he'd been sedated overnight, had they started experiments on *him?*

He knew that some of the buzz about stem cells involved the fantasy that someday they might be used to forestall the aging process. Responsible researchers all said that they weren't trying to extend life; they were only hoping to make a normal lifetime more livable. Rejuvenative medicine. Winston Bartlett, however, had just taken stem cell potential to its obvious conclusion; he was talking about doing what others did not dare. Regenerative medicine.

"What would we give to be able to look forward to thousands of mornings like this, ending it all only when we chose?" he declared, his hands sweeping over the dense green beneath them. "Time would become something that merely flows endlessly through us, ever renewing. So-called old age would cease to exist, at least for those with the courage to take the necessary risks."

Now they were moving above the pine forests that comprised the outer ring of the Greater New York suburbs, as below them the green wilds of New Jersey, north of the GW Bridge, were sweeping by.

Hmmm, Stone pondered, *if a man somehow stopped growing older and nobody else did, at some point he'd end up being the same "age" as his grandchildren.* That caused him to think again about Amy and wonder if Bartlett would ever reconcile himself to her existence. . . .

A few minutes later, he looked down and saw a wide clearing in the trees and a red-tile roof. They had arrived, but from the air, the Dorian Institute gave no clue to the momentous research going on inside.

Bartlett said nothing as they began their descent, and in moments they were settling onto the rooftop landing pad. The downdraft from the rotor cleared away a few soggy leaves, which had somehow blown there, and then the Japanese pilot cut the power and the sound died away. When Bartlett opened the side door, the first thing Stone noticed was the fresh, forest-scented morning air against his face.

He found himself wondering whether the roar of the engine had disturbed the patients, but that was almost beside the point. The Dorian Institute was not, he now realized, merely about using stem cell technology to heal the sick. Bartlett had been letting him know that it was also about an experiment that was much, much more profound.

In the silence that followed, Bartlett stepped onto the pad and lit a thin, filtered cigar. (For somebody who'd just been talking about how long it was possible to live, the act confounded credulity.) He took a deep drag, then tossed it onto the paving and peered back through the opening.

"Are you able to walk yet?"

"I think I can manage," Stone said. He actually wasn't sure at all. The vibrations of the chopper had done serious damage to his sense of equilibrium.

But he did find he could take small steps. As they moved to the stairwell leading down to the third-floor elevator, Bartlett said, "I know you've been here once before. You tried to sneak in. Grant saw you and sent you packing. Well, this time you're here for real. The full experience. We're going to start by taking you down to the lab and checking you in."

The man, Stone suspected, was trying to hide everything that was going on in his mind. He wanted to talk about grandiose themes, but his mind was really somewhere else. Beneath all the braggadocio, there was the smell of deep, abiding fear. Winston Bartlett was in some kind of major denial.

"You know, life has been good to me," Bartlett declared as though thinking out loud. "I've done and seen things most mortals can only dream of. I'm sixty-seven, but I feel as though I've only just begun to live. And that's what I intend to happen." He turned back to Stone. "Whether I have a son to share this with remains to be seen."

A son? Stone glanced back at the man Bartlett had called

Ken, who was now shutting down the McDonnell Douglas. Maybe he was a surrogate son for Bartlett. He was clearly a lot more than a bodyguard. He'd been the one who nabbed Kristen and returned her to the reservation. So what did *he* think of whatever was going on? Or what about Ally's brother, Grant? He'd claimed *he* was the son Bartlett longed for and had never had.

Winston Bartlett already had a surfeit of sons.

When they walked through the door and into the hallway of the third floor, it was milling with the breakfast crowd, nurses and patients, but no one took any special notice of Winston Bartlett, the man who had made it all possible. Did they even know who he was? Stone wondered.

"We're going downstairs." Bartlett directed him toward the elevator. "I'm still offering you a choice. You can be part of the biggest medical advance in human history, or you can be just another impediment."

Stone glanced at his watch. The hour was just shy of nine.

Where is Ally? What kind of procedure has she under-gone? Is she okay? He had to find her.

As they headed down, he felt like it was a descent into some pit of no return. Winston Bartlett had not elaborated on what awaited down there. It was as though he couldn't bring himself to face whatever it really was.

What was the worst-case scenario at this point?

What he had to do was figure that out and then plan a countermove.

Chapter 32

There are sounds of doors opening and closing, with whispered words that are like alien hisses. She senses she is in motion, on a bed that is gliding past powerful overhead lights.

She doesn't know where she is, but that doesn't matter, because wherever it was, she knows it surely is a dream.

All she remembers is that Karl Van de Vliet had told her he wants her to undergo a second procedure with the telomerase enzyme, which possibly might create sufficient antibodies to reverse . . . It's all a jumble now in her mind.

Or had she just dreamed all that? Now her life seems a flowing river that has no beginning and no end. Her mind is drifting, a cork bobbing helplessly in the current.

Then her brother, Grant, drifts alongside her. At least she thinks it's Grant. She recognizes his voice.

"Ally, can you hear me?" he seems to be asking. "Is there anything you want to tell me? Do you still want to go through with this?"

It's the kind of dream where she can hear things around

her, but when she tries to speak, no sounds will come. Instead, she's talking inside her head.

I'm afraid. I'm just afraid.

"I can still try to get you out, but you have to help. I waited for you last night but you never came."

She wants to say, *yes, get me out,* but she can only speak in the dream.

Now the lighting changes and she feels like she is falling. No, she realizes, she's just on an elevator.

"Talk to me, Ally," whispers the voice one last time. "I can try to stop them, but I have to know what you want."

Then a door opens and she floats through it and out. Then comes the clanking of a door that reminds her of the steel air lock she'd gone through last night looking for Kristen. The smells. She's in the laboratory.

"We can take her from here," comes a voice, drifting through her reverie.

She fantasizes it's Karl Van de Vliet. Or maybe he really *is* there. In her dream state it's hard to know. But he isn't alone.

"You said you'd make one more attempt to create the antibodies. Is . . ."

It's Winston Bartlett. Or at least it sounds like him.

"I said I would do all I could, W.B. The first attempt . . . you know what happened. I got almost no results, but I gave you an injection of all I managed to garner. Today I spent the day doing simulations. We're working closer to the edge than I thought. That's why I needed her down at the lab tonight. I want to run some more tests and then try to make a decision. Tonight. There's just a hell of a lot more risk than I first thought."

The voice trails off and Ally finds herself trying to comprehend "risk."

She hears "beta" again and it floats through her mind, but now its meaning is unclear. It's something she'd heard but can no longer place.

"Ally," comes a ghostly voice. Surely this is a dream, and

she recognizes it as her father, Arthur. Now she can see him. He's wearing a white cap and they're boating in Central Park. He shows up in her dreams a lot and she feels he's the messenger of her unconscious, telling her truths that she sometimes doesn't want to hear.

"Ally," he says, "he's going to perform the full Beta procedure on you. He didn't tell you, but you *know* it's true. He thinks he's finally calculated everything right. Can't you see? Is that what you want?"

She isn't sure what she wants. And right now she isn't entirely clear where she fits on the scale of sleeping/waking. It is so bizarre. The two parts of her mind, the conscious and the unconscious, are talking to each other. Her unconscious is warning her about fears she didn't even know she had. Or at least she hadn't admitted to yet.

Then she hears Winston Bartlett's voice again.

"Karl, we can't save Kristen now. I've finally realized that. She's gone too far. It's just a tragedy we'll have to figure out how to live with."

"The body is a complex chemical laboratory that sometimes gets out of balance. There's always hope. I think—"

"Know what *I* fucking think?" Bartlett cuts him off. "I think I'm in line for the Syndrome if you don't get this right."

What Ally wants to do, more than anything else, is to make sense of what her options are. The most obvious one—in fact, maybe the only one—is to flow along with that infinite river she feels around her, just to lie where she is, in this sedative-induced reverie, and let her body be taken over by Karl Van de Vliet. Perhaps he has marvelous things in store for her. Except she has no idea what's real and what is imaginary.

"The simulations are giving me some idea of what went wrong with the Beta before." The voice is Van de Vliet's. "I have one more test to run, but if I handled this the way the simulation now suggests, I think I could actually generate the telomerase antibodies we need *and* get the Beta to finally work, avoiding the Syndrome. But to prove it would require a full-scale experiment. I'm reluctant to do that without Alexa's permission."

"Christ, Karl, are you getting cold feet? This is a hell of a time for that."

"Call it a pang of rationality."

"But everything is at stake."

"I don't know what's eventually going to happen with the Syndrome, but it's criminal to jeopardize any more lives." Van de Vliet sighs. "Look, you had the procedure of your own free will, and you knew the risks. Alexa Hampton didn't volunteer for the Beta. She's not a lab rat. At the very least, we ought to get her to sign a release. The liability is . . . In any case, I'm not doing anything till I run this last test. Then maybe I'll have some idea exactly how much risk is involved."

"And then, by God, we're going to do it. Tonight. This is it."

She feels a cold metal object insinuate itself against her chest. Time rushes around her, sending her forward on a journey that seems increasingly inevitable. Where it's taking her, she has no idea, but she senses she no longer has an option of whether she wants to go or not.

Now her dreamscape has become crowded as Grant drifts in once more. He seems to be wearing a white lab coat like the others. He settles beside her and takes her hand.

"Ally, it's going to be okay. I'm going to be here for you."

Grant, why are you here? Do you really give a damn *about me?*

She wants to talk to him, but the words aren't working. *Why is this happening?*

Don't let them give you more medications, she tells herself. *Get your mind back and get out of here.*

Chapter 33

Friday, April 10
8:45 P.M.

Ellen O'Hara had not left after the day shift ended at six P.M. Instead, she had told Dr. Van de Vliet that she wanted to reorganize some of the NIH paper files she kept in her office on the first floor. The truth was, she had become convinced that the culmination of something deeply evil was scheduled for later that night.

The evil had begun when Kristen Starr's mother arrived looking for her and declaring that she'd been kidnapped. Then after Dr. Vee categorically denied he knew anything about her (a blatant lie), Kristen was brought back to the institute from wherever she'd been moved to, and she was visibly changed. She was whisked down to the subbasement the moment she arrived and immediately sealed off in intensive care, but it was clear she had no idea who she was or where she was. Something horrible had happened to her. And maybe it was imagination, but she no longer even looked like a grown woman.

Then this morning, Bartlett and his Japanese bodyguard brought in the young man who had accompanied Alexa

Hampton, but he wasn't put through the admissions formalities. Instead, he was taken directly downstairs.

May at the front desk said she thought he was a newspaper reporter she'd met once when they were on a public-health panel together. That was when Ellen realized he was Stone Aimes, that feisty medical columnist for the *New York Sentinel*.

Now Stone Aimes might be able to save Alexa Hampton.

Dr. Van de Vliet and Debra had carried out a special stem-cell procedure for her aortic stenosis, the first that they had attempted for that particular condition. The results, as shown by her file, were nothing short of astonishing. She'd begun responding in a matter of hours.

She should be in a room upstairs, so why was she still down in the subbasement?

Now Ellen O'Hara knew the reason.

She had seen in the file that they were going to perform the Beta procedure on Alexa Hampton. When they'd performed it on Kristen Starr, the result was a horrific side effect. And now they were going to do it again. Tonight.

The criminality that started with Kristen Starr and Katherine Starr was going to be compounded. She was about to become part of a criminal conspiracy. She had to put a stop to it.

She was nervous about confronting Van de Vliet, but she didn't know what she could say that wouldn't sound like an indictment. Still, she was damned well determined to do it.

If nothing else, it would provide a diversion.

She put away the files and walked out into the dim hallway, then made her way into the reception area.

"Everything all right, Grace?" she asked the nurse at the desk.

"My, you're working late," came the pleasant reply. "Quiet as a mouse around here. I guess it'll be even quieter when the clinical trials are finished. I mean, after the celebrating is over."

"Right." *But they're not over,* Ellen thought. *And there may not* be *a celebration.* "I'm going down to sublevel one. Is Dr. Vee down there now?"

"I think he's in his office. Everybody else went out for a bite, probably that diner down the road. I think something's scheduled for later on. I don't know. Everybody looks kind of worried."

"Well, nobody has said anything to me." *They don't need to,* she thought. *I saw the file.*

She swiped her card through the security slot and got onto the elevator.

When she stepped off, the laboratory was dark and a light was showing under Dr. Van de Vliet's office door.

Good. She swiped her card in the reader next to the laboratory air lock and went in. Another swipe and she was on the elevator down to the subbasement, where she was not authorized to be.

She went to the second door and slipped her card through the slot, wondering what she would see.

The room was dark and smelled of alcohol and disinfectant. She quickly closed the door behind her before turning on the overhead fluorescents.

Alexa Hampton was secured to the bed with restraints, and she appeared to be sedated, though she did slowly open her eyes as the light flickered and then stabilized. There was a wheelchair in the corner.

"Ms. Hampton, can you hear me?" she whispered, hoping not to alarm her. "Do you remember me? I was the one who helped you when you were first admitted."

She watched as Alexa stared at her for a moment and then quietly nodded.

"I . . . I want to get out of here." Her eyelids fluttered and then she closed her eyes again. "But I'm too weak. I can't move."

"You're strapped down, love. Let me help you."

She reached for the Velcro straps and then paused. Was this a decision she wanted to make?

If I do this, it's the end of my career here. Have I lost my mind? What will I do after this?

But if I don't try to stop them, God knows what . . . we could all end up convicted of criminal conspiracy and in prison.

"That reporter friend of yours is here." She pulled open the straps, then helped Alexa sit up in the bed and swing her legs around. "I'm going to take you to him."

"It's so horrible," Ally went on. She was settling into the wheelchair as though she expected it. Then she looked up, her eyes dazed. "Where are you taking me? 'Reporter'? Do you mean—"

"Like I said, I'm moving you into your friend's room."

She rolled her to the door, then stopped and cracked it and peeked out.

"Don't say a word, dear," she whispered as she began pushing Alexa down the hall. There was a pale flickering light under the door at the end. "Debra and David and the others have all gone out to the diner down the road, and Dr. Vee is in his office, probably running some last-minute computer simulations. But we need to be quiet."

The fluorescent lights seemed to swirl overhead. *This all feels so familiar,* Ally thought. *This is where I saw Kristen. Does Ellen know what happened to her?*

"You two have to decide what you want to do."

"Stone? You're sure he's here?"

"Yes," she said, "and he's in some kind of battle of wills with Mr. Bartlett."

When they reached the door at the end, she tried it and it was locked. She pulled out her magnetic card and zipped it through the slot.

As they went through, Ally realized the room was lit only by the glow of a laptop computer screen.

"Stay here," Ellen said, turning to leave. "I'm going to try to talk to Dr. Vee."

As the door closed, Stone finally looked up. He was wear-

ing a sweater and jeans and had been typing furiously on a
Gerex laptop.

"Hey, how're you feeling?" He paused to glance down
and save what he'd been writing, then clicked off the computer.

"I have no idea." Something about him didn't seem quite
right. It was like he was on happy pills or something. "How
about you? The last time I saw you, I was passing out."

"I don't actually remember all that much of what happened
after that. I think I went back to the city. But I feel great now.
Like I went through a dark tunnel and came out the other
side. I feel very different. I don't know what's next, but right
now I'm just happy to be in the middle of the biggest story in
the history of medical science."

What's going on with him? she wondered. *He's spacey. He
has to be on some kind of drug.* What *have they done to him?*

He closed the laptop, then reached and clicked on a light
by the bed. "Come on. Want to see something incredible? It's
a marvel of medical science, never before happened."

"What—"

"Come with me. I guarantee you've never seen anything
like it."

He tossed the laptop onto the bed, then swung his feet
around and settled them onto the floor. She noticed that the
room was a pale blue, with white linoleum. There was a pair
of white slippers next to the bed.

He slipped them on and then opened the door and
grabbed her wheelchair.

The hallway felt colder now, yet it was also stifling, as
though someone had drawn the air out of it.

"There's nothing we can do," Stone said.

There was a hint of madness in his voice. It was as if he
were trying to convince himself that he was still sane, and it
wasn't working. He was just barely holding it together.

Then she realized he was about to go into intensive care,
where Kristen had been.

"So Kristen's still here?"

"Oh, you'd better believe it," he said. "She is most definitely still here."

When they got to the door, he revolved back.

"Ally, you really don't *have* to see this, you know. Not if you'd rather . . . Nothing remotely like this is going to happen to you. They assured me."

What the hell is he talking about?

"On the other hand," he went on, "maybe you *should* see it. Maybe everybody in the world should see it. It's so astonishing."

He pushed open the door and rolled her in. Then he reached down and lifted her to her feet. Standing wasn't that hard, and somehow he had known that.

The room seemed to be captured in mist, though surely that was her imagination. Everything must be her imagination.

Kristen was in the corner of the room, in a wheelchair, but now her body was shriveled. No, shriveled was not the right word. In fact, there might not *be* a word to describe the change. Her skin was smooth and flawless. She didn't look like this the last time Ally saw her and now she wondered how long ago that actually was. How many hours, or days?

The bones were the same as always; in her cheeks the underlying structure was sharp and severe and elegant. But there wasn't enough flesh on them. They were reminiscent of what happens at puberty, when the body starts changing in ways that aren't well coordinated.

That was it. Kristen had become a child—it was in her innocent eyes—except that her body was now the flesh of a child over the bone structure of an adult.

It scarcely seemed like the same person from the last time. She had crossed some mystical divide. She was holding a large rag doll—where did she get that? Ally wondered—and humming the tune of the ditty that ended with "Now I know my ABC's. Tell me what you think of me."

"She can't talk," Stone was saying. "I mean, actually communicate. Or at least she doesn't seem to want to. I've already tried. But isn't what's happened incredible? There's never been anything like this in history. The replacement cells are making her body newer and newer, so she's getting younger and younger."

Ally walked over, slowly, and tried to take her hand. She was grasping the doll and she violently pulled back.

"Hey," she said, trying to muster a matter-of-fact air, "how's it going? Do you remember me?"

"I don't think she recognizes you," Stone said in a stage whisper. "I wish I knew more about the biology of the brain, but I think there's some kind of aggressive replacement of memory synapses under way. I think it's one of those LIFO things. Last in/first out. She's regressing chronologically, but in reverse. Maybe she's lost use of language, the way Alzheimer's patients do. I don't know."

Ally felt herself near to tears. "Van de Vliet was going to use antibodies from me to try to . . . something."

"That was always a long shot," he said. "But now the preliminary tests he's just done on you indicate that the level of enzyme in you can be controlled very accurately. He's very excited."

She turned back to him. "How do you know all this?"

"I've become part of the story, Ally. That's not supposed to happen, but this is the only way to get it all firsthand. I have to *live* it. And guess what, I now know enough to write the book I've been waiting all my life to write. I have the punch line."

"Which is?"

"Stem cell technology goes to the very origin of life, and it may turn out that for once Mother Nature *can* be fooled. Dr. Vee's venturing into areas now where even *he* doesn't know what's going on. Ally, what's happening in this room is the biggest medical story since . . . Nothing begins to compare."

Stone had lost it. There was true madness about him now. She walked back over to Kristen and leaned over and kissed her. Kristen stared at her in unfocused confusion, but then she smiled.

"I'm alone in here. Will you take me outside? I want to find my mother."

The voice was that of a five-year-old and it sent a chill through Alexa. The "grown-up" memory cells in her brain had been replaced by blanks. It was "last in/first out" and thirty-plus years of life experience were being replaced with brand-new nothingness.

The Syndrome. Time had to move in one direction or the other. The body either went forward or in reverse. There was no equilibrium.

Then she had a further thought. Winston Bartlett was not going to let this Beta disaster run to its natural conclusion— a horrifying exposure to the world. He was going to inter-vene. Kristen was not about to leave this room in her current condition. Either she left cured—which seemed wholly im-plausible at this point—or she departed in a manner that left no trace.

Then yet another thought crossed her befuddled mind. She and Stone knew about Kristen. *What does that mean for us?*

"Stone, we can't leave her here."

"What are you proposing we do?" he queried. "Take her to an ER somewhere? Frankly, I don't know how you would describe her problem to an emergency room admissions staffer."

"I'll think of something."

"By the way, Ally, so you should know, she's wearing dia-pers. This is the real deal."

"And how do *you* figure in all this?"

"I told you. I'm going to be the James Boswell of stem cell technology. I'm going to report on this miracle from the inside. But now, Ally, if the Beta procedure is going to suc-ceed, you have to be the one to make it happen."

She looked at him, still stunned by the wildness in his eyes.

And she had a feeling like her heart was being wrenched out.

"You're working with them, aren't you?" She was fuming with anger. She no longer knew who could be trusted. He'd taken leave of his senses. Or had his senses been taken from him? Which was it?

"I'm thinking about you. And hopefully about us. You're being offered something you'd be a fool to turn down. That's all I have to say." He took her hand and helped her back into the wheelchair. Then he whispered, "Let's get out of here."

He quickly opened the door and rolled her out into the empty hall. When he closed the door behind them, he whispered again. "Didn't you see the surveillance camera and microphone in there? There's one in the room where they had me locked up. They just put them in."

"To watch Kristen?"

"And me. I heard Bartlett and Van de Vliet talking. If any of this Beta screwup with her gets out of this building, Bartlett's conglomerate is toast." He bent over near to her and continued whispering. "Listen, we don't have much time. They've got your procedure scheduled for later on tonight. I'm still somewhat of a zombie from something they gave me, but maybe I can help get you out of here. Let me tell you what I've found out so far. Van de Vliet gave you a low-dosage version of the Beta procedure, in hopes he could harvest telomerase antibodies and use them on Bartlett. But there was only a trace. He did inject those into Bartlett, but he doesn't think it's enough to have any effect. So now Bartlett is demanding he give you a massive dose of telomerase. Van de Vliet is freaked about the risks, but Bartlett thinks it's his only chance to head off having what happened to Kristen happen to him too. However, what Bartlett doesn't know is that Van de Vliet has just finished a new computer simulation and he thinks he's finally figured out how to do a successful Beta procedure. For him, that's the Holy Grail."

"How do you know all this?"

"I heard him talking to his assistant Debra. I was supposed to be sedated. The reason he wants to perform it on *you* is because he now has so much data on you, as a result of the first procedure. He thinks he's got a real shot at redemption. Ally, if he's calculated wrong, you could end up like Kristen."

"What about *you?*" she asked. "You should get out too."

"I should, but . . . Look, I've been trying to get in here for a long time. Now I'm finally in. You could say I'm under duress, but I'm here and this is where it's happening. If I get out alive, I have a hell of a story."

Is he thinking clearly? she wondered. *He seems to be drifting in and out of a mental cloud.* What *is wrong with him?*

"Stone, there's an emergency door on the first level of the basement. If we can get up there, we might be able to escape. And while we're doing it, you might want to seriously reconsider staying in this place. We've both seen Kristen. What makes you think they're planning on either of us ever living to tell that tale?"

"I'm having some trouble thinking just now." He was helping her out of the wheelchair. "But I do know *you've* got to disappear. Whatever plans they have for me remain to be seen, but I know exactly what's in store for you. So come on and try to walk. We can't use the elevator, but there's a fire door at the other end of the hall, which leads up to the lab floor."

It's probably alarmed, she thought. Then *what do we do?*

Walking was easier than she'd expected. The strength was rapidly coming back in her legs. But more than that, there was no sense of tightness in her chest as she might have expected. She was always aware of traces of stenosis, but now she felt nothing. Maybe there *were* miracles.

The hallway was dimly lit, and she wondered, *Is a surveillance camera tracking our every move?*

"Shit," Stone announced when they reached the fire door, "it's alarmed."

That's exactly what I was afraid of, she thought.

"Any chance they're bluffing?"

"Don't think so." He pointed. "That little red diode says it's hot."

God, she thought, *we've got to get out of here.* "Maybe we could just make a dash for it?"

He looked at her and shook his head. "Like you're in shape to *dash?* No, what's called for is stealth."

He was pulling out his wallet. "The thing about these card readers, some of them, like those that get you into bank ATMs, sometimes will open for other cards. I've got four kinds of plastic. Might as well give them a try."

"Well, just hurry." She leaned against the wall. "I'm starting to get weak."

He slipped his Visa through and nothing happened. He immediately tried MasterCard. Again nothing.

"Maybe I should try my all-purpose bankcard." He slipped a Chase plastic through, but once more nothing happened.

"This isn't working, Stone." She sighed, feeling her legs weaken as she clasped the wall. "I think we're going to have to chance the elevator."

"Don't give up yet." He took out his American Express, kissed it, and swiped it through. "One last shot."

The red diode blinked off.

"Never leave home without it," she whispered.

"We will now proceed very, *very* quietly." He carefully pushed open the door, inches at a time.

The stair had metal steps and was lit by a single fluorescent bulb. As he helped her up, Ally was wondering if there was any way to extract her mother too. She couldn't imagine how she could do it, and besides, Nina might well refuse to go.

No, just get out. And make Stone understand that no way was Winston Bartlett going to let him go free to tell the story of Kristen. He clearly wasn't thinking with all cylinders.

Stone Aimes was about to disappear, just like Kristen had.

The entry to the laboratory level was also alarmed, but American Express once again saved the day. When they pushed open the door, however, the lights were on in the office at the far end of the hallway.

Where's that door that Grant was going to use to get me out? she wondered. Then she saw a door marked EXIT next to Van de Vliet's office.

Shit, it's all the way at the opposite end of the hall.

"Stone, we have to get to that door before anybody sees us. I don't know if it's alarmed or not, but that's the ball game." She reached for his hand. "If we can get there and get out, please come with me. We can make it to the highway. You can't stay here."

"Let's get you out. Then we'll talk."

"I'll drag you if I have to."

As they moved quietly along the wall, they could hear an argument under way. She recognized the voices as Ellen O'Hara's and Karl Van de Vliet's.

"I won't allow my staff to be part of this," Ellen was declaring. "I've seen Kristen. Any form of the Beta is dangerous. If you do anything involving that procedure again, you'll put everybody here at risk."

"Don't you think I've thought about that, agonized about it? We have one chance to turn all this around. This is it."

"I don't want to be involved, and I don't want any of my people involved, do you hear me?"

"Then keep them upstairs." He was striding out of his office, flipping on the lights in the hallway.

"Oh shit," Ally whispered. She opened a door and pulled Stone into the examining room, where her mother had first been admitted. Just as she did, she heard the *ding* of the elevator and caught a glimpse of Debra and David, Van de Vliet's senior researchers, getting off.

When she closed the door, the room should have been pitch black. But it wasn't. A candle was burning on a counter and there was a figure at the far end of the room.

He was sitting on the examining table, in the lotus position, his eyes closed.

"Are you ready?" Kenji Noda asked. "I think just about everyone is here now."

Oh my God, Ally thought. *What are we going to do?*

She watched helplessly as he reached over and touched a button on the desk. A red light popped on above the door. A moment later, it opened.

"What are you doing here?" Debra asked, staring at them.

"Getting some exercise," Stone said.

Then Winston Bartlett appeared in the doorway behind her.

"How did *they* get up here?"

"Ally, I'm not going to let them do this to you," Stone declared, seizing her hand. "We're going to—"

"Ken, please get him out of here," Bartlett said. "Take him back downstairs, anywhere."

"You shouldn't be out of your wheelchair," Debra was saying. She turned to Ellen. "Would you get—"

"I'm not getting *you* anything," Ellen O'Hara declared. "I've just submitted my resignation. Effective three minutes ago. I don't know a thing about what's going on here and, from now on, I don't want to know."

She got on the elevator and the door closed.

"Ken," Bartlett said, "first things first. Go after that woman. Don't let her leave the building."

Now Debra was rolling in a wheelchair. David had appeared also, deep disquiet in his eyes, and he helped her in.

"There's very little risk to this," he said. "Believe me."

She felt him giving her an injection in her left arm.

No, don't . . .

As the room started to spin, she reached out and grabbed Stone's arm and pulled him down to her.

"Downstairs," she whispered. "Look around. There's—"

She didn't get to finish because Debra was whisking her out the door and toward the laboratory. Stone had just grinned confusedly, seemingly not paying any attention to what she was saying. Instead, he ambled toward the open stair door and disappeared.

At this point, however, no one appeared to notice or to care. They were rolling her through the steel air lock. On the other side, Winston Bartlett was already waiting, standing next to a gurney with straps.

No!

Chapter 34

Friday, April 10
9:34 P.M.

She was still conscious as David and Debra lifted her onto the gurney. There was no operating table in the laboratory, but this procedure did not require one. It consisted of a series of small subcutaneous injections along both sides of the spine, followed by a larger injection at the base of the skull.

As the injections began, she drifted into a mind-set where she was never entirely sure how much was real, how much was fantasy, how much deliberate, how much accidental. She remembered that she felt her grasp of reality slipping away, but there was no sense of pain. Instead, images and sensations in a sequence that corresponded to the passage of time drifted through her mind. It was couched in terms of the people she knew.

The first image was her mother, Nina, and they were together, struggling through a dense forest. Initially, she thought they were looking for her father's grave, but then it became clear they were searching for some kind of magic potion that would save her mother's life. As they clawed their way through tangled tendrils and dark arbors, she became increasingly convinced their quest was doomed, that she was destined to watch Nina pass into oblivion.

But then something happened. The forest opened out onto a vast meadow bathed in sunshine. In the center was a cluster of snow white mushrooms, and she knew instinctively that these would bring eternal life to anyone who ate them.

"Come," she said to Nina, "these can save you."

"Ally, I'm too old now. I don't want to be saved. There comes a moment in your life when you've done everything you feel you needed to do. You've had the good times and now all that's left is the slow deterioration of what's left of your body. It robs the joy out of living."

"No, Mom, this is different," she said, plucking one of the white mushrooms and holding it out. "This prevents you from growing any older. You'll stay just the way you are. You can have a miracle."

"To never escape this vale of tears? To watch everyone you love grow old and wither and die? Is that the 'miracle' you want me to have?" Then she looked up at the flawless blue sky and held out her arms as though to embrace the sun. "My mind, Ally. You've given me back my mind. Now I can live out whatever more life God will see fit to give me and actually know who I am and where I am. That's miracle enough for me."

As she said it, a beam of white light came directly from the sun and enveloped her. Then the meadow around them faded away and all she could see was Karl Van de Vliet, who was bending over her and lifting back her eyelids.

"Alexa, I can't tell you what you're about to feel, because no one has ever been where you're about to be. God help us, but we're on the high wire without a net here. But any new cell configurations should immediately form tissue that's a facsimile of what's already there. That's what the simulations show."

She was listening to him, not sure if he was real or a dream. Then she heard Bartlett's voice.

"Why are you talking to her, Karl? She can't hear you."

"We don't actually know whether she can or not. At some level I think she's aware of her surroundings. In a way we should hope that she *is*. If there are going to be impacts on her consciousness, I'd rather she be alert and able to remember what it was like."

Then the voices drifted away, but she was sure she had no control over anything. The white mushrooms. She was thinking about them again. Only now they were above her and growing toward the sky and then she realized she was underground, buried and looking up from her own grave.

What happened next was a journey through time—somewhere in the far-distant future. She seemed to be watching it through a large window, unable to interact with what was happening on the other side.

Time.

She felt a sensation at the back of her neck and the images faded away.

"This damned well better be right," came a voice. "There's not going to be another chance."

"I did an activity simulation for a range of antibodies, just to make sure she wouldn't automatically reject the enzyme because of the earlier injection." The voice belonged to Karl Van de Vliet. Her mind was clearing and she recognized it. "But all the results indicate that the effect of the antibodies is essentially washed out at this concentration of active enzyme. Have the good grace to let me try to get this right."

She was listening and trying to understand what was going on. Her mind had been drifting through time and space, but now she was aware that something new was happening. The hallucinations, the conversations around her, all were beginning to focus in, to build in intensity.

But that was not what was really happening; it was merely a mask over something that had entered the laboratory, some kind of force.

Then her vision began to work in a strange way that felt more like a sixth sense. She was "seeing" what was going on in the room, even though her eyes were shut. Or perhaps they weren't. She didn't know and she was still strapped to the gurney, so she had no way to check.

"Kristy," Winston Bartlett said, dismay in his voice, "you shouldn't be in here. You should be resting."

"What the hell are *you* doing down here?" Van de Vliet demanded. The pitch of his voice had noticeably gone up.

Who? Ally wondered. *Who's he talking to?*

There are definitely new people in the room.

"Come on, Ally," said a voice in her ear, urgent. This time she knew who it was. It was Stone. "Damn them all. I'm getting you out of here. *Now.*"

Chapter 35

Friday, April 10
10:07 P.M.

She felt the straps on the gurney loosening and then she started prying her eyes open. She thought, hoped, it was Stone, but she couldn't see well enough to be absolutely sure. Her mind and her vision were still overflowing with horrifying nightmares of time gone awry. What did all those bizarre dreams mean?

She was groggy but was coming alert. Perhaps it was the sense of electricity in the room, but something very unscheduled was going on.

When she finally got her eyes open and focused, what greeted her was a blinding row of white lights directly overhead that seemed to isolate her. But there was tumult all around her in the lab, a cacophony of alarmed voices echoing off the hard surfaces of glass and steel. She squinted into the light as she felt Stone slip his arm around her shoulders and raise her up.

Thank God, he's here, she thought.

"Come on," he was saying. "She's not interested in you. She just wants Kristen out of here. This is the only way."

"Who . . . ?" She was startled by the sound of her own voice, mildly surprised to discover she was even capable of speech.

She gazed around, trying to find her when . . . *Jesus!*

Katherine Starr was standing next to Kristen. She was moving in a surreal way, gripping Kristen's hand and pulling her along.

Stone had found her. *He had understood.* Katherine Starr appeared to be wearing a blue bathrobe under a gray mackintosh, but the part that got Ally's attention was the knife she was holding, glistening like a scalpel.

No, it *was* a scalpel, shiny and sharp as a razor.

Tough luck, guys. No pistol this time, but she still managed to come up with a convincing substitute.

She didn't look any saner than she did the last time. Now, though, she finally had what she'd come for. She had her daughter. Could it be that Kristen was about to be liberated? Had the world come full circle?

"No." The voice belonged to Winston Bartlett. "I want her with me."

"You're the prick responsible for this." Katherine whirled on him, brandishing the scalpel.

"Mrs. Starr," Van de Vliet interjected, eyeing the sharp metal, "you can't take Kristen away now. She's at a very delicate stage of her procedure."

"I seem to be doing a lot of things I can't," she declared, turning back. "I'm not supposed to be out of my room, but I am. And now I'm getting us both out of here. We're going through that air lock and onto the elevator. So whose throat do I need to cut to do it?"

Winston Bartlett was edging away, and his eyes betrayed he was more concerned than he wished to appear.

"Look at her," Katherine Starr continued, shoving Kristen—who was completely disoriented, her eyes blinking in confusion—in front of Van de Vliet. "She doesn't know me; she doesn't know anything. She's acting like a baby. What in *hell* have you done to her?"

"She had the procedure she wanted. At the time I warned there might be side effects we couldn't anticipate."

"She's lost her mind. That's what you call a *side effect!*"

All this time Kristen was just standing and staring blankly into space, but there were growing storm clouds welling in her eyes. It caused Ally to wonder what was really going on with her. Had this troubled girl been made permanently childlike, or was there a split personality at work? Did she have a new mind now, or a parallel mind?

"We're still trying to stabilize her condition," Van de Vliet said in a soothing tone. "We just need a little more time."

That was when Kristen wrenched free of her mother's grasp. Her eyes had just gone critical, traveling into pure madness. She strode over and seized a glass jar containing a clear solvent.

"I want them all to die," she said in a little girl's voice. "They're going to kill me if I don't kill them first."

Now Katherine Starr had turned and was staring at her. "Kristy, honey, put the bottle down. I'm going to take you home. I don't know what he's done to you, but I'm not going to let you stay here anymore. You're coming with me."

This is not going to end well, Ally thought. She began struggling to her feet, trying to clear her mind enough for an exit strategy.

Nina was upstairs, or at least that was where she *had* been. *Okay, the first order of business is to get her out. Stone could probably manage on his own. . . .*

Now Kristen was walking over to an electric heater positioned on a lab workbench. She switched it on and the tungsten elements immediately began to glow. Then, still holding the bottle, she turned back to Van de Vliet.

"I see things that I never saw before. My mind has powers it never had till now."

He nodded knowingly. "I always suspected that—"

"I'm able to think just like I did when I was little," she continued, cutting him off. "Sometimes I'm there, in that world. Then sometimes I flip back. But I can always tell when grown-ups are lying to me. What did you do to my mind?"

"Kristen," Van de Vliet said, "the brain has many functions that we still only barely understand. With the Beta procedure, we don't really know what activates general cell replacement or what the nature of the replacement tissue actually is. We're just at the beginning of a marvelous—"

"I'm seeing a future in which nothing exists," she muttered despairingly, still holding the glass bottle of solvent. "I don't want to be a part of it."

Van de Vliet was staring at her, his eyes flooded with alarm. "What . . . *what* are you seeing, Kristen?"

"I'm seeing you dead." She glared around. "All of you."

Then, with an animal scream, she whirled and flung the glass liter bottle at the electric heater on the laboratory workbench. It crashed into the shiny steel case with a splintering sound, followed by an explosion that sent a ball of fire and a shock wave through the room. In an instant the entire end of the lab was engulfed in a sea of flame.

Ally sensed herself being knocked to the floor, but she also felt a surge of adrenaline. This was endgame, the moment when everybody found out who they were.

A hand was gripping her like a vise. It was Stone's, but the blast had knocked him to the floor too and he was now motionless, slumped against the side of a laboratory bench. It was like she was being held in a death grip. Was she going to have to carry him out? She wasn't even sure she had the strength in her legs to get *herself* out.

Now something even more horrible was slowly beginning to happen. The central part of the lab had several sets of steel shelving arranged in rows, and each supported a carefully organized arrangement of sample vials filled with some kind of organic solvent. She saw with horror that the first towering set of shelves, easily seven feet high, was slowly tipping from the force of the blast. It teetered for an instant and then fell into the set of shelves next to it with all the ponderous majesty of a giant sequoia.

What happened next sounded like the end of the world. As the first set of shelves crashed against the second, like a row of massive steel-and-glass dominoes, each subsequent tower tipped and fell against the next, and on and on.

All the while, as the tumbling racks were spewing flammable solvents across the smoky lab space, they were ripping out electrical wiring and sending sparks flying.

The whole danger-dynamic of the room had been turned upside down. Katherine Starr and Debra and David now lay pinned beneath a tangled mass of angle-iron supports that had collapsed in the wake of the falling shelves. All three appeared to be unconscious.

Winston Bartlett was at the far end of the room. He'd been slammed against the wall by the force of the explosion but was pulling himself up. He seemed to be unhurt, though it was hard to see through the billowing smoke.

Karl Van de Vliet was standing in the middle of the laboratory, his eyes glazed, flames and smoke swirling about him.

What does this mean to him? Ally wondered. *Years of research data being obliterated in an instant.*

But the horror wasn't over. The fire was depleting the hermetically sealed room's oxygen. Ally sensed that anybody who didn't get out of the lab in the next five minutes wasn't going to be going anywhere standing up.

But what was happening with Kristen? She was walking through the flames as though on a country stroll. It was like the fires of hell were all around her and she was ambling through them unscathed. *She must be experiencing third-degree burns,* Ally thought, *yet there's a sense that nothing can harm her. How could it be?*

And then an astonishing possibility began to dawn on her. With the stem cell enzymes working at full blast, was it possible her body was immediately replacing its damaged cells? Could it be that the telomerase enzyme didn't know the difference between a cell that had aged and one that had been damaged by its environment?

"Jesus," Stone said, finally stirring, "what's—"

At that moment the overhead lights flickered and died and the emergency lights clicked on, sending battery-powered beams through the smoke.

"Christ, Ally," he declared, gazing around, still dazed as his consciousness seemed to be slowly returning. "We've got to get people out of here."

There didn't appear to be a sprinkler system. Probably, she thought, because an onslaught of water would wipe out all the computers.

Now she was thinking about the automatic air locks. How did those steel-and-glass doors work without electricity? Did they have a battery backup, or some kind of fail-safe mechanism, which provided a manual override in case of a power outage?

Now Winston Bartlett was striding toward the center of the room. From the dazed look in his eyes, it wasn't clear whether he knew where he was or not. Kristen was walking toward him, on a collision course.

"You let this happen," she said. "You wanted to ruin my life."

"Kristy, nobody *made* you do anything," he said, choking from the smoke. "But now we've got to—"

"It's too late," she declared, lashing out with the side of her hand against his neck. He staggered back, flailing, and seized an iron girder.

There was a blast of voltage, a shower of sparks, and he screamed as he crumpled sideways. Then the force of his fall broke his hand loose from the electrical short. He lay prostrate on the smoky floor of the lab, twitching.

My God, Ally thought, *she really is determined to kill us all before she's through.*

"Kristen," Van de Vliet was saying, "please. There's still time. I'm going to do everything I can for you."

He was gasping for air and now more vials of flammable liquid were exploding from the heat and igniting. He turned and stumbled toward the air lock. There were sounds of yelling on the other side.

The people outside can't get through, Ally realized. *The security lock has no override.*

We're going to die.

Van de Vliet pounded on the button controls of the air lock, but there was no response. Smoke was billowing around him and he choked, coughing and dropping to one knee.

Then Kristen walked up behind him. She appeared not to notice the flames and smoke swirling around her.

"This is where you get what's coming, you bastard. I warned you you'd better do something for me. But you never really intended to help me. I was just an experiment. That's all I ever was. For both of you. You *fuckers.*" And she lashed out with a powerful fist, sending him to the floor.

Outside there was now the wail of a siren, the sound faintly filtering through. And the pounding on the other side of the air lock continued, though now it had the force of authority.

At last, Ally thought, *somebody finally got serious and called the fire department.*

Now Kristen had bent over the prostrate Van de Vliet and was doing something, though Ally couldn't tell what.

"Keep your face close to the floor," Stone was yelling. "It's where the last of the air is. Hang on. We'll be okay."

She had a premonition they were *not* going to be okay. They all were going to suffocate.

All, that was, except Kristen. She seemed to possess some magic immunity from the horrors around her. She had risen and was standing over Van de Vliet like a statue, while everybody else was on the floor.

As Ally watched her—a serene figure in the middle of chaos and death—she began to have an odd sensation. The burning in her lungs, from the smoke, started to dissipate. And strength felt like it was pouring into her limbs. The tongues of flame around her had become dancing white figures that invited her to rise and join them.

She did, slowly, not quite knowing what she was doing. Then she walked to the jammed air lock. She stepped over

Karl Van de Vliet's collapsed frame and placed her hands on the steel. It was already scalding, but she only took fleeting notice of that.

While a firefighter's ax futilely pounded on the outside, she seized the wide bar of the door and ripped it open, to the sound of wrenching metal.

It was a superhuman effort she didn't realize she was capable of. And it was the last thing she remembered. The space around her had become a blazing white cloud and she didn't feel the hands of the two firefighters who seized her as she fell through the open air lock.

Chapter 36

Friday, June 5
8:39 P.M.

Days later, Alexa Hampton was still considering herself one of the luckiest people alive. When she'd regained consciousness the next week in Lenox Hill Hospital, hooked up to oxygen and being fed by an IV, she noticed that the nurses were looking at her strangely and whispering to each other. Finally she couldn't stand it anymore and asked why.

"It was what you did," a young Puerto Rican woman explained, gazing at her in awe through her rimless glasses. "No one can believe it."

Then she explained. What they couldn't believe—as reported by the New Jersey firefighters—was that she had single-handedly wrenched open the steel-door air lock of the laboratory at the Dorian Institute. At the time firefighters were on the other side vainly trying to dismantle the door with their axes. Yet she'd just yanked it aside like paper. It was reminiscent of those urban legends of superhuman strength in times of crisis, like the story of a panicked woman who hoisted an overturned Chevy van to free a pinned child. Later, though, some of the New Jersey fire crew went back and looked again. The steel hinges had literally been sheared off. . . .

How did she *do* that? More important, though, symptoms of her stenosis had entirely disappeared and she felt better than ever in her life. The stem cell technology pioneered by Karl Van de Vliet had indeed produced a miracle. She even had a new kind of energy, periodically. It was unlike anything she'd ever felt.

Other things were new as well. She'd been seeing a lot of Stone Aimes and helping him finish his book on the Gerex Corporation's successful clinical trials with stem cell technology. After all the publicity following the fire at the Dorian Institute, the manuscript was generating a lot of buzz. A paperback auction was already in the works, with a half-million floor, and *Newsweek* had abruptly taken a second look at the "first serial" excerpt his agent had been trying to place with them and come up with six figures. The only part Stone hadn't reported was the ghastly side effect of the early Beta experiment, the Syndrome, because Kristen Starr had disappeared. He had no proof and his publisher refused to print potentially libelous speculation.

In the meantime, Winston Bartlett hadn't been seen in public since that tragic day. The business press speculated he had become a Howard Hughes–like recluse in his Gramercy Park mansion. Ally had tried several times to reach him through his office to find out what he wanted to do about the design job, and each time she was told he would get back to her. He never did.

Maybe he was still recuperating. When the firefighters pulled him out of the flaming wreckage, his clothes were singed from the electricity that had coursed through his body, his heart was stopped, and he appeared to be dead. In fact, he *was* dead.

The paramedics immediately began intensive CPR. Moments later, his heart was beating again. Then he declared he was well enough that he didn't need to go to a hospital. He had his Japanese henchman, Kenji Noda, help him to his McDonnell Douglas and he disappeared into the night.

Oxygen had not been to his brain for . . . No one knew how long. The paramedics said he awoke in what seemed another reality.

Was he still alive? There had been no reports otherwise, but he most certainly had withdrawn from the world.

Karl Van de Vliet, for his part, had been hospitalized for severe burns. He remained in the trauma unit at St. Vincent's Hospital, but when Alexa tried to go visit him, she was told he wasn't accepting visitors but was doing well. Katherine Starr was dead from a massive concussion, along with the two researchers, Debra Connolly and David Hopkins, who had been in the wrong place when the steel racks collapsed. And Alexa never been able to find out what happened to Kristen Starr. Officially, nobody by that name was there.

But business was business. With the clinical trials over, the pending sale of the Gerex Corporation to Cambridge Pharmaceuticals was proceeding on autopilot, handled by Grant Hampton, who stood to make a bundle or so he bragged to Alexa. The Dorian Institute had been closed and all the remaining records moved to a converted facility near Liverpool.

After six days in Lenox Hill, Ally went home, and three days after that she had returned to her desk at CitiSpace. Now, inevitably, she was back to her workaholic habits and grueling hours.

Today, though, she had knocked off early, since Nina had taken a cab down to join her for supper.

She marveled just thinking about it. Her mom taking a cab. By herself. It truly was a miracle.

Their "light" repast had consisted of cold roast beef and room-temperature stout, two of Nina's favorites. She had never been much for cucumber sandwiches with the crust cut off. Afterward, she elected to have a brandy.

"The trouble with having your mind back," she said as she settled onto the couch, snifter in hand, "is that sometimes you remember things you'd just as soon forget." Outside thunder boomed from an early evening rainstorm, which had blown in from the northwest.

"Well, Mom, at least now you can pick and choose what you want to remember and what you want to forget." She didn't really mind the storm. Having her mother back was such a blessing.

It still felt odd, though, having her rescued from what had to be an inevitable, ignominious fate. It was as though time had gone in reverse. A miracle was very much in progress. . . .

She was experiencing a miracle too, though of a slightly different sort. She felt pretty much normal, if occasionally shaky and uncertain on her feet. But at unexpected times she would have bursts of energy that defied reality. They were, in fact, scary, like that thing with the steel door. Something weird would sometimes take control of her body and she didn't really know what it was. . . .

Truthfully, she was feeling some of that tonight. She had joined her mother with a brandy and was thinking about taking Knickers for an early walk, downpour or not. She wanted to see the river through the mists of a storm.

That was when the phone rang. She got up and made her way to the kitchen and took the receiver off the wall.

"Hello." She was hoping it was Stone. He'd usually call early in the evening to see what she was doing and ask if she wanted some company.

"Alexa, I need to see you," came a voice. The other end of the line was noisy, as though a loud motor was running.

"Who—"

"I think you know who this is. If you would come down to the river, right now, I will make it very much worth your while."

For some reason, maybe it was telepathy, Knickers had begun bouncing about the kitchen, angling for a walk, even though she normally was mortally fearful of thunder.

Now Ally did know who it was.

What was *he* doing calling her here at home, in a rain-storm? After all these weeks.

Well, she thought, *I have nothing left to fear from him or any of them. Why not?*

"It's raining," she said. "This had better be fast."

And she hung up the phone.

"Who was that, honey?" Nina asked. "I hope it wasn't anybody I know. You were somewhat abrupt."

"Mom, they deserved whatever they got, and it's no big deal. But I think I'm going to take Knickers out. She's mak-ing me nuts."

Ally couldn't focus on what had just happened. He had a lot of nerve. On the other hand, she loved to be down by the river when it was this way, shrouded in pastel mist.

"Honey, it's raining cats and dogs," Nina declared. "You're apt to catch your death."

"No, Mom, it's letting up now. I'll be all right. Really." She was digging out her tan raincoat and rubber galoshes from the closet by the door. Knickers immediately realized what was up and began a dance of joy, barking as she raced to find her leash.

"Come on, honey," Ally said, taking the braided leather. "I want you close to me."

The ride down in the elevator felt ominous, though Knickers failed to share any of her apprehension as she bounced around the glass dome and nuzzled Ally's legs. The thunder she was sometimes fearful of had lessened, and that, Ally thought, had doubtless improved her courage.

The condominium no longer had a doorman. In hopes of trimming costs, the condo board had sent out a secret ballot on the subject. By a narrow margin the owners had voted to dispense with that particular frill. Although she missed Alan and his early morning optimism about his Off-Broadway hopes, she realized the economy was probably timely. All those weeks when she hadn't been pulling her weight at CitiSpace, the nut on that operation hadn't diminished any.

As she stepped onto Barrow Street, the late-spring air was unseasonably brisk and the rain had blanked visibility down to almost nothing. On other days this would had been that magical moment just after the sun went down, when gorgeous fiery orange clouds hung over the Hudson, but now there was a hint of brooding in the bleak rain. It fit the dark mood she felt growing around her.

He wanted to meet her down by the river. Gripping Knickers's leash, she checked the traffic lights, then marched across the West Side Highway. The new esplanade along the river was awash in the rain and was uncharacteristically empty.

That was lucky for Knickers. Off-the-leash time. Ally drew her close and clicked open the catch that attached it to her collar. With a "woof" of joy, she dashed off toward the vacant pier, then headed out.

"Baby, slow down," Ally yelled, but it was to no avail. A second later, her fluffy sheepdog was lost in the rain.

But she couldn't go far. The refurbished pier extended out into the river for maybe the length of a football field and change. Beyond that, there was at least half a mile of river before the shores of New Jersey. For all her enthusiasm, Knickers wasn't about to dive into the chilly Hudson and swim for the horizon.

So where was he? He'd said "down by the river."

What to do now? She decided she might as well walk out after Knickers.

Now she was noticing something odd. The air was chilly; actually, raw was a better description. A last blast of unusual arctic air had accompanied the rain. She could feel the temperature on her face. She had stupidly gone out with just a light shirt under the raincoat, yet she didn't feel the slightest bit cold. It was as though her metabolism had sped up, the way it did during a run, though she wasn't breathing heavy or anything. It felt like one of those strange moments she'd been having, when she felt superalive.

Now Knickers was returning, but she was slinking back as though fearful of something, the rain running off her face.

"Come here, baby," Ally said, reaching out. "What is it?"

The darkness of the river flowed over her now, and for the first time ever, she wished she'd brought along a flashlight. . . .

That was when, out of the rain, she finally heard the sound. It was an engine lowering from the sky, which Knickers must have already heard. Then a helicopter, a McDonnell Douglas, materialized, lowering onto the empty sports space on the pier.

The downdraft of the rotor threw spray against the FieldTurf and into her eyes. But she gazed through it, unblinking, feeling an unexpected sense of power entering her limbs. The rain should have felt cold, but she didn't really notice.

Maybe, she thought, they *had* to meet. They were bonded.

As the pilot cut the power, the engine began to wind down—*whoom, whoom, whoom*—until it came to a dead stop and there followed an unnatural silence. Finally the door on the side opened and a metal step dropped down.

After a moment's pause that seemed to last forever, he appeared, at first a vague figure in the rain, but then he stepped down and came toward her. He was wearing a white hat with a wide brim and a tan raincoat that seemed more like a cloak than a coat.

"Alexa, I so appreciate your making time for me."

It was hard to tell in the rain, but he appeared to be strong, and there was actually a kind of radiance about him, as though he carried his own special luminosity. He seemed completely transformed. The question was, transformed how? He looked years younger than the last time she saw him.

"I thought we should talk. I've been meaning to call you. I wanted to see how you're doing."

That's not it at all, she told herself. *What do you really want?*

"Actually, I've been wanting to thank you," Winston

Bartlett went on. "It turns out that you saved me after all. Your telomerase antibodies finally kicked in. The initial ones Karl injected in me. It just took a few weeks."

"And what about Kristen?" she asked.

His look saddened.

"You didn't hear?" He shook his head. "She . . . died in the fire."

That doesn't sound right, Ally thought. *She looked like she was the only one who* was *going to survive it.*

"Oh yeah? How did that happen?"

"You might as well know. She was burned beyond recognition. The body still hasn't been officially identified. When the firemen found her, she had a shard of glass through her throat. They thought she must have fallen on something, but I fear it's entirely possible she could have done it to herself."

Was that story true, or a bald-faced lie? Ally wondered. Were they still hiding her someplace?

But why was he here? He certainly hadn't come to discuss the kitchen design job for his Gramercy Park mansion. That was now long ago and far away.

"Alexa," he said, moving toward her, "please don't be frightened, but there's something I have to find out."

He reached out with his left hand and seized her wrist. She only saw the glint of the penknife in his right hand for an instant before he slashed it across her palm.

"What!" she screamed, and yanked her hand away. Knickers gave a loud yelp and then howled mournfully.

Only then did she notice that there'd been just a momentary flash of pain.

"It's okay," Bartlett said, reaching to soothe Knickers. "Just a superficial scratch. Now watch it. I want to know if Karl had time to finish the procedure."

My God. She didn't have to watch. She could already feel it beginning to heal.

"What's . . . what's going on? Is this—"

"He had hopefully completed the Beta on you just before

Kristy's mother showed up. But did it work the way it was supposed to? We didn't know. Until now."

"My God. I knew I was feeling—"

"You received just the right amount of telomerase injections," Bartlett interjected, "to induce the Beta without any side effects. It was the 'Goldilocks dosage' Karl had been trying to calculate, just enough that only aged or damaged cells are replaced, while healthy tissue is not altered."

She now realized that was why she'd been having bouts of incredible energy.

"We're the only ones," he went on. "Just us. You and me. We've been given this gift, Alexa. And now we have the responsibility that goes along with it." He glanced down at her hand. "By the way, how's that cut doing?"

"What are you getting at?" It was definitely healing.

A wave of thunder boomed over the river, sending Knickers scurrying to Ally's side.

"What I'm getting at is that you and I are now two very special people. We both are living proof of what the Beta can achieve. The question is, what are we going to do about it?"

She was still stunned.

"This is a lot to absorb. I'll have to think—"

"I've already thought about this and I believe it must be kept secret at all cost. At least for now."

"But why? It's a miracle that—"

"That must be handled prudently. I need your cooperation with that."

She was having extreme difficulty getting her mind around what he was talking about.

"I don't really know what's going on. I think I'd better see some doctors. And Stone is finishing his book about . . . I've got to tell him—"

"Those things cannot happen, Alexa." He looked out at the river for a moment, then turned back. "A brand-new world has dawned. Finally all things are possible." He moved closer to her, then reached out and took her wrist again. She looked down and realized the cut on her hand was all but healed. "For now, this has to be our secret, yours and mine. Just us."

She thought about all that had happened in the weeks since her wayward brother had accosted her running along this very river. It felt like an eternity.

"I'm asking you not to talk about this," he continued. "To anyone. You must give me your solemn word."

She felt the grip on her wrist get stronger.

"Now that we know the Beta can work," he went on, his voice piercing through the rain, "I am forming an elite association, the Methuselah Society. Membership buys a guarantee that you can stop aging; in fact, you can pick the age you want to remain. Karl is sure he can do that, assuming the Beta worked with you. And now we see it has. The first memberships will naturally be somewhat expensive, but as time goes by, the cost will be gradually scaled down to respond to market forces. One may *only* join with a companion, but for obvious reasons all those who undergo the Beta must be sworn to secrecy, on pain of death, since there's bound to be a hue and cry and government intervention if word leaks out that only individuals with significant resources can have this miracle."

"I think that's obscene," she said.

"I suspected you might feel that way. Which is why we're having this talk. As I've explained, the Methuselah Society will be contingent on the utmost secrecy, at least initially. So the question is, are you on board with this?"

"The answer is, I'll do what I please." She was thinking what a bombshell this would be to have in Stone's book. Stem cells—the Fountain of Youth was no longer a dream.

Winston Bartlett had won his dice game with God. And now he was planning to sweep the table. But he also was smart enough to realize he had to cash in quickly and discreetly.

"Don't you realize how irresponsible that is?" he insisted.

"We stand on the threshold of a new era for humankind. But if we let small-minded politicians get involved with this, they might decide to forbid . . . Keep in mind that using stem cell technology to regenerate organs is already controversial. Just imagine what the self-appointed zealots would do with *this*. The good of humanity is less important to them than their narrow-minded, bigoted constituencies."

That was when it finally dawned on her why he had lured her down here by the river on a rainy night. What better place for a convenient "accident" if it came to that.

She watched as he turned and raised a finger toward the open door of the McDonnell Douglas.

The motor started and then another figure emerged and came down the steps. She squinted through the rain and recognized Kenji Noda, Bartlett's ever-present bodyguard. He was carrying a plastic bottle, along with a small white towel.

He's going to chloroform me and then God knows what. I'm about to disappear the same way Kristen did.

She stared at them both, wondering what to do.

"Alexa, I regret to say that you are either with me or you are a problem I cannot afford to have," Bartlett said, and then he nodded to Noda.

Shit.

She backed to the edge of the pier as Noda advanced on her menacingly, dousing the cloth. He was a foot taller than she was and he weighed over two hundred pounds.

Her first instinct was to run, but then she sensed an impulse to stand her ground. Something told her to try to use her strength against him. He wouldn't expect it.

Out of the corner of her eye, she noticed that a white car had pulled onto the pier and was cruising down the side, slowly inching their way. It looked like a police vehicle, probably a couple of cops curious about the presence of a helicopter on the FieldTurf.

They were approximately half a minute too late to make any difference. Kenji Noda was five feet away and they were fifty yards away. And they probably couldn't see what was going on anyway. The rain had chosen that moment to begin to gush, shrouding everything in sheets of water.

Knickers was nudging at her leg, as though urging her to flee. And again she thought about running, but an instinct told her to stand her ground. She was feeling a sensation of power growing in her limbs.

She found herself oddly calm as Kenji Noda reached her, then wrapped his left arm around her neck and with his right hand clamped the cloth over her nostrils. It was infused with chloroform—she knew the smell—but she held her breath.

Then it happened. She casually reached up and took his left arm and pulled it away from her neck.

It was so easy. There was the same feeling of strength she'd had when she wrenched open the air lock. Yet it was something that came and went. She had no inkling how long it would last this time.

"I don't think you should do that," she said, continuing to pull his arm around behind him. Then she twisted it to the side and there was a sickening snap as it came out of its shoulder socket.

He groaned lightly but did not speak. Instead, he reached with his right hand and pulled an automatic out of a holster at the back of his belt, dropping the chloroformed cloth in the process. While his left arm dangled uselessly, he brought around the pistol and tried to aim it at her torso. Her senses, though, were coming fully alive now and she seized his wrist and pushed it away just as he fired.

The round caught her at the outer edge of her shoulder. She felt it enter and exit, but there was no pain, merely a mild itch. Still holding his wrist, she picked up the white cloth and buried his face in it. She held it against his nostrils until his body twitched and went limp.

That was when the spotlight hit them.

"Drop your weapons and show your hands," came a basso voice over a megaphone.

Who had a weapon? she wondered. The one pistol around was lying on the ground next to the crumpled frame of Kenji Noda.

The police must have heard the shot and assumed they were being fired on.

She turned around to search for Winston Bartlett and saw him retreating to the McDonnell Douglas. Running, actually.

He saw what happened, she told herself. *He's afraid of me.*

"Stop and identify yourself," came the police megaphone. The spotlight was now squarely on Bartlett, who was bounding up the retractable steps.

Without looking back, he pulled up the steps and slammed the door. The rotor had already begun revving higher, and in moments the chopper had begun its ascent out over the dark river.

"You have been warned to identify yourself," came the futile megaphone. The chopper had all but disappeared into the dark and rain when she heard a shot fired from the direction of the police car.

It must have been an accident, she told herself. *There's no way—*

But the smooth hum of the engine dying away in the fog abruptly changed tone, then started to sputter. Ten seconds later, there was silence.

She was so engaged she didn't notice the stirring at her feet. A moment thereafter, she saw the towering bulk of Kenji Noda rise up beside her. Then she felt his grip on her wrist and realized he was dragging, and pulling her to the edge of the pier. Then she felt a shove and a swirl of dark air around her, followed by the splash of cold water. Surprisingly, it didn't really feel freezing—it just felt refreshingly brisk. With one hand she grabbed one of the square concrete pillars that was supporting the pier. The mysterious strength she'd had from time to time was coming back once more.

That was when she heard a vicious howl, wolflike, that transmuted into a growl, and the next thing she saw was a hazy form hurtle past her and splash into the water.

Actually, it was two forms, and the darker one was flailing while the lighter one bore down on him, her teeth on his throat.

"No!" she screamed, *"Don't."*

As the pair drifted past her in the current, still linked, she reached out and seized Knickers's collar, yanking her back. Then she watched helplessly as Kenji Noda disappeared into the dark. Could he swim with one arm?

The cops were futilely searching the wide river with their searchlight, looking for the helicopter, for anything, but there was nothing left to see.

She quietly made for shore, even as she and Knickers were being swept downstream by the current. When they finally reached the bank, it was somewhere around Morton Street. Oddly enough, she wasn't cold and she wasn't tired when she drew herself up onto the rocks, Knickers at her side. She just lay panting for a moment.

"Come here, baby," she said, drawing Knickers to her. The dog was shivering and she knew she had to get her home soon. "Thank God you can't talk. I think something very evil just passed from the world."

Epilogue

Thursday, June 25
10:49 P.M.

"You're really something," Stone declared, falling back onto the rumpled sheets. "What's come over you lately? Don't you ever get tired?"

"Maybe I'm just happy to be alive," Ally said, smiling as she ran a finger down his chest. "I'm catching up on all the living I've been missing out on."

Her heart was definitely on the mend, in several ways. She was beginning to think she was in love. After Steve went missing, she thought that love would never happen again, but maybe it had.

"Know what," he said, rising up, "I've really worked up an appetite. How about you? Think I'll make an omelette. Got any eggs left in the fridge?"

"Should be some," she said. "But I'll pass. Anything I eat after ten goes straight to places on my body that don't need further reinforcement."

It was so nice just to have someone to be near again. Her nervous system was still recovering from the harrowing experience down on the pier. In fact, she wasn't really sure what actually had happened. The crashed McDonnell Douglas was retrieved from the water the next day, but there were no bodies aboard. Had Winston Bartlett drowned and his body been swept out to sea by the tide? Also, there must have been a third person, a pilot. And what about Kenji Noda, who also was missing? Did he make it to shore? In any case, they all had disappeared. The case was closed. And since nobody had found a will, New York State was currently the executor of his fortune. Eileen Bartlett was sole heir. Her waiting game had paid off superbly. The price of her Gerex shares was doubling every two weeks. She was about to become a very rich woman indeed.

But had Winston Bartlett really gone to a watery grave? Ally somehow doubted it. He had too much invested in life to cash in so easily.

As she watched Stone get up and swathe himself in a huge white towel before heading for the kitchen, she found herself replaying that harrowing scene at the pier. She kept trying to remember something Bartlett had said about forming some kind of society. Was she fantasizing or had he said he was going to do that and then offer the Beta procedure to its members? What was he going to call it? Try as she might, she couldn't remember. She had developed a mental block that her mind was using to shield her psyche from the horror of that evening.

That night she'd first considered going to St. Vincent's Hospital emergency room for the gunshot wound, but then she'd thought it over and decided there were too many things to explain that couldn't be explained. Instead, she just went home and washed the wound and filled it up with Neosporin. She didn't even tell Nina. The next morning, scar tissue was already forming. Now it was completely healed and even the scar had all but disappeared.

Had the Beta really worked? She wanted to tell Stone about that possibility, but she wasn't sure how he would take it. And she absolutely did not want to end up in the book.

She pulled on a terry cloth robe and slippers and padded

her way into the kitchen. She wasn't hungry, but she felt like a glass of wine. She poked around in the wine rack in the kitchen closet and came up with a bottle of Bordeaux. Stone was cracking large white eggs into a stoneware bowl.

"Sure I can't make some for you?" he asked, leaning over to buss her hair as she searched in the drawer for a corkscrew. "I'm gonna throw in some cheddar, but I'll leave it out if that doesn't work for you."

"I just want a glass of red wine," she said, retrieving the corkscrew. "And I need a memory jogging. What's a word that makes you think of living a long time? I . . . I want to look up something on the Internet and I don't know how to start."

"What kind of word is it?" he queried. "I'm a wordsmith. Twenty questions. Is it a noun, a verb, an adjective?"

"If I could remember that, I might be able to come up with it."

He was tossing a quarter stick of butter into the pan. "Hey, I once learned hypnosis. Why don't you let me take you under?"

"Does that really work?"

"It's how I come up with interview stuff sometimes, from years ago. We really do have a complicated memory system. I think *everything* you ever knew is buried somewhere, maybe in a tiny little wrinkle."

She suspected he might be right. In this case the repressed info was still there; it just had been deliberately covered over and hidden.

"So do you want to hypnotize me? You're sure you know how?"

"I'm not boasting, but I could make Methuselah remember the day he first got out of diapers."

She stared at him. "My God, I think that's it. Methuselah. I think that's the word I couldn't remember." She kissed him on the mouth enthusiastically. "I've got to check something."

She popped the cork and poured herself a glass.

"Want some?"

"I'm not sure what goes with eggs at this time of night. Probably tequila."

"Good luck. You know where to find it. There're some limes in the fridge. Right now I'm going to fire up the Dell and do a little search."

"Now?" His face dropped. "How about a little romantic . . . whatever?"

"Come and join me. Bring your plate. We'll go exploring in cyberspace. It'll be a romantic voyage. I've got a hunch about something."

She walked back into the bedroom and clicked on the computer. She sipped at her wine, deep but still fruity and delicious, as it booted up.

"What's going on?" he asked as he wandered in. He was carrying a shot glass of tequila and a white plate with the cheese omelette. The aroma was seductive.

"I want to check out something. I have to be honest and confess I've been holding out on you a little. When I saw Winston Bartlett that night on the pier, something he said—"

"Ally, I need to do some confessing too. The time never seemed quite right. I need to tell you something about him."

"Well, don't tell me now. I don't think I can handle anything else to worry about tonight. Please save it."

She was logging on to AOL. Then she went to the search engine Google, which she had found to be the best.

"I want to check out that name you came up with. It rang a bell."

She typed in *Methuselah,* supposedly the guy who lived for nearly a thousand years.

There were pages and pages of references relating to that word. It started with a five-thousand-year-old pine tree, then an article from *Modern Maturity* on how to extend life, then Caltech research on a longevity gene, then a rock band in Texas (undoubtedly *very* retro), a short story by Isaac Bashevis Singer, and so it went.

"What, exactly, are you looking for?" he asked, holding out a fork. "Here. Want a bite?"

She reached and tore off a fluffy corner. He did eggs perfectly.

"Thanks," she said, chewing. Now she was moving to the third page. "I think I'm looking for an organization. And Methuselah was in the name. At least . . . that's what I seem to remember. I'm definitely repressing a lot."

"Well, what about that one?" he asked, pointing.

The line read, *the Methuselah Society.*

"That's *it,*" she declared. "Now I remember. That's the name he used. I swear. So it's real. I'm not crazy."

"What are you talking about?"

"It's him. That's what he said he was going to do."

She clicked on the name.

The Web page came up and it was strictly in black and white, with small print. And there it was again. THE METHUSELAH SOCIETY. There was no information beyond a request for a secure e-mail address.

"Looks like they want to check you out," Stone said.

"To make sure you're not connected to politics or law enforcement."

"Then why not give it a shot," Stone said. "You're on AOL. You'd have to be a civilian."

She typed in her address and entered it. Immediately a little yellow padlock appeared in the lower right-hand corner, indicating their communication was secure. Then a notice materialized, a small square flickering to life. It contained her phone number and then her name. Next a complete financial record began to scroll down. It had been elicited from banks, mortgage companies, credit services. There was Value of Real Estate owned, Mortgages Outstanding, Bank Accounts, Outstanding Obligations, Estimated Net Worth. It had all appeared in a time span of seconds.

"Wow," Stone said. "There are no secrets left from these guys, whoever they are. They are *wired.*"

Then a message appeared: *The minimum net worth required to be a member is 500 Million Dollars. The fee for membership is 100 Million Dollars. A 10-Million-Dollar retainer is required while your application is being processed. Please be prepared to designate the ages you and your companion wish to remain.*

"My God," she said, "that's him. He's done it. Winston Bartlett is alive and well, and selling immortality, real or not."

Then another message came up: *Welcome, Alexa. Please be advised you are already a member. But you have not yet selected a companion.*

Afterword

How much of the foregoing is true or even plausible?

In late 2002, medical researchers in Düsseldorf announced they had successfully treated heart-attack victims using stem cells harvested from the patients' own bone marrow. The stem cells were delivered to damaged heart muscle via angioplasty catheters, a minimally invasive procedure. Subsequent monitoring indicated that the stem cells had reduced the damage to heart-muscle tissue and had improved their heart function when compared to similar patients in a control group who had declined the procedure.

It's already happening.

The miraculous stem cell cures in this story are essentially an extrapolation of research well underway that has been the subject of magazine covers and is possibly the most promising and, yes, problematic field of medical research. The clocks at the Dorian Institute ran faster than ordinary timepieces, and research areas and cures that currently are only speculation were made real there. But that's why it's called fiction. As with the example cited above, many stem cell miracles conjured here may be just over the horizon.

As for Kristen and the Methuselah Society, they are a fictional embodiment of misgivings given voice by many, including no less an authority than Professor Leonard Hayflick, whose Hayflick limit, defining the process of how cells grow old, could be said to be the underpinning of modern stem cell research. He is now a leading bioethicist who is sufficiently convinced of our potential to use stem cells to arrest the actual aging process that he has worried about its ramifications in print. He makes no claim that such a thing is imminent, but he doesn't dismiss its possibility either. He has far-reaching societal concerns about this, and he also raises biological issues such as, if you've treated your brain malady by using stem cells to grow new neural tissue, have you altered your mind? Are you still you?

It's called Regenerative Medicine. Watch for it.

ABOUT THE AUTHOR

Thomas Hoover lives in New York City. *Syndrome* is his seventh novel.

BOOK YOUR PLACE ON OUR WEBSITE AND MAKE THE READING CONNECTION!

We've created a customized website just for our very special readers, where you can get the inside scoop on everything that's going on with Zebra, Pinnacle and Kensington books.

When you come online, you'll have the exciting opportunity to:

- View covers of upcoming books
- Read sample chapters
- Learn about our future publishing schedule (listed by publication month *and author*)
- Find out when your favorite authors will be visiting a city near you
- Search for and order backlist books from our online catalog
- Check out author bios and background information
- Send e-mail to your favorite authors
- Meet the Kensington staff online
- Join us in weekly chats with authors, readers and other guests
- Get writing guidelines
- AND MUCH MORE!

**Visit our website at
http://www.kensingtonbooks.com**